X

BY JANE THYNNE

The Scent of Secrets
The Pursuit of Pearls

THE PURSUIT
OF PEARLS

DOUBLEDAY CANADA

THE
PURSUIT
OF PEARLS

A NOVEL

JANE
THYNNE

Originally published in hardcover in the United Kingdom by Simon & Schuster UK
under the title *Faith and Beauty*, in a different form, in 2015.

This book contains an excerpt from Jane Thynne's forthcoming book.
This excerpt has been set for this edition only and may not
reflect the final content of the forthcoming edition.

Library and Archives Canada Cataloguing in Publication

Thynne, Jane, author
The pursuit of pearls / Jane Thynne.

Sequel to: The scent of secrets.
Issued in print and electronic formats.
ISBN 978-0-385-68294-7 (paperback).--ISBN 978-0-385-68295-4 (epub)

I. Title.

PR6070.H96P87 2016   823'.914   C2015-906233-0
                                              C2015-906234-9

The Pursuit of Pearls is a work of historical fiction. Apart from the well- known
actual people, events, and locales that figure in the narrative, all names,
characters, places, and incidents are the products of the author's imagination
or are used fictitiously. Any resemblance to current events or locales, or
to living persons, is entirely coincidental.

Cover design: Victoria Allen
Cover photograph: Alfred Eisenstaedt/The Life Picture Collection
/Getty Images

Printed and bound in the USA

Published in Canada by Doubleday Canada, a division of
Penguin Random House Canada Limited

www.penguinrandomhouse.ca

10 9 8 7 6 5 4 3 2 1

Penguin
Random House
DOUBLEDAY CANADA

For John Carey

We want girls who believe unreservedly in Germany and the Führer, and will instill that faith into the hearts of their children. Then National Socialism and thus Germany itself will last for ever.

DR. JUTTA RÜDIGER, HEAD OF THE FAITH AND BEAUTY SOCIETY

In the peoples of Germany there has been given to the world a race unmixed by intermarriage with other races, a peculiar people and pure, like no one but themselves.

TACITUS, Germania

BERLIN, APRIL 1939

I T IS COLD IN THE DENSE WOODS OF THE GRUNEWALD AT seven on an April morning. Even though spring has dotted the moss with bluebells and wild daffodils and filled the tops of the pines with nesting birds, the temperature is still chilly enough to goose-pimple the arms and cause the hardiest hiker to shiver. It's gloomy, too, even in the glades, where the early sun filtering through the boughs casts only a greenish, watery light and leaves most of the tangled ferns and mulch in darkness. The mist hangs low between the closely packed trees, confusing any traveler unwise enough to stray from the path. The mix of wood here—pine, oak, and birch—has remained unchanged for thousands of years, and wild boar forage for beech mast in the undergrowth as they have always done. Hunters search for deer and pig along dirt tracks that have been trodden since the Middle Ages. Though the city is only a few miles away to the west, the forest could be the same primeval place it was in the Ice Age, when meltwater first created the lakes surrounding Berlin's flat, sandy plain and the early German tribes first emerged from the boggy swamps.

In the Grunewald, history slips by like a leaf falling to the forest floor.

HEDWIG HOLZ SQUINTED DOWN the barrel of the Walther PPK pistol, released the safety lever, cocked the hammer, took aim, shut her eyes tightly, and squeezed.

Nothing happened.

She dropped the pistol with a sigh, aligned it again. Keeping two fingers wrapped around the grip and her little finger curled beneath the magazine the way she had been shown, she aimed again. Despite the freezing air, she could feel a trail of sweat running down her brow and a maddening itch from her woolen vest just below her arm that she longed to scratch. What was more, in her hurry to dress that morning she had chosen the tighter of her two skirts, and the waistband was now digging in uncomfortably. Yet she had to stop these trivial bodily sensations from distracting her, just as she must ignore the thrushes flitting between their nests in the high pines, the squirrels scrambling among the branches, and the whole awakening Grunewald around her. She must concentrate. Straighten her arm, feel the cold metal of the pistol burn against her palm, find the target, and shoot. Even without her glasses, how hard could that be? She aimed, shut her eyes again, and fired.

Although the gun worked this time, the shot veered wildly off course, ricocheting around the tranquil woods and provoking a chorus of screeches from the crows overhead. Hedwig flinched, brushed the sweaty trails of hair from her brow with the back of her sleeve, and aimed again. The rustling in the trees above had broken her concentration; her next shot went even wider, sending a flutter of birds up into the sky and provoking muffled laughs from the gaggle of girls behind her.

They had been there for an hour now, a group of twenty young women, all startlingly alike from a distance, with blue eyes, braids of various shades of gold pinned up on their heads, and white smocks with neckties over navy serge pinafores. All wore ankle socks, and clumpy black boots. They made a curious sight as they threaded their way along the woodland path behind their leader—an Amazonian figure named Fräulein von Essen, wearing a leather jerkin and carrying a satchel of ammunition and a target, which she set up a hundred meters away from the firing site. They could expect to be there for another hour at least, Hedwig decided despondently, until Fräulein von Essen was satisfied every girl among them could shoot a man at a hundred paces.

Shooting was the last activity Hedwig had expected when she joined the Faith and Beauty Society. Far from shooting a man, all most girls wanted was to capture one. The Glaube und Schönheit society was, after all, the Third Reich's elite finishing school for young women. Its girls were the pearls of the Reich, and the plan was to equip them with the poise, polish, and talent required to marry into the top ranks of the Nazi hierarchy.

To this end, every weekend, and several evenings in the week, a select group of girls would gather at the Faith and Beauty community house in the picturesque woods outside Neubabelsberg to be educated in the finer points of civilization: history, the arts, music, dancing, and dinner party conversation. How to discuss Beethoven intelligently and dazzle a man with knowledge of the Franco-Prussian War. How to make tapestries and play chamber music. How to waltz, sketch a head, and paint a decent landscape in watercolors. Any old Bride School or Mother Class could teach a girl to cook a herring, the wisdom went, but some German girls should be setting their sights on higher things. That was why Reichsjugendführer Baldur von Schirach, head of all Nazi youth groups, had hit on the idea of a society for the cream of the nation's young women. Faith and Beauty girls were the Third Reich's Vestal Virgins, according to the introductory talk—a comparison that made Hedwig blush profusely when she heard it for the first time.

Every girl applying to the Faith and Beauty Society must be blond and blue-eyed—the precise color was measured against a chart containing sixty different shades—but there was no actual stipulation that they must also be beautiful, which was fortunate for Hedwig, whose moon-like face was earnest, rather than exquisite, and whose mousy hair could be called blond only by a vivid stretch of the imagination. She was tall and bosomy, a born worrier with a perpetually anxious air that vanished only when a good-natured smile lit up her face, exposing her crooked teeth.

Hedwig's appearance was in stark contrast to that of her only friend in the society. Lottie Franke was a slender beauty with thick, honey-gold hair, a bold gaze, and a full mouth. She looked like a girl in a Renaissance portrait, with eyes as blue as gas flames and skin like whipped cream. Although Faith and Beauty girls were encouraged to acquire a suntan, Lottie maintained that sunlight caused wrinkles and insisted on coating herself with Nivea and remaining as pale as wax.

Despite their physical differences, the two had been close since they met on the first day of school, with their satchels on their backs and the traditional cones of sweets in their hands. Frau Mann, the Faith and Beauty principal, never lost a chance to boast that the two girls proved the egalitarian nature of the society. In the Third Reich, elites weren't just for the rich. The other girls might come from middle-class homes with pianos and maids, but Hedwig and Lottie were unambiguously from the wrong side of the tracks. Hedwig and her five brothers inhabited a cramped apartment in Moabit, four rooms with a cuckoo clock in the parlor, a pervasive aroma of pork fat, and a bathroom they shared with another family. Lottie's family was even poorer. It had been a great sacrifice for the Frankes to find the fees, but Lottie was an only child, and generally Lottie got what Lottie wanted. And what she really wanted was a ticket to a better life. To meet all the right people and leave working-class Berlin behind forever.

Lottie was passionate about fashion, and as part of her Faith and Beauty course she had chosen to study costume design at the nearby Ufa film studios in Babelsberg. She had met any number of film stars—Lilian Harvey, Willi Fritsch, Brigitte Horney, and Marika Rökk—and she was full of snippets of celebrity gossip. Which actor was sleeping with someone else's wife, who had undergone cosmetic surgery, what girl had caught Reichsminister Goebbels's eye. All the Faith and Beauty girls crowded round her. Lottie was the type who knew secrets, and even though she probably made most of them up, hearing about a film star's drug habit was infinitely more diverting than a lecture on Napoleon's retreat from Moscow.

Hedwig braced herself, focused, and once again took aim. The gun was heavy—half a kilo of iron that had to be aimed with a straightened right arm. Her next shot went even wider, provoking unrestrained shrieks of laughter from her fellow students. Damn pistol shooting! And archery. What on earth was it for? Fräulein von Essen told them archery would re-awaken their sense of the medieval, but Hedwig had a nine-to-five job as a librarian. She had never had a sense of the medieval and didn't want one now. When would she ever need to handle a bow and arrow? Let alone a gun?

As if reading her thoughts, Fräulein von Essen glared at her, flint-eyed, and signaled, with an infinitesimal dip of the head, that she should try again. Hedwig needn't think that mere ineptitude would reprieve her from pistol practice. They could stay there all day, as far as Fräulein von Essen was concerned. Didn't Hedwig remember taking that oath to the Führer about loyalty, sacrifice, and achievement?

Hedwig was distracted—that was the problem—and it was Lottie who was distracting her. She had not turned up for pistol practice that morning, nor had Hedwig seen her at their previous community meeting. She was out during the day, of course, but everyone was supposed to congregate at the community house at six for dinner and evening instruction, and Lottie had already missed a two-part talk on medieval tapestries.

Hedwig knew what the problem was, of course. Lottie was in love. When Hedwig asked who the lucky man was, her friend had turned secretive, so Hedwig assumed he must be unsuitable. She had no idea who it could be, but Lottie had been making endless outings over recent weeks and refused to tell Hedwig where she had been. God forbid she had eloped. The thought of what that would do to Herr and Frau Franke, who worshiped their clever daughter and had gladly donated their savings for her Faith and Beauty training, made Hedwig wince.

When her next shot veered even farther from the target, prompting a further burst of hilarity from the others, Fräulein von Essen put an unexpected end to Hedwig's misery by ordering her to give someone else a try, so she moved gratefully to the back of the group, leaned against the trunk of a tree, and miserably surveyed the dank, mushroomy woods around her.

Hedwig knew she was supposed to like the forest. The Faith and Beauty girls were constantly sent on hikes with a knapsack and compass, the branches whipping in their faces and the undergrowth threatening to trip them up, and besides, true Germans belonged in the woods. They had learned that in the weekly race ancestry lessons; according to the Roman author Tacitus, the German race had originated in the forest before giving birth to the whole of human civilization. The original Germans were blue-eyed with golden hair and vigorous bodies, and life in the forest had made them a tough warrior race.

But the silence of the forest unnerved Hedwig. Berlin was a cacophony of noise, yet here were only pigeons rustling and cooing, the occasional sound of a deer crashing through the undergrowth, and the sporadic crack of the girls' guns.

That morning, however, the silence had been shattered by a bevy of construction workers who had begun work a few hundred meters away, building an air-raid shelter for the film studios. Because of the warmongering of the British, the whole of Berlin was digging air-raid shelters now. Wherever you went in town the rattle of drills and clang of spades could be heard in the background, preparing for the day that British bombers appeared in the skies. Everyone was talking about war, but Hedwig didn't believe it for a second. As far as she was concerned, the chances of any actual fighting were as remote as those ancient battles between the rival tribes of Europe that Tacitus wrote about. No foreign country had stood in the Führer's way before, and there was really no reason to suppose they would now.

On the way back, Fräulein von Essen couldn't resist another dig at Hedwig's hopeless aim. "Back again tomorrow, ladies. And perhaps this time Hedwig Holz will be able to manage just a single shot on target."

THE PURSUIT
OF PEARLS

1

BERLIN, IN APRIL 1939, WAS PARTYING LIKE THERE WAS no tomorrow.

The Führer was fifty and the whole of Germany was in a frenzy. The day itself had been declared a National Holiday and the largest military parade ever held—five hours' worth of storm troopers, hurricane troopers, tornado troopers, and every other type of trooper—was proceeding along the new East-West Axis, the great triumphal boulevard that ran all the way from Unter den Linden to the Olympic Stadium. Guns and tanks glittered in the morning air as the boots of fifty thousand soldiers thudded rhythmically into the ground. One hundred and sixty-two Heinkel bombers, Messerschmitt fighters, and Stuka dive-bombers performed flybys at five-minute intervals, leaving lightning flashes of vapor in the sky. Deputations of the Hitler Youth and League of German Girls had arrived from all over Germany. There were armored cars, cannons, Howitzers, and antiaircraft guns. And more than a million spectators, most of them carrying black bread sandwiches, bottles of beer, and swastika flags.

Clara Vine shuffled her feet and looked down at her glossy Ferragamo leather pumps. They were hand-stitched in Florence, had cost the earth, and they hurt like hell.

Why on earth had she not worn comfortable shoes?

She was hungry and thirsty and longing to sit down. She had been there since nine that morning, but had only managed to secure a place three deep opposite the Führer's saluting podium on the Charlottenburger Chaussee. The view to her right was obscured by a large woman with a squashed felt hat, accompanied by two boys of around six and seven. At first Clara had pitied the children, doomed to spend the morning fenced in by a forest of legs, but after hours of their relentless wails, demanding to know when *exactly* the Führer was coming and how much longer would he be, her sympathy was wearing thin. To her left stood a war veteran, medals pinned proudly to his chest, saluting frenetically like someone with uncontrollable muscle spasms. He had come all the way from Saxony, and he was not the only one. Thousands of visitors had poured into Berlin. The stations were teeming, and every hotel from the Adlon down was booked solid. People who couldn't afford anywhere else had pitched their tents in the parks.

Like all birthdays, Hitler's special day had begun with presents, but that was where the ordinariness ended. Vast marble tables had been assembled in the Reich Chancellery to display Meissen porcelain, silver candlesticks, and Titian paintings, alongside rather more modest gifts from ordinary people, largely made up of swastika cakes and cushions. The Pope, the King of England, and Henry Ford had sent telegrams. The engineer Ferdinand Porsche had presented Hitler with a shiny black convertible VW Beetle. Rudolf Hess had acquired a collection of priceless letters written by the Führer's hero, Frederick the Great, and Albert Speer had given him an entire scale model of "Germania"—the new world capital, with buildings made out of balsa wood and glass and a thirteen-foot model of the proposed triumphal arch. This was, without doubt, Hitler's favorite present, and he pored over it like a boy with a train set until he could be persuaded to tear himself away.

On the face of it, Berlin was putting on a magnificent show. Gigantic white pillars had sprouted all along major thoroughfares. The newsstands groaned with souvenir birthday issues. Swastikas sprouted from every conceivable surface. Spring was a riot of color in Berlin, so long as the colors were red and black.

Beneath the birthday bunting, however, everything was a little shabbier in Germany's capital. The tablecloths in the restaurants were spotted because there was no detergent, the bread was sawdust, and the ersatz coffee undrinkable. People looked the other way on the trams because there was no toothpaste, precious few razor blades or shaving foam, and the sour odor of humanity and unwashed clothes hung in the U-Bahn. Even high-class nightclubs like Ciro's stank of low-grade cigarettes, and taxis home were nonexistent because of the gas shortage.

After the previous year's Anschluss, when Germany annexed Austria, followed by the bloodless seizure of Czechoslovakia that March, most of Europe guessed a war was on the way. When it happened, it would be Poland's fault, according to the Ministry of Public Enlightenment and Propaganda, which ensured that newspapers were black with seventy-two-point headlines screaming belligerent revenge on the Poles for their atrocities against Germans in the disputed "Polish corridor." POLAND, LOOK OUT! There had been murderous attacks on Germans in Danzig. God help any country that stood in Germany's way.

Looking around her, Clara guessed that despite the marching and the machines, no one in this great big birthday pageant really wanted war. The ghost of the last war was still in their eyes, and the thought of what another would do haunted all but the very young. Only the little boys beside her, who now had squeezed between the legs of the storm troopers guarding the route, saw anything thrilling in the inexorable wall of men and tanks rolling past. Everyone else was getting by on an edgy cocktail of hope and denial. Everywhere you went, nerves flashed and shorted, like violet sparks above the tramlines. Tempers frayed. The whole city was as pumped up and jittery as a dog being forced to fight.

Above their heads, loudspeakers strung along the street barked out radio broadcasts of Joseph Goebbels between bursts of military music. Goebbels was cheerleading the nation as though the Führer's birthday was synonymous with facing up to the Poles. Enthusiasm for both was compulsory.

"No German at home or anywhere else in the world can fail to take the deepest and heartiest pleasure in participation."

Clara winced. The voice of the short, clubfooted minister for enlightenment and propaganda still got under her skin like shards of glass. Even now, after six years in Germany, hearing it daily on the radio and at the film studios where she worked, Joseph Goebbels's wheedling tone could make her flinch like chalk screeching on a blackboard.

Clara was there only because of a solemn promise she had made to her godson, Erich Schmidt, who at sixteen had been chosen to lead his battalion of Hitler Youth in the parade. It was a great honor, he had reminded her numerous times. But from where she was standing there seemed little chance of even glimpsing Erich, let alone of him registering her loyal presence.

It didn't have to be that way. As an actress contracted to the Ufa studios, Clara had qualified for a place in the VIP enclosure, alongside prominent personalities in their finery and portly Party dignitaries trussed up in field gray. The viewing stand, garlanded with golden laurels and tented drapes like a marquee at a country wedding, offered a far better view and a gilt chair to sit on. That was why she had risked the Ferragamo shoes, as well as the skirt suit and the tip-tilted hat, which now looked far too smart amid the stolid burghers of the Berlin crowd. Only, when she reached the gates of the VIP enclosure, she realized she couldn't face it. She spent enough of her life in close confines with Nazi officials without wanting to join them behind a velvet rope with no chance of escape.

A frisson of excitement ran through the crowd. A posse of steel-helmeted, black-jacketed SS officers had appeared and were elbowing their way through, glancing from left to right. Joseph Goebbels, who was recording this extravaganza for posterity, was clearly controlling every last detail. No one was allowed to take their own photographs, and police were deputed to arrest anyone in the crowd who wielded a camera or failed to perform the Nazi salute. As the SS men barged past, Clara saw an elderly couple at the back of the throng, the man a teacher or a pastor perhaps, and his gray-haired wife beside him, being hustled off to a side street and lined up against a wall to await the police wagon.

Mirror periscopes swiveled like reeds in the wind, and the yells around her intensified, rising into a wall of sound. The cordon of SA and SS officers linked arms to prevent the surge of sightseers spilling into the road.

"He's coming!" The excitement of the moment caused the stolid woman beside Clara to burst into a cry of joy.

First came a fleet of motorcycle outriders, then Hitler himself, upright at the helm of his seven-liter Mercedes Tourer, with his arm raised in the trademark salute he could apparently hold for two hours straight. His peculiar, impersonal stare traveled like a searchlight across the crowds as his head flicked intermittently right and left, his eyes seemingly seeking out individual faces. Flowers were hurled through the air, hitting the sides of the Mercedes with soft thuds. Surprisingly, only two members of the Adolf Hitler Leibstandarte bodyguard were at the Führer's side. The usual car of followers was absent.

How vulnerable he was. All it would take would be a single shot and the leader of all Germany, the object of all this adulation, would be extinguished like a lightbulb, along with the fears of an entire continent. Clara wondered if she was the only person who had such a thought. German civilians were never told about attempts on the Führer's life, but Clara had heard that in Munich several years ago, during a parade like this, a pistol had been found in a newsreel camera mounted on the roof of a car, the barrel of the gun pointed down the lens. Another couple of other assassination attempts had been averted at the last minute. Each lucky escape only served to convince Hitler more firmly of his deepest belief: destiny was on his side.

As he came parallel to Clara, a shaft of sun lanced through a rent in the clouds, and a finger of light pointed down towards his car. Hitler's bright blue gaze turned in Clara's direction and seemed to penetrate right to where she was standing.

Clara ducked her head, turned sharply, and pushed her way back through the throng. She had a long day ahead of her and a party to attend that evening. And today of all days she had chosen to move.

2

STEPPING OVER THE BAGS SHE HAD DUMPED IN THE hallway and shrugging off her coat, Clara looked around her new home.

For an actress working in the Babelsberg studios, just a short distance away through the Berlin forest, this place couldn't be more perfect. It was set in a colony of houses built in the nineteenth century by rich Berliners seeking respite from the city on the bucolic shores of the Griebnitzsee. The villas, all of them by up-and-coming architects, boasted a variety of styles—sweet, gabled cottages in the early nineteenth-century Germanic domestic fashion and turreted mock-baronial palaces, alongside modernist constructions with clean lines and open-plan spaces. Since the 1920s, the original owners—the bankers and industrialists—had given way to film stars, and now the little group of houses was known locally as the Artists' Colony. It was Berlin's version of the Hollywood Hills—an oasis of luxury just a short drive from the city center for those who could afford privacy and architectural distinction.

Not a category that included Clara Vine.

Although her acting contract with Ufa kept her in regular film work, she was far from the heights of stardom that promised a place in the Artists' Colony. It might have been her half-English heritage or the rebellious twist to her smile that prevented directors from casting her in leading roles. Or perhaps it was merely that the preferred template for a Reich film star was blond and buxom—a pattern fitted perfectly by her friend Ursula Schilling, who had been one of Ufa's top actresses until the previous year, when she joined stars like Marlene Dietrich and Billy Wilder in the sanctuary of Hollywood. This was Ursula's house, and Clara was here only until Ursula decided when, or if, it was safe to return.

If she didn't know better, Clara might have wondered how Ursula could bear to leave it. Though small, the house, like every other in the Artists' Colony, was exquisite in every detail. It had been designed by Mies van der Rohe, with a steep-gabled, red-tiled roof, vanilla-painted façade, and teal-blue shutters on the windows. Beech, oak, and pine trees grew all around, shielding each house from any sight of its neighbor, and giving each dwelling a sense of total rural isolation.

The front door opened directly into a paneled, open-plan drawing room running the entire length of the house, furnished with bookshelves and a piano. Expensive rugs covered the polished wooden floor, and there was an armchair soft enough to sink into and never get up.

Ursula had been gone for months now, but the way she had left the house, you would think she had taken a shopping trip to the Kurfürstendamm rather than an ocean liner across the Atlantic. Everything was still there—cushions, lampshades, curtains. The rubble of lotions, stubby kohl pencils, and cratered powders on the dressing table. She had abandoned all her books and furniture, not to mention crockery in the sink and withered rosebuds in a dry vase. Even Ursula's clothes were still in the bedroom, draped carelessly across chairs, falling out of drawers, and hanging in scented layers of silk and satin like gleaming ghosts.

Fortunately Clara didn't have much luggage of her own. She had always traveled light, ever since her days in repertory theater in England. All she had with her was a few changes of clothes, her leather jewelry box, Max Factor makeup, a book of Rilke's poetry with a duck-egg-blue cover, and the sheaf of mail she had grabbed from her apartment as she left.

Wandering into the kitchen, she set down a bag containing black rye bread, eggs, potatoes, and an onion. She had stood in line that morning for the eggs and onion and had every intention of enjoying them in an omelet as soon as she had unpacked. As she ran a tap to fill the kettle, she opened a cupboard to rummage for a cup and discovered, with the delight of an archaeologist making an antique find, a gigantic jar of real Melitta coffee beans, shiny nuggets of black gold, almost untouched. The only coffee to be found in Berlin right now, *Kaffee-Ersatz,* was a gritty concoction of chicory, oats, and roasted barley mixed with chemicals from coal, oil, and tar; so a jar like this was real treasure. Unscrewing the lid, she inhaled greedily. Everyone in Germany obsessed about food now. They dreamed of potatoes fried in butter, crispy chicken, and fragrant roast meat. Of real coffee and cream. Being half English, Clara fantasized about thick wedges of Fuller's walnut cake and solid chunks of Cadbury's chocolate, which were even more impossible to find.

Cradling her fragrant, smoky-flavored coffee—black, no milk—Clara went over to the far window, from where a long sliver of the lake was visible, its hard silver surface marbled by high clouds, and a dark fringe of woods beyond. A narrow jetty protruded into the water and a duck stood on it, frisking a rainbow of water across its back. Shielding her eyes against the dazzle of light, she opened the French windows and stepped outside. She had not had a garden since childhood, when nine acres of Surrey at the foot of the North Downs had formed the limits of her world. There she; her elder sister, Angela; and her brother, Kenneth, had raced snails, collected tadpoles, and played French cricket.

Resting against the sun-warmed brick, she breathed deeply, inhaling the scent of narcissus and sweet woodsmoke from a bonfire, letting the smell of nettles and grass float through her. In the city a hundred different noises made up silence, like the colors that together constitute white light—the rumble of traffic, the bang of a shop door, the jangle of a milk cart, the whine of a wireless—but out here the silence had a different texture. It was a deep, medieval quiet, the kind you never found in the city. Thick and tangible, oppressive almost. Clara could see why no one bothered locking their doors. The only sounds were the distant chug of a steam cruiser, squabbling squirrels in the high branches of the pines, and her own breathing.

But it was no good. Whenever Clara relaxed, her mind would return to the same matter. The matter that she tried to keep buried, but that became increasingly urgent as time passed.

Leo Quinn.

Leo was the British passport control officer who had first suggested her other—and what felt increasingly like her real— role. At Leo's urging, Clara had begun to feed details of the gossip and feuds of the senior Nazi women to British intelligence. Moving, as she did, in the regime's high society, Clara had become a spy on the private life of the Third Reich. For years now she had formed a link in the shadowy chain that stretched across Europe, passing news of the Nazis to her contacts in Britain's Secret Intelligence Service, learning from Leo the tradecraft and secrets of a spy's life.

And in the process she had fallen in love with him.

At the thought of Leo, sadness swelled and images of their last two weeks together flared in her brain. They had spent the time enveloped in each other, driving a borrowed car out to the lakes and plunging into the chill water, slippery fronds beneath their feet. Making love in a bedroom, the morning light spangled across his face. Walking in the forest, beneath the shifting leaves. Talking about the future, and Leo's longing that she should leave Berlin for the safety of England. She thought of his fingertips tracing her face as though committing it to memory. Holding her so tightly she could feel the blood pulse through him, his mouth on hers and his arms encircling her as though he would never let her go.

And yet he had let her go. Without a second's hesitation.

It happened quite abruptly one morning. He had received a message the previous night, requesting that he return to work in London without delay. Clara didn't even know what Leo's job entailed—only that it was something to do with encrypted communications and that he was based in a London office block somewhere near Oxford Street but also made frequent trips abroad. Yet as soon as he had told her, he was knotting his tie and glancing at his watch. Then he pulled on his jacket, gave one last look back, and headed out of the door.

That was six long months ago, and she had not heard a word from him since. Not so much as a postcard.

Where are you, Leo?

The questions ran through her head like beads on a rosary.

Most evenings after she had finished at the studio, she would have a solitary supper and bury herself in the latest novel her sister had sent from Hatchards bookshop in London. Occasionally she would be dragged out by friends, and other times she took Erich to the cinema or a meal. At night she might stretch out a hand across the satin counterpane to where Leo had been, but more often she fell asleep the moment she climbed into bed, exhausted by the constant busyness she had adopted to keep thoughts of him at bay.

Yet increasingly a mutinous anxiety arose in her, one that she tried and failed to suppress. Why had Leo not been in touch? For someone whose work involved communication, it seemed ironic that he had failed entirely to communicate with her. Agents learned to compress their words into codes, but what code did silence contain?

On one side of the room a gigantic rococo mirror was angled to reflect a photograph of Ursula on the opposite wall, an icy peroxide fantasy swathed in fur. Gazing into the mirror, Clara tried to see what Leo saw.

He had always said she had a face that was easily able to conceal her feelings, or to project other emotions entirely. The glossy, dark hair with its russet streaks had been cut short for her current film role, and the effect was to frame her face more closely, emphasizing the widely spaced blue eyes with the brows high and thinly plucked, in the current fashion. Her sleek dress, flatteringly nipped in at the waist, gave her an air of self-assurance, even if it was worn in patches and the cuff was starting to fray.

Yet that self-assurance, like her identity itself, was a lie. The document she carried in her bag at all times, certifying that Clara Helene Vine was a full member of the Aryan race, disguised the fact that she was, in Nazi terms, a *Mischling*, with a Jewish mother and grandmother, who under the strict race laws now in place could not marry a gentile, work for one, or even sleep with one without the threat of imprisonment.

At the thought of it, she pulled out her Max Factor compact, dabbed a little powder on, ran a layer of Elizabeth Arden's Velvet Red round her lips, and gave a defiant smile. If she was going to present a false face to the world, it may as well be an immaculate one.

She turned to her bags, began unpacking, and placed three photographs above the fireplace. One of a smiling six-year-old and another of the same boy ten years later, grown dark-eyed and somber. Her godson, Erich, who was even now burning to join the Luftwaffe and perhaps would soon get his chance. The third photograph was of her mother, Helene, throwing her head back in laughter. Acting, as she had been from the day she arrived as a new bride in England at the age of twenty-two, leaving Germany behind and with it any mention of her Jewish heritage. Clara had no picture of Leo.

THOUGH URSULA'S HOUSE WAS far more luxurious than Clara's last home, that had nothing to do with the actual reason for her move. In recent weeks Clara had been increasingly convinced that her apartment in Winterfeldtstrasse was being watched. Far too frequently there were men around to clean the windows of the block opposite, or to paste new advertisements on the billboard outside. Clara had carried out all her usual precautions. She placed a dish of water for the cat just inside her front door. She didn't have a cat, but anyone entering the apartment surreptitiously would bump the dish and spill water on the carpet. She left a tube of lipstick balanced on the casement window latch; it would easily be upset if the window was opened. Although she was certain there had been no actual intrusion, the previous week she had dashed home in an unexpected rainstorm and almost collided with an unfamiliar figure in the lobby.

"Can I help you?"

He was a sinewy young man with a lean, evasive face.

"Just sheltering from the rain."

But he was bone dry. No pearls of water clung to the fabric of his umbrella or dripped from its spokes, nor was there any drop on his coat, dampening his felt hat, or soaking his scuffed leather shoes. He carried a bulky case and avoided her eyes when she spoke to him.

That was the moment she decided. Clara was experienced enough to distinguish between the instinctive feeling of being observed—that constant prickle of self-awareness all actresses develop—and the insidious lick of nerves prompted by Gestapo surveillance. She had learned to trust what her instincts told her, and at that second they told her it was time to switch locations without delay. She had no desire to check the face of every street sweeper or sneak a glance into every idling car on the curb. Fortunately, she remembered Ursula's offer of housesitting. Out in Griebnitzsee there was very little chance of passing strangers. It was almost too isolated. But then, she might not be spending that much time at home.

She propped an invitation on the mantelpiece. It was printed on stiff, heavy ivory card with shiny engraved lettering and gold edges—the kind that Angela ordered from Smythson in Bond Street for her cocktail parties and at homes. Just the feel of it gave Clara a jolt of nostalgia for her sister's smart society gatherings, the Mayfair ballrooms filled with actors and politicians, the theater people and poets. She pressed it to her nose and inhaled the faintest trace of cigarette smoke.

CAPTAIN MILES FITZALAN

REQUESTS THE PLEASURE OF THE COMPANY OF

MISS CLARA VINE

AT A BALL AT THE ST. ERMIN'S HOTEL

VICTORIA,

LONDON SW

CHAMPAGNE AND CARRIAGES AT 1:00 A.M.

The only difference about this invitation was that Clara did not know any Miles Fitzalan. Nor had she heard of the St. Ermin's Hotel. And she guessed, whatever this meeting was about, it would certainly be no party.

BEING SEDUCED BY JOSEPH GOEBBELS WAS EVERY
starlet's worst nightmare, but for foreign journalists it
was a rather pleasanter experience. The Press Club he
had established at a cost of half a million marks on
Leipziger Platz was a comfortable mansion of gleaming
wood and chrome, superbly fitted out with ornate restaurant, reading room, library, and bar, where journalists were encouraged to congregate in the clubby
armchairs and write their stories in luxurious ease. The
restaurant served the types of white-fleshed schnitzel,
buttery vegetables, and rich, flaky pastries that were no
longer available elsewhere in Berlin, accompanied by
fine wines and the holy grail of Viennese coffee. All the
international newspapers were available, a Tannoy system was in place, and journalists could obtain anything
from reduced-rate opera tickets to special red identifica-
tion cards for procuring taxis. They could also write
their copy on the typewriters there and have it cabled
directly back to their own newspapers, if they didn't

mind the censors crawling over every word. The club was practically in earshot of the Propaganda Ministry in Wilhelmplatz, but that was irrelevant because beneath every plush leather banquette was a listening device to collate conversations, and anything the listening devices missed was scooped up by the superbly attentive waiters, who doubled as Goebbels's spies. All the journalists knew the Press Club was an eavesdroppers' paradise, but the quality of the food and the prices at the bar made it a popular destination, just so long as you didn't mind your thoughts being shared by a wider audience, which journalists by their very nature generally didn't. The level of comfort encouraged harmonious conversation, and the only permanent disagreements came from the three clocks on the wall, telling the time in Paris, London, and Tokyo.

Clara made her way towards Leipziger Platz with some difficulty. Battling the throng of people who had spent all day at the birthday parade was like wading through a drunken river upstream. It was as though every one of Berlin's four million souls had turned out to glimpse the Führer. Whole family groups walked several abreast on the pavement, the fathers carrying cameras slung over their shoulders by straps and the mothers lugging picnic baskets and folding seats. Clara breasted the flow, passing bars belching beer breath through open doors and navigating crash barriers, skirting the boozy crowds and dodging the sharp sticks of flags trailed by exhausted children who had been up before dawn.

Eventually she escaped up the porticoed steps of the Press Club, edging around a twenty-five-foot portrait of the Führer in the lobby proclaiming OUR LOYALTY: OUR THANKS, and entered the party.

Like everywhere else in Germany, the Press Club was celebrating with unrestrained joy. Goebbels had allocated a large quantity of *Sekt* to assist the celebrations, and despite the fact that the drinks came accompanied by a liberal sprinkling of bureaucrats from the Reich Chamber of Press, the foreign correspondents had decided en masse to take full advantage of it. Clara looked round for the plump, sandy-haired figure of Mary Harker, the journalist she had met when she first arrived in Germany and who was now a close friend. Mary, with her passionate concern for the underdog and her deep sense of justice, had been reporting from Europe for the *New York Evening Post* since 1933. Recently, though, she had been in Prague, and Clara hadn't realized how much she missed her. Being good-hearted, wholly on Clara's side, and, most important, having an inkling of Clara's secret role meant Mary Harker was the only person with whom Clara could genuinely relax.

Mary's hearty laugh and distinctive New Jersey accent were instantly recognizable from the far side of the room. She had scarcely changed since they met six years ago. She still had the same mordant sense of humor, the same favorite old black dress, her hair was a corn-colored tangle, and her lively eyes were hidden behind heavy-rimmed black spectacles. As usual she was at the center of a throng, and loudly enjoying herself.

"Clara, let me introduce Bill Shirer, from CBS, and Louis Lochner, head of the Berlin bureau of the Associated Press." She indicated a short man with a mustache, waving a pipe, and his balding colleague, with horn-rimmed glasses. "You already know Sigrid Schultz of the *Chicago Tribune*." She gestured at a tiny, china-complexioned woman with a fierce stare. "Guys, meet Clara Vine. A star of the Ufa studios, as I expect you know."

The group nodded politely. American correspondents were thick on the ground in Berlin. There must have been at least fifty, staffing the wire services, broadcast stations, and newspapers, but you rarely saw so many together.

"Quite a turnout," said Clara.

"We're congregating for safety." Shirer laughed. "Roosevelt has refused to send Hitler a birthday card, so we Americans aren't flavor of the month anymore."

"At least you remember what it's like to be popular," came a voice. "We British haven't been popular for years."

Clara didn't know the voice, yet in another way, she recognized it instantly. It was the kind of voice that echoed across expensive school playing fields and down the corridors of the British civil service in Whitehall. The same voice that belonged to friends of her brother's back in England; precise, understated, and slightly mocking. A tone that said most things should not be taken too seriously and very little should be taken seriously at all. Clara turned to see two men, one tall and lanky in a three-piece suit of Harris tweed with a lock of oiled hair jutting over his brow. Beside him stood a shorter figure with a shock of blond hair, a freckled face, and alert blue eyes, his old school tie secured with a tiepin.

"Clara, meet Charles Cavendish and Hugh Lindsey. Your fellow Brits," said Mary, eliciting a look of pure puzzlement on the men's faces.

"Clara's half English, didn't you know?" she continued. "She's the daughter of Sir Ronald Vine."

"*The* Ronald Vine?" asked Cavendish, with the look of disdainful astonishment that always accompanied a mention of Clara's father's name. Almost immediately he concealed it with a polite smile and stuck out a hand, but not before Clara had noticed.

"The same," she replied evenly.

Being known as the daughter of one of England's most prominent Nazi sympathizers had been invaluable in gaining the trust of senior members of the Nazi regime. Her father's loyalties had been Clara's ticket into the inner circles of the Third Reich. Yet still, it was an uncomfortable façade to maintain, especially with the British.

Somehow, the second journalist, Hugh Lindsey, seemed to understand. His eyes traveled over her with intuitive sympathy.

He said, "None of the Nazis love us Brits anymore. Despite the Duke of Windsor's best efforts."

"Hugh's just arrived," Mary explained.

There was a rapid turnover of foreign journalists in Berlin. Reporters were constantly having their visas withdrawn for overstepping Goebbels's mark, or allowing criticism of the regime to creep into their stories.

"Hugh's Rupert's replacement," added Mary.

"Not that Rupert could ever be replaced," said Hugh, gallantly. Clara gave Mary a quick, private glance. At one time Mary had been half in love with Rupert Allingham, the aristocratic head of the *Daily Chronicle*'s Berlin bureau. Eventually his increasing frustration with the regime, combined with increasing drinking, had the predictable results. When his friends gathered on Lehrter Bahnhof to wave him off, they agreed that, however much they were going to miss him, Rupert's expulsion from Germany had been an accident waiting to happen.

"You have big shoes to fill," Clara told Hugh.

"Big beer glasses too," he replied lightly.

"Rupert's well out of it," Cavendish remarked. "There won't be any war. I've heard Chamberlain is having a nervous breakdown. Whenever people try to talk to him, he just stands feeding pigeons through the Downing Street window."

"You wonder how the Nazis would even have the time for war," added Shirer. "They're so busy being at war with each other. Von Ribbentrop and Goering aren't even on speaking terms I hear, and Goebbels can't stand either of them."

"I'll be able to update you on that," said Mary. "I've been granted an interview with Goering tomorrow. My new minder just told me."

"Your minder?" asked Clara.

"Over there." Mary tilted her Martini glass towards a cluster of officials all towering over Goebbels's five-foot-six frame. They were vigorous, hard-faced men, mostly in uniform, and those in civilian dress wore the Party emblem in their button-holes.

"We have one each. Mine's the one with the face like Babe Ruth and the charm of Al Capone. They've been appointed to keep an eye on us."

"Don't they have enough spies?" complained Shirer.

Every newspaper office in Berlin had its quota of govern-ment informers, from the translators to the secretaries, follow-ing the reporters like wasps at a picnic and keeping a watch on their contacts.

"Goebbels says Germany's message needs to be better con-trolled than ever. The minders have to note every word we write and every place we go. Mine's going to be spending a lot of time at the Adlon bar."

"Mine too." Hugh had an easy laugh and an expansive man-ner that seemed to put people at their ease.

Clara glanced again at the men clustered around Goebbels, and as she looked, one man caught her gaze and boldly returned it. He was a haughty figure in a crisp uniform, his hawkish nose and cheekbones as sharp as an SS dagger. Even from across the room she felt his eye travel over the contours of her silk cocktail dress, down her body, then up again to her face. As their eyes met, a brief smile lifted the corners of his mouth. Then he nodded and raised his glass very slightly in her direction.

"Did you see all those presents being taken into the Chancellery this morning?" Cavendish asked. "Weren't we always told it was frightfully spoiling to have too many presents? What's wrong with cake and champagne?"

"You can forget the champagne," Mary teased. "I asked. The Propaganda Ministry informed me that the birthday dinner consisted of asparagus tips and artichoke hearts in cream sauce. And the only alcohol on offer was beer at one percent proof. I'd kill to see the guests' faces when that was served up."

"I heard our host gave Hitler a hundred and twenty feature films," said Hugh. "But then what *do* you give the man who has everything?"

"Poland, probably," said Mary.

Clara glanced again at the tall figure who had caught her eye. She had evolved many tricks for remembering faces, and one of them was to think of which animal she was reminded of. This man would be a large, powerful creature, a panther perhaps, with his dark coloring, black livery, and sleek, muscular demeanor. There was an impatience about the flare of his nostrils and the brief glance he cast towards the door, which said that as far as he was concerned, this party couldn't end soon enough. As she looked, their eyes met again, and he gave a smile that suggested amusement at some private joke only they shared.

She looked away.

She wandered over to the window to watch streams of people returning from the parade, their flags turning the street below into a shimmering sea of swastikas. Having spent all day offering rigid salutes at every opportunity, the crowds were relaxed now, drunkenly loud, singing off-key. Overhead, the last squadrons were passing, their drone fading into the distance. The crash barriers were being folded away, and litter collectors were busy picking up the occasional abandoned flag and empty cardboard wurst carton. More than any city on earth, Berlin liked to be immaculate. On the surface at least.

"It's a historic occasion."

Clara turned. The man who had been surveying her from across the room had come up behind her. At closer quarters, he was more than merely good-looking—there was a kind of perfection to his features. His eyes were gray as pewter, his silver-flecked hair swept precisely from the kind of face Clara had seen on statues in the British Museum—haughty, aristocratic, chiseled by generations of breeding, with a nose that in relief would fit perfectly on an ancient Roman. The only unambiguously German things about him were the four silver pips and stripe on his collar badge, which marked his rank as an SS Obersturmbannführer.

"I suppose. We have an awful lot of historic occasions nowadays. Sometimes one longs for a simple, unhistoric day."

The Obersturmbannführer raised a dark eyebrow. "Aren't you enjoying the holiday?"

"I'm not a great one for holidays. I'd rather get back to work."

Close up he smelled of fresh leather. No one, except soldiers, smelled of that anymore; the rest of the leather in Berlin was worn, scuffed, and long overdue for replacement.

"Personally, I'm finding it a welcome respite. But perhaps that's to do with my current occupation." He rocked backwards on his heels and followed her gaze down at the street.

Clara didn't ask him to elaborate, so he continued.

"Herr Doktor Goebbels has suggested I acquaint myself with all aspects of the Reich Chamber of Culture. I can cope with the concerts, but the minister thought I should watch as many films as possible, and frankly, I'm finding it a formidable job. He's provided me with a list of movies, and I'm having them screened as often as I can bear it."

"Tiresome for you."

"Indeed." He drained his glass. "I'm managing two per evening."

"Almost as many as the Führer, and he watches movies for pleasure."

"Well, it wouldn't do to compete with the Führer," he replied smoothly. "Though watching these films does rot the brain, don't you find?"

"Considering I spend my time acting in them, I suppose not."

If the Obersturmbannführer was abashed by his obvious faux pas, he didn't show it. A small sardonic smile danced on his lips.

"So you're an actress! That's the work you're so eager to get back to. And what are you acting in at present?"

"A romantic comedy."

"Tell me about it."

Clara kept her eyes concentrated pointedly on the street below. "Not much to tell. It's nearly finished," she replied tersely, hoping he was not going to ask the name of her current project.

"And what's it called? Just so that I can look out for it?"

There was a sarcastic composure about him. It was clear he enjoyed prying the information out of her. Turning, she met his gaze and said, "It's called *Love Strictly Forbidden*."

His smile broadened slightly.

"Very stirring. And is it *your* character who is forbidden to love?"

"You could say so."

Liebe Streng Verboten was a romantic comedy of the most frivolous kind. It was set in occupied Vienna, and Clara played a ditsy secretary who fell for her boss. Although the movie was sure to be a cast-iron success, secretly Clara understood the officer's disdain. *Love Strictly Forbidden* had as much in common with cinematic art as ersatz coffee had with a rich blend of Ethiopian Arabica. It would take no more than a couple of weeks to film, and the result would be the same as ninety percent of the Ufa output—frothy romance, as light and forgettable as a Haribo marshmallow candy. But although she knew this, Clara was not about to sympathize with this man's patronizing remarks. She wondered exactly who he was. He must be fairly secure if he was prepared to disrespect Goebbels so airily. She inclined her head.

"It's not often you meet someone who never visits the cinema. Presumably you never see the newsreels either. You must feel awfully out of touch."

"Sometimes I think it's the only way to live at the moment," he murmured; then the supercilious expression returned, and he said, "But you're right. The cinema is important and I'm attempting to embrace it."

"Which films have you embraced recently?"

"I tried watching *Dance on a Volcano.*" He paused with a soupçon of scorn, his lips curled. "It was billed as a historical drama, though I'm still trying to work out what it had in common with history. But then, perhaps history is whatever Doktor Goebbels says it is."

"A word means what I choose it to mean, neither more nor less," mused Clara.

"*Alice Through the Looking-Glass,*" the officer replied in English. "Lewis Carroll is a much underrated philosopher."

Startled, by both his comment and his flawless English, she stared. "Have you read it?"

"I spent two years living in England. I was an aide to von Ribbentrop when he was ambassador there. So yes, I've read it. But I've omitted to introduce myself." He clicked his heels and bent to kiss Clara's hand. His mouth was softer than seemed possible from such chiseled perfection.

"My name is Conrad Adler. And you are Fräulein . . ."

"Vine."

"Vine?"

"That's right."

Could she be mistaken, or did a transitory frown cross those perfect features, like a shadow momentarily darkening the sun? Clara was used to her name provoking an immediate reaction. Often it caused people to widen their eyes, or refer at once to her films, but the expression that flitted across Adler's face seemed more puzzlement than recognition. Almost as soon as she noticed it, however, it had vanished, to be replaced with a courteous smile.

She retrieved her hand. "Clara Vine."

"*Clara Vine.*" He repeated her name experimentally, as though tasting it in his mouth like a fine claret. "Yes. That's a good name for an actress."

The smooth mask was back in place.

"So if you work for von Ribbentrop, Obersturmbannführer, what are you doing here?"

"I've been assigned to another task for three months."

"Can I ask why?"

"I'm afraid not. I'm on loan." He shrugged. "Like a painting in a museum."

A gale of laughter reached them from across the room and

Clara glanced instinctively over at the Propaganda Ministry bureaucrats, gathered tightly around Goebbels and guffawing unctuously at his remarks.

Adler followed her gaze. "And you're English . . ."

"Half English."

"Yet you choose to live in Berlin? Why?"

Could he tell that this was the question she most often asked herself?

"It's an interesting time. Germany is changing fast."

"I agree with that. To think ten years ago there were soup kitchens and people standing on the streets with boards around their necks and camps for the unemployed outside the city. And now this."

He nodded towards the street, from where faint strains of the Horst Wessel song, the informal Nazi anthem, floated up. "No unemployment. Autobahns everywhere. Germany is great again. And all without a shot being fired."

"I saw some pretty large guns in the parade this morning."

A glimmer of amusement flickered behind his well-sculpted countenance.

"Ah. We must never forget there's a narrow boundary that separates the savage from the civilized. So, Fräulein Vine . . ." Still that teasing, probing smile. "At first glance you could be pure German. You have Aryan features, yet there's something distinctly English about you, too. A certain look you have—the one you're giving me now. It's like fire behind ice."

He held her gaze deliberately, provocatively. For a moment, it was as though he was seeing through her, to the Clara Vine who hid behind the carefully composed surface. Heat entered her face, the sounds of the room fell away, and a silent connection sparked between them. It was an unspoken understanding, a charge of sheer energy between a man and a woman. His gaze swept over her body like a physical touch, and Clara found herself speechless.

"Perhaps," Adler murmured, moving closer. His uniform exuded an aroma of starched linen and some sharp, citrus-scented pomade. "You might like to help me in my research."

"How exactly would I do that?"

"As you're evidently the expert on these things, you could accompany me to the cinema."

"I'm a little busy right now."

"Busy filming *Love Strictly Forbidden*. Of course." Amusement glimmered in his eyes like candlelight. "All the same, let me give you my card."

He slipped a card into her hand, and she transferred it to her bag.

"You could tell me if I'm watching high-quality art or low-grade trash."

Instantly Clara regained possession of her senses. The presumption, the arrogance of the man, took her breath away. She had told him she was an actress, yet still he was intent on disdaining her profession. She was about to issue a curt riposte when Hugh Lindsey appeared, inserted himself bodily between Adler and Clara, and thrust a glass of sparkling Sekt into her hand.

"Got you another drink, Clara. Oh, sorry. Am I interrupting?"

"Not at all," replied Adler, his mouth tightening slightly.

"We're making plans to go to Erich Carow's cabaret soon. Have you heard of it?"

"Fräulein Vine is already acquainted with my deficiencies as regards popular culture."

"Mary says it's unmissable." Hugh turned to Clara. "There's a whole group of us going. Care to come along?"

"I'd love to," said Clara.

"Excuse me, Fräulein. I should leave."

Adler clicked his heels, nodded at her, and melted away.

"Thought you needed rescuing." Hugh grinned. "Who was that?"

"Probably another of Goebbels's lackeys," said Mary, coming to join them. "They never leave Clara alone because they've seen her onscreen."

"Actually, he works for the Foreign Ministry. And he'd never heard of me." Clara finished her drink and checked her watch. "You know, I'd better be getting back. The S-Bahn will be crammed."

Mary's face creased in concern. "Be careful, after the news."

"What news?"

"It just came through on the ticker tape."

The ticker tape of the DNB, the German news agency, was stationed in a corner of the Press Club, from where it spewed out important information at all times of the day and night. Generally this important information concerned improved crop yields and record steel production numbers, but occasionally some actual newsworthy incidents seeped through.

"Everyone's talking about it. A girl's body was discovered by some construction workers close to the studios. They were building an air-raid shelter for the Artists' Colony. And that's where you're living, isn't it?"

"A body?" said Clara.

"In a shallow grave, apparently. Barely even covered. It was one of the Faith and Beauty girls."

"Faith and Beauty?" Charles Cavendish frowned. "What on earth is that?"

"It's the Nazis' finishing school for young women. Hitler's ideal women. They join at seventeen, and they're groomed as consorts for senior Nazi men. They have a community building near there."

"Extraordinary," said Hugh, taking out a notebook as though he was about to begin a news report there and then. "They're groomed, you say?"

"What about this girl then?" interrupted Cavendish. "Could it have been an accident?"

"No. She was murdered apparently." Mary checked the piece of paper in her hand. "Shot. Lottie Franke, aged twenty."

Until then, Clara had been silent, but the girl's name went through her like an electric jolt and she tore the paper from Mary's hand.

"It can't be!"

She stared at it, but the name was there in stark type. *Lottie Franke.*

"Oh, Clara, did you know her?" asked Mary, gently.

"She's my student. She was assigned to me from the Faith and Beauty Society to study costume design. I was looking after her. She's such a talented girl. It has to be a mistake."

Mary put a hand on her arm. "I hope so, too, Clara. But I can't see how it can be. The Criminal Police have announced it. They think the killer took advantage of the Führer's birthday because he knew everyone would be in town. What was she like, this girl Lottie?"

"She's . . . was . . ." Clara paused, and conjured up Lottie's exquisite face, with its wide cheekbones, ivory skin, and pale blue eyes. The slender, feline grace. "She was quite beautiful, but very intelligent, too. When I showed her round the studio she knew all sorts of details about the sets of *Metropolis* and *Nosferatu,* and she was terrifically knowledgeable about photographic technique. Hardly any young people in Germany know that kind of detail about Expressionist film anymore. I thought it was pretty daring of her even to talk about it."

"Liking Expressionist film may not be encouraged, but it's not enough to get you killed," remarked Mary somberly. "The police are telling women to be careful in isolated areas. There's a dangerous man on the loose."

"Will you be okay going back on your own?" said Hugh, laying a solicitous hand on Clara's arm.

"Of course. But thank you."

Mary looked doubtful. "Remember what I said, Clara. Please be careful."

CLARA LEFT THE CLUB and walked north, letting herself be carried in the tide of straggling crowds all the way to the S-Bahn at Friedrichstrasse. The news about Lottie Franke had obliterated all traces of Herr Conrad Adler and their conversation from her mind. As the cool air played on her flushed cheeks, her head filled with images of the girl she had known for just a few weeks, the flaxen hair cropped in a *Bubikopf*—the short bob frowned upon in these more conventional times— striding along the corridors of Ufa as if they were catwalks, impervious to admiring glances. Lottie had been unusually beautiful, yet her beauty was matched by an exceptional intelligence. Though Clara was supposed to answer Lottie's questions and show her around, quite often Lottie had been the one to provide information about Ufa's past, and the films she had seen. What a waste of a life. Clara tried not to imagine that slender figure sullied with earth, the perfect limbs crumpled and askew in a shallow grave.

At Friedrichstrasse the station was predictably packed, but

the crowds that surged onto the trains were different from the normal commuting throng, more jovial and less truculent. Wedged in one of the steamy carriages, jammed with jubilant day-trippers, Clara looked out at the darkness flashing past, the necklace of lamps strung like pearls along the track, and the chill spring night fizzing with neon. Everyone on the train was tired and content. The Führer's fiftieth birthday had been a moment of excitement, a firework flash against an ever-darkening horizon. Yet for one family, she thought, the day would always be marked by loss. Clara had no idea where the Franke family lived, but she knew the Faith and Beauty building was nearby in Neubabelsberg, and she resolved to call there the following day and ask for Lottie's address. The least she could do was to visit the girl's parents as soon as possible.

LOTTIE FRANKE'S PARENTS LIVED IN SCHULZENDOR-ferstrasse in Wedding, an industrial area of cavernous, gray streets and barracks-style, five-story tenement blocks grouped around dank courtyards. The blocks were more than six apartments deep, accessed from the street by a grimy archway and cramming together individual apartments with workshops, shared kitchens, and communal privies. All around, iron-framed chimneys belched smoke and men with cloth caps and collarless shirts trudged by carrying bags holding wurst and sandwiches for lunch.

As she climbed off the tram, Clara was instantly assailed by the yeasty stink of malted barley, wheat, and fermenting hops. It seemed to permeate everything from the bricks of the buildings to the paving stones beneath her feet. It issued from the Schulzendorf brewery, which provided jobs for hundreds of local workers and barrels of cloudy, sour *weiss* beer for their relaxation afterwards. Consumption of the traditional Berlin brew had soared in the past few years, and not even the new craze for Coca-Cola could begin to rival it.

Clara consulted her map and looked around. Wedding was a solidly working-class district, and before Hitler took power it was the scene of regular street fights between Communists and storm troopers. Though the ugly tenements dominated, Clara remembered that Mies van der Rohe's architecture could also be found here in the form of a series of experimental residential cubes he had designed and built in the 1920s.

The Frankes' home was not one of them.

Three floors up a stone stairwell reeking of urine and cooking, Marlene and Udo Franke's apartment was three cramped and dingy rooms. Lottie's father was moored on a sofa, his face stripped of animation and his eyes red-rimmed and pouchy from lack of sleep. A day's growth of stubble shadowed his chin. Marlene Franke was, by contrast, seized by frenetic activity, rushing in and out to fetch photographs of Lottie and asking repeatedly how Clara took her coffee. It was clear to see where the daughter's good looks had come from, though Marlene's blond hair was tied in a lank bundle and her startling blue eyes were crazily bright.

Everything about the apartment testified to an ardent faith in the Führer. The regulation picture of Hitler hung above the stove in a cheap gilt frame, its lurid coloring giving him a somewhat consumptive air, and set out on a veneer table dressed with a lace doily was the Führer corner. These shrines were everywhere now—in shops and offices, cafés and restaurants, as well as family homes. People believed they brought good luck. Mostly they featured a picture of Hitler and a candle, but the Frankes' shrine was an elaborate affair, with a copy of the *Jubiläumsausgabe*, anniversary issue of *Mein Kampf*, in honor of Hitler's birthday, and flanking Hitler, head shots of

Goebbels and Goering, like the two criminals at some devilish crucifixion.

Marlene Franke backed into the room with a tray of trembling crockery, set it down, then sat next to her husband, rocking slightly.

"Lottie was a wonderful daughter. I don't know how we're going to cope without her," she said, twisting a damp rag of handkerchief between her fingers. "She had such promise, didn't she, Udo?"

With a twitch of shaggy eyebrows, Udo Franke assented. "She wanted to be a costume designer. She saw all the movies."

"I was impressed by how much she knew about film when she came round the studio with me," Clara told them. "She was very intelligent."

"And artistic," said her mother, with a nod at the wall. "She modeled all her own designs. She had even been photographed by the fashion photographer Yva. Have you heard of her?"

Everyone had. Yva was one of the most celebrated fashion photographers in Berlin. Her pictures were in all the glossy magazines, *Die Dame, Elegante Welt*, even *Life* magazine.

"We kept them all."

Every wall in the room was indeed plastered with photographs of Lottie wearing dramatic, elongated costumes in shapes that were plainly inspired by Expressionist film.

"My daughter said fashion was Art," said her mother, with a touch of defiance. "And Art couldn't be categorized into acceptable and unacceptable. There's only good and bad Art. I'm sure we're not meant to think that—it's not what the Führer says, is it?—but you couldn't tell Lottie what to think. The most you could do was tell her not to say such things out loud. Now I'm tormenting myself thinking it was ideas like that which got her in trouble."

"I can't imagine her views on Art could have led to her death," said Clara gently. "Have the police anything to say about the investigation?"

"Nothing. They've just left. A Kriminal Inspektor Herz and some other rank. They said everyone was out of town. The Führer's birthday, you see. No one saw anything strange. They asked if our girl had a boyfriend, but I said there was no one."

Marlene's face darkened with misery. "So much for that Faith and Beauty Society," she spat savagely.

Clara couldn't help but agree. When she had called at the Faith and Beauty community home earlier that day, the grim-faced principal, Frau Mann, had met Clara's inquiries with a transparent lack of sympathy. It was as though Lottie had corrupted the whole idea of Faith and Beauty. If Faith and Beauty girls had to die, it should be gloriously for the Fatherland, not sordidly at the hands of an unknown murderer.

"They're supposed to look after the girls. Instead they filled her head with ideas about getting away. They took her to London, did you know?"

"To London?" Clara looked up, surprised.

"A couple of months ago."

"What were they doing there?"

"It was a deputation." Marlene Franke stood and began to scrabble in a drawer. "I kept the invitation. It was so beautiful." She handed Clara a piece of card—precisely the same kind of stiff, high-quality invitation with embossed black italics as rested on her mantelpiece at home.

THE BRITISH WOMEN'S LEAGUE
OF HEALTH AND BEAUTY
AT HOME
CLARIDGE'S HOTEL

Clara had heard of the British Women's League of Health and Beauty. It was an organization dedicated to improving the health of England's young women. It regularly held outdoor galas, where groups of trim girls in navy gym shorts performed synchronized athletics. Photographs of these events frequently appeared in the press, not always for the reasons the organizers imagined.

"Do you know Claridge's Hotel?" asked Udo Franke. "It's very grand. As big as the Paris Ritz and almost the equal of the Adlon. Marble everywhere, our Lottie said. And beautiful food, much better than you expect English food to be."

"The people were charming," added Marlene. "The dinner was given by something called the Anglo-German Fellowship. That sounds like a nice group of people."

"I've heard of it."

Clara had more than heard of it. Her father, Sir Ronald Vine, and her elder sister, Angela, were two of its most trenchant supporters. It was the last outpost in England of sympathy for the Nazi regime. With a jolt Clara realized that if the fellowship had organized the dinner, there was every chance that Angela would have been there. Angela might even have met Lottie, without knowing that her own sister knew her, too. Clara shivered as she felt the tectonic plates of her existence shifting beneath her, the two parts of her life clashing unawares.

"They said a visit to London would be valuable for her education. She would meet educated people, and converse with them about high-minded subjects. London!" The way Marlene spat the word out, the city might have been a sink of unimaginable depravity. "It must be a dreadful place. I wouldn't be surprised if she met the madman there!"

She burst into a torrent of sobs and buried her face in the sodden handkerchief.

"Now then, Marlene." Udo Franke roused himself from his trance and placed a hand on his wife's juddering arm. "You're imagining things. Nothing happened in London. Lottie loved that trip. It was a big opportunity for her. How many girls get to visit London?"

"So much promise, and a few months later she's dead!"

Udo trained his weary gaze on Clara. "Fräulein Vine. My wife and I are touched by your visit. It's a great comfort to hear how talented our daughter was, and we would like to hear more. But I implore you, if you hear anything which could help us find the monster who killed her—anything, no matter how small—you will come back and let us know."

Clara took his large, moist hand. She knew there was no possibility that she would be privy to any information that could help catch Lottie's killer, yet she also knew how unbearable she would find the grief if anything befell her godson, Erich, and he was not even her flesh and blood. Could people ever be truly happy again after the death of a child?

"I promise I will."

On the way to the door, her attention was caught by a small, framed photograph of Lottie.

"It's special, that one," Udo Franke told her. "It's from the dinner in London. It's only a snapshot, but it's the last one we have of our little girl, which is why we put it by the door."

The photo was entirely different from the artfully posed and backlit studio portraits on the other walls. In it, Lottie sat beaming at the camera across a snowy tabletop, a picture of composure between the crystal decanters and silver bread baskets, surrounded by a gaggle of Faith and Beauty girls. Although it was a group photograph, the eye was instantly drawn to Lottie, the candlelight forming a dazzling halo that accentuated the flawless complexion and the perfect proportions of her face. Next to her, leaning into the picture, was a much plainer girl, with a round face and unbecoming braids.

"Who's that?" Clara asked.

"That's her best friend, Hedwig. They knew each other since they were tiny," said Marlene. "Hedwig looked up to our daughter because Lottie was so good at everything, and so much prettier, of course. But Hedwig's a nice girl. Very upset, too."

Clara stared at the picture for some minutes, far longer than she needed. It was full of the terrible poignancy that freights photographs of the past. Those smiling faces, so joyful in the present, so optimistic for the future, and so innocent of what was to come. A sadness washed over her as she realized she was really searching for another image—the face of her own sister, Angela.

She didn't find it.

OPPOSITE THE TRAM STOP outside the Frankes' block, as if in direct mockery of the commuters shuffling their aching feet, was a poster featuring a gleaming new Volkswagen car with the slogan: "Save five marks a week and you will drive your own car." Most people in the queue looked as likely to buy a rocket to the stars as a Volkswagen car. Erich's grandmother, Frau Schmidt, a nurse at Berlin's biggest hospital, the Charité, was saving from her meager salary and had worked out that it would take her five years before she could afford one. After another few minutes shuffling alongside the others in the queue, Clara decided to walk.

Berlin was changing. It still looked like Berlin, but every day it was a little different, as subtle as fashion that shifts from one season to the next, raising hemlines, adjusting shoulder pads, and tightening waists. It even smelled different. People used to talk about the famous *Berliner Luft*, the fresh air that blew into the city from the Grunewald, but now the city reeked of sour breath, bitter cigarettes, and stale, unwashed bodies. The only soap available was gritty and impossible to lather because there was no fat in it. People had taken to carrying their own soap with them, if they had any, because leaving it lying around risked finding it missing.

Clara's mind went back to the photograph of Lottie Franke, and the certainty that Angela would have been at the same event. Yet again she regretted the estrangement between her and her sister. She thought of the last time they were truly close, when she was sixteen and their mother had died. They'd been standing in a ragged group around the graveside, and Angela had hissed the reminder *Dig your nails into your hands to stop yourself crying*. Repressing emotion was an article of faith for Angela. Concealment was more than courtesy, it was a way of life.

Behaving properly. Being properly British! That was Angela's code. Yet surely the quick, intelligent sister Clara knew was still there—buried beneath the visits to Harrods and bridge nights and society teas. Angela's letters tended to focus on the interminable round of charity events that she conducted, the deaths of relations, and the relentless progress of her husband's political career. *Gerald is in line for a big promotion. Chamberlain is so impressed with him.* Clara responded with a dutiful list of parties, premieres, and work reports. Nothing intimate. Nothing political. Nothing real.

Right then she resolved that she would write to Angela very soon, and attempt something they had not managed for ten years. Communication.

———

CLARA PASSED A LOUDSPEAKER lashed to the side of a building, blaring out *"Deutschland über Alles"* and obliging everyone to give a perfunctory right-armed salute. She generally avoided giving the *Führer Gruss* by ensuring she was carrying something in both hands, but that day, distracted by thoughts of Lottie, she failed to comply.

A hand on her shoulder made her jump like a coiled spring. A man was standing in her path.

"Documents please."

He had a complexion the color of concrete and an expression that epitomized the *Berliner Schnauze*, the direct, graceless, skeptical manner so many of the city's inhabitants perfected. He flicked the lapel of his jacket to reveal the aluminum disk marking him out as Gestapo.

Clara handed over her ID and watched the stupidity and aggression warring in his face as he scrutinized it. Although the small piece of card was beginning to fray at the edges, she never had any doubts about the quality of her identity documents; such was the skill of their forgery. All the same, even if papers were in order, a policeman or Gestapo official could confiscate them if he didn't like you. Clara wondered what this man saw in her. The usual Berliner, cowed in the face of authority and determined to keep a low profile? How much did her face give away? Into her head floated the remark of Conrad Adler.

Like fire behind ice.

"Alles in ordnung."

Gracelessly, the man returned her identity card, and she stuffed it back in her bag.

She walked on, remembering Mary Harker's warning. *We*

have one minder each. They've been appointed to keep an eye on us. Might that apply not only to foreign journalists but to actresses as well? She thought again of the man in the lobby of her apartment block: the lean, expressionless face, the trench coat belted loosely, the way he avoided her eyes.

In the fortnight before he had disappeared, Leo had talked a lot about the techniques of espionage. One afternoon he had told her about a list that all agents were being trained to memorize, to be used if they believed they were being followed.

Number One: look out for the unobtrusive. A shadow could be anyone. The young woman who clicked her painted fingernails on the counter beside you in a shop. The newspaper seller who slipped you a friendly remark each day with your change. The runner at the studio, or the parking attendant who joked about how he would always save the best space for you. Or a head-scarfed Frau, like the one a few steps behind, gray-skinned and footsore, weighed down by the kilo of potatoes in her shopping basket.

Number Two: watch for anyone walking at a steady pace. A shadow would be neither nonchalant nor too purposeful, though as far as vehicles went, the opposite applied.

Number Three: listen for a car that moves either too fast or too slow.

If surveillance was suspected, there was *Number Four: change your appearance.* Find a fresh coat, ditch your jacket, remove a hat. The slightest change could help to evade detection.

But whereas it was simple to put on a head scarf, or abandon a briefcase, a mustache could not easily be shaved off, nor hair color disguised. Thus *Number Five: check for distinguishing features.* A shadow rarely had time to change his shoes. There was also *Number Six: listen for what you don't hear.* And if surveillance was certain, there was *Number Seven: stick to public places.* Finally, in case of arrest or capture, *Number Eight: stay calm. Don't react instinctively.*

There were a couple of other points on the list, and Leo had made Clara commit them to memory and recite it back to him. "That list will keep you safe, Clara," he'd told her. "It'll be more use to you than any creed."

That was one relief about the trip she was about to make. In London, there was no chance of being followed. And it would not be the Gestapo she had to worry about but Captain Miles Fitzalan, whoever he might turn out to be.

OF ALL THE BEAUTIFUL PLACES IN BERLIN, COULD THERE be any lovelier than the sunlit drawing room of the Faith and Beauty community building, with its marzipan-yellow walls, icing-sugar plaster whipped like a meringue, and tall windows propped open to allow a freshening waft of pine from the woods beyond? Outside, a flock of hens pecked in the shade of the orchard and horses were being saddled up for riding lessons. A group of rowers were preparing for an outing to the lake, and on the lawn, two girls in face masks were taking instruction from the fencing master, their bodies as quick and flexible as the sleek silver foils they wielded. The quiet of the morning was punctuated by the solid, comforting *clunk* of the grandfather clock, and the faint scrape of a violin issued from the music room on the other side of the house. It was impossible to imagine that near this idyllic place just a few days earlier, a crumpled body had been found beneath a heap of leaves.

When Hedwig Holz first saw the Faith and Beauty

home, she was openmouthed with amazement. She had grown up in a drab apartment, with nothing but a window box to tend and a dank cobblestone courtyard below. Even though their apartment was slightly better than their neighbors' on account of her father's managerial job, it had still taken weeks to accustom herself to the refinement of the Faith and Beauty home. When she told her parents about the classes in Art, home décor, fashion design, needlework, flower arranging, and conversation, her mother could barely contain her amazement. *Conversation!* Who needed classes in that?

Hedwig felt much the same about Art. Sitting in front of her easel, she sighed, squinted at the life model, made some further experimental cross-hatching, then rubbed out the face she had drawn. Already a murky patch testified to the number of times the sketch had been erased—the model was beginning to look like something from one of those old horror films, *The Cabinet of Dr. Caligari,* starring Conrad Veidt, with nothing but a shadowy void where her features should be. Hedwig dreaded the moment Herr Fritzl, the art master, turned up to linger at her easel, twirling his mustache while he tried to think of something constructive to say. Their portraits were supposed to mirror the correct proportions of the Nordic form—every figure must have broad shoulders, a long body, and slender hands—but Hedwig's sketch could have been straight out of Grimms' fairy tales.

The Saturday life drawing class had been Lottie's idea. Hedwig didn't have an artistic bone in her body and would gladly have signed up for skiing, rowing, even high-board diving rather than humiliate herself with Art. Her younger brothers would actually beg her not to sketch them. Hedwig's father, a stolid production line manager at the AEG engineering works, thought art training, like everything else on the Faith and

Beauty curriculum, was a lot of effete nonsense, but he deferred to her mother, who had ambitions for her only daughter. Privately Herr Holz told Hedwig to concentrate on her job and think about her promotion prospects. If indeed she had time for promotion, before marriage and motherhood came along and put an end to all that.

Hedwig agreed. She had never imagined getting a job as a librarian, and she loved it. Although her most taxing duty involved looking interested while doing very little, she enjoyed sitting at her desk, greeting visitors, and being the only female in the building. She could think of a thousand better ways of spending her weekends than attending Faith and Beauty art classes, but Lottie had set her heart on it.

It was agonizing to think that Lottie had sat in this class only two weeks ago, sketching costumes, her bold, confident lines delineating impossibly glamorous women, their outfits carefully annotated in her flowing handwriting. Hedwig could picture her now, high, plucked eyebrows arched above aquamarine eyes, chin jutted forward as if she was born to it all. As if, indeed, it was all slightly beneath her.

Hedwig knew Lottie only wanted company, yet where Lottie was concerned she could never say no. Faith and Beauty girls were encouraged to think of themselves as a spiritual sisterhood, but Lottie was more like an ordinary sister. When they were children their two families had sometimes taken holidays together in the countryside outside Berlin, and Hedwig and Lottie had shared a room. Hedwig recalled Lottie's grave face, reciting German poetry or expounding on her ambitions for life, requiring only that Hedwig be a devoted listener. And when Hedwig had confided her most precious memory, of the first time a man kissed her, Lottie had burst into peals of most unsisterly laughter.

Sister or not, she was dead now, and Hedwig felt an utter desolation.

The murder had sent shock waves through the Faith and Beauty community, but although no one could talk of anything else, they were forbidden to talk about it at all. That was useless when it was all over the newspapers and a pair of steel-helmeted soldiers were shuffling their feet on permanent guard outside the front gate. A new set of regulations had been hastily formulated for the girls. Shooting was curtailed for as long as the killer was at large and replaced with rowing. No girl was permitted to walk alone the short distance from the Griebnitzsee S-Bahn through the forest, though that was quite unnecessary advice because being alone was frowned on. The Party disapproved of solitude on the grounds that faithful citizens would always prefer communal life, and privacy in all its forms was strongly proscribed for Faith and Beauty girls.

Hedwig stared out the window and wondered if her mother would agree to her leaving now. Etta Holz adored the idea of her only daughter being here. Faith and Beauty training gave German girls such an advantage. No going to the Nuremberg rally and getting pregnant by the first Hitler Youth you encountered! Hedwig would be invited to parties with senior Party members. She would be cultivated and polished and pass into the top echelons of society with ease. *Once you've finished you'll hold dinner parties for all the top SS men and you'll be able to talk about . . .* Here Frau Holz had paused, having no idea what top SS men might possibly talk about. *The Merry Widow,* she'd finished lamely, recalling the Führer's favorite operetta. "It will pay for itself, you'll see."

But the real reason that her mother favored the Faith and Beauty curriculum was that it meant her daughter would grow out of Jochen.

Jochen Falke did not have the kind of looks deemed hand-some among Hedwig's friends. His high, Slavic cheekbones and skinny frame were far from the muscular athletes modeled by the Führer's favorite sculptor, Arno Breker. But he had lively hazel eyes that missed nothing and a swagger about him that reflected his inner confidence.

He was an artist, too—in a way. He worked at an art manu-facturing plant in Kreuzberg, a humdrum place that carried out all forms of printing and publishing, as well as commercial art-work, signs, and advertising. But the real money-spinner was merchandising the Führer. Hitler souvenirs were big business. Birthday figurines, postcards, ashtrays, medallions, posters, cocktail forks, and bottle stoppers. There was a whole variety of jewelry, and cameo brooches were especially popular because every woman wanted her Führer close to her heart. Jochen's specialty was pictures. On a good day he could reproduce Adolf Hitler a hundred times over.

"What takes the Fräulein's fancy?" he would ask with a laugh, parodying an unctuous shop assistant. "We have Hitler in a gilt frame, Hitler with children, Hitler at the Berghof, Hit-ler with Bismarck, or would Fräulein prefer the Führer's hands alone?"

He worked with a photograph in front of him, softening the nose and making the eyes larger, adding a tint to the cheeks. *Just doing a little cosmetic surgery*. He brought one back for Hedwig's mother, who hung it proudly opposite her bed. Hed-wig thought seeing the Führer's scowl like that last thing at night would give her nightmares, but her parents seemed to like it.

She looked up to see Herr Fritzl approaching. He was bound to say something uncomplimentary about her efforts. Last time he'd claimed Hedwig's approach smacked dangerously of Degenerate art, which was tantamount to accusing her of treason. Apparently in the Weimar period Berlin had been a hell pit of sexual depravity, and obscene nudes by Degenerate painters like Otto Dix had corrupted the morals of the entire nation.

The thought of Otto Dix's nudes only reminded Hedwig of Lottie, her graceful gymnast's limbs askew in the clumsy crush of death. She pictured the diaphanous wings of flies glittering like cut coal in the air above her friend's body. What had Lottie ever done to deserve that fate?

Hedwig picked up her charcoal stick and turned back to the horror on her easel, but found she could no longer see it because of the tears slipping down her face.

6

ON LONDON'S KING'S ROAD THERE WAS A QUEUE TO collect gas masks from Chelsea Town Hall. Whole families were waiting, the children jumping up and down, wriggling with excitement, the parents, anxiety etched on their faces, keeping up appearances because they were lining up alongside their cooks and housemaids. One little boy kept singing "There's going to be a war!" until he was abruptly hushed by his father. Those who were leaving, already issued with masks, were rather more subdued. Now that they had had their first taste of the acrid rubber contraptions with their bleary glass panels at the front and straps fastened behind the head, perhaps the dangers of the future seemed suddenly more real.

Watching from the top deck of the number 11 bus, however, Clara was transported to the past. She had a vision of herself on this same bus with her mother, sitting in exactly the same spot—front row of the top deck—Helene Vine upright and proper, handbag balanced on her knee, and Clara herself, a small simulacrum, pressed warmly against her mother's side. Angela, meanwhile, sat aloof across the aisle. Clara had always been her mother's daughter—the only one of them named for a distant German ancestor rather than a resolutely English relation—and the only child who resembled her, too. Angela, with her honey-blond hair and long, gangly legs, was already exhibiting the first coltish inklings of the glamorous model she would become.

Now Clara was alone, in a mac and a printed silk scarf with a copy of *Picture Post* unread on her knee. "Miss Penelope Dudley-Ward, the English heroine of the London-Paris–New York hit *French Without Tears*, wears a rose, turquoise, and gold brocade lamé jacket and a full satin skirt in a deep rosy red."

The bus halted before men hauling sheets of corrugated iron for bomb shelters. Clara wondered if Angela had a shelter of her own, and if she did, whether she would ever need to use it. It was hard to imagine the elegant Angela shivering in a damp construction of earth and corrugated iron that flooded when it rained, or cramped in a basement, with a flashlight and a book. Angela liked a pink gin and a rubber of bridge in the evenings. Listening to Cole Porter at the Café de Paris or visiting the cellar of the Embassy Club in Bond Street, where until recently the Prince of Wales and Wallis Simpson had danced the quickstep on the tiny dance floor.

Clara had an impulsive, fervent desire to get off the bus and visit her sister, but she knew that was impossible. How would she explain this sudden appearance in London? What cover could she credibly construct that Angela would not instantly penetrate? Despite her long practice in controlling impulsive urges, it still took an almost physical strength for Clara to stay in her seat and not dash down the winding stairs and jump off the back platform of the bus.

After six years away, she scanned the familiar surroundings as though hunting for changes in the face of a long-lost friend. There were the same advertisements for Wrigley's Spearmint gum, Ovaltine, and Eno fruit salts, and Peter Jones had changed its Victorian red-brick frontage to a sleekly modernized tower of glass and steel. But now its windows were pasted with criss-crossed strips of brown paper to protect against potential bomb blast, the curbstones had been painted white, and sandbags, ex-uding a smell of damp jute, were shored against the side of every building. A giant recruitment advertisement for the RAF, "Sa-lute to adventure!" towered beside Sloane Square Tube, and a group of young men, subjects of the first wave of conscription, sailed past in a National Service truck. There were other changes, too, Clara could not help noticing. Women wore little hats tipped slightly forward and to one side. Jackets were more boxy and defined, coats had puffed shoulders, shoes were tightly laced, and the whole female silhouette had become harder and more defi-nite, as though fashion itself was bracing for what was to come.

Disembarking at Westminster, she made her way across Par-liament Square, past Methodist Central Hall, and along the elegant Georgian terraces of Queen Anne's Gate. Bright, lu-minous bursts of laburnum and wisteria blossom hung over sun-warmed walls. Through the pellucid blue sky, the bells of Westminster Abbey marked four o'clock. The abbey's bone-white frontage of pleated stone was draped with a veil of soot, and placards along the railings announced that it was now open day and night as part of a "Vigil for Peace." Passing a poster for *The Spy in Black*, Clara was startled to see the movie starred Conrad Veidt. Just a few months ago she had passed the vener-able German actor in the corridors of the Ufa studios. Now he was established in a new life and a new career in England.

It could happen to her, too.

As she walked, she felt her body tense and her shoulders knot in the familiar brace. It was impossible to shake the tension that clenched her stomach. She thought for a moment it might be the dizzy rush of nostalgia, set off by everything from the pillar boxes and the plane trees to the copper pennies with the king's head on them. Even the newspaper seller outside St. James's Park underground station, advertising the first sight of the new pandas at London Zoo, prompted a yearning for the city she had not realized she missed so much. In reality, though, Clara knew it was only nervous anticipation of what this meeting might bring.

THE ST. ERMIN'S HOTEL was a shabby, late Victorian, red-brick mansion block in Caxton Street, set back from the road and only a few hundred yards from 54 Broadway, where the Secret Intelligence Service was based. On a quiet afternoon it was the last place on earth one would associate with espionage. The lobby, all tartan-trimmed upholstery and dusty carpet, was hushed and gloomy. Watercolors of the Lake District hung alongside a painting of the king, and the smell of congealed vegetables and floor polish exuded a distilled essence of Englishness. A couple of ladies in hats and fur capes taking tea at a side table were the only sign of life.

Clara hesitated. It had not occurred to her until that moment how exactly she would make contact with the mysterious Captain Miles Fitzalan, who had invited her to his fictitious ball. She approached a girl reading a copy of *Woman's Weekly* behind the mahogany reception desk.

"Is there a Captain Fitzalan staying here?"

The girl gave an insultingly perfunctory smile. "Can I ask who wants him?"

"Miss Clara Vine."

Putting down her magazine, the receptionist reached wearily for the telephone. "They're fifth floor."

"Thank you."

"The lifts only go up to fourth, but if you press the button to the left, it'll take you all the way up."

Clara emerged from the lift to find a long, dingy office partitioned by panes of frosted glass and plywood, filled with men in pin-striped suits lounging at their desks. A fug of cigarette smoke hung in the air, lit by broad shafts of sunlight penetrating the murky windows. Though she was dressed quietly enough, in a skirt of houndstooth check, a blouse with scalloped collar, and a small pearl necklace, curious eyes swiveled immediately towards her. One man, with rumpled hair and tie at half-mast, one ear pressed to the telephone, gave her a wink, but Clara barely had time to look around her before an imposing figure with a scarlet carnation in his buttonhole approached.

"Miss Vine. So pleased you could come. What do you think of our offices? None too decorative, but very handy for clubs and so on." Pumping her hand, he detected her incomprehension and added, "I'm sorry. You don't know me from Adam. I'm Major Grand. Lawrence Grand."

"Clara Vine."

"Precisely. Please follow me."

Anyone who did not know that Lawrence Grand had recently been assigned from the army could have detected it instantly from his ramrod bearing, his tanned complexion, and the military exactitude of his pencil mustache. Clara recognized his type immediately. He wore his politeness like a uniform, buttoned up against the possibility of revealing the merest snippet of extraneous information.

Striding ahead, he led the way to a corner office with a view of budding plane trees and a line of pigeons shuffling along the soot-dappled rooftops of Westminster.

"Do sit down, Miss Vine. Smoke?"

"Thank you." She took the proffered Senior Service, and he slid across his desk a cut-glass ashtray, studded with ocher stains like pollen in a lily.

"Who are all those people?"

"Ah." Major Grand fired up her cigarette and assessed her, head tilted. "That, Miss Vine, is a question I can't possibly answer. Not only would it endanger my people if I identified them to you, but it could put you at risk, too. Let's just say we have all sorts from all walks of life. Often the very last sort you would expect."

"Of course. I'm sorry."

"On the other hand, seeing as you've been so good as to come all the way here, you're entitled to ask a few questions. You'll probably want to know what we're about."

Clara guessed this was her cue. "Can I ask who you are, for a start?"

"Certainly. The fact is, we're a bit of a fledgling venture. We're called Section D. Connected to the Secret Intelligence Service. Physically connected, in fact—there's a tunnel that runs under this building all the way to Broadway, not that anyone I know has used it. We've been up and running for a few months—ever since SIS concluded in the wake of the Czech invasion that war is unavoidable—our intention being to establish agents in those countries that face being overrun by the Wehrmacht."

For Clara it was still a shock to hear, utterly so casually, the idea that war was "unavoidable." Every fiber of her hoped that wasn't true. She dreaded what would happen to her friends, and most of all to Erich, if war came.

"We've already placed officers in Sweden, Norway, Holland, and Spain, not to mention Austria of course, but infiltrating people into Germany, let alone being able to do anything useful once they're there, is a very different challenge. Which is why, Miss Vine, your name has come up."

"You want me to apply?"

Grand bent his head to the complex task of extracting another Senior Service from his jacket pocket and fitting it into an ebony cigarette holder, then rose and strode over to the window.

"People don't apply to us, because we don't officially exist. We approach those we think might be valuable. You've been in Berlin now, what, five years?"

"Six."

"Quite so. They've just been celebrating the Führer's birthday, I hear. What was that like?"

"Not exactly understated."

He laughed drily. "So I understand. As a matter of fact, Noel Mason-Macfarlane, our military attaché in Berlin, offered to shoot Herr Hitler during the parade. He has a sixth-floor flat on the Charlottenburger Chausee with a clear line of sight to the saluting podium, and he swore it would be easier than bagging a stag at a hundred yards to pick the beggar off. This chap's an excellent shot, so we put the plan forward to the prime minister."

Grand stared down at the street below as though Hitler was saluting right there on the pavement.

"If you can believe it, the PM overruled it as unsportsmanlike."

Clara could barely contain her astonishment. So she had not

been the only person to contemplate the idea. Hitler might have been assassinated, while the eyes of the world were on him. What would the Ufa newsreel have made of that?

"Unsportsmanlike?" she echoed incredulously.

"That was his precise word."

"I'm surprised."

"Good."

He wheeled round, all jocularity replaced by an expression of intense seriousness.

"Our feeling here is that even at this late hour Mr. Chamberlain badly underestimates the danger of Herr Hitler. I hope if you were ever in the same room as him you would have no qualms. If the opportunity arose, we would not want you, Miss Vine, to be hindered by fears of 'unsportsmanlike' behavior."

Her heart bucked with fear, but she replied calmly. "I can't imagine the opportunity would arise, Major."

"Perhaps not."

He sat and crossed one leg over the other, stroking his trousered calf and scrutinizing her, as if trying to decide something.

"I'm aware that life in Berlin is not a bed of roses. But it's going to get much worse now that war is on the horizon. We all have decisions to make, but yours is especially acute."

Clara bent her head and smoothed the skirt on her knees, as though the mere action would help straighten out the questions in her mind. She had guessed that this summons would be a request from the British Intelligence Service—those shadowy men in Whitehall who had over the years been the ultimate recipients of all the gossip and information she relayed. She knew too that, just like Conrad Veidt and a host of other actors, if she chose to return to England she could make a fresh start in the British film industry. Yet mentally she had shied away from the question facing her. That same question which, beneath the penetrating gaze of Major Lawrence Grand, she must now face.

"We need to know, when hostilities arise, whether you intend to stay in Germany. It's going to get a lot more dangerous."

Something about Grand's patrician assurance suddenly rankled. Who was this man, in his smart suit and comfortable office, to talk of danger? What could he know of what she went through on a daily basis?

"You forget I've already been arrested and interrogated by the Gestapo, Major Grand. I've had plenty of opportunity to understand how dangerous Berlin can be. I'm not even living in my own apartment because I believe I'm being watched."

An apologetic smile transformed his face, and she could glimpse the kindly man beneath the gruff exterior. "Forgive me. So I take it you *have* decided to stay?"

Suddenly Clara quailed at the direct question. The twists and turns that had determined her life had always been impulsive ones. The decision to leave England for Berlin in 1933 had come after a chance meeting at a party. The agreement to spy for British Intelligence came about because of an episode of Nazi brutality she had witnessed in the street. None of the decisive events in her life had ever been premeditated. Ultimatums made her nervous. She remembered how she had shied away from Leo Quinn's proposal of marriage because he insisted that she leave Germany. Was avoiding decisions her own personal form of cowardice?

"Actually, I haven't quite made up my mind."

"I see." Grand was plainly taken aback. "Your prerogative, of course. But there was a specific task I had in mind . . ."

"Which is?"

Suddenly the major sprang to his feet, eyes on the door. Clara registered the clatter of china, and the next moment, with a perfunctory rap, a large woman in a floral apron backed in, pulling a tea trolley containing a large steel urn and a stack of pale green civil service crockery, as well as a plate of rich tea biscuits.

"Milk and two, Major Grand?"

"You know me so well, Mrs. Fairclough," said Grand, helping himself to a biscuit, snapping it mathematically in half, and dabbing up the crumbs with a forefinger. "And for my guest?"

"Just milk please."

The sight of the malty, copper stream of British tea splashing into the cups prompted in Clara another jolt of nostalgia. Although her time in Germany had introduced her to the pleasure of coffee, no one else in Europe made tea the English way, well brewed, refreshing in all weathers, and the answer to every crisis.

After Mrs. Fairclough had dispensed the tea, plunked in the sugar lumps, and maneuvered the trolley out of the office, Grand perched on the desk in front of Clara and fixed his eyes on her.

"To answer your question, this is a task of the utmost delicacy. One that goes to the heart of the future peace of Europe. I don't mind saying it will determine whether all those gas masks we've been given will ever get used. There are rumors going round intelligence circles that a Nazi-Soviet pact is in the offing."

Clara looked up from her tea with a frown. "A pact with the Bolsheviks? Surely not?"

"A marriage of convenience is I think what they call it."

"But the Nazis and the Bolsheviks are ideological enemies. It could never happen."

"My feelings precisely," said Grand. "I would have thought hell would freeze over first. However. If the rumors are true, there would be very grave repercussions for the rest of us. From what we hear, the idea of a pact is being propelled by von Ribbentrop. He has a pathological loathing for the British, so he's presumably working on the basis that my enemy's enemy is my friend."

"Even so, it's so unlikely."

"Personally I agree. It's arrant nonsense. Besides, our own people are negotiating with Comrade Stalin right now. But we need more solid intelligence. Something concrete. We need an inside track to the Foreign Ministry, and that's where you come in."

Into Clara's mind came the impatient, chiseled face of Conrad Adler. *I'm on loan. Like a painting in a museum.*

"Von Ribbentrop is a stupid man," continued Grand. "Vain and foolish. His wife, however, is another matter. And I think you know her."

Grand slid a newspaper photograph out of a manila file on his desk, and craning across, Clara saw with astonishment that it was a yellowing page from the *B.Z. am Mittag* showing herself talking to Annelies von Ribbentrop at the launch of the Reich Fashion Bureau in 1933. The passage of six years had done nothing to soften the rigid composure of the foreign minister's wife, the iron set of her jaw, or the dyspeptic smile that could so easily be mistaken for a grimace.

"What do you make of her?"

Clara thought back to the first time she'd met Frau von Ribbentrop, just after the regime came to power. Then the woman was an arriviste, desperate to impress with dinner parties at her Dahlem home, and now she was half of one of the most powerful couples in Europe. Kings, presidents, and prime ministers came to her parties. She was a far more ardent Nazi than her husband, yet their marriage could not be more different from the marital catfight the Goebbelses waged. The von Ribbentrops were said to share everything, especially political plans.

"She's a formidable woman," Clara remarked carefully.

"Indeed. A couple of chaps here met her when von Ribbentrop was ambassador to Great Britain, and they were frankly terrified. She was always cornering them to complain about the weather—as though they could do anything about it—and insanely jealous about her husband's behavior with the ladies. He was said to send a daily bunch of red carnations to Wallis Simpson, and his wife couldn't tolerate it. She was a bit of a laughingstock actually. She brought over a marching squad of SS guards, who created the most frightful atmosphere, and above all she had the most dreadful nouveau riche taste. Decked out the whole of Carlton House Terrace in marble cladding. It looks like a public lavatory. It's going to take years to unpick."

Clara finished her tea and returned the saucer to the table. "I take it, Major, it's not her artistic tastes you're concerned about here."

"Precisely. More her knowledge of diplomatic maneuvers. To what extent she influences the husband's decisions."

"Goebbels always says von Ribbentrop bought his title, married his money, and got all his political views from his wife. They say even Hitler is wary of her."

A flicker of a smile. "I suppose that's the thing about marriage—one can never tell what goes on inside. Do you see much of her?"

"Hardly. Last year she tried to have me arrested as a spy."

Clara hesitated. Something Mary Harker had mentioned came to mind.

"But she is holding a press reception to show off the refurbishment of the new Foreign Ministry building. The Reich Chamber of Culture always likes actresses to attend these events if possible."

"To supply a touch of glamour."

"That's the idea. But even if I went, I can't imagine she would give me the time of day, let alone confide any military secrets."

"I'm sure she'll come round," declared Grand, as though Clara's objections were negligible. "Find a way to get closer to her. From what we've heard, Frau von Ribbentrop frequently formulates political policy, which is later passed off as her husband's."

"She's not like him, though. Not the kind to be easily taken in."

"Then you'll need to find another way in. Any way we have into the Foreign Office. It's urgent, I don't need to remind you. If the German Foreign Ministry is contemplating a marriage of convenience with the Soviet Union, it's vital we know as soon as possible."

Grand paced across the room, thumbs tucked into his waist-coat pockets.

"The Soviet Union is the key to everything, Miss Vine. It's a complicated dance. If Germany attacks Poland and the Red Army joins in on Poland's side, and Britain and France come to her aid, then Germany would be in a parlous position. They would never choose to fight on two fronts. But if the Nazis are making advances to the Russians, it's essential that we uncover every piece of information that we can. And we have only a matter of months to do it."

"Months? How can you be so sure?"

"If Hitler's set on war, he won't attack before harvesttime.

But he'll want to make a move before winter. It's a tight window."

He slid his cuffs and checked his watch, as though setting a deadline.

"If you decide to stay in Germany, we'll need to brief you. We'll set up another meeting. Shall we say a fortnight's time? In Paris?"

Clara laughed. "That's impossible. I already had to plead a family emergency to come to London. I couldn't make a trip to Paris without Goebbels finding out."

"Then tell him."

"I don't think you understand," she said, as patiently as she could. "Travel is severely restricted for members of the Reich Chamber of Culture. You need permission to go abroad, and nowadays it's not often given. Certainly not without a plausible explanation."

For a second, Grand steepled his fingers in thought, then he aimed them towards her in the shape of a gun.

"How about if you were to feature in French *Vogue*?"

"*Vogue?*"

"You know, the fashion magazine."

"I know what *Vogue* is, Major Grand. But why would they want to feature me?"

"Well, it's not a magazine I'm intensely familiar with— *Horse and Hound* is about my limit where periodicals are concerned—but we have a friend who works as a photographer there, and I daresay a spread on European cinema might be the kind of thing he does. My sources tell me you've done some modeling in the past."

Clara nodded, suddenly realizing how much detail about her lay in that manila file in front of her interviewer. In 1933, shortly after her arrival in Berlin, she had been invited to model outfits for the Reich Fashion Bureau, an establishment set up by Hitler. That was how she had first come into contact with Magda Goebbels, Emmy Goering, and the other senior Nazi wives.

"Excellent then. Our friend's name is Thomas Epstein. He occupies apartment four, number eleven Rue Léopold-Robert in the Fourteenth Arrondissement of Paris. Can you remember that?"

"Of course."

"I'll tell him to expect you. Shall we say two weeks today? And we'll need to have whatever information you can obtain within the month."

"A month! But, you see, I don't actually think . . ."

"I hope I did impress on you, Miss Vine, that time is very much of the essence."

Grand walked briskly to the door, as though Clara's objections, let alone any further pleasantries, were a dangerous waste of time. Suddenly she sensed her chance slipping away. She couldn't leave without asking the question that was tearing her apart.

"Major Grand, do you know Leo Quinn?"

Outwardly, his genial expression remained intact, but minute study of his face revealed that her question had disturbed him. A muscle tensed in his jaw; he gave the barest nod of assent.

"Would you have any idea where I could contact him?"

"Contact Mr. Quinn? Now why would you want to do that?"

Clara hesitated, wondering if Grand knew the truth. He knew so much else about her, there was every reason he would. Every reason except Leo's careful, meticulous attempts to keep their love affair secret.

"He's an old friend of mine. He's the one who got me into all this in the first place when he was a passport control officer in Berlin."

Grand paused with his hand on the doorknob. "If I were you, my dear, I should forget Mr. Quinn."

It took everything Clara had to prevent the alarm that arose in her showing on her face. Blindly she trained her eyes on Major Grand's mustache and gripped the cotton handkerchief inside her pocket.

"Forget him? What do you mean by that?"

"Just what I say."

"Is it bad news?"

"Need-to-know basis, I'm afraid."

"But I do need to know." She clenched her teeth. "Has something happened to him?"

Grand gave another businesslike smile, but his voice was softer. "I don't like telling you this, my dear. I *shouldn't* be telling you this, frankly. But our networks in Europe have taken a bad hit. We lost a couple of agents in Austria, and Mr. Quinn was involved. Our network there was blown."

"In Austria? I thought . . ." What did she think? She had no idea what Leo did, where he went, or what his job really was.

Grand stared beyond her, a pained expression on his face, his mouth grim as though fighting to contain emotion. "There's a break in the chain somewhere. An informer somewhere on the continent. I can't be any more precise than that, but it behooves all our people to be doubly, triply cautious about who they trust."

"But Leo—you don't know what's happened to him? Not for sure?"

Grand touched a hand to her shoulder. "I'm sorry. Your friend was a brave man, my dear. You should be proud of him."

"He *was?*"

He imprisoned her hand momentarily in a tight clasp. "Thanks once again for coming. Can I take it you remember the way to the lift?"

Numbly, Clara retraced her steps along the corridor. Tears welled in her eyes, blurring the partitioned offices and the men on telephones. She was barely aware of the clack of typewriters and the chatter of secretaries carrying files clipping alongside her. A tall, tawny-haired man with a narrow toothbrush mustache glanced quizzically at her, as though about to inquire if she was all right. As their eyes met she noticed that he had irises of two different colors, one blue and one brown, and the irrelevant thought went through her head that such a distinguishing feature would make undercover work impossible; this agent must be office based. Ducking her head, she walked on to the lift.

She did not look back. If she had, she would have seen Major Grand poised at the entrance to his office, an unusually sympathetic look replacing his rigid military demeanor.

IN CAXTON STREET A brisk wind rose, rustling the leaves on the plane trees and causing women at the bus stop opposite to clutch their hats. In a breeze like that, it was unsurprising that anyone should have tears in their eyes, and no one gave Clara the slightest attention apart from a grinning bus conductor, sailing past on the platform of his bus, who called, "Penny for your thoughts, darling!"

She walked like someone dazed by an explosion, the exterior world locked off behind an invisible wall. The bomb that had gone off inside her had caused everything around to resettle in unrecognizable disarray.

She progressed blindly, wondering what to do in the hours before heading for Liverpool Street station and the boat train. Suddenly, the shock she had received overcame her instincts. Turning impulsively on her heel, she caught up with the bus that had just passed and jumped aboard, heading for Elizabeth Street.

She sat numbly on the lurching bus. *If I were you, my dear, I should forget Mr. Quinn.* It was as though all the ballast was knocked out of her and she might simply collapse without the coarse red and blue backing of the seat beneath her. All she could think was of knocking on Angela's door and feeling her elder sister's sinewy arms enfolding her in a stiff but heartfelt embrace. She was aching to breathe in Angela's trademark perfume and bury her face in soft, sensible cashmere. She had not seen her sister for two years. They may disagree politically; they may have avoided any intimate exchanges for a decade, but Angela was, after all, her only sister. And at a time when she felt desolately alone, Clara yearned for the visceral comfort of flesh and blood.

SHE HAD NEVER VISITED Angela's home in Elizabeth Street, but it was exactly as she expected. Wedding cake white stucco, window boxes trimmed with box and ivy, expensive cars parked outside, and a black door so polished you could see your face in it. It was hard to believe her sister had come so far. In her mind's eye Clara still saw her in an Aertex shirt, cotton skirt, and white leather T-bar shoes, standing in the garden of their Surrey home, arguing over a tennis racquet.

Her heart was thumping as she waited on the step and raised the lion's head knocker, but it was a while before the door opened, and then it was only an indifferent maid who peered out and did not invite her in. Her cap was askew, as if she had only hurriedly fixed it on, and her hair badly pinned beneath.

"Mrs. Mortimer is out. Mr. Mortimer is at the House of Commons."

"It's Angela I want. When will she be back?"

"I can't say, I'm sure. The mistress left instructions that she's away."

"Away? Away where?" Emotion made Clara abrupt, but she didn't care.

The maid hesitated, as if deciding whether she needed to elaborate for the sake of this insistent stranger, then resolving that to be on the safe side, she did. She poked a strand of hair defensively beneath her cap.

"She's visiting her sister. She's been gone for days. Would you like to leave a message?"

Visiting her sister? What was that supposed to mean? Angela only had one sister, and she, Clara, was standing right there on the doorstep. She knew for a fact that Gerald Mortimer had no sisters. Yet it was inconceivable that Angela could have embarked on a trip to Berlin unannounced; her normal traveling requirements made the Queen of Sheba look casual. Angela was the last person to turn up in a foreign country without the most complicated advance arrangements about luggage and hotels, which usually changed several times. She liked to be met at the airport and lunched in the appropriate restaurants, which in Berlin meant the Esplanade and the Kaiserhof, before attending both the theater and the opera. Unlike Clara, Angela never did anything on impulse, so it was unthinkable that she should have packed a suitcase and slipped away to Berlin without a word, as Clara had done all those years ago.

Yet a second before she opened her mouth to protest, some deep, acquired caution prevented Clara from blurting out these objections and she divined a possible explanation. Angela's excuse must have been dreamed up to cover some less innocent activity. The only explanation was that she was indulging in an illicit affair. Further questions would only give this maid something to gossip about.

"Shall I tell her who called, miss?" inquired the maid, offhandedly.

"No. Thank you. It doesn't matter."

Clara turned and made her way along Elizabeth Street, skirting around the workmen who were removing a set of wrought-iron railings, presumably for airplane manufacture. As she went, Clara tried to see her sister from this new, surprising perspective. Glamorous Angela, modeling Jean Patou in her brief dalliance as a fashion mannequin, had always been elegant and unflappable. She was a Vine to the ends of her racehorse-long legs, and when their mother died, Angela was seamlessly co-opted into the circle of their father's sister, Lady Laura Vine, and an endless round of society parties, tennis matches, and charity events. She enthusiastically participated in their father's Anglo-German Fellowship and, from everything Clara knew, was still fundraising for closer ties between Germany and England.

In every respect Angela's life could not be more different from Clara's own, except one. Neither of them had gotten around to having children. Perhaps that was the reason. Maybe Angela was engaged in an affair because her marriage to Gerald Mortimer, MP, was already crumbling. If so it was sad, but given her brick-faced brother-in-law's manner, not entirely surprising.

Clara progressed up to Knightsbridge, past Harrods, and along Piccadilly until, eventually, her steps took her to a Lyons Corner House on the Strand, where she drank two cups of tea and ate a bun pocked with currants and smeared with a dab of oily margarine. Then she retraced her route, skirted the soot-stained lions of Trafalgar Square, and found herself outside the National Gallery.

It was only when she was sitting on one of the leather benches, surrounded by glimmering gilt frames and blankly studying a painting in front of her, that she gave in to her feelings. Major Grand believed that Leo had died and that Clara should consign his memory to the past. *I should forget Mr. Quinn.* But how did anyone forget? In one way, it was treacherously easy. She thought of Leo's face fading, like a photograph left out in the sun, until no image remained. If it blanked out entirely, she would have nothing but his words to resurrect him; just the letters he had written to her and the book of Rilke's poetry that he gave her. Yet how could Leo be dead when her body still held the memory of him, pressed into every muscle and tendon? A wave of stubborn denial engulfed her. Why should she believe it? Just because someone told you something, didn't mean it was true.

When at last her focus cleared, she saw the painting she had been staring at was Jan van Eyck's *Arnolfini Marriage*. The Bruges merchant in wide-brimmed hat and sable-lined robes clasping hands with his young bride in her sage green gown. Crystalline daylight streamed through the window and glanced off the oranges on the window ledge. The bride, with her little dog at her feet, seemed frozen in reflection, poised at the threshold between concentration and distraction. What was she thinking? Was she happy to be betrothed to this older, wealthy merchant? Or was the ornately opulent room merely a gilded cage? Was the marriage a love match, or an aristocratic contract, so appropriate to the times? *That's the thing about marriage—one can never tell what goes on inside.*

Major Grand's request rose in her mind. Might von Ribben-trop really be attempting a pact with the Soviets? *A marriage of convenience,* Grand had called it. It seemed unthinkable, yet hadn't so much of what seemed unthinkable come to pass in Germany in the last six years?

Suddenly, Clara's focus was razor-sharp and she was no lon-ger looking at the tranquil Belgian interior with its subdued and pensive bride but looking through it, to a garishly refur-bished German Foreign Ministry and the steely, square-jawed grimace of Frau Annelies von Ribbentrop.

FIFTY YOUNG WOMEN, OUTFITTED IN THIGH-SKIMMING WHITE dresses and matching knickers, their hair in coronets of radiant blond braids, filed into the Faith and Beauty canteen for lunch after gymnastics practice. An aroma of sweat mingled with clouds of steam rising from trays of meat, potatoes, and overcooked cabbage as the girls, in their pristine ankle socks, formed a line every bit as precise as a storm troopers' honor guard.

Above them, Hitler hung, brooding eyes inclined downwards to the tanned legs and heaving breasts, and a slogan beneath him blaring, "Future German mothers! Your body belongs to the Führer!" Three passing police-men, part of the investigation into Lottie's death, pointed to the picture, and one made a ribald remark. Although Hedwig couldn't hear what he said, she could guess.

The Faith and Beauty girls had been practicing for a "special event." No one yet knew what it was, only that it was on the Führer's command, and that the eyes of the world would be on them. Hedwig assumed it would be something complicated involving hoops. Hoops always made her nervous, because of having to throw them in the air and catch them and the terrifying possibility that one's hoop would escape and roll away to the eternal shame of herself, her family, the community, and ultimately the Fatherland itself.

Gym was compulsory here. On their first day the leader of National Socialist Youth, Baldur von Schirach, had turned up in person to address them and told them gymnastics focused "the harmonic cultivation of body, mind, and spirit." Privately, Hedwig wondered what the point was of learning social graces that expressed their individuality when gymnastic displays made everyone look the same.

Everyone, that is, except Lottie. She had been the star gymnast of them all, lithe and acrobatic, her lissome body curling obligingly into extreme poses with no apparent effort. She claimed gymnasts had better sex because they were more in tune with their bodies. That was the kind of thing Lottie said, and Hedwig had long since gotten used to it.

She rubbed the places beneath her armpits where her outfit chafed and left angry marks on her skin. Being tall meant that from the moment she joined the Jungmädel at ten, followed by the Bund Deutscher Mädel at fourteen, the regulation uniforms had never quite fit. Lottie, even though she was five foot ten with big feet, was as graceful as a cat and could make the frumpiest outfit look like something from *Elegante Welt*. Hedwig's body was always awkward. She sprawled on a chair like a disjointed puppet and stooped to make herself less tall. Watching her one day, wrestling with a blouse, Lottie had joked it was not the clothes but Hedwig herself who didn't fit. It was a light remark, but secretly it terrified Hedwig. It was something she had always feared about herself—that she was different from the others. That everything the Fatherland demanded from a woman—obedience, enthusiasm, and utter loyalty to the Führer—was somehow missing in her. And one day it would be found out.

In a way, it had been found out already.

Jochen was the only son of Eastern immigrants who came over in the years after the war and settled among the grim tenements of Prenzlauer Berg. He was as tough as any Hitler Youth, but his strength came from digging vegetables rather than paramilitary exercises. Often his pockets were filled with dried seeds in mysterious, leathery pods that he was planning to plant in his allotment. Despite the fact that he spent all day painting Hitler, he had never joined the Party or talked excitedly about army service or the chances of war. On the Führer's birthday he had taken the train out to the borders of the city and spent all day harvesting asparagus, while everyone else traveled in the opposite direction.

It was inevitable that when Hedwig's parents met Jochen the encounter would be a disaster. In their cramped parlor, with its dark brown walls and sooty stove, Jochen had sat dumbly, making monosyllabic comments, eyes fixed stubbornly on the tabletop. Hedwig felt her mother wince when he fetched out a rag of a handkerchief to wipe his face and saw her father frown every time he heard Jochen's rough Berliner accent. Herr Holz had fired off questions to Jochen as though conducting one of the questionnaires that every German now completed in the workplace. What were his interests? Botany. What was his ancestry? Polish. What was his Party membership? Nonexistent. The answers could not have been more disappointing, and as Jochen wolfed down the sausage stew as though it might be taken away from him, and wiped his plate round with a piece of bread, Hedwig could read the verdict in her parents' eyes. He had failed the test. This boy was not what their daughter had joined the Faith and Beauty for. Precisely the opposite, in fact. What was she thinking of?

Afterwards, there had been an argument. Frau Holz claimed Jochen would never amount to anything, and if Hedwig stuck with him, the only house she could hope for was a greenhouse. Herr Holz went further, demanding she end the relationship there and then. Hedwig knew that from that moment on her assignations with Jochen would have to remain secret. Which was why, perversely, her staying in the Faith and Beauty Society suited everyone. Her parents wanted her there so she would not see Jochen; she wanted to be there so that she could.

After lunch that day there was Dinner Etiquette, focusing on how to lay the correct knives and forks, fold napkins into swastikas, and use sugar icing in clever ways. The entire topic was fiendishly complex. There were guidelines for which flowers went with different dishes. Roses with beef. Orchids with fish. The Führer's favorite, edelweiss, if you could find it, with anything.

Everything was about rules now. The girls had been given a Rule Book to mark down everything they learned. How to talk, how to look, how to conduct yourself correctly. Girls should always, for example, wait for the men to pick up cutlery and start eating first. Hedwig studiously noted everything she learned, but in truth, it was like taking life lessons from a fairy tale. No one in Berlin would be holding five-course dinners in the near future. You couldn't get sugar icing, and finding a side of beef was about as likely as the Führer himself dropping by to eat it.

Gloomily she selected a hunk of rye bread to accompany the thin gravy. Today's lunch was sauerkraut, bread soup, and fake meat. Everything was fake now; not just the coffee but the rice cooked in mutton fat molded to make artificial chops, rice mixed with onions and oil, which was called fake fish, the nettles in soup, and the horse chestnuts in bread. It reminded her of a joke Lottie had told. *What's the difference between India and Germany? In India one man, Gandhi, starves on behalf of millions. In Germany, millions starve on behalf of one man.*

Lottie was the only woman who dared tell jokes in public, with a rich, full-throated, gurgling laugh. That was also against the rules, of course. Laughing was inelegant for women, according to the principal, Frau Mann. It implied criticism and did not befit a German woman. Smiling was a different matter—indeed, Faith and Beauty girls should always smile when a man addressed them—but laughing, well, the way Frau Mann talked, it was as though a healthy dose of female laughter could bring the whole edifice of the National Socialist Party crashing down.

"Are you eating that?"

Hilde Ziegler was eyeing Hedwig's slice of rye bread, and Hedwig shrugged. She used to be hungry all the time. A hunger that filled her dreams with fat pork chops, chocolate, and cake with real cream and pastries made with butter, but since Lottie's death, her appetite had disappeared.

She glanced out of the window to the woods at the far end of the garden. At the place Lottie was found, the police had erected arc lights, the kind you saw in film studios, bathing the area in a dazzling phosphorescent glow. But there was one secret that no amount of police spotlights were going to uncover.

Everyone in Germany kept a place in their mind, like a cellar in a house or an attic concealed by a study door, that nobody knew about. A place where they thought their own thoughts and examined their true feelings. And when Hedwig retreated to this place and shut the door behind her, what she mainly felt was guilt.

8

E VEN THOUGH HE WAS STANDING IN THE SHADOWS, CLARA could feel his eyes on her. Calculating, malign, dangerous. Attempting, with the precision of an interrogator, to dissect her performance and separate pretense from reality. Analyzing every minute facial movement, every glance and gesture, to pounce on falsity and drag the truth from where she had concealed it.

Despite the heat of the stage lights, she shivered.

She was wearing a flimsy pink silk dress and spectacles and standing next to Heinz Rühmann on stage five of the Ufa studio—the very same soundstage on which Marlene Dietrich had only a decade earlier filmed *The Blue Angel* and Fritz Lang made *Metropolis*. Now, in contrast to those cinematic masterpieces, stage five was playing host to the final scene of *Liebe Streng Verboten*. *Love Strictly Forbidden* was pure, high-octane candy-floss for the eyes. The plot revolved around an ambitious mother who wanted to marry her daughter to the lord of the manor, while the daughter was in love with a lowly hotelier. It was a farcical procession of mistakes and confusions with a satisfyingly happy ending and just the kind of escapism Herr Doktor Goebbels prescribed to soothe a nation's frazzled nerves.

In truth, Clara was glad that the film required a minimum of effort. Her visit to London and the news of Leo occupied all her thinking space. She felt stunned, as though she had left part of herself in England, and *Love Strictly Forbidden,* whose script had as much depth and sophistication as the back of a cornflakes packet, was the ideal vehicle to occupy her. The love-lorn secretary was a popular role in German cinema, and she had played it a number of times over the last few years, so it was easy to go through the motions. It helped that Heinz Rühmann, one of the biggest blond heartthrobs of German screen, was an old friend, so kissing him was no great hardship.

Yet even the most intimate of love scenes required an army of people in the studio: director, assistant director, crew, clapper board loader, piano player. Continuity girl, props manager, cameraman, and gaffer, and a makeup artist with brushes and palette primed for a last-minute touch-up. Boys with belts of tools hung from the cranes, and in distant glass cubicles sound engineers fiddled with knobs and microphones. All morning everyone's attention had been focused on the small pool of light occupied by Clara and Rühmann, but when the minister for propaganda entered, suddenly no one was watching the actors anymore.

As soon as Clara saw Goebbels take shape in the shadows, assistants fluttering around him and the violet haze of his cigarette smoke coiling up into the studio roof, she knew there was no point going on. The man in charge of all filmmaking in the Third Reich was not the type to linger respectfully in the shadows. Once he registered that she had seen him, he gave an infinitesimal nod, and Clara, with a quick, apologetic smile to the director, threaded her way through the camera cables and followed Goebbels as he hobbled in his built-up patent leather boots along the corridor to his office.

The propaganda minister's limp was the first thing everyone noticed about him and the last thing they dared mention. In the early days of the regime, the Society for the Aid of Cripples had brought out a pamphlet celebrating Goebbels as the supreme example of mental powers triumphing over physical disabilities. The charity got a taste of those mental powers shortly afterwards, when their pamphlet was burned and the society closed down.

Reaching his office, Goebbels flung open the door.

The office was a symphony of gleaming light, polished oak, and pale leather furniture. Chrome lamps graced a desk of immaculate walnut. Stills from Ufa's greatest hits were displayed in tasteful black frames on the walls. Pride of place was devoted to an enormous close-up picture of Goebbels's own face, cadaverous, hollow-eyed, and exuding all the gravitas of a wanted poster. The office also came fitted with the standard accoutrements of any minister of the Third Reich—microphones concealed in the walls, lamps, and picture frames—invalidating the need to close the door quite so firmly as he gestured her to a seat.

Goebbels stalked across to his desk and threw himself down. Generally, his charm was as polished as his own furniture, but that day his bony visage was grimly set and his pomaded hair visibly graying. Despite the immaculate Hugo Boss herringbone suit and shimmering silk tie, he looked more wretched than Clara had ever seen him. A twitch flickered in the corner of his left eye. Something serious was plainly troubling him, and though there was no shortage of troubles that might concern a senior member of the Nazi government in the spring of 1939, Clara guessed Goebbels's misery had nothing to do with the prospect of European war.

She wondered if it was the stomach complaint that had forced him into hospital recently, or the fact that Lida Baarová, the Czech actress he had been besotted with, had been banished from Germany on Hitler's orders. Yet instinct told her it was the same old story—the ongoing marital war with his wife, Magda, who according to studio gossip had taken revenge for her long humiliation by initiating an affair with Karl Hanke, her husband's aide, and was now disporting herself in an unseemly manner around the city's nightclubs. On Goebbels's desk Magda stared out from a silver picture frame with a look that could freeze blood. Clara wondered how he managed to stop himself turning it to the wall.

He eyed her coldly.

"I must say you look totally unrecognizable with those spectacles. You don't need them, do you?"

"Not yet."

"Good. They're hideous. Take them off. Spectacles on women are worse than trousers. They lend a dreadfully academic air, and I loathe academic women. Besides, it makes it harder to tell what you're thinking."

Unbidden, Conrad Adler's phrase again floated into Clara's head. *Like fire behind ice.*

"Actresses are supposed to project their feelings, not suppress them. It doesn't do to look sly. Especially—"

He broke off to reach for the silver cigarette box, a gift from Hitler himself, and extracted one cigarette, tossing it carelessly in Clara's direction and offering a light. Having savored this hesitation, he resumed.

"Especially when you're about to appear in the most ambitious film that Germany has ever seen."

"Love Strictly Forbidden?"

Goebbels cast his eyes to the ceiling, as though beseeching divine help, and tapped a finger on his patent leather boot.

"Don't be ridiculous, woman. *Love Strictly Forbidden* is a piece of nonsense designed for brainless secretaries on a night out whose highest ambition is to seduce their employer and entrap the poor sap into marriage. I'm talking about something of immense artistic importance." He exhaled a weary stream of smoke, as though the woes of the world had settled on his narrow shoulders.

"You, Fräulein Vine, have been plucked from—well, perhaps not obscurity"—he gave a sardonic wince—"but very far from stardom, to feature in a documentary film about the making of Germania."

"But I . . ."

"Don't interrupt. It's the inspiration of the Führer himself. He feels the time is right for a full-length film about the triumphs of our nation and a celebration of our cultural conquests abroad."

What exactly could Goebbels be referring to? The remilitarization of the Rhineland? The annexation of Austria? The seizure of Czechoslovakia?

"Which cultural conquests did you have in mind?"

Goebbels's eyes narrowed to check for subordination, then he said, "I take it you've heard of the Ahnenerbe?"

"I'm not sure I . . ."

"Herr Reichsführer Himmler's hobby."

The mention of the sinister, moonfaced SS chief was like an ice cube down the spine. Himmler had that effect on most people. Generally his hobbies involved building new concentration camps and expanding the Gestapo's state-of-the-art surveillance system, but no one, as yet, had suggested making a film about them.

Goebbels crossed his skinny legs and sighed. "I can see I'm going to have to explain. You must have seen newsreels about the trip to Tibet?"

"Oh yes," she said quickly. "That."

The weekly newsreel was shown before every feature film. Clara had dozed through one just the other evening when she visited the Ufa Palast with Erich. Vaguely she recalled footage of scientists disembarking from a plane at Tempelhof airport. From what she could recall, the expedition had been dedicated to proving one of Himmler's most cherished notions—that the Aryan race was preeminent on earth. They had been examining Tibetan natives for evidence.

"Himmler's full of these obsessions," grunted Goebbels. "If it's not the Ahnenerbe, it's that place down in Wewelsburg."

Sensing that he had imparted a little too much information, he drew himself together, rose, and clasped his hands behind his back.

"Anyway. The Ahnenerbe is a scientific institute established to research the cultural history of the German race, and whatever our private thoughts about the SS Reichführer's—*enthusiasms*—its work will be the centerpiece of this film. It's got foreign locations, history, adventure." A little, dismissive wave. "Everything people love."

"It sounds very ambitious." Clara made a mental note to grill Erich about the Ahnenerbe as soon as possible. As an ardent member of the Hitler Youth, he always knew about these things.

"It is. As the Führer sees it, the Ahnenerbe is at the very

heart of our work as National Socialists. It seeks to propagate the eternal values of the Germanic races. Et cetera, et cetera." Goebbels waved his hand to signify the kind of officialese beloved of his own newsreels and newspapers. "I'm giving you the broad-brush picture here, but you're going to need to familiarize yourself fairly swiftly, because from what I hear Himmler is taking a close interest in this film and he's perfectly likely to turn up on the set without warning."

Goebbels's face twisted with distaste at the thought. The prospect of another senior Nazi intruding on his own department was plainly a serious irritant. He strode over to the window to look out on a small square of lawn in the style of a medieval cloister, where actresses and secretaries liked to relax between takes, gossiping and catching the sun and, all too often, the minister's eye. Although his gaze traveled automatically over the tanned legs and golden figures on display, his mind was plainly elsewhere.

"I would have thought, Fräulein Vine, you would be flattered to be involved."

"I am. Very. Who's the director?"

He swung round, his expression, if possible, even more dyspeptic. "I was coming to that. *Germania* is to be directed by Fräulein Leni Riefenstahl."

Leni Riefenstahl.

Leni Riefenstahl was, without doubt, the most famous female director alive. Her film about the 1934 Nazi party rally, *The Triumph of the Will,* had seduced not just Germany but many around the world. Her documentary about the 1936 Berlin Olympic Games had just won Best Film at the Venice Film Festival. If *Germania* was anything like Leni Riefenstahl's previous epics, it would make all Clara's previous films look like home movies.

"I'm honored, Herr Doktor. I really am. But . . ." For a moment Clara's habitual composure had deserted her. "I don't understand why I should have been given the privilege of presenting something quite so . . . high-profile."

"That makes two of us," said Goebbels gracelessly. He rubbed a hand over a cheek silvered with stubble. His complexion was dull with fatigue.

"It's the obvious question, and the first thing I asked, too, but Fräulein Riefenstahl has not deigned to honor me with an explanation. She just said the Führer had given her a free hand and you were what she wanted. She's irrational like that."

He examined his beautifully manicured fingernails and regarded Clara with disdain.

"You seem very cool, considering the honor that's being handed to you. You're invited to star in a movie made by the world's most famous female film director about the most powerful country on earth. I can't imagine you've received many more significant propositions recently. Or perhaps you're too busy? Possibly you have too much on your plate?"

"Of course not. I'm very grateful."

If he was mollified, he didn't show it.

"Good. Well, there's a tight deadline, so you'll need to start right away. I'll have Fräulein Riefenstahl get in touch. Where are you living now? Winterfeldtstrasse, wasn't it?"

"Not anymore. I'm very near here actually. At the Artists' Colony in Griebnitzsee."

"Griebnitzsee?"

She had surprised him. No doubt he assumed he knew everything about her movements, so his surprise provided a crucial piece of information.

Whoever had ordered surveillance on her apartment, it wasn't Joseph Goebbels.

"Strange choice. I've never seen you as the country type."

He was more accurate than he knew. Already Clara wished she was back in Winterfeldtstrasse, watchers or not. She'd never realized how much she loved the comforting racket of the city around her, the clank of the trams and trains on Nollendorf-platz a few blocks away, which started early in the morning and didn't end until late at night, the rattle of shopkeepers rolling up their blinds, the shouts of the newspaper men, and the crash of bottles from the local bars. Some things you never knew you loved until you missed them.

There was a knock on the door, and a secretary's head craned around. "Your sitting, Herr Reichsminister."

"Already? Show him in then!"

Goebbels's face brightened, and he straightened his tie. "An-other official portrait, I'm afraid. I'm not a vain man. I don't like the idea of ministers flaunting themselves, but the minis-try will insist. It has to do with official prestige."

A shock-headed figure with an easel had edged into the room and was hovering uncomfortably by the door.

"Herr Messel! Come in! You have precisely nineteen min-utes of my time."

Goebbels moved to the window so that the light sliced onto his cadaverous cheekbones, fixed his gaze on the sunbathing girls outside, and assumed a philosophical air.

"At least Herr Messel is a decent German artist. My fellow ministers have not been so scrupulous. Von Ribbentrop actually asked André Derain to come from France, and the chap turned him down. Extraordinary, don't you think?"

Clara was saved from replying by a clatter and a soft excla-mation of dismay. Beneath nervously fumbling fingers, Herr Messel's easel had collapsed.

"For God's sake, man!"

Goebbels gave Clara a brusque wave, and she realized that if she didn't act now, she might not have another chance.

"As it happens, Herr Doktor, I have a request. It's another kind of cultural expansion really. *Vogue* magazine in France have asked to photograph me for their September issue. In Paris."

She might as well have proposed flying to the moon.

"*Vogue?* You? Why?"

"They first suggested it when I was there last year," she lied.

"Why not Brigitte Horney or Marika Rökk?" Goebbels protested, cruelly citing two better-known actresses. "Or Zarah Leander?"

She shrugged. "It's a feature called 'Cinema and Fashion.' Apparently the article's a tribute to German cinema. Under the aegis of the Reich Chamber of Film," she added politely.

The idea prompted an explosion of vicious laughter from Goebbels, long, hacking guffaws culminating in a spluttering cough, like a chain saw refusing to start. He bent his heaving shoulders over to recover.

"I shouldn't laugh. I can see how desperate they are to curry favor. But it'll take more than that."

"I'm sorry?"

"Nothing. Just thinking ahead."

"I was hoping you would give your permission for a few days' travel."

He was certain to refuse. Why, after all, should he grant permission for such an insignificant jaunt? Nazi Germany had never been interested in accommodating the French, precisely the opposite. Many more powerful artists had had requests for foreign travel turned down. Since Marlene Dietrich's defection to Hollywood, Goebbels lived in eternal suspicion that his stars were about to jump ship and thumb their noses at the Nazis from the safety of America or Britain.

Clara tried valiantly to remain unruffled beneath his skeptical gaze until Goebbels spread his hands in mock surrender and said, "Go, if you want to. But I can't spare you for more than forty-eight hours. I'm all for the cultural conquest of Europe, but this film is far too pressing to be held up for some trifling magazine piece. Particularly if it's *French*."

IF THERE WAS ONE OCCUPATION THAT OFFERED TRUE JOB security in the Third Reich, it was manufacturing uniforms. From the field gray of the Wehrmacht to SS black, from the attractive slate blue of the Luftwaffe right down to the dark brown overalls of the Reich Labor Service, uniforms were the only product that was never in short supply. And amid the plethora of uniforms lay numerous fine degrees of difference. A universe of trimming, braid, buttons, silver oak leaves, daggers, insignia, and gleaming death's-heads existed, all of them signifying specific titles and ranks and requiring meticulous attention to detail. Contracts to dress the armed forces sparked fierce competition among tailors, and those who were lucky enough to win business were keen to advertise their skills. To this end, twin life-size mannequins in black SS death's-head uniforms had been erected in the window of Fromm's tailor shop, in a narrow street just off the Königsallee, scaring late-night drunks and terrifying children on their way to school.

Clara averted her gaze from the mannequins and checked the address again. It was hard to imagine a less appropriate workplace for a Jewish seamstress, but this was where she had been led to find her old friend Steffi Schaeffer.

The bell clanged behind her as Clara entered the shop and looked around. It was a hushed, deep-carpeted space, perfumed by a tangy mixture of polish, leather, and expensive pomade. Bolts of cloth were stacked at every level, dull gray, blue, pin-stripe, and herringbone, rolled up and reverently folded like vellum manuscripts in a medieval library. Against one wall a dresser of gleaming mahogany with ivory-handled drawers was stacked with containers of braids and buttons, tortoise-shell, horn, ivory, bone, visible through the glass compartments.

On the opposite wall was a gallery of Fromm's more famous clientele. First came the ordinary stars, the actors Gustav Fröhlich and Hans Albers, and the boxer Max Schmeling sporting immaculately cut dinner suits, and above them, at eye level, hung the true celebrities of modern Germany: Heinrich Himmler, with his trademark wide gray breeches and clinical grimace, mad-eyed Rudolf Hess, and Reinhard Heydrich, head of the SD security service, as skeletal and expressionless as any catwalk model.

From the interior gloom a stooped figure emerged with a measuring tape around his neck, peering at Clara through a pair of pince-nez. She guessed this must be Herr Fromm. He nodded towards Himmler's photograph. "We are honored to have the SS Reichsführer as a regular customer."

"So I see."

"And Herr Reichsminister Goering is also a most rewarding client," he added unctuously, intertwining his fingers.

"I can imagine."

Anyone who loved dressing up as much as Goering did would

keep a team of tailors in full-time occupation. Clara peered at a picture of Hitler's second in command cavorting in the bejeweled guise of a Roman emperor, in toga and fur-trimmed slippers, with hair freshly permed, a gold dagger at his waist, and blue diamonds on his pudgy fingers. He was clearly wearing full eye shadow and lipstick. German women might be constantly informed that makeup was degenerate, but different standards applied to German men, it seemed. Senior ones, at least.

"We turn our hand to all varieties of costumes," continued Herr Fromm smoothly, as Clara examined another shot of Goering, looking absurd in an orange suede jerkin and green Tyrolean hat with an animal tail sticking out of it.

"That's Herr Goering's uniform as Reichsforst Jaeger. It required the most exquisite stitching, but here at Fromm's we pride ourselves on attention to detail. Hugo Boss, of course, makes uniforms for everyone—the Sturmabteilung, Hitler Youth, National Socialist Motor Corps . . ." He waved his hand in a faint gesture of deprecation. "But his are made in factories. Discriminating gentlemen prefer bespoke uniforms. And ours, of course, are entirely handmade."

He halted the advertisement inquiringly. "But may I ask how I can help? Is it concerning a uniform for your husband, perhaps? Or something for yourself?"

Although there was no one else in the shop, Clara lowered her voice. "I'm looking for Steffi Schaeffer."

The poker-faced demeanor did not change, but there was a flicker of scrutiny behind Herr Fromm's shuttered eyes.

"Please." He gestured towards the back of the shop and ushered Clara through a velvet drape into an even gloomier room, where volumes of swatches were distributed like open books and a slender woman was measuring out lengths of field gray serge.

At the sight of Clara the other woman jumped up and embraced her, then, keeping hold of her hands, she stood back and looked her up and down.

"How on earth did you find me?"

It was hard to equate the figure before her with the poised and beautiful woman Clara had first met in the Ufa costume department six years before. Steffi Schaeffer still had an air of elegance, but her caramel-blond hair was now liberally threaded with gray and hollows of worry shadowed her face. The lines bracketing her mouth might have been carved there with a knife. The hand that held Clara's was still soft enough to accomplish the most delicate stitching, but her eyes had hardened. Steffi Schaeffer was no longer a costume designer, nor a seamstress with her own premises and a list of private clients. She was not even a German. All Steffi Schaeffer could call herself now was a Jew, and like all the other Jews who made up ninety-five percent of Germany's textile trade, she relied on people like Herr Fromm to make use of her skills. She was lucky, probably, that he had been prepared to take her on.

Instinctively Clara waited until the tailor had melted from view.

"Don't worry about him," Steffi told her. "He's been a godsend. I've lost all my customers, but he gives me what work he can. If anyone important arrives at the shop, he shouts 'Get on with that jacket, Elsa!' up the stairs. It's our code. How did you find me?"

"I went to your old studio. Several times. It was only by chance the block warden saw me and said you might be here." Clara looked around the minuscule room. "What happened?"

"What happened?" There was bitter acid in Steffi's voice that had not been there before. "Kristallnacht happened." The night the previous November when synagogues were burned, Jewish homes and shops demolished, and thousands of Jews arrested all over Germany. The carpet of shattered windows had spawned its own sinister, poetic coining, known the world over. *Kristallnacht.* The Night of Broken Glass.

"The authorities demanded that we repay the cost of repairing shopfronts. Then there was the new law—the Exclusion of Jews from German Economic Life—which meant I couldn't run a business. It was the same for all of us seamstresses. Until a few years ago almost every seamstress in Germany was Jewish. Now, can you believe it, they claim all Jewish influence has been eradicated from the German clothing industry! Who do they think makes the clothes? The Nazis are very demanding; they want the best, and that only comes from Jewish tailors."

"Is Herr Fromm taking a risk, employing you?"

"Of course he is. Officially I need a permit to be here. We're banned from almost everything now. Swimming, going to the cinema, walking in the park. Any sentence with a verb in it, that's what we're banned from. They'd probably ban us from breathing if it were possible."

Steffi hesitated, as if she was still, after all these years, calculating what metal Clara was made of.

"You asked if Herr Fromm is taking a risk employing me. He is. But he's taking an even bigger risk than that. My dressmaking business may not be flourishing, but my other business is."

Clara understood at once what she meant.

After she lost her job at the Ufa studios, Steffi had found another, more urgent line of work, assisting a network of underground resistance workers who helped Jews disappear. Steffi's network provided clothes, food, and disguises for those who needed to vanish fast, helping them to move from safe house to safe house as they kept one jump ahead of the Gestapo's net.

"In fact, there's something you should see. Come with me."

Steffi led the way up two flights of worn wooden stairs and into a room divided in two by a floral curtain.

It was a stark contrast to the polished leather and gleaming mahogany cabinets below. The window shutters were three-quarters closed, casting a dim shadow across the battered sofa and cheap chest of drawers. There was a pungent smell of compressed humanity, stuffy and fetid. In the midst of the room a young girl sat at a Singer sewing machine, bent over a pile of blue gauze.

"This is Esther Goldblatt."

The girl raised a pair of inscrutable almond eyes in brief acknowledgment. She had a haunting gaze, level and unblinking. She could be no more than fifteen, with jet-black hair twisted up in a bun and a slight, resentful twist to her mouth.

"Everyone's learning something now—infant care, mending, glove making, millinery," said Steffi brightly. "So I suggested Esther train as a seamstress. She's a very promising pupil."

"Frau Schaeffer is exaggerating," said Esther, tersely.

"Not at all. You'll pick it up in no time. You're artistic, after all."

Steffi turned away, and as she did, subtly but distinctly, the girl rolled her eyes. It was the gesture of teenagers the world over, the one that expressed an utter disconnect between the world of adults and adolescents, and Clara was instantly reminded of Erich.

"How long have you been here?" she asked.

Clearly the girl's presence in the stuffy attic had nothing to do with dressmaking lessons.

"A whole week."

It showed. Her skin was pale from lack of sunlight, and her hair was lank.

"She sleeps on the sofa bed, and if anyone comes"—Steffi tilted her head at the cushions—"she can hide in the bed frame. It lifts up, and I've fixed the catchment so it looks as if it's broken. I've tacked material on the underside and drilled holes for air. A friend who runs a restaurant on the Ku'damm brings us food."

"But . . ." Clara hesitated. "Why?"

Steffi lowered her voice, as though hoping in vain that Esther would not hear. "The police want to question her about one of her schoolbooks."

"I don't understand."

"It was a drawing book, but I made it look like a schoolbook," explained Esther, refusing to be excluded from the conversation. "I covered all my sketchbooks with blue waxed paper and stuck labels on them from school, with titles like *Algebra* and *Racial Theory*, and hid my pictures inside."

"What did you draw?"

"People being arrested," she answered tonelessly. "I did some of the day when they lined us all up against the garden wall and forced us to watch while they smashed our possessions. They threw a hammer at the mirror, and they tore all the keys out of the grand piano. Then I did drawings of the Gestapo men on the day they took our father away. I draw everything. Here. I did another one today." She passed a piece of paper to Clara.

"It's only people's faces." The girl's voice was deliberately blank, as though challenging Clara to protest. "Steffi can't complain about that."

Esther was right. The drawing was nothing but a panorama of faces. Ordinary Berliners' faces. Grinning, interested, indifferent, heartless. Clara had seen those faces a hundred times, when people were being arrested or loaded into trucks. Or an old man was hauled off by a policeman from a station platform while onlookers stood by.

"Father said I should draw what I liked."

"Well, your father's not here now, is he?" snapped Steffi, exasperated.

"So what happened?" Clara asked.

"The police came. They said our house had been requisitioned by a high-ranking SS officer and we would have to move. They started combing through all our rooms. They'd already taken all our jewelry, but then they found my books."

Clara imagined the hulking forms of the policemen crammed into the apartment, guns at their hips, eyes flitting everywhere, rough hands reaching into drawers.

"Once they looked inside they came back for her that night," added Steffi. "Fortunately her mother had already brought her to me, and she and the older sister are in hiding, too."

Esther's eyes dropped, as if acknowledging for the first time the gravity of her predicament.

"I hate it here," she burst out. "There's nothing to do. I can't even wash because there's no soap."

"Have you seen your mother?"

"She came yesterday, just for an hour. The worst thing is, I miss my cat. What's going to happen to him? Who will look after him while we're gone?"

It might have seemed strange that the girl should expend her anxiety on a cat, rather than her mother and sister, or her father, imprisoned in a camp, but Clara was not so easily fooled. Esther was focusing all her anxieties on one, easily identified treasure. It had been the same for Clara when her mother died. She recalled the obsession she had with her horse Inkerman and his lame leg. She remembered burying her face in his glossy pelt, and inhaling leather and straw and sweat.

"He'll be fine," she told the girl.

"He's only a kitten."

"Cats are good at looking after themselves."

"My mother kept saying nothing would happen. My father won the Iron Cross in the war. He didn't believe in running away. My uncle came back from Palestine because it was too dirty, and then in the Olympics he said no city on earth could compare with Berlin. Father said Jews always thrive under pressure. He said pressure turns coal dust into diamonds."

Suddenly the vulnerability of Esther Goldblatt, with her narrow shoulders and solemn, mistrustful eyes, touched something deep within Clara—a protective urge that was both mysterious and utterly familiar.

"How old are you, Esther?"

"Fifteen in July."

"Fourteen!" She turned to Steffi. "She's a child still. How can they be looking for a child?"

"She's a young woman in their eyes and she has disseminated subversive material," said Steffi.

"It's not material!" Esther jerked her chin proudly. "It's Art!"

"If your drawings were passed around they could influence other people," snapped Steffi. There was a harshness about her that had not existed in the early days of Clara's friendship with her. It was born of exhaustion and worry, no doubt, but Clara felt for the girl on the receiving end.

"Now get on with that hem, Esther, while I have a word with Fräulein Vine."

Steffi descended the flight of steps and stared out of the window to the street below.

"Poor kid," said Clara.

Steffi shrugged. "She doesn't make it easy. Perhaps it's harder for her than for others because she came from a wealthy background and the family sheltered her from what was going on. They had a large apartment in Charlottenburg, and the father was a boutique owner with a smart shop on the Ku'damm. But she tries my nerves, Clara. I'm at my wit's end, and she complains constantly about being shut up in an attic and not having enough to eat. What does she think this is? The Hotel Adlon?"

She gripped the banisters with clenched hands.

"Esther's situation is not hopeless. Her father may be in Sachsenhausen, but her mother and sister are safe and they have an uncle in America who has given them an affidavit to move there. The problem is, Esther's quota number is very far down the list and it will take years before it comes up. The only country that gives transit visas to people with American quota numbers is England, but Esther needs someone in England to guarantee for her because she's too young to earn a living there. She would have to be adopted by a British citizen."

"Officially adopted?"

"Only until the age of eighteen. But that's not all. The person in England must deposit a large sum of money to sponsor a refugee."

The complexity of the situation dimmed Steffi's countenance, and her face creased again into a lattice of lines.

"We can supply most things. We have a doctor who brings medicine and a young man who produces passports and identity papers for us. He turns his hand to anything. Work permits, release papers, travel permits. Tickets for buses and trains. His work is superb, but he can't conjure up an English sponsor. And on top of that, Esther can't stay here for long. Herr Fromm has been very good, but he generally only takes Jews in for one night at a time. The other day Heydrich came in and Herr Fromm said measuring the inside leg of the top man in the SS with Esther one floor above was enough to give him a heart attack. His nerves are in shreds."

"What will you do?"

"If we could just find some way to get her to England . . ."

"You're asking me to help."

"I'm sorry. You don't have to get involved in this. You can't have expected this when you came today. I wouldn't blame you if—"

"No, of course. I'll do everything I can."

A clatter on the street below caused them to turn, but when they looked down they saw only several large rolls of black cloth being unloaded from a van and carried inside.

"Herr Fromm got his orders in early," said Steffi quietly. "There's going to be a boom in black. Black crepe, black cotton. Black serge to cover windows in a blackout. Black felt to conceal the car headlights. Black voile."

"Why voile?"

"War means widows. And there'll be clothing cards, too, so materials will be rationed. Herr Fromm is wise to stockpile early."

She reached out a hand. "I forgot. I have something for you, Clara."

She went over to her bag and brought out a velvet pouch, from which she withdrew a box containing a three-stranded string of pearls. The pearls were old, Clara could see, and of the highest quality, with an intricate gold clasp and a soft gleam that seemed to hover around them as they nestled on their bed of crimson velvet. She looked on in astonishment as Steffi fastened them around her neck.

"What's this?"

"It's not a gift, I'm afraid. More a loan. I've sewed hundreds of necklaces and rings into the linings of women's dresses, but the Gestapo are getting wise to our scheme now, and they routinely rip up people's clothes, so I thought of a better hiding place. These pearls are valuable. They belonged to my grandmother, and you know the thing about pearls—they come from the sea and they need moisture to keep their luster. They must be worn, and I can think of no one better to wear them for me."

Clara touched the necklace and smiled. "I'd be honored. But only until you need them again."

"I don't need them. In fact, I want you to sell them."

"Sell them! Are you sure?"

"Next time you go to England, sell them and keep the money there. That way, if Esther manages to leave, we can have something to pay her sponsor."

Steffi stood back and studied the necklace with an approving smile. "In the meantime, pearls suit your skin. They have a way of lighting up the face, don't you think? But my necklace does show up that dress you're wearing. Look at this rent in the sleeve. Let me darn it while you wait."

Clara felt ashamed at the original purpose of her visit.

"For heaven's sake, Steffi. You have more important things to do than darn dresses."

A hint of the seamstress's old self returned as she examined the sleeve critically, assessing its texture and precise shade.

"Allow me. It's relaxing. And besides, you are, almost certainly, the only customer I have left, Clara."

10

ALBERT SPEER LOOKED MORE LIKE A MAN TOURING THE stations of the cross than someone inspecting his own, recently completed refurbishment of the Foreign Ministry in Wilhelmstrasse. The Führer's favorite architect was a good decade younger than most of the Nazi elite, and it showed; his chestnut hair was lustrous, his muscular frame filled a finely cut suit, and Hitler's fondness for him was said to border on the homoerotic. True, by the standards of the Nazi elite—obese Goering, mad Hess, and crippled Goebbels—Speer was practically an Adonis, but as he toured the room on the queenly arm of Annelies von Ribbentrop, the architect's handsome face was not a happy one. Indeed, behind the bland, professional composure it was possible to detect outright dismay at the sight of the journalists, celebrities, and actresses gathered to toast the new décor at 73 Wilhelmstrasse.

Perhaps because the end result was far from what he had planned. Speer, whose own style was cool, severe, and neoclassical, favoring shimmering colonnades of pristine marble, must have winced at the grandiose swags of cerise velvet that now gussied up each window, the silk wallpaper and mounds of soft furnishings. Opulent chandeliers had been fitted, and the walls were plastered with old masters in handsome gilded frames—Rembrandts and Goyas hanging in tiers three and four high, displayed in order of expense. Every pillared hall, every marbled vista, every polished wall now bore the flamboyant personal stamp of Joachim von Ribbentrop. Or to be more accurate, his wife.

Clara stood amid a group of journalists at the far side of the room, Major Grand's request resounding in her head. *From what we've heard, Frau von Ribbentrop frequently formulates political policy, which is later passed off as her husband's.* It was true, the foreign minister's wife was very different from those of other senior men. Magda Goebbels was too depressed to care about politics, and Eva Braun, the Führer's girlfriend, probably couldn't spell Czechoslovakia. Annelies von Ribbentrop, by contrast, was highly educated and politically motivated. She knew more, and would impart far less. How could Clara possibly find a way into her mind?

That day the châtelaine of the new Foreign Ministry was wearing a suit of hairy mauve, a pussy bow blouse, emerald earrings, and a welter of pearls at her throat. Powder settled into the lines round her eyes like wrinkles in old paint, and her hair was set like concrete. Frau von Ribbentrop's delight at parading Albert Speer was all the greater because of the hot competition for his services. He had already redecorated Goebbels's Propaganda Ministry with lacquered walnut fittings and installed a home cinema in the minister's townhouse. He had renovated 11 Leipziger Platz, the grandiose, turreted monstrosity that was home to the Goerings, and in January he had signed off on the brand-new Reich Chancellery, on which eight thousand workers toiled night and day. Now he was starting his most ambitious commission to date—rebuilding Berlin as the capital of a continental empire. Speer would be the man responsible for turning the Führer's dreams into stone. No wonder he seemed anxious to get away from the von Ribbentrops' soft furnishings.

"Poor Speer," remarked Hugh Lindsey, who was standing at Clara's side. "He's the only one who seems remotely modest, and he has the least to be modest about. Some of his buildings are genuinely exciting."

"Not so exciting for the Jews whose homes are being razed to make way for them," commented Mary.

"You've heard about his next commission?" asked Hugh, helping himself to a canapé proffered by a waiter in silk stockings. "Hitler wants Speer to build a Führermuseum in Linz. His hometown. It's going to house his collection."

"What collection is that?"

"Clara, you must be the only person in Germany who hasn't heard. The Führer's planning to create the greatest art gallery ever seen."

"The only problem is," added Mary conspiratorially, "so is Goering. When I had my interview with him the other day, I thought it was going to be about the Luftwaffe, but it was all about art. Goering is boasting that his country villa, Carinhall, will house the biggest private collection in the world."

"Makes sense," said Hugh. "Nothing about Goering would be small."

"Goering told me his collection will be far more important than Hitler's. He wants to track down all the valuable art of Germanic origin, whatever that might be, and return it to the

Reich. It's quite a spat. Apparently, Speer's calling it the picture war."

"Thank heavens I've found you, Clara."

The voice that broke into their conversation was the kind of theatrical whisper designed to reach the back row of the upper circle.

"What do you make of it? Not exactly cozy, is it?"

Emmy Goering, the wife of Hitler's second in command, sailed unopposed through the goggling throng. Frau Goering had been an actress herself before fate decreed that Hermann Goering, on a rare outing to Weimar, should catch sight of her and fall in love on the spot. Now her fortunes were transformed—she was married with a child, and universally known as the first lady of the Reich. Yet despite having accumulated more wealth than she could have dreamed of, Emmy Goering had also accumulated enemies, and none more potent or bitter than Annelies von Ribbentrop. As Mary and Hugh melted discreetly into the background, Clara recalled Major Grand's motto.

My enemy's enemy is my friend.

"Poor Annelies," continued Emmy, watching acidly as the foreign minister's wife shepherded Speer around the room. "All that money and no taste whatsoever. You know she's announced that all German embassies should be redecorated as precise replicas of the Reich Chancellery? Can you imagine the expense? Now she has a whole ministry to play with, her extravagance knows no bounds. The woman doesn't understand restraint."

It was hard to know how to respond to this. The Goerings' own palatial villa would make a Borgia feel at home. Besides the gem-encrusted gold chairs and mosaic floors inlaid with lapis lazuli swastikas, it was a temple to taxidermy. You could scarcely move for stags' antlers protruding from the walls, and cases containing pheasants, vultures, and eagles. The first artifact to greet visitors in the hall was a stuffed giant panda, a gift from the King and Queen of England.

Frau Goering steered Clara into an alcove, away from the throng.

"Thank God the Winter Relief drive is over. We had to spend an entire morning with the von Ribbentrops rattling collecting boxes in Wittenbergplatz."

The annual Winter Relief charity, the Winterhilfswerk, was always crowned with the appearance of party VIPs on street corners jovially touting lapel pins and coin boxes.

"It took everything Hermann had to keep smiling, but now everything's much worse. Something terrible has happened. You'll never guess."

She paused dramatically, and Clara tilted her head, awaiting the bombshell.

"The Italians have gone and awarded von Ribbentrop the Collar of the Annunziata!"

"What on earth is that?"

"You mean you've never heard of it? I wish I hadn't. It's Italy's greatest chivalric order. It's a gorgeous piece, solid gold, and studded with diamonds. The holder becomes the honorary cousin of the Italian king. Hermann has wanted it for so long. When he heard that von Ribbentrop was to have it, he was almost physically sick. You know he adores jewels."

Clara recalled the photograph of Goering in Herr Fromm's shop, adorned with gold dagger and blue diamonds in the persona of a Roman emperor.

"That's why he admired your Duke of Windsor and his American duchess. All their jewelry! Hermann couldn't stop

talking about the duke's Art Deco cuff links and the duchess's
Cartier diamonds. He says you can tell a lot about a person from
their taste in jewels."

"I bet you can," said Clara, recalling Wallis Simpson, studded all over with pearls the size of pigeon eggs.

"Jewels are an absolute obsession with Hermann. I fret
about him. It's an addiction."

There was every reason why Frau Goering should worry
about her husband's predilection. His addiction to morphine
tablets—originally prescribed for war wounds—was part of
the reason for his monstrous size, which led to his nickname
Der Dicke—Fatso.

As if on cue, a waiter materialized with a tray of smoked
salmon sandwiches, and Emmy popped a couple in her mouth.

"You should try not to worry," Clara told her.

"That's easy for you to say," said Emmy through a mouth of
crumbs. She sighed and patted the corn-colored hair wound
round her ears in thick braids. "It's driving him crazy. But it's
not just that. It's something else." She frowned in genuine per-
plexity. "We're just back from a rest cure in San Remo—in fact
I wish we were still there—but all the time he's been in the
most terrible mood. He's preoccupied with something, but he
won't tell me what it is."

Clara wondered if she should point out the obvious. "Could
it be the international situation?"

"That? Oh no. Don't be silly. Hermann assures me there will
be no war. We need another three or four years of peace. The
English—with respect—are terrible warmongers, but the future of Danzig can hardly concern them. And besides, the Führer won't want to see all his new buildings bombed. No." She
paused, as though trying to solve some incomprehensible puzzle. "All I know is, it's definitely to do with a jewel."

"This golden collar, you mean?"

"No. Another jewel. Hermann's been cheated out of it. That's all I can get out of him. He said it again at breakfast this morning. He's been cheated out of a jewel. He's looking for it high and low, and God help anyone who gets in his way."

"It's hard to imagine anyone cheating your husband."

This remark prompted a peal of laughter from Emmy. "Don't you believe it! Von Ribbentrop spends his life trying to cheat him." Belatedly realizing the consequences of being overheard, she lowered her voice. "Only yesterday Hermann told me von Ribbentrop is cozying up to the Russians."

The Russians? Suddenly all Clara's nerves were on alert. Could it be possible that her questions were to be answered this easily?

"Well, one Russian in particular. I think you know her. Frau Olga Chekhova. Annelies's new best friend."

The letdown was instant. Clara had acted with Olga Chekhova many times over the years. Although she was Russian by birth and a niece by marriage of the great Anton Chekhov, Olga had lived in Berlin for decades and had even been given the honorary title of Staatsschauspieler, state actor. However skillful the acting talents of the kindly Olga Chekhova, one role she was surely not playing was that of spy. She was a motherly woman behind the silk and pearls, and the last person one could imagine meddling in the murky waters of Stalin's henchmen.

"Olga Chekhova's a huge supporter of the Führer. I don't think there's anything suspicious about her."

"Oh, don't you?" said Emmy, with a distinct air of affront. "Well, just between us, Hermann has heard some quite unsettling things about La Chekhova. Her brother is a senior official with the NKVD."

The NKVD was Stalin's secret intelligence service. As cunning and brutal as the Gestapo themselves, they formed a fear-some network of ruthless agents stretching across Europe. Yet while this revelation surprised Clara, she had no doubts about her friend.

"You think it's strange that a woman whose face is on every billboard in Berlin could be working in the shadows? That an actress could also be a spy?"

"I do."

"Trust me, these times bring out the strangest behavior in people."

She paused primly.

"So what are you doing at the moment?"

"I'm about to start a film about the Ahnenerbe."

Frau Goering rolled her eyes. "Ugh. Heini Himmler's little passion. All that archaeology and measuring skulls. If men must have obsessions, give me Hermann's jewelry craze any day. Why on earth do we need a film about the Ahnenerbe?"

"Herr Doktor Goebbels said the Führer was attaching the highest importance to it."

Emmy's eyes gleamed with mischief. She pounced on this information. "So you've seen Goebbels? How was he?"

Clara hesitated. It was always risky to give Emmy Goering too much detail unless you wanted it to reappear at some future date with your name attached.

"I thought he looked strained."

"Doesn't he! The man's a bag of nerves. He's just been in the hospital with kidney pains, but I'm sure it's all because of Magda. You can't imagine the stories I've been hearing!"

Clara guessed she was about to find out. "Are they having troubles again?"

"Troubles! You have no idea! Far be it from me to feel sorry for the Herr Doktor, but I think it behooves the wife of a senior man to behave in a certain way, and the way Magda is carrying on would try the patience of a saint, which, as we all know, the Herr Doktor most certainly is not. Fortunately my Hermann is in the pink of health. He was up to two hundred and eighty pounds—he seeks comfort in food, you see—but he lost forty pounds on his diet. I know because he was trying on his outfit just this morning. Oh, but of course . . ."

Her face brightened.

"That's why I was looking for you, Clara. We're holding a reception for Prince Paul of Yugoslavia. It's a state visit. There are eight days of celebrations, but our party will be the high point. It's at the Schloss Bellevue. We've had to invite the von Ribbentrops unfortunately, but it should still be great fun. As a matter of fact, we're having a deputation of those Faith and Beauty girls come." She grimaced. "We had no choice. It's Himmler's wish. They're being trained up to take their place in polite society. We have to let them loose on diplomatic guests so that they can practice their conversational skills. God help us, but at least they'll look decorative."

"Thank you. It sounds very glamorous."

"Don't thank me. It was Hermann's brother who wanted you to come, actually. It was his particular request."

"His brother?"

"Albert's in the film business, but he's fearfully shy. You'd never believe the pair of them could be brothers. Quite Hermann's opposite."

Clara was astonished. In the world of celebrity, the brother of Germany's second most powerful man could hardly remain low-profile. Yet she had never heard of Goering having a brother, let alone one in the film business.

"I had no idea the minister even had a brother."

"Nobody does. Albert works in Vienna for Tobis-Sascha. He's

nothing like Hermann, just an ordinary little chap, and he hates these grand affairs. You can keep him company. Stop him being overawed."

She gave a small, indulgent smile.

"We want it to be really special. The Goebbelses are hosting something for the royal couple at Schwanenwerder—the usual gemütlich picnic-on-the-lawn affair—but we thought international visitors deserved something a little classier."

Between Goering and Goebbels, competition to entertain foreign dignitaries was fierce. As the visit of Prince Paul was part of Hitler's plan to pressure Yugoslavia into supporting his moves in Europe, not an inch of red carpet would be spared in the wooing.

"Prince Paul's practically English, as you know, Clara. He's a great friend of the British royal family, and our dear Duke of Windsor, of course, so it will be nice to have some English people to greet them. Anyway, I'll say goodbye now."

Emmy Goering spun rapidly on her heel, and Clara turned to find the reason. Annelies von Ribbentrop was heading in her direction. She aimed a speculative glare towards Clara, and as she swept past, a smile parted her lips, thin as a chink of light through metal shutters.

"Lipstick, Fräulein Vine? Better hope the Führer doesn't see you wearing that."

"Better hope Goering doesn't see either," muttered Mary, sidling up from behind. "I hear Elizabeth Arden's Velvet Red is his absolute favorite."

CHAPTER

11

"WHAT YOU NEED TO UNDERSTAND ABOUT HITLER is that he regards himself as first and foremost an artist. His ultimate desire is to sit in the Berghof and paint mountains for the rest of his life."

Leni Riefenstahl leaned back, crossed her legs, and blew a plume of cigarette smoke into the middle distance. At the age of thirty-six she was the most famous female film director in the world and, with her deep-set eyes, cascading curls, and full mouth, certainly the best looking. Her form was encased in that season's Chanel wide-legged trousers teamed with an open-necked silk shirt and chunky amber beads nestling at her throat. Her voice was like gravel dipped in treacle. Leaning back on a pelt of bear fur, she seemed for all the world like some rare and endangered creature herself, svelte and powerful and wild. The Führer's very own femme fatale.

She paused for a sip of coffee before adding, "If you want to know how I know what Herr Hitler thinks, it's because only a few weeks ago he was sitting exactly where you are now."

Clara suppressed the urge to leap out of the chair immediately.

"The Führer comes to your home? That's quite an honor."

Leni gave a slight leonine toss of her head. "He likes to confide in me. He says this house is one of the few places he can properly relax."

Leni Riefenstahl's villa at 30 Heydenstrasse was a modish, low-built, white-faced house in Dahlem, a neighborhood popular with Nazi bureaucrats, high-ranking Party members, and industrialists. Towering hedges screened a succession of handsome villas with stucco detail and mansard roofs, and the leafy peace was punctuated only by the occasional dog's bark and the low growl of a lawn mower. Owning a villa like this was a testament to Leni Riefenstahl's success. And, lest anyone forget it, a gigantic self-portrait of the director herself, holding a Leica camera, hung on the drawing room wall, alongside a framed cover of *Time* magazine on which she posed as seductively as possible on a pair of skis. It was all a long way from her origins as the daughter of a Berlin heating engineer, yet while Leni Riefenstahl may have made her name in the German craze for films about mountain climbing, social climbing was just as much her forte.

"Here. I bought Linzer torte in his honor."

She drew a tray towards her, fingers glimmering with opal and moonstone rings, and cut a fat slice of the tart for Clara. Linzer torte was named after Hitler's birthplace, but despite its unfortunate associations, Clara could not stop her mouth from watering at the crumbly pastry with lemon zest and ground nuts, filled with plum butter. Gratefully, she took a piece and bit into it. Leni ate nothing but fished out a packet of Rothmans in a battered gold case and lit another cigarette.

"How did you first meet the Führer?" Clara inquired.

"I read *Mein Kampf* cover to cover on a train journey and it changed my life. I wrote to him at once, and to my astonishment he invited me to spend the afternoon with him. He told me he had seen all my films and the one he loved best was *The Holy Mountain*. He said my dance on the shore was the most beautiful thing he had seen in his life."

Clara remembered the footage of Leni capering on the beach in a barely-there scrap of gauze. This in itself said a lot about Hitler's taste in films.

"He told me once he came to power I would be the person to chronicle his Third Reich. It was a huge honor."

"Which you have certainly repaid."

She gave a gracious toss of her head. "I can't deny it. Josef von Sternberg—the director, you know—was in love with me. He asked me to go to Hollywood with him in the twenties. I could have gone, but I sacrificed myself. I felt it my duty to stay and support the Führer."

"That must have been a difficult decision."

And an ill-judged one. Yet Leni seemed pleased by this idea. She ran a hand through her lustrous mane, stroking it like an expensive pet.

"It's true. Loyalty is my weakness. Unfortunately, because I am loyal and the Führer loves me, the Party hierarchy hates me. I'm not one of their drab little hausfraus or neurotic wives. I like Frau Hess, but the rest of them I could take or leave. For Magda Goebbels I feel nothing but pity, I despise Frau von Ribbentrop, and as for that puffed-up actress Emmy Goering, well, the less said the better. You see, Fräulein Vine, I'm not the kind Goebbels can push around. I'm my own woman. If I have any problems I go straight to Hitler himself."

Springing to her feet, she crossed to the wall, which alongside the portraits was festooned with advertisements for her work.

"Tell me, Fräulein Vine, or Clara as I'm going to call you, have you seen all my films?"

"I'm a great admirer."

"Good. I knew I was right to choose you."

Leni spun around and beamed at her. "I like the fact that you're half English. I've been to England. I spoke at Oxford and Cambridge. They loved me. How is it you're living in Berlin?"

Clara thought of Leo, his green-eyed gaze and the reddish tint in his hair. The day six years ago that she had gone to him in the British passport control office and taken up his offer to spy for the Secret Intelligence Service. The weeks of patient schooling in the arts of espionage, surveillance, and evasion. Then the love affair, which had never been part of the plan.

"I fell in love," she answered bluntly.

"With Berlin?"

"No." She laughed. "With a man."

"Anyone I know?"

"I shouldn't think so. Besides, he left in 'thirty-three."

Leni nodded sagely. She would assume that Clara's lover was Jewish—an actor or director from the film studios perhaps. The day Hitler came to power an exodus of Babelsberg's greatest talent—Fritz Lang, Peter Lorre, Paul Henreid—had taken the first train across the border.

"I know how it feels. I'll probably always be single, even though so many men have been desperately in love with me. My life often feels like a movie itself. They're always trying to make a film about me. When I was in Hollywood they wanted Marlene Dietrich to play me. I soon put a stop to that."

"I wondered, Fräulein Riefenstahl. Leni. Could you explain a little more about my role?"

The director's attention snapped back to the present.

"I'm glad you asked. You see—and please don't take this the wrong way, Clara—your face has a useful quality. It's a blank canvas. It's like I can project anything I want on it." Her eyes misted, as though the entire storyboard already existed in her mind. "You will be the anonymous German woman who accompanies us from the forests of Berlin, where the original Germans lived, to today's Berlin, and the new world capital as created by Herr Speer. We begin with an aerial shot of Berlin, and as the plane comes closer we find you, the nameless woman, standing by the Brandenburg Gate."

"And the script?"

Breaking out of her reverie, the director gave a slight, dismissive shrug. "There is no script. You don't need one. You will project no distinct identity. Basically, you are the soul of Germany. Just like the French have their Marianne. You will be the spirit of *Germania.*"

The spirit of *Germania?* No wonder Goebbels had been astonished at the choice of Clara for the part.

"Herr Doktor Goebbels did wonder . . ."

"Don't talk to me about Goebbels."

Leni Riefenstahl flared her nostrils like a thoroughbred racehorse, came to sit beside Clara, and placed one hand on her knee. Her voice lowered to a husky whisper. "You know he's infatuated with me."

"I had no idea."

"My dear, from our very first acquaintance, when he invited me to the opera and shoved his clumsy paw up my gown, he has never let up. In fact he has virtually stalked me. I've tried so many ways to put him off, endless chats about Magda, talks about my boyfriends. I once spent an entire evening recalling what a wonderful time I had at his wedding. None of it worked.

When I rejected his advances, Goebbels did everything he could to sabotage my career."

"That didn't work."

"Thankfully, not. But he banned any reports about me in the press for an entire year. He lied to the Führer about me. My advice is, don't believe a word he says. I've never met a man who lies like him. He was determined to ruin me, but I was bold enough to stand up to him, and the Führer backed me. In fact, that's one reason I wanted you presenting the film."

"Because . . . ?"

"I knew Goebbels would want some buxom Nordic blonde to do it. Probably some little idiot he was screwing. There's no end of them, as you well know. So I decided to choose the precise opposite. Which was you."

Clara could not help smiling at this display of willfulness. However manipulative and deceptive Leni Riefenstahl may be, it was refreshing to find a woman so different from the downtrodden Nazi wife. That was, no doubt, what Goebbels found attractive, too.

"There was another reason, of course."

"Really? What's that?"

Leni sprang skittishly to her feet again.

"Oh, never mind. You don't need to know. Besides, I liked the look of you. I'd seen a couple of your films and I thought we would work well together. Did Goebbels brief you at all? We have a scene at the Ahnenerbe, Himmler's institute. You should take a look around it. It's a couple of streets from here."

Was it visible, the shiver of apprehension that ran down Clara's spine?

"Is Himmler often there?" she asked carefully.

"Whenever he gets the chance. He's terrifically proud of it. But mostly the place is full of fusty scientists. I've arranged for one of them—Herr Doktor Kraus—to show you around the day after tomorrow. I've asked him to give you a feel for their work. It's all rather eccentric, but Himmler has decided that no stone should be left unturned. In fact, he's just agreed to give this film an unprecedented honor. His most precious project in the entire world is going to be opened up for the purposes of the movie."

"What's the project?"

"His castle. You must have heard of it. Wewelsburg in West-phalia. It's marvelously photogenic. Fearfully gloomy and im-pressive."

She yawned like a cat and began flicking through a calendar.

"So we'll need to discuss the shooting schedule. Preproduc-tion is well advanced; my location managers have been working overtime. I've already hired all the crew and set up the camera positions. We're on a tight deadline. The Führer wants *Ger-mania* to be ready for this year's Nuremberg rally."

"Five months! For an entire film? That's impossible!"

Leni Riefenstahl sniffed, fished in her bag, and extracted a blue glass atomizer encased in gold net. She pumped a fine sheen of perfume around her.

"That's what I said. But the Führer told me we aren't the only ones. He said the whole world's on deadline now."

"The problem is . . ." Clara hesitated. "I have go to Paris for a couple of days."

"Paris? What on earth are you doing there?"

Clara calculated that now that she had told Goebbels, she may as well establish her cover story as solidly as possible.

"I'm to be photographed for *Vogue* magazine. For the Sep-tember issue. They have a feature on European actresses."

A slow smile lit Leni Riefenstahl's lovely face; then she burst into peals of laughter.

"The September issue? That's ambitious. Who knows what will be happening by September! Let's hope they're still keen on German actresses by then."

MAKING HER WAY HOME, Clara passed a news kiosk by the S-Bahn, and her eye was caught by the face of Lottie Franke, peering out of the front page of the *Berliner Zeitung*. The newspapers had seized on Lottie's death with a kind of ferocious delight. Beside the political complexities of Danzig and Poland, the murder of a single German girl was somehow more outrageous and far easier to contemplate. There was a salacious edge, too, to their interest. The Faith and Beauty girls were supposed to be a cut above the ordinary. They were the pearls of German womanhood, being groomed as consorts for the top men. Yet what did that grooming entail? Who knew what went on in these places? Were the morals there any different from the Bund Deutscher Mädel, which everyone nicknamed the League of German Mattresses? Despite everything Himmler said about producing more babies for the Reich, the promiscuity of the German girls' associations still shocked the more stolid citizens of Berlin. Who was to say the Faith and Beauty Society was any different?

Clara hated to think of the ponderous, devastated Udo Franke and his distraught wife, anxiously awaiting some fragment of intelligence that could explain the inexplicable murder of their only daughter. She was already regretting having told the Frankes that she would find out what she could. It had been a thoughtless promise, uttered in a moment of emotion. There was nothing Clara could uncover about Lottie's death and no chance that she would learn anything more than any other regular newspaper reader. No man had been caught. No details of the murder weapon had been given out. No lines of inquiry had proved fruitful. All the police were saying was that women should be careful around the Grunewald at night.

As she exited the pretty red-brick station at Griebnitzsee, Clara noticed that two policemen had been freshly stationed there, stamping their feet, studying the commuters as they straggled out of the station tunnel. The man who killed Lottie Franke was still at large. What if he returned?

HER UNEASINESS LASTED ALL evening. Clara made a simple meal of sausage and bread and tried to relax by reading. She picked up *Jane Eyre* and put it down again. It might have been her favorite novel, but recently she had found herself craving detective stories—a world where problems arose, then were solved and the world put right. She searched for her old copy of *The Thirty-Nine Steps* and took it to bed.

It was impossible to sleep. At one point she jolted up, her heart racing, all her nerves alert at some strange noise, a distant creak in the house. She sat, her mouth dry, and gazed round, disoriented by the unfamiliar room, lit by a wash of bright moonlight creeping through the curtains.

She was convinced that someone had entered downstairs, only to conclude that it was the wind in the distance banging the gate. Yet she always made sure to latch the gate. A few moments later, she heard it again. A faint creak. And from outside a sound like the crunch of the gravel on the drive. Her heartbeat quickened, but when she drew the curtains there was nothing there but the rain-pitted Griebnitzsee and beyond it the black emptiness of the forest.

She lay down, regretting again that she had sought refuge so far from the city, wishing herself back in Winterfeldtstrasse in the busy heart of Berlin, with the comforting presence of millions of fellow citizens slumbering nearby. She missed everything about her old apartment. Her beloved blue and white china, her comfortable red velvet armchair with its stack of novels alongside, and her chic little mirrored bathroom. The tree-lined, cobbled streets with the old-fashioned green water pump, operated by its dolphin handle. She even missed her unlovely view of cluttered rooftops patrolled by pigeons, the pipes extending down the backs of houses and the washing cobwebbing the narrow alleys below.

Eventually, her thoughts turned to the other issue—the issue that was crowding out every other concern in her mind. Major Grand's request. How was she going to discover von Ribbentrop's plans? The idea of a casual, gossipy chat, the kind she could have with Frau Goering, was an impossibility with the foreign minister's wife. Yet how else would Clara discover if the Nazi regime was genuinely contemplating an alliance with their old enemy?

It was an hour before she fell asleep, and when she finally did, Leni Riefenstahl's parting remark echoed in her mind.

The September issue! That's ambitious. Who knows what will be happening when September comes?

12

IF THE MARRIAGE OF JOSEPH AND MAGDA GOEBBELS REALLY was one long screaming match, then their children had inherited their tendencies, judging by their shrieks as they tore around the garden of the propaganda minister's residence. The window of Mary Harker's room in the back wing of the Adlon hotel had a clear view of the Goebbelses' garden, which was located on a street that had been, to the propaganda minister's great irritation, freshly renamed Hermann-Goering-Strasse. As Clara waited for her friend to finish typing a dispatch, she gazed in fascination at the little blond Goebbels children, who had arrived in yearly installments as regular as the products of any Volkswagen production line. The eldest, Helga, in a white smocked dress, was chasing Helmut, the only boy, rumored to be slow and a great disappointment to his father, while Hilde, a ringleted five-year-old, was pushing two-year-old Holde around the paths on a wheeled wooden horse. All the while the latest addition, Hedda, slumbered in her baby carriage in the shade of a lime tree. Of their mother there was no sign. Perhaps it was true what everyone said about Magda Goebbels, that she was too busy engaging in an affair in bitter retribution for the public way her husband had humiliated her.

"See what you think of this."

Behind Clara, Mary Harker sat back from her Remington, removed a sheet of paper, and read aloud:

"*A few years ago Adolf Hitler declared war. It was war on 'degenerate' art—which to him meant any work in a modernist style, or colors 'not found in Nature,' and, most of all, any work by Jewish artists. Georg Grosz, with his emaciated prostitutes and bloated plutocrats, was declared cultural Bolshevik number one. To comply with the Führer's wishes, Propaganda Minister Joseph Goebbels instigated the seizure of thousands of artworks from the Reich's museums by modernists like Picasso, Dalí, Léger, Miró, and Van Gogh. German Jewish artists have fled: Max Beckmann to Amsterdam, Max Ernst to America, and Paul Klee to Switzerland. Others live in internal exile, forbidden to paint, or even buy paintbrushes. Some of them carry on secretly with the most ingenious of means. One of them has switched to watercolors so his neighbors will not notice the smell of oil paint. But now the war against degenerate art has been taken to new levels.'*"

"So what's happened?" Clara asked.

"As a matter of fact"—Mary leaned forward—"it's something rather shocking. Even by the standards of the Nazis, and they do know how to shock. My editor, Frank Nussbaum, wants it on the front page. Last month a fresh stash of confiscated artwork from Austria arrived in Berlin. There's supposed to be a system. They store the art in a warehouse in Kopernikusstrasse, and a dealer named Hildebrand Gurlitt has been appointed to separate the so-called Degenerate pieces from the rest. Then they sell them, supposedly so that they can make money out of what they call garbage. But Goebbels has done something drastic. He held a symbolic bonfire."

"You're not going to tell me he burned all those artworks?" Clara was appalled.

"A thousand paintings and sculptures, nearly four thousand drawings and watercolors. All burned to ashes in the courtyard of the Berlin Fire Department."

"Just like he burned the books on Opernplatz in 1933. I can hardly believe it."

"They're saying Goebbels did it deliberately to spite Goering because Goering was desperate to have some of those paintings for himself. I suppose it makes sense. They're at each other's throats all the time."

Clara sat in contemplation, trying to puzzle something out. Slowly she said, "I heard something else about Goering. I don't know if it's significant, but he's very upset about a jewel."

"A jewel?" Mary frowned.

"You saw me talking to his wife at the Foreign Ministry, re-member? Frau Goering told me he had been cheated out of this jewel and that it was obsessing him."

"Who cares? It wouldn't be his jewelry anyway, would it? It probably belongs to some poor Jew. Everything they touch is stolen."

"So how did you find out about the bonfire?"

"Hugh Lindsey discovered it. He had a contact down at the warehouse who told him everything that had happened, and Hugh told me."

"Nice of him to share a scoop like that."

"Well, Hugh *is* nice. As I'm sure you've noticed."

"I have. He seems charming."

"So . . . what are you saying?" Mary snatched off her glasses and narrowed her eyes.

Clara laughed. "I'm saying he's charming! I think he's very good-looking, but I'm not interested."

"Good, because I rather like him myself. There's something about him that reminds me of Rupert."

Clara could see that. The humor, the laconic English drawl, the underlying implication that there was nothing in life that could not be solved by a dry sherry and a quiet chat between gentlemen. A way of talking that made the other person feel like the wittiest, most amusing person in the room.

"He's such a contrast to his friend," said Clara. "Cavendish is so patronizing. He's the worst kind of Englishman. I wonder how Hugh can bear him."

Mary's face lit up. "The one thing I've discovered about Hugh in the short time I've known him is that he's utterly loyal to his friends. Even the objectionable ones."

Clara smiled. She dearly hoped a romance might flourish for her friend. Mary was popular with the male reporters, but too often her dry humor, rapier wit, and raging interest in politics ensured that she was treated as a colleague first and a woman second. Perhaps this time she could do a little matchmaking to help it along.

As these thoughts went through Clara's head, Mary was studying her with a forensic attention. "How about you, Clara? I have the feeling there's someone in the picture. I hope it's not that Nazi we met the other night at the Press Club."

"What do you take me for?"

Clara had never told Mary that Leo had returned to Berlin the year before, or that their love affair had resumed. So, however much she longed to, she now could not share the anxiety that was tearing her apart.

"Well, if there's no one keeping you here, you need to think about the future."

Mary was giving Clara one of her direct looks, the kind that brooked no evasion. That quality must be what made her such a fine journalist, Clara decided. Her friend never shied away from asking the important question, and she never let tact, delicacy, or embarrassment hinder her pursuit of the truth.

"Your two countries are on the brink of war. You don't have journalistic protection, like me."

"I have my identity documents. I'm a member of the Reich Chamber of Culture."

"They're pieces of paper, Clara! The Nazis never let pieces of paper stand in their way. If they decide that your loyalties are divided, it will get very difficult for you. Let alone if . . ."

Mary fell silent and raised her eyes to the light fixture. Both women knew that rooms in the Adlon allocated to foreign journalists came accessorized not just with tea-making equipment, telephones, and soda siphons but with high-quality listening devices, monitored and changed as regularly as the bed linen.

"Don't say anything you wouldn't like to see on the front page of *Der Angriff,*" cautioned Clara.

Der Angriff was Goebbels's own paper, full of the worst kinds of accusations and propaganda.

But Mary didn't need to say any more. Her face said everything. Despite a passionate concern for her friend, she knew Clara's existence in Berlin was not as straightforward as it seemed.

"As it happens, I *am* thinking about the future. I'm off to Paris in a couple of days."

"Paris!" Mary's eyes lit up. "How did you swing that? What wouldn't I do to be in La Coupole right now, drinking with Hemingway, or living at the Hôtel Scribe and having cocktails at the Crillon. And the food! Foie gras sautéed with grapes. Blanquette de veau. What are you going for?"

"A magazine shoot."

Despite her friend's delight, Clara wondered what Mary must truly think. What would anyone think of a woman who tripped off to model the latest fashions when the only outfit on everyone's mind was an army uniform and the color of the season was field gray?

Mary sighed. "Just thinking about Paris makes me want a vodka Martini. Let's get to the bar."

FROM THE TINKLE OF a piano to the soft patter of the famous elephant fountain and the murmur of moneyed voices, everything about the Adlon said that, despite all circumstances, it was still the social epicenter of Berlin. It was far too grand to display signs reading NO JEWS OR DOGS, which graced less smart establishments, although a discreet placard next to the lifts announced that they were barred for non-Aryan use. Yet while superficially the Adlon was the same, there were indications that all was not well. The hotel was crowded, but that was because people thought there was no point holding on to their money. The same three-piece orchestra played in the lobby, the same women in satin evening gowns congregated for parties, and the famous grill room and bar were still the central meeting points for foreign journalists mingling with diplomats, military attachés, and businessmen in fur-collared coats. But now their conversations were more guarded. Everyone wanted to know what was going on, but no one wanted to be the person imparting privileged information. Gossip was less likely to concern marital indiscretions than military maneuvers. Scraps of information would be pounced on and passed around. The

Adlon was one of the few places in Berlin where foreign news-papers were available, and hotel staff could be seen in the corridors leafing quickly through the papers before delivering them to guests.

Hugh Lindsey was standing amid a cluster of reporters at the bar, reading aloud from the classified advertisement section of that day's *B.Z. am Mittag.*

"Listen to this! 'Two vital, lusty, race-conscious Brünnhildes, with family trees certified back to 1700 desiring to serve their Fatherland in the form most ennobling to women, would like to meet two similarly inclined Siegfrieds. Marriage not of essential importance. Soldiers on leave also acceptable.' Who said romance was dead?"

" 'Desiring to serve the Fatherland'? Does that mean what I think it means?" asked Mary.

"It certainly does. Fidelity and chastity are out of fashion, didn't you know? And not just for race-conscious Brünnhildes. The whole of the top echelon of the Party are at it. Heydrich is a regular womanizer. Rumor has it he's established his own brothel up in the west end called Salon Kitty's. He's wired the place throughout so he can spy on his own men. And we all know about Goebbels, not to mention the gossip about his wife."

Mary took the newspaper from Hugh and turned it over. It was folded into a rectangle, and the other side bore a large photograph of Lottie Franke. She gave Clara a sympathetic glance. "Still no news on your Faith and Beauty girl?"

Clara looked, but a quick scan confirmed that nothing had changed in the investigation. The press was merely seizing the opportunity to run another picture of a photogenic young woman. Death had given Lottie the celebrity that life had never offered.

"The way they're reporting it, it's a national tragedy," complained Charles Cavendish loftily. Clara felt a stab of dislike. Cavendish reminded her of the snobbish young men of Angela's set, who would only talk to women as a last resort, and then only to those whose fathers or brothers they knew.

"Presumably it feels like that to people who knew her." Mary glared.

"Ah yes," said Cavendish, with a light apologetic shrug. "Sorry, Clara. How's work?"

"Busy, thank you. I've been cast in Leni Riefenstahl's latest film."

He raised a laconic eyebrow. "That's quite an honor, isn't it? The Führer's favorite film director. Goebbels says Riefenstahl is the only woman in Germany who truly understands what the Party is about."

"I'm a woman, and I have a pretty good idea of what they're about," interjected Mary.

"So what's this film going to be?" asked Bill Shirer. "Thousands of storm troopers goose-stepping up Unter den Linden?"

"Not exactly. It's about the Ahnenerbe."

"What's that?"

"Some cultural project of Heinrich Himmler's," said Hugh.

"Himmler has a cultural project?" Mary laughed. "Hope I never have to see it. I think I've had all the Nazi Party culture I can manage for one day. I was telling Clara about the bonfire at the art warehouse."

Shirer's kindly face wrinkled in disdain. "Obscene, isn't it? I must mention it in my next bulletin."

Already Shirer had attracted some attention for his broadcasts for CBS. He stared gloomily into the depths of his brandy. "Not that anyone back home will be interested. I've almost given up trying to persuade Americans of Herr Hitler's true intentions."

"Think there's anything in this talk of the Nazis building bridges with the Russians?" asked Cavendish.

Shirer waved a dismissive hand. "How could there be? Hitler's entire goal is the occupation and annexation of a great part of Russia. How do you play ball with a man who covets your house and intends to settle in it if he can, even if he has to hit you over the head with his bat?"

"What makes you so sure?" Clara wanted to know.

"Ever read *Mein Kampf,* Clara? Of course you have. Hitler spells it out very obligingly there. If Uncle Joe Stalin hasn't read it yet, someone should put it on his reading list."

Their talk drifted on to other subjects—their forthcoming trip to the cabaret, the rumors about the feuding Goebbelses, the frustration that visiting Americans still enthused about the clean streets and the absence of crime. But as they talked, Clara's eye was caught by a stately figure progressing along the far side of the gleaming marble lobby, beyond the palm court and its celebrated elephant fountain, towards the revolving doors.

Tall and dignified, she seemed to glide rather than walk, and lurching in her wake were two burly men in ill-fitting dark suits, like a pair of tugs accompanying a ship in full rig. As she passed, a momentary hush descended on the matrons taking cake and tea and the Party members quaffing cognac at the bar. The Adlon may be the epicenter of glamour in the Third Reich, but it was not every day one had a close-up sight of the biggest star of German cinema, the beloved grande dame Olga Chekhova.

Everything about Chekhova emphasized her star status, from the ropes of fat, lustrous pearls to the beautifully cut dress and mink stole, strong Slavonic face and high cheekbones. Her immaculate complexion glowed as though lit by an internal lightbulb. She had a star's innate charisma, an invisible force field of energy that rippled through the space around her, causing heads to swivel magnetically and voices to hush. Impulsively Clara called out.

"Olga!"

Hearing her name, the actress looked over, and a flash of recognition passed between them, yet almost immediately she turned again without replying and moved on.

Olga Chekhova had cut her dead.

Clara was baffled as much as hurt. She had worked with Olga on several films and had been invited to numerous dinners at her smart Kaiserdamm apartment, hung with icons and Fabergé enamel frames and always thronged with White Russian émigrés in astrakhan coats. The evenings were long and sentimental, filled with anecdotes about Olga's Moscow childhood and fueled by red caviar and blinis, borscht, poppy seed strudel, and delicious Russian vodka. Despite her fame, Olga had always taken an eager interest in Clara's career. She had treated her more like a daughter than like a rival actress. So why, when it was patently obvious that she had seen Clara just yards away, should she choose to ignore her?

Clara had a sudden, devastating flash of intuition. It must have to do with the two business-suited men, swarthy, anonymous types whom she could not place. They didn't look like film industry figures. They didn't even look German. Was it possible that Olga did not want Clara to see who she was with? Although the incident had lasted only a matter of seconds, Clara had a sense of sinking dread. Perhaps it was true, what Emmy Goering said. That as well as being Hitler's favorite actress and the greatest star of Third Reich cinema, Olga Chekhova, the sister of an NKVD operative, was herself a Soviet spy.

THE HEADQUARTERS OF THE ANCESTRAL HERITAGE
Research and Teaching organization—the Ahnenerbe
for short—were situated in a handsome building in one
of the most upmarket areas of the city, 19 Pücklerstrasse,
Dahlem, just a few doors from Martin Bormann's townhouse. Its vine-covered walls and gleaming stained-glass
windows projected a hallowed air of academic respect-
ability, as though this center of German heritage combined a sacred chapel and a university in one. The
strongest impression, however, was that everything about
the building, from its ivory sandstone façade to the new-
model cabriolet parked on the gravel drive, reeked of
money. Whoever was funding Germany's search for its
own cultural identity wasn't short of a few Reichmarks.

Crunching across a half-moon of pristine gravel,
Clara stood for a second at the door, summoning her
courage, before entering and looking around the expensive wood-paneled hall. The place seemed deserted.
Ranks of display cases lined the walls, filled with stone

carvings and wooden figures. There was a tortoiseshell—a vibrant swirl of orange and black—a papery snakeskin, and a glass-eyed fox. There were photographs of cave drawings and eerily lifelike plaster casts of human faces momentarily reminding her of visits to the Natural History Museum in London during the long school holidays of childhood. But that was where the resemblance ended. Approaching the first cabinet, she saw with a shudder that it contained a selection of human skulls alongside a series of instruments that resembled calipers. On inspection she discovered that they were steel measuring implements, designed to record the size of noses, cheekbones, and jaws. Alongside each skull was a note about the previous owner's racial characteristics.

DALIC: high stature, robust and heavily built, rosy skin, blond hair, light eyes, brachycephalic cranium, big mouth, and thin lips

EAST BALTIC: medium to low stature, fair skin, strong build, brachycephalic, light hair and eyes

DINARIC: wedge-shaped profile, receding forehead, large nose, weak receding chin

NORDIC: dolichocephalic. Forehead and chin scarcely receding. The Nordic people are the spine of the human race

A clatter of boots behind her alerted Clara to a man trotting down the gleaming staircase. His face, with its full complement of blond hair, blue eyes, flawlessly symmetrical features, and long horse's nose, might have been torn straight out of the textbook illustrating the final race in the display case, the Nordic. He also possessed an immaculate SS uniform and a penetrating, aquiline stare.

"Admiring our Untermenschen? We use them as teaching aids to instruct students in racial typing. We can tell so much from skull form, size of brain, and so on. Compare the features of Nordic dolichocephalism—lofty brow, narrow temples, large eyes, aquiline nose—with this Slav—see his round facial structure and small nose? Our founder, the SS Reichsführer, believes a man's entire character can be told from anatomy alone." He clicked his heels. "Herr Doktor Kraus."

Clara gave him her hand and felt his eyes flicker speculatively over her face, reading the shape of her forehead and the spacing of her eyes as if mentally pigeonholing her pedigree. She repressed a shudder.

"And you, I take it, are Fräulein Vine. Was no one here to meet you? That useless girl." His eyes roved across to an empty desk in the corner of the hall. "I told her to expect you. Are you aware of our work? I would give you a copy of our magazine if our young librarian had not deserted her post."

As if on cue a tall, pink-cheeked girl dashed into the hall, almost invisible beneath a towering stack of magazines, which she proceeded to drop on the floor by the desk.

"I'm sorry, Herr Doktor! I was just getting these!"

"Don't worry," Clara said, directing a consoling smile at the girl, who was scrabbling around collecting the litter of papers. "I've seen the latest copy already."

Clara had found the Ahnenerbe's magazine on a newsstand the previous day and spent several dispiriting minutes flipping through it. From what she saw in it, there were forty separate research projects in subjects ranging from musicology, astrology, linguistics, and Sanskrit to runes, all devoted to proving the existence of the lost Aryan master race.

"Perhaps you'd like to see some of our exhibits," said Kraus, directing a savage stare at the flustered young woman.

He stalked along a corridor flanked by more glass cases into a grand drawing room lined with shelves crowded with books, paintings, pottery, and tiny primitive figurines. African fertility sculptures and tribal masks rubbed up against turquoise Egyptian shabti figures. Thighbones rested casually alongside panpipes. Long, curved yellow teeth grinned beside flint spear tips. They had the dusty, jumbled, abandoned air of holiday souvenirs assembled by an especially undiscriminating tourist.

"The Herr Reichsführer is an avid collector," commented Kraus.

He drew her over to a series of photographs of Orientals.

"The elites of Asia—the Brahmin priests, the Mongolian chiefs, and the Japanese samurai—are all descended from Aryan invaders. Take these chaps . . ." He indicated a row of Tibetan tribesmen in shawls, clustered like scouts around a campfire and gazing at their SS guests with a mixture of hostility and bewilderment. "Even the most casual observer can see at once that the higher Tibetan classes possess Nordic characteristics. Note the long heads, narrow faces, receding cheekbones. They are quite clearly descended from the same race as we Germans. It is an added pleasure that the swastika should also be an ancient Tibetan symbol."

"Fascinating," said Clara, neutrally.

"Isn't it?" He removed his glasses and polished them with a handkerchief before replacing them. The tiny rimless spectacles almost vanished in the folds of his face.

"The same measurements of skulls allowed us to prove that the Antarctic was once inhabited by Germanic peoples. Physiognomy is destiny. We can tell any number of qualities—intelligence, honesty, propensity to criminality—simply from a person's racial characteristics."

"It must take a lot of training to recognize all that just by looking at a person."

If he detected her sarcasm, he did not show it. "You're quite right. It does. It's a whole new specialism, the discipline of criminal biology. And I flatter myself that I am at the forefront of it. Of course, I was already something of an expert on race science. Are you familiar with that?"

"Very."

Race science was one of the biggest growth sectors in Nazi Germany. Universities were hastily establishing new lecturing posts in the subject, and schools held twice-weekly lessons in it. At Erich's school it had now entirely replaced biology. Clara had recently helped him with his homework and waded with horror through a pyramid diagram of racial hierarchy, which placed the Master Race at the top, Goths, Franks, Vandals, and Normans beneath, and "subhuman" Russians, Romani, Serbs, Poles, and Jews on the bottom row.

"We have aural displays, too," persisted Kraus. "The Ahnenerbe has recorded folk dances in Finland. I would have the equipment set up for you but . . ."

"Honestly, it's fine."

"In that case, you should see our library." He flung open a further door. "We keep a complete archive of ancestral German history."

Clara stepped in with relief. Somehow, no amount of books could be as depressing as the contents of the previous room. The library was a soft gleam of dark, polished leather, with volumes of books stacked floor to ceiling, shimmering with gilt tooling. None of them looked like they had been disturbed since they were placed there. The girl she had seen before, wearing an owlish pair of spectacles, was bending over a manuscript.

Kraus hovered as Clara surveyed the shelves.

"An early copy of the Bhagavad Gita. A Sanskrit epic. It tells how thousands of years ago a pure Aryan race invaded India. The SS Reichsführer finds its teachings inspirational. He carries a copy wherever he goes."

Kraus was hovering uncomfortably close. To escape him, Clara moved towards a glass display case where a piece of text was framed.

THE PEOPLES OF GERMANY HAVE NEVER CONTAMINATED THEMSELVES BY INTERMARRIAGE WITH FOREIGNERS BUT REMAIN OF PURE BLOOD, DISTINCT AND UNLIKE ANY OTHER NATION.

"Magnificent, isn't it?" said Kraus. "It's *Germania*. Written by Cornelius Tacitus in A.D. 98. One of the greatest historians and prose stylists who ever wrote in Latin. You know it, of course?"

"I don't think so." Clara was racking her brain for any fragment of knowledge that might linger from Miss Herbert's classical civilization lessons, conducted in a stuffy classroom in Kensington a lifetime ago.

"Really? All German schoolchildren are taught him from the age of six. Tacitus was the first historian to study the early Germanic clans. And what he discovered is very pleasing for us. As far back as when they wore the skin of wild beasts, Germans had a natural nobility, inured to corruption or servility. They scorned luxury and prized military courage above all things."

He sighed, reverently. "The *Germania* is a precious work for us. In many ways it's a blueprint for the National Socialist revolution."

"So which one is it?" asked Clara, her eyes roving round the library shelves.

Kraus gave a short, bitter laugh at this question. "Oh, but we don't *have* it."

"Would it not be good to have?"

"My dear Fräulein, I don't think you understand. There is only one copy of *Germania* in existence. The Codex Aesinas. And that's in Italy. Herr Mussolini was aware just how much we National Socialists revered that book, and three years ago he promised Herr Hitler that he would make a gift of it." His expression stiffened. "Unfortunately, the Duce went back on his word."

"That must have been quite frustrating for the Führer."

"You have no idea." Kraus allowed himself a pinched smile. "However, we have the typed texts. And most of us have learned the important passages by heart. Rather like medieval monks learned the Bible."

The story of Mussolini's treachery seemed to put a damper on the tour. Kraus paused and checked his watch.

"I trust I've answered all your questions, Fräulein Vine. Although it is of course an honor for our work to be immortalized in film, today does happen to be especially busy. I have the SS Reichsführer arriving shortly. I'm not sure . . . Would you like to meet him?"

Clara managed to prevent herself from recoiling in horror.

"No. I mean . . . No, thank you. I must leave, too."

She looked across to where the librarian was sitting. The girl had clearly been listening to their conversation. Even though she was pretending to leaf through a pile of papers on her desk, the tips of her ears had gone pink and there was a high flush on the apples of her cheeks. As Kraus clicked his heels and left the room, she said softly, "Excuse me, Fräulein Vine?"

Clara turned.

"Your magazines?"

"It's okay, thank you, I don't think I'll be needing them. I've seen enough for one day."

Clara left the building and set off down the gravel path, but as she did she heard footsteps pattering rapidly behind her and turned to see the librarian heaving breathlessly into view.

"I'm sorry, Fräulein. I mean. I wonder . . ." She hesitated, then cast her eyes down again. "I'm sorry. I shouldn't interfere."

"What did you want?"

"It's just. I know who you are."

Clara was used to being recognized, and direct approaches from strangers usually involved autograph requests. Automatically she pasted a friendly smile on her face and reached for the pen in her bag as the girl before her continued.

"You're the actress, aren't you?"

"That's right."

Though she was flushed with agitation, the girl had a sweet smile and soft, heavy-lidded eyes.

"No. You see, I'm a member of the Faith and Beauty community. Where the girl was killed."

"Lottie Franke?"

"She was my best friend."

She uttered this sentence with an air of incomprehension, as though even now she was struggling to understand the desolation of death.

"I'm Hedwig. Hedwig Holz."

Instantly she came into focus. The girl from the photograph in the Franke family apartment. Large and clumsy in her regulation uniform, an awkward foil to Lottie's eye-catching beauty.

"I'm so sorry," Clara said.

Hedwig hesitated, twisting her hands on the edge of her unbecoming tweed skirt. "The thing is . . . Maybe it doesn't matter, but . . ."

Clara recognized the first rule of her training. *When a door is ajar, push it open.*

"Of course it matters. Whatever you have to say, if you were a friend of Lottie's, I'd love to talk. You must be devastated by what happened. Would you like some lunch?"

Hedwig's eyes lit up and then dipped again, like a dog denied a treat.

"I can't. I need to be at my desk when SS Reichsführer Himmler arrives."

"Why don't we take a short walk? Just round the block. We're bound to see the official car when it passes. And if Herr Doktor Kraus is angry, I'll tell him I asked you to walk with me."

"Would you?"

"Of course."

"Just five minutes then."

With a reluctant look behind her, Hedwig Holz slipped through the gate. "I shouldn't complain. Herr Doktor Kraus has been extremely kind to me. It was he who offered me this job actually, right after his lecture on mate selection."

"Mate selection? What on earth is that?"

Distractedly the girl said, "Oh, we have to select genetically suitable mates according to the Nordic-Greek ideal."

Select mates? What kind of young woman referred to her boyfriends like this? Come to that, what kind of girl talked of love and marriage in terms of genetic suitability? Almost as soon as she had asked herself, Clara knew the answer. Girls in Nazi Germany.

"We have these social evenings. We Faith and Beauty girls

have been specially selected by Herr Himmler as suitable mates for his future warriors, so there are dances and dinners with SS officers. I hate them, to be honest, but one of our group is already engaged to a man she met. They're getting married in a few weeks. The trouble is"—Hedwig's face clouded and she shot a quick glance at Clara as if calculating whether she could trust her—"I already have one. A boyfriend, I mean. That's why I'm in the Faith and Beauty Society."

Clara frowned. "But if . . . ?"

"My mother hopes I'll meet a handsome SS officer and forget Jochen altogether."

"And might you?"

"Not a chance." She smiled softly. "Especially if they see me dancing. Fräulein von Essen—she's our instructor—says I dance like a pantomime cow. There's a ball next month and I'm terrified."

Clara laughed. "They have something like that where I grew up. In England. They were called debutante balls."

Angela had done the season. It began in May with presentation to the king at court, followed by a series of dances packed with aristocratic young men, the weak-chinned, the graceless, and the brutish, who steered the girls around the dance floor while their chaperones, a formidable jury of matrons perched on gilt chairs, scrutinized from the sidelines. Every deb had her own dance—Angela's had been held at their aunt's home in Piccadilly—but high-society husband hunting had horrified Clara. She didn't want to learn any old-fashioned etiquette. She remembered Angela's lofty incomprehension.

But how will you ever know how to behave?

The Faith and Beauty girls were Hitler's debutantes—groomed to take their places in the ranks of Nazi aristocracy. Only, as well as learning what fork to use at dinner and how to arrange roses, Hitler's debs were drilled in every last detail of National Socialist ideology.

"You'd understand then," Hedwig told her. "We're supposed to learn all the social graces because we guard the spiritual health of the nation."

"That's asking a lot."

"That's what Lottie used to say." Her face fell. "Lottie admired you so, Fräulein Vine. She said you were the only one who showed real interest in her ideas. You said she had a bright future."

"She did."

"She worked as a photographer's model sometimes. At a studio in Schlüterstrasse. They paid her."

"Lottie had real talent. It's a tragedy you've lost her."

"She told me you were half English. We went to London once."

"I heard. Did you like it?"

For a moment, Hedwig's face glowed as if all the lamps in Claridge's Hotel had lit it from within.

"I loved it! We both did. It was the last time I saw Lottie really happy."

They came to a bench and sat down, and Hedwig began to unburden all the anxiety and pain of the last few weeks in a torrent of words that Clara only occasionally interrupted.

"Lottie wasn't what people thought she was. I mean, she had another side that people here didn't see. A different side."

"In what way different?"

Hedwig knitted her fingers and gazed around her for inspiration.

"She wasn't this perfect specimen of Aryan womanhood that the principal always says we are. Lottie was very . . . ambitious."

"That's good, isn't it?"

"Yes," agreed Hedwig hesitantly. "What I mean is, she knew what she wanted. She liked talking about people like Marx and Engels. Sometimes I had to tell her to keep her voice down, but she didn't care what people thought. And . . ." With a quick, desperate glance at Clara, she lowered her voice. "Men liked her very much."

"I'm not surprised. She was beautiful."

Clara recalled the slight, defiant lift of Lottie's head when men's eyes flicked over her and stuck to her all the way down the corridor.

"She was a magnet for them, Fräulein Vine. They followed her like dogs. It didn't matter if they were married or single. You could see their eyes glaze over when they looked at her, as if they were imagining things, you know? Like they were picturing her with no clothes on."

"Did she like them, too?"

Hedwig blushed. She was twisting her braid around a finger and gazing sightlessly into the middle distance. There were layers of shadow in her voice, of things that remained unspoken.

"She slept around—even when we were over in London. She slipped away a couple of nights and made me promise to cover for her. I tried to talk to her about it, but she said what was wrong with that? She wasn't married or anything. She didn't feel at all guilty. She couldn't get hold of condoms anymore, no one can, but she carried a bottle of vinegar with her and used it as a douche. It works perfectly"—Hedwig blushed more profusely—"apparently."

"Did she have a regular boyfriend?"

Hedwig pushed away the hanks of mousy hair that had escaped her braids. There were beads of sweat in her hairline, Clara noticed, and even though they were sitting in a deserted side street, her gaze flitted around as though fearful someone might be watching.

"That's just it. When the principal, Frau Mann, asked me, I said no. But now I've been feeling so guilty about it. I think I should have told the truth."

Clara was silent.

"Lottie *had* met someone, Fräulein Vine. She wouldn't tell me who. Usually she'd talk for hours about her boyfriends." A shy sideways glance. "I'm sorry, Fräulein, but she liked boasting about what they . . . did in bed. Only this time it was different. She was infatuated with this man, but she wouldn't even tell me his name. She just said he was very interesting. An artistic type. And he had a secret."

The chill breeze sent a fragile confetti of petals spiraling down from an apple tree, and a petal stuck to Hedwig's cheek. Clara reached across to brush it away. "What sort of secret?"

"She wouldn't say. He was on her mind all the time. But this man didn't make her happy. I think perhaps he saw other women. One of the last times I saw her, Lottie said that she had had enough. She would show him he couldn't play around with her. She had something on him. But at the same time . . ."

The roar of a passing car caused Hedwig to startle. Turning back to Clara, she took a soft breath and lowered her voice.

"The fact is, I think she was terribly frightened of him."

Clara wanted her to keep talking, but she could see it was no use. The girl was as nervous as a kitten.

"Why should she be frightened of this man if she was in love with him?" Clara asked gently.

"I don't know."

Clara noticed a café across the road.

"Would you like to have a cup of coffee with me?"

Hedwig sniffed and squeezed the bridge of her nose to hold back the tears. Then she shook her head.

"That's kind, but I'd better get back. Herr Doktor Kraus will have noticed by now, and God help me if the SS Reichsführer has already arrived." She paused. "If you hear anything about . . . about Lottie, would you tell me? I need to know. She was my dearest friend and I would do anything I could to find who killed her."

"I feel the same."

Clara took out a tan leather Smythson notebook and scribbled her address and telephone number in it with her silver pen.

"Take this. And if you remember anything else, just call me. It might be useful." She tore the page out and pressed it into Hedwig's hand.

"Thank you, Fräulein Vine. And please—be careful. If that monster who did this to Lottie is still out there, all of us women need to watch ourselves until he's caught."

"SO WERE YOU REALLY THERE? I DIDN'T SEE YOU."
Erich regarded Clara suspiciously, his dark brows knitted above skeptical eyes.

"I told you. Right opposite the Führer's saluting podium."

"And you definitely saw me?"

Goebbels was fond of saying that for a lie to be believed, it had to be a big one, but Clara thought that, at certain moments, a little lie was a better choice.

"I was very proud of you."

It was Saturday, and they had just finished one of their regular weekend pursuits. A swim at the Charlottenburg public swimming baths. It was a lovely old building—the pride of the district—decorated with porcelain dolphins, the high glass ceiling with its turquoise blue struts echoing with the shouts of parents and children.

Clara loved these weekend meetings with Erich. She found herself looking forward to them throughout the week—moments of sunny respite from the darkening political scene. Young people lived so much more in the moment. She liked hearing about his friends, their fights and feuds, and talking about books, films, and her own childhood. Erich especially liked to hear about his dead mother, Helga, who had befriended Clara when she first moved to Berlin. Although he had only come into her life six years ago, some of the happiest times in her life had been with Erich. Rowing in the Wannsee, the sun bouncing off the clear water of the lake as Erich learned to handle the oars, or seeing his enthralled face beside hers in the silvery glimmer of the cinema as they sat through innumerable war films.

Clara knew very little about teenage boys and had no more expected to find herself entrusted with one than she might have an elephant or a giant panda, but she had come to love Erich as if he were her own.

The best part of the swimming mornings came afterwards when, exuding the tang of chlorine and the virtuous flush of exercise, they would wander a couple of streets along to the vast Rogacki market hall and sate their appetites. Despite the food shortages, the market always gave an impression of plenty, and the café she and Erich liked best was famous for its generous portions. They sat among the market traders surveying a whole panorama of food—glistening haunches of meat, slabs of cheese, and rainbow-scaled fish on beds of ice. Over the years Erich had grown almost visibly as he devoured mountains of spätzele and wurst and cakes and ice cream.

That day Clara had selected *Pflaumenkuchen*, sweet, doughy plum cake topped with cinnamon sugar and a dollop of whipped cream, while Erich went for *Pfannkuchen*, a kind of jam doughnut. To Clara's secret pleasure he also ordered *Himbeersaft*, the sugary raspberry juice so loved by children in Berlin. It consoled her that perhaps he was not growing up quite as fast as she feared, despite the fact that he outgrew every shirt she bought for him within months.

"Anyway"—Erich seemed mollified by Clara's admiration—"you can watch me march again if you like."

"So soon?" said Clara, trying hard to inject some enthusiasm into her voice.

"In the cinema. It's a movie already. Hitler's fiftieth birthday. We've watched it twice in the HJ film hour."

"That's great."

He shrugged. "I suppose."

He pulled out a packet of cigarettes, but at the sight of Clara's face put it away again.

"Anyway, I've got better news than that. I've been appointed to the HJ-Streifendienst."

Clara beamed at him lovingly. She had no idea what it was, but any achievement of Erich's gave her a lift. She gave a little shake of his arm.

"Darling, that's wonderful! Clever you. What is it?"

"It's the Patrol Force. We keep order at meetings and watch out for troublemakers. We make a note of anyone criticizing the Party, you know, or disrespecting the Führer, and we put that in a regular report to our divisional office. It's a way of keeping the HJ strong and united."

"Oh." Clara couldn't help the disappointment seeping into her voice, and Erich flared with annoyance as if she had rubbed a raw wound.

"I knew you'd be like that! You should be pleased. Anyone else would be. It's a privilege. A position of responsibility. If you get into the Streifendienst, you're on track for recruitment to the SS, and sometimes you go directly to SS officer training school. You can't believe what an honor it is!" He had a high flush on his cheeks. "But you're never pleased when I have good news."

"That's not fair," she reproved gently. "But all this talk of the SS is quite new. I thought you wanted to join the Luftwaffe. You've spent so much time building gliders and taking rides in fighter bombers."

"I know." Erich frowned and fiddled with his glass. Clara guessed that she had hit on the heart of his dilemma, but that didn't mean he was ready to forgive her. She knew his mother, if she had lived, would have been proud of him.

"It's true. I did want to join the Luftwaffe. I do. But when someone gives you a chance like this. The SS, Clara! All the others were green with envy. It means I've been singled out for leadership."

Clara forced a smile. The HJ was all about spotting future leaders. Once a likely candidate had been identified, the boys were plucked by the leadership schools, in Vogelsgang and Krossinsee and Pomerania, and trained in political science and administration as well as obedience, zeal, and mental fitness for the struggles they would face enacting the Führer's wishes.

"You just don't understand."

"I suppose I don't. I'm sorry."

"It's all right." Erich never sulked for long, and besides, it was Saturday, and a *Pfannkuchen*, glistening with sugar, had just landed on his plate. "Everything will change if we go to war with Poland anyway, and that's only a few months away."

"You seem quite sure."

"I am," he said, through a mouthful of sweet dough. "We're not supposed to say, but our battalion has already been issued luminous paint for painting the curbstones. So people can see their way in a blackout when the Poles begin their aerial bombardment."

The news gave Clara a chill. Everyone knew Goering had laid elaborate plans to defend Berlin in case of bombing, and the HJ were endlessly practicing air-raid precautions, but the idea that these plans were now being put into action made the threat of war seem even more real.

Erich licked his sugar mustache. "It's quite exciting. They're saying we'll be pushed to fight over Danzig by the autumn. The Poles are refusing to see reason."

"There's *nothing* exciting about war, Erich." There was steel in Clara's voice, but she couldn't help it. "Don't *ever* make that mistake."

Erich shrugged and returned to his glass of *Himbeersaft.* Clara knew what was going through his head. Men were better judges of these things than women. Male reasoning powers were scientifically superior to women's, and the woman should never presume to argue with the man. That was the kind of thing he had learned in the HJ, where they were taught that even the highest BDM leader in the land could not issue orders to the lowest HJ boy.

She reached a hand across to Erich and patted his arm. "Why don't we talk about something else?"

She hated talking politics with Erich. Subjected to weekly political conditioning at the HJ, and gifted with a naturally quick, analytic mind, he loved to pursue political debates. Having to maintain a façade with the boy she so loved, while dreading what might happen to him in a war, was draining. Erich's argumentative nature would have made him a good barrister, but instead he was probably destined to become cannon fodder in Hitler's deluded war. She looked at his face, still puppyishly rounded, and his eyes, shining with a sense of absolute rightness, the clarity of conviction so common in the young and dangerous in the old.

"Have something else to eat. It's a treat, remember," she told him.

It was a treat because Erich was to leave the next day for a three-week Hitler Youth camp north of Berlin. Clara had first taken him there when he was fourteen and entered the senior Hitler Jugend; that was when he'd acquired his short brown trousers, black boots, and belt with its iron eagle buckle. Above the camp entrance was a banner with the slogan "We were born to die for Germany," and Clara's sarcastic comment on it had caused a predictable squabble between them. But it was soon forgotten. Even though the marching, bayonet drilling, grenade throwing, and pistol shooting went against Erich's naturally studious nature, and he was often so tired that he would fall asleep in class, he embraced the HJ with fervor.

"What's this favor you wanted to ask?" asked Clara, wrenching her mind back to the present. She had already guessed that the answer lay in the wicker basket that Erich had tucked beneath the table.

"It's only for a couple of weeks. Just while I'm away."

He lifted the basket's front grille to show Clara its tiny, trembling cargo: a pair of young rabbits huddled together. Erich and his grandmother, like a vast number of Berlin citizens, had taken to breeding rabbits for meat, and the animals were kept in a hutch on the balcony. As Erich was off to camp, his grandmother had suggested that she wring their necks to save herself some work, but instead he had brought them to Clara.

"They're so young. It's far too early to kill them. You will look after them, won't you? Just while I'm at camp."

Clara poked a finger through the grille and felt the animals' impossibly soft fur. Beady eyes blinked at her and soft noses twitched, too young even to fear a predator.

"I would, darling, but I'm going to be in Paris for a couple of days."

"Leave them some cabbage leaves and water. They'll be okay. Better off than if they stay with Oma, anyway. Please."

He opened the basket, lifted one rabbit onto his lap, and stroked it. The tiny creature remained motionless, ears flattened, nose still quivering.

She felt a pang of tenderness. Even now, with all his Hitler Youth bluster, his cigarette smoking and adolescent edginess, the child in Erich still surfaced. She remembered their trips to the zoo, in the early days after Helga had died, and Erich's fury that wild animals should be caged.

The thought of exotic animals brought yesterday's trip to the Ahnenerbe back.

"All right—and I meant to ask. Have you ever heard of the Ahnenerbe?"

Erich rolled his eyes. "Everyone's heard of it. *You've* heard of it, Clara. We saw a newsreel about the latest expedition, remember?"

"I wasn't concentrating."

"It's very interesting. They're scouring the world for the origins of the German race."

"You would have thought the German race originated in Germany."

He frowned. "It did, I think. But the Ahnenerbe has discovered that the Aryan race used to rule all sorts of places. That's exactly why our soldiers must fight to reclaim our original lands."

The urge to put him right rose in her, but she suppressed it. So that was what Erich and his friends had been told.

THEY PARTED AT THE S-BAHN, and Clara kissed his cheek fleetingly, because he hated public displays of affection. Then she sat on the platform, with the basket of rabbits alongside her, waiting for the train. On the next bench was a mother with two children—a little girl of around a year old, thumb in mouth and dark-lashed eyes fluttering shut, and her older brother, who was hanging off the handle of the stroller impatiently, longing for the train to arrive. As he caught sight of Clara's rabbits and stared with fascination, his mother reached down a hand and ran it idly through his shock of hair.

The gesture, so ordinary, sent a shaft of longing and loss through Clara. It was something she remembered from when she first knew Erich. How casually, fondly, she had run her fingers through his dense, springy tuft of hair. And now such gestures were forever out of bounds. Never again could she ruffle his hair or pass a proprietorial hand across his face. It was only a tiny, incidental loss when set against the scale of losses that faced everyone now, but she felt it, and it ached.

Erich had been damaged by the Nazis, too. Nowhere near so much as Esther Goldblatt, in silent hiding, lying awake every night in fear of footsteps coming up the stairs, yet the wounds Hitler's regime inflicted on him were lasting and real. His mother had been murdered by the Nazis when he was ten years old. He had lost all his security and was left with only a grandmother and Clara herself. No wonder he reserved his ardor for dreams of heroism. No wonder he poured all his passion and loyalty into that other family, the Hitler Youth—the family that never left him with a second to himself.

And what if she went back to England for good? Clara didn't want to leave Erich, even if sometimes he did everything in his power to make him easy to leave. But if she stayed in Berlin she would be trapped, just like on the saluting podium at the birthday parade, confined by velvet ropes to a world that was harder and harder to escape.

A voice jerked her back to the present.

"Fräulein?"

It was a lottery ticket seller, coming along the platform with a tray-load of orange, sealed tickets. The Reichslotterie, the German state lottery, was all the rage. Everyone played— except Jews, who were banned from buying tickets—and the money supposedly went to a variety of noble causes: job creation, winter relief, mothers and children. Whether the odds were entirely as pure as mathematics would suggest, or rigged to minimize payouts, was another matter. Some people said the Party ensured winning tickets were few and far between. Despite that, everyone had their favorite numbers, and in a vote for improbability as well as a protest against her own mathematical brain, Clara always selected primes. Now she handed over the requisite fifty pfennigs, the ticket seller saluted, and she picked five numbered orange envelopes. Only each one she opened had a blue ticket with the single word *Nicht* written on it.

She might have seen it as an omen, had she not long since learned to disregard them.

15

"WHY DID YOU WANT TO MEET HERE?"

Hedwig sneaked a quick look around her and frowned. They never went to restaurants, let alone ones like this. They couldn't possibly afford it. Alois's restaurant, at 3 Wittenbergplatz, just across from the ritzy KaDeWe department store, was a pretty smart place. The building had belonged to a Jewish family until it came under the uncomfortable scrutiny of a tavern proprietor whose influence was out of all proportion to his pale, sweaty, unprepossessing form. For the bespectacled Alois, who had set his sights on the Jewish family's home and subsequently had them beaten up and evicted, was not just a former Bavarian waiter and petty criminal but the half brother of the Führer himself. Even though relations between the two men were not what anyone would call brotherly, no one in the Third Reich felt like questioning the strength of that particular sibling bond.

"It's amazing what a powerful brother can do for

you," muttered Jochen as he surveyed the menu and selected a dish of liver dumplings. "From a petty thief and drunken waiter to owning a classy joint like this."

"The Führer's brother's a thief? That can't be true."

"He served a couple of prison sentences in Austria before he fled to Britain to start a new life. Then he married another woman without bothering to divorce the first. He's a family disgrace. His brother even made him resign from the Party."

"That may be," Hedwig said softly, trying to avert her eyes from three rowdy storm troopers leering in her direction. "But I don't see why that would make you want to come here."

"I thought I'd give it a try," he replied curtly. "If it's good enough for the SS. And aren't you supposed to be mixing with SS men now? I thought that was what the Faith and Beauty Society was all about. Moving in the right circles."

"Jochen, please." She placed a hand on his arm. She knew he was jealous, seeing his girlfriend being primped and groomed as a consort to senior Nazi men, and it hurt her to think it. "I told you I'd never be interested in any man but you."

He managed a smile, a quick flicker that transformed his face and, just for a second, erased all the worry lines.

"Any news about Lottie?" he asked more gently. "Are the police still searching? Have they found anything yet?"

"Nothing. They were there again this morning. They kept asking if we had seen anyone."

In a matter of a few weeks, the Faith and Beauty home had transformed into a full-blown crime scene. Kripo cars cluttered the driveway, and the corridors were full of detectives, their boots ringing unnaturally loud on the polished parquet floor. Police tape fluttered across the lawn like ribbons on a maypole. Why would a girl like Lottie go into the woods? That was the question they all asked. Faith and Beauty girls were not the sort to make unlikely assignations in the Grunewald, unless some-one had forced them. It tormented Hedwig, too. Lying awake at night, she tried to imagine the man who had killed Lottie, yet she couldn't conjure any features. Only a face that seemed to compress into it all the horrors of the night.

"I'm surprised they haven't questioned me more, but no one wants to know. It's as though no one really cares."

"Of course they care."

"They don't. Or if they do, it's only because it's in the news-papers, and it might look bad if they don't arrest someone soon. I miss her, Jochen."

"I know."

"Do you think I should ask the police if I can help them more?"

"No." He was firm about this. "Don't do that. If they need anything they'll tell you."

He lit two cigarettes and gave her one. "How's that other friend of yours? Irna? She's getting married, isn't she?"

It was true. Irna Wolter had scored the greatest triumph of them all—the jackpot of the Faith and Beauty lottery. She had won the heart of an Ubersturmbannführer and was to wed him later that month. She was currently at the Reich Bride School on Schwanenwerder Island, studying for the certificate she needed to qualify for marriage into the SS.

"She's at Bride School now. Getting ready for the wedding."

"Are you invited?"

"I wish I was, but it's not in Berlin. It's at a special SS train-ing school. A castle, can you believe it, in Westphalia. Women aren't allowed in."

"Some wedding. Is that the kind you want then?"

"Don't be silly. You know I don't want anything special. Besides, there's only one man I want to marry, and he doesn't have much time for castles."

Jochen looked down at his fingers, which were stained yellow by nicotine. Usually they had traces of ink on them, too, from work. It was always this way when the subject of marriage came up. He would immediately clam up and avert his gaze. Hedwig felt the familiar, agonizing tear at her heart. She tried not to talk about marriage, but it was he who had brought the subject up. If he couldn't bear the idea of a future with her, then why didn't he come right out and say so? Lottie had always insisted she should tell Jochen the truth, but Hedwig feared that if she pushed too hard, Jochen would back away. And then she would be left without the only man she had ever loved.

Being with Jochen was like being with a dog that had been ill-treated and had never lost the distrust in its eyes. Sometimes she wondered if he would ever form a commitment, at least to her, but at other times she thought she should simply be patient and loving. Perhaps it was still too early, or maybe Jochen cared more than he showed about her parents' entrenched hostility. Often she found herself scanning his face like a cryptologist, trying to divine a hidden meaning in his silence. Usually she would cover up any pauses by saying all the things that she didn't mean, rather than saying what she did, but this time she stayed silent, and unwelcome tears stung in her eyes. Since Lottie's death she found herself crying at the slightest provocation.

"At last."

Their *Leberknödel* arrived, and though the dumplings turned out to contain far more bread crumbs than liver, maybe that was for the best. Hedwig always felt guilty eating meat these days. More and more people were turning vegetarian because they wanted to follow the Führer's example, and they had been told that even the top men in the Party, like Hess and Himmler and Goebbels, regularly enjoyed vegetarian meals, though Jochen said this was all made up. It was important to be thrifty, too. The newspapers were full of recipes for cakes without fat or eggs. They had been told that bread, sugar, and coffee were in short supply because the Führer wanted to increase the racial fitness of the nation. Just as Hitler was preparing for war by building tanks, so his people must prepare their bodies for war through frugal eating. Only the other day on the radio Doktor Goebbels had condemned Berliners who complained about the coffee shortage as "cosmopolitan," which was as good as calling them Jews. If people really wanted to please the Führer they should become vegetarians, like him.

"We were learning about the Führer's love of animals," she said, for the sake of conversation.

Apparently, the Führer had decided some animals were never acceptable to eat. Snails were all right, though just the idea of their little eyes on tiny gray stalks made Hedwig queasy, but lobster and frogs' legs were out. That hardly mattered as Hedwig couldn't afford lobster and she was scarcely likely to encounter frogs' legs any time soon. "He's banning scientific research on animals. And there are to be new regulations on the care of horses. Hitler says all Germans love horses."

"Preferably in a stew," said Jochen, bitterly.

"Germany is the first country in Europe to make laws to protect animals."

"Tell that to the bombers," he replied sourly, forking a dumpling into his mouth. "Nothing's going to protect animals if a war starts. And it will."

He gave a quick glance behind him, then leaned closer. "At

work they're already printing rationing coupons. Color-coded ones, white for sugar, blue for meat, purple for fruit and nuts, yellow for dairy, and green for eggs."

"Rationing?" She was wide-eyed.

"Sure. Twenty-four hundred grams of bread a week, five hundred grams of meat, two hundred and seventy grams of fat, whole milk for children and invalids only. It's serious, Hedy. The authorities are making preparations." He looked up at her, inscrutably. "As it happens, I am too. I've joined the RLB."

The Reichsluftschutzbund, the Reich Air Protection League, was busily organizing blackout provisions and shelters in event of war.

"I had my first outing yesterday, inspecting cellars. All blocks have to convert their cellars, and in some streets all the cellars will interconnect, in case escape routes get blocked. You wouldn't believe what there is underneath your feet, Hedy. There's a whole network of underground canals, tunnels, and shelters already constructed. You'd be astonished."

She was bewildered at this initiative. "That's not like you."

"Why not?"

"You hate thinking about war, or the Führer's attempts to protect Germany."

"Perhaps I've changed my mind."

A terrible thought seized Hedwig. "Does that mean you're going to enlist?"

"Your father would like that, wouldn't he?"

So her suspicions were correct. Her parents' hostility bothered Jochen far more than he let on.

"Of course they wouldn't. They just need time . . ."

"Then I could go off and get killed and not bother their dear daughter again."

Her eyes filled with tears. "Please stop talking like that. You know I hate it. It tears me apart."

The savage look fell instantly from his face, and he reached out a hand towards her. "Don't cry," he whispered. "I'm a cruel beast, but I don't mean it."

He wiped away a tear that was dripping off the bottom of her spectacles.

"I thought you'd be pleased that I'm spending my evenings in cellars rather than nightclubs or bars, Hedy."

"There are plenty of nightclubs in cellars," she joked with a brave sniff. Any quarrel with Jochen engulfed her in alarm, but being Hedwig, she didn't stay miserable for long. Jochen was the only person in the world to call her Hedy. She hated her name. Her parents had named her after St. Hedwig's, Berlin's Catholic cathedral, an uninspiring place whose pediment was lined by ranks of stone saints, surveying all comers like police officers inspecting the faithful. There were no glamorous Hedwigs in history, or literature, or any kind of culture. Even the Viennese movie actress Hedwig Kiesler had moved to Hollywood and changed her name to Hedy Lamarr.

"Anyhow. How's work?" she inquired, pulling herself together.

"Busier than ever. You can tell your father, our company's supporting the Reich just as much as any soldier. Our products make millions for the Party. The Führer makes a pretty packet out of it too. He charges for the use of his image. He makes a pfennig every time his face appears on a postage stamp."

"I'm sure he gives it to the Winterhilfswerk. The Führer wouldn't want any money for himself."

"Wouldn't he? That makes him different from the rest of them then. I heard old Joey Goebbels was making money selling all those Degenerate paintings they took down from the museums."

"That's only Jewish art, though, isn't it?"

His eyes sparked dangerous fire. "What does that mean exactly?"

"I mean"—Hedwig labored on, trying to remember what Herr Fritzl had told them—"it's disgusting, isn't it? Not like your kind of art."

"Not like my kind of art," he repeated in a tone that seemed slightly menacing. Hedwig knew she had said something wrong, or stupid, but she didn't know how to fix it. She worried the edge of her skirt with a nail.

"What's my kind of art then, Hedy?"

"You paint faces."

"Not faces. I paint *a face*. The same face, day after day after day. Sometimes making his cheeks a little pinker, his eyes a little darker blue. Flattering him. Touching up his mustache. Shortening his nose. Making him into a matinee idol. A little more hair, fewer wrinkles."

"That's nothing that the old masters wouldn't do. They had patrons and they needed to please them so they flattered them."

Herr Fritzl had definitely said this.

"We're not talking about Michelangelo here, Hedy. What I do is hack work. I know Hitler's face better than I know my own. I've painted it on plates and dishes and canvases and candleholders and beer steins. Sometimes I wonder how he can bear it, seeing his face everywhere. It's on everything except the money, and that's only because he remembers the inflation and thinks he had better keep his head off the banknotes in case it happens again."

Fortunately, their conversation was interrupted by a cheer and a round of applause from the far side of the restaurant.

The Führer's brother had emerged and was standing, incongruously, beneath the portrait of his sibling, a cigar in one hand and a beaming smile across his face. At the sight of him, Jochen seemed to forget their argument instantly.

"As a matter of fact . . ." He was scratching at the surface of the table with his finger. "I'm going to ask you something."

Hedwig was bathed in relief. "Anything, you know that."

She was rewarded with one of his true smiles, a tender beam that lit up his face, and made his hazel eyes shine. It was the smile that had first made her love him. It opened up a chink in his cynicism and revealed the gentle and protective man that other people would never have believed possible. That was what love did, she supposed. It made you see below the surface of a person, to the soul beneath.

"Is it about a book?"

She guessed it would be something to do with literature. Jochen was a fervent reader. He was like Lottie in that. Always quoting little snippets of poetry and talking about writers she had never heard of. Hedy suspected that he kept a stash of banned books somewhere in his home, too. Perhaps he wanted to borrow something from the library at the Ahnenerbe.

"Not exactly."

"What is it then? Don't keep me in suspense!"

"I can't tell you quite yet."

"How mysterious!"

"It is. Shall we meet at the usual time next week?"

"Any time. I can tell Mutti I'm needed at work. There's a lot going on at the moment. They're making a film about the Ahnenerbe. Leni Riefenstahl is to direct it."

He gave a whistle. "Riefenstahl! Will you be in it?"

"I certainly hope not. I'm going to keep well away."

"You're far too shy."

She took off her spectacles and began absently cleaning them on her skirt. "I'm not exactly film star material."

"Don't say that." He grasped her hand. "You know what? I spend my whole day beautifying the Führer, straightening his nose, giving him a bit of color in his cheeks, touching up his hair. So it's nice to come out in the evening with someone who doesn't need any beautifying."

He reached up to brush a curl from her eyes.

"You're perfect, Hedy. You know I think that."

ERICH CAROW'S *LAUGH IN* WAS A CELEBRATED COM-
edy act staged at the Valhalla theater in an appropriately
cavernous cellar on Weinbergsweg, north of Rosenthaler
Platz. Just a few years ago Berlin had been the nightclub capital of the world, a neon-lit, champagne-fueled
extravaganza of singing, dancing, and most of all sex.
Sex for every taste, no matter how specialized or how
depraved, could be found in dimly lit caverns off the
Friedrichstrasse and openly in the rooms above. For two
decades straight, nighttime Berlin had been a dazzling,
decadent, nonstop party, played out at the Wintergarten,
the Admiralspalast, and the Residence Casino. But the
party stopped abruptly in 1933, and most of Berlin's cabarets closed down. The risqué acts were replaced with
musicals, and the only variety on offer was the choice
between folk singing and operetta. Jazz was degenerate
Entarte Musik, and Goebbels issued all musicians with
instructions on how to hold their instruments so they
didn't resemble Africans. All the dangerous glamour

had been swept up by the broom of National Socialism, and the only traces of it were left in a few dark corners, one of them being the Valhalla. Everyone went there—actresses, journalists, artists, politicians—and while the comedy survived, the laughter was darker and more bitter. At a time when blackout paper and black material were everywhere, black humor was the only kind in vogue.

Navigating down the stairs, past an enamel plate reading JAZZ DANCING FORBIDDEN, Clara made her way into the shabby cellar and looked around for her friends. Immediately in front of her a table of soldiers were amusing themselves by trying to shove ice cubes down the cleavages of a pair of buxom waitresses. The waitresses, struggling with large trays of beer and trapped amid the knot of young men, were laughing, but Clara glimpsed the alarm in their eyes. The soldiers' faces were lean and savage, as though they were already inured to cruelty. Anyone of their age had already spent years in the Hitler Youth being trained to ridicule, taunt, and bully, and their sport with the barmaids was no different from that of cats playing with a mouse. These women existed for entertainment, and their distress was simply part of the fun.

Clara prayed that the same did not happen to Erich.

The foreign correspondents were up by the bar. She detected the lanky frame of Charles Cavendish towering over an animated Bill Shirer, who was jabbing with his pipe to emphasize a point. Hugh Lindsey, a Burberry coat slung across his shoulders, was deep in conversation with Mary Harker. As Clara approached he caught her eye and winked, but she had no intention of interrupting, so she approached Cavendish, who swiveled towards her, sweeping an oiled hank of hair from his eyes and baring his tombstone teeth in a patronizing smile.

"The lovely Clara Vine."

She guessed that he disliked her, and that was to be expected, given what he must assume. What else should he make of an Anglo-German actress who mingled in the top circles of the Nazi Party and whose father was one of Britain's most prominent Nazi sympathizers? When you looked at it like that, it was a wonder that he was even prepared to welcome her as a drinking companion.

"How are you, Charles?"

"As well as can be expected for a man who has sat through two press conferences and an interview with Robert Ley."

"You've come to the right place, Cavendish," said Shirer. "Apparently Himmler has decreed that an evening at the cabaret counts as therapy. He's recommended it for any German soldiers suffering trauma inflicted during their role in Czechoslovakia."

"Maybe he should suggest it for some of his colleagues." Cavendish smiled. "They're a dreadfully unhealthy bunch. The Führer is said to be suffering from appalling digestive problems. Goering's diabetic, has sciatica, and is always exhausted. Von Ribbentrop is in constant pain because he has only one kidney. And Himmler suffers from the most agonizing abdominal attacks and lives in terror of stomach cancer."

"Even Goebbels is fresh out of a clinic," added Shirer.

"One thinks one knows what caused that. Or rather *who*," said Cavendish knowingly, and following his eyes Clara saw a figure she recognized.

Joseph Goebbels may have censored all the cabarets in the city and even dictated which dances could be performed in them, but there was one thing in the Third Reich he could not control: his wife. Magda Goebbels, thirty-eight-year-old mother of six, was seated at a table in the center of the club in full, embarrassing view. Around her, a circle of dazzled young men clustered, topping up her glass, lighting her cigarettes, and hanging slavishly on her words.

"Apparently Goebbels was forced to spend Christmas in the guesthouse," remarked Shirer. "She won't have him in the house."

Since her husband's affair with the Czech actress Lida Baarová the previous year, Magda had resorted to her own style of revenge. It involved the conventional combination of a make-over, an affair, and an awful lot of alcohol. Her wheat-blond hair was now ashy and stiffly strained into rolls against her head. Her slinky plum dress—an elegant design by Paul Kuhnen—was ostentatiously modern, though its slender silhouette did her bulky form no favors. And the Elizabeth Arden foundation she had always used was now painted as thickly as a Van Gogh sunflower.

"She's in nightclubs several nights a week around town," murmured Cavendish waspishly. "She likes to invite young men to share her table. She even asks sailors home."

There was a malicious gleam in Cavendish's eye at Magda Goebbels's predicament—a malice that was, thought Clara, not too far from the savage laughter of the SA youths with the bar-maids. She thought back over the years she had known the pro-paganda minister's wife, a brittle, nerve-racked, unsympathetic figure, locked into the gilded cage of a Nazi spouse by her own disastrous choices. So what if Magda chose to play out her mis-ery on the public stage? Who could blame her given the horror of her marriage and the remorseless barbarity that her hus-band's regime perpetrated? Clara was about to reply when Magda Goebbels turned in her direction and lurched to her feet.

"Bad luck," murmured Cavendish. "Looks like she's seen you."

Magda, it was immediately clear, was drunk. Very drunk. Drifts of powder had collected in the crevices of her face, and her lipstick might have been applied by one of her own little girls. The depths of her cleavage glistened with sweat. Yet beneath the blowsy exterior she was more agitated than Clara had ever seen her. A gold-tipped Sobranie trembled in her hand, and her address was far more familiar than she would allow herself in daylight hours.

"Fräulein Vine. Our own little actress. Fancy seeing you here." She swayed to a stop. "I wouldn't have thought this was the kind of place you frequented. They tell jokes against Party leaders here, didn't you know? I always had you down as a loyal member of the Chamber of Culture."

"As I am."

"Not so loyal as to sleep with my husband, I hope."

"Certainly not."

"Well, you can always join the queue," Magda said with a harsh laugh, which brought a sour gust of schnapps and tobacco. "Though there's quite a waiting list."

A hush had descended. Most of the customers had turned in their direction, their faces agog with expectation, if not surprise. Magda Goebbels had, in recent months, become an alternative cabaret. She was a living, breathing one-woman stand-up comedy show, firing off unspeakable quips about the Nazi leaders. An act like that by anyone else would be closed down instantly, and the performer sent to a camp the same evening, but who would dare denounce the propaganda minister's wife? In what newspaper or magazine could the allegation be printed, and what court would hear the accusations? Besides, why denounce her, when you could laugh at her instead?

Clara felt a wave of sympathy. "Why don't we sit down? There's a seat over there. In that alcove."

"Don't let me take you away from your friends. Especially not that handsome young man," commented Magda, eyeing Hugh Lindsey.

"They're not really my friends," said Clara hastily. "Just some journalists."

She hoped the mention of journalists would be enough. Surely Magda was not so reckless that she would risk getting drunk in front of the cream of the foreign press? God forbid she should ask to be introduced to Hugh, or invite him back to the Goebbelses' villa for a drink.

"I barely know them," Clara added.

But Magda's interest had flagged, and all her attention turned inwards again, to her own troubles. She plumped herself down on the banquette with a noisy sigh.

"I have a terrible headache. You have no idea how much I suffer, Fräulein Vine."

"I have aspirin——" Clara began to fumble in her bag, but Magda waved her away.

"It's a spiritual suffering. There's no pill for that, no matter how much my husband keeps booking me into clinics and sending the frightful Doktor Morell around with his prescriptions."

Theo Morell was Hitler's own doctor, who had been slavishly taken up by all the senior Nazis and as a consequence enjoyed lavish premises on the Kurfürstendamm and a country villa on the Wannsee. The contents of his pills were top secret, but generally thought to be amphetamines, designed to combat the sleepless nights of the top men.

"God knows what he has in those pills. I wouldn't be at all surprised if I ended up poisoned one day. At least Joseph would be pleased."

So they had reached the heart of the matter, in one easy step.

"How is the Herr Doktor?"

"How should I know? He's barely speaking to me. The Füh-rer might have ordered him to break up with that marriage wrecker, but you wouldn't know it. He went on a grand tour of Europe to 'soothe his wounded heart,' but when he came back it was just as bad. Do you know what he's done now?"

Clara could only imagine.

"He's commissioned a film from Veit Harlan to tell the story of his affair."

It was, of course, the talk of the studios. Veit Harlan, an actor turned successful director, had been allocated an eye-popping budget for his latest project, *Die Reise nach Tilsit.* The movie told the story of an honorable man torn between his exquisitely beautiful mistress and his dumpy wife, struggling to resolve the conflict between head and heart. The lovelorn Goebbels was constantly popping in to watch the action or ex-amine the rushes with manic attention to detail.

"Joseph denies it's about himself, of course. And he refuses to discuss our marriage. Whenever I complain he stuffs his ears and shouts, 'It's the same old song! Even Bormann is allowed a mistress!' Apparently Bormann has taken up with one of your little actress friends. I expect you know her."

Clara did, slightly. Manja Behrens was a dental assistant whose aspirations to a film and stage career had undergone a meteoric rise since she had come under the eye of Hitler's en-forcer, the vicious, bull-necked Martin Bormann. In a grotesque parallel of Magda Goebbels's own plight the previous year, it was rumored that Bormann was planning to move Manja under his own roof. Only the browbeaten Gerda Bormann might prove more amenable than Magda, who had tolerated her hus-band's ménage à trois precisely one week before storming off to Hitler and demanding a divorce.

"Joseph may have a broken heart, but it hasn't stopped him of course. He's built a new villa for his whores, out at Bogensee. It cost three million marks and it's supposed to be the property of the German Film Industry. Though I suppose that makes sense, given the number of German actresses who pass through." Magda's face hardened. "In a few weeks it's our annual trip to Salzburg for the Wagner. I can see it already. All that operatic passion, and Joseph snuffling away next to me, moaning about his wounded heart."

Magda sniffed, blinking away the tears of alcohol and self-pity in her eyes. Despite her prickle of sympathy, Clara knew she must not pass up the opportunity of this confessional mood.

"Have you heard much of Frau von Ribbentrop?"

"Unfortunately, I never hear the end of her."

Since their first encounter in 1933, Magda Goebbels had not bothered to conceal her view of Annelies von Ribbentrop as a nouveau riche social climber, and despite the fact that she had now achieved the dizzy heights of Wilhelmstrasse, Magda saw little reason to revise her opinion.

"I went on tour to Italy with Albert Speer. I was desperately in need of a break. We went all round the Doric temples of Sicily and southern Italy. It should have been so fascinating, but all anyone could talk about was the von Ribbentrops. Joachim is bordering on insanity, they say, and Annelies is goading him on to all sorts of rash decisions."

She leaned forward confidentially. "In fact, they worry that von Ribbentrop's advice is badly misleading the Führer in his military planning. Some of the senior men have been consulting a psychic to find out if the auspices are right for what Hitler has planned."

Clara could barely believe it. "They're asking a fortune-teller?"

"A good one. Her name is Annie Krauss. She has a place up in Wilmersdorf. She read my palm once actually, and it was completely accurate. Every bit of it! She said if I stay with Joseph I'll be dead by the age of forty-five. I can well believe it. I feel half dead already."

The clatter of percussion and a roar from the audience alerted them to the beginning of the cabaret. As the performers made their entrance onstage, Magda rose unsteadily to her feet.

"My friends will be wondering where I've gotten to."

Clara picked up her bag. "Of course. Mine too."

"I thought you said they weren't your friends."

Magda lurched forward and gripped her wrist so hard that Clara flinched. Flushed and sweating, she loomed in Clara's face.

"What is it about you, Fräulein Vine? I've known you on and off for what is it, six years, and I don't think I have ever seen you with a proper boyfriend. Not even my husband, which is quite an achievement, given his penchant for brunettes. And I've never heard scandal attached to your name until now."

Clara felt the blood freeze inside her, but on the surface she was merely cool. "Really? Scandal?"

"You want to watch out . . ." Magda smiled cruelly. "People are keeping an eye on you. Somebody has been saying some very unkind things about you."

"I wonder who?"

"I can't tell you. And I'd be lying if I said I cared. But for the sake of our long acquaintance, I'd advise you to be careful. Unless you want to spend more time enjoying your own company."

AT THE BAR MARY was still deeply ensconced with Hugh, and he had taken her arm to emphasize some point, making her flush with unexpected pleasure. Clara's encounter, however, had not escaped her notice.

"I didn't realize you and Magda Goebbels were such great friends."

"It was just a friendly chat."

"I've seen friendlier Alsatians."

"She says some of the regime are consulting a fortune-teller about their military plans."

"Astonishing," said Hugh.

"You'd better believe it," said Mary. "Most of them are intensely superstitious. Even Hitler had his own astrologer until the SA discovered the man was Jewish and shot him in a field outside Berlin. Goebbels was joking about it for years afterwards."

"Our minister enjoys jokes, doesn't he?" said Hugh drily. "I heard today that he's appointed his own joke writer in the ministry."

"He certainly needs something to improve those speeches."

"It's not for the speeches. It's rather more ingenious than that. The idea is to create jokes about the senior men and then track their spread across the country. Apparently it's an effective way of monitoring dissent."

"Aren't these people incredible?" Mary shook her head. "They're more of a joke than any cabaret act."

"If the Nazis are a joke," said Hugh, "I'd hate to hear the punch line."

CLARA MADE HER WAY back through the shadowed streets. *Someone has been saying very unkind things about you.* The shock of Magda Goebbels's remark only heightened the anxiety that had first prompted her to move out of Winterfeldtstrasse. The fear that she was being watched and that her every movement was under close scrutiny was all-pervasive. Yet still she had no clear idea who might have ordered such a surveillance, or why. To distract herself from these circling fears, she turned her thoughts to the fortune-teller Annie Krauss. Berliners were indeed famously superstitious. The city was thick with psychics and palm readers. Their advertisements peppered every newspaper and advertising column. Nor was a tendency to superstition limited to the general populace. Not only Hitler but Himmler firmly believed that psychic forces controlled his destiny. How perilous that the future of Europe might hinge on the prognostications of a palm reader or an astrologer.

And yet, thought Clara, as she boarded the last S-Bahn and sat in the warm, rumbling darkness, was she not herself in thrall to a kind of superstition? Wasn't she also longing to believe her own personal faith? That unexplained sixth sense, like a quiet flame in her heart, that told her that while Leo was missing, while he had disappeared without a trace, he might yet not be dead?

17

HEDWIG WAS SITTING IN THE CRAMPED FRONT ROOM of the apartment with all five of her brothers, quizzing Reiner on air raids. It was his homework, but all the boys were listening—all of them except one-year-old Kurt, who was drifting to sleep on her lap. Kurt was too young to understand about bombs or fire or death, and when he had been given a picture book about air raids, he had torn it up and cheerfully stuffed the pieces into his mouth. Hedwig wished she could do the same with Reiner's quiz.

As she ran through the list of questions, she was trying to keep order while all three of the other boys attempted to compete. Wolfgang, who at eleven was younger than Reiner but brighter, kept butting in. The oldest, Peter, bent over his schoolwork, contributing answers in a tone of bored superiority that infuriated his younger brother. Even little Ludi, who at five was too small for the Pimpf, but who had regular air-raid lessons at kindergarten, kept jumping up and trying to interrupt.

"Stop it, Ludi. It's my homework!" shouted Reiner, with a mounting flush on his cheeks. "I need to get it right because there's a big test coming up!"

Reiner always found himself left behind by his cleverer brothers. He was hopeless at school. Perhaps that was why the HJ meant so much to him. It played to his strengths, which were running, fighting, and swimming. Placing a soothing hand on Ludi's head, Hedwig continued.

"What do you do if you see a fire, Reiner? Who would be the right person to tell? What do you do if someone's injured? How would you deal with poison gas?"

War was by far her brothers' favorite subject. It occupied all their thoughts. Even when they weren't studying it, the boys were playing it in a variety of military board games, Tanks Forward, Without a Propeller, We Sail Against England— a new one involving U-boats—and Bombs over England, a game where Heinkel bombers attacked London Bridge. That was Wolfgang's favorite, and when Hedwig told him she had seen the real London Bridge and hoped it wouldn't be bombed, he'd stared at her in disbelief.

But who needed board games now that the whole of the city had turned into one big practice site? Mock air raids and black-outs went on all the time in Berlin. In a recent drill, soldiers trussed up in decontamination suits had hosed down the streets as if clearing poison gas. The Luftwaffe had been co-opted to drop smoke bombs for a more realistic effect, and fire engines raised their ladders up the sides of buildings to stage rescues. The Hitler Youth dedicated a couple of evenings every week to air-raid drills, and Reiner's battalion had a large-scale exercise coming up. When war came, it would be the HJ that the city would rely on to coordinate the air-raid precautions, check blackouts and sound sirens, and cope with casualties. That was why Reiner's homework mattered so much, and why Hedwig needed to drum the answers into his head.

She was devoted to her brood of brothers. Sometimes she felt she was never happier than when settled in this drab, untidy, cramped apartment, parrying their backchat and adjudicating over their squabbles. There was Peter, at seventeen serious and ambitious; Reiner and Wolfgang always fighting; Ludi, a burly miniature of their father; and tiny, boisterous Kurt, who called for Hedwig before he called for his mother and whose care Mutti seemed quite happy to delegate. In the evenings when she was not taking Faith and Beauty classes, Hedwig cooked and washed the plates, and after her father departed for the nearest *kneipe* bar, divided her time between homework, storytelling, and keeping order. Not to mention patching Kurt's clothes, which had been shed by four brothers before him like the skins of a snake. This humdrum existence could not be less like the gracious, elegant life that the Faith and Beauty Society was preparing her for. Here in Moabit there was no art, or dancing, or conversation to speak of, unless you counted their father bellowing at the children or Mutti moaning about the amount of washing she had to do. There was no music, apart from the light dance music on the radio, which Mutti used to drown out the squabbling of the boys. And yet it could not suit Hedwig better.

Plowing through the pages of questions on Reiner's list, she felt a pang of sympathy for him. It had been the same for her in the BDM—endless lists of questions that she could still reel off like some leaden poetry imprinted forever in her mind. *What is the date and place of birth of the Führer? What are the clauses of the Treaty of Versailles? What is the date of the Beer Hall Putsch? What is the significance of November 10*—the an-

swer to that was Martin Luther's birthday, rather than Kristallnacht, which had raged through the city last year.

At times it seemed citizens of the Reich spent their entire
lives answering questionnaires. At the Faith and Beauty Society
they marveled at the form issued by the office responsible for
maintaining the racial purity of the SS to women hoping to
marry. It was seven pages long and spelled out cumbersome
requirements of the hopeful girl, including the precise date
that she learned to walk, and photographs of herself in a bathing suit taken from three angles. Worse, some of the queries
seemed as daunting as a university examination.

"Is the woman positively addicted to housework?" was one.
How did you answer that?

"Does she hold fast to the values of German womanhood?"

And the one that had particularly floored Hedwig. "Does
she cherish the high ideals of German philosophy?"

God knew how she would ever answer them, yet with any
luck there would be no need. The only question she was interested in just then was the one that Jochen had mentioned the
other evening in the restaurant. And if it was what she guessed,
then it would be both thrilling and terrifying in equal measure.

18

PARIS IN THE SPRING HAD A REPUTATION TO LIVE UP TO. The air was soft as a peach. The sunshine had obliged, and the smart ladies at the Auteuil races showed off that season's striped silk suits. Hats were worn flowered. Eau de Nil, sorbet, champagne, and sky blue were the colors of the moment. The bateaux mouches slid beneath the bridges of the Seine, the used book sellers set up their stalls on the parapets, and artists in broad-brimmed hats propped their easels as ever beneath the façade of Notre Dame. The chestnuts were blooming in the broad boulevards, and in the exquisite spring light the elegantly peeling façades of soft mushroom stone and the bleached shutters with their window boxes of tumbling scarlet geraniums seemed almost impossibly beautiful.

Paris, above all cities, was good at putting on a show.

If the French were preparing for war, it was with all the elegance and nonchalance that only Parisians could muster. Young men at café tables still whistled and tried to catch the glances of passing girls in imitation silk dresses, who stalked the pavements as haughtily as fashion models. Policemen still wore brass-buttoned jackets, flat-topped caps, and white cotton gloves to conduct the traffic round the Place de l'Opéra. Even the air-raid precautions were undertaken with a view to appearances, and the statues and monuments were fringed with spotless lines of sandbags. Perhaps the French thought the great Maginot Line would protect them from anything the Germans could attempt, or perhaps they trusted that no one, not even Hitler, would dare sully the splendor of their most elegant city.

Clara was wearing a silk day dress—white zigzags on a dark pink background—and the Chanel scarf that Erich had given her the previous year knotted casually round her throat. She rarely risked bright colors in Berlin. The ideal demeanor for a spy was nondescript, which translated as workday, inconspicuous clothing or at the very least muted shades, but here in Paris she felt more relaxed, and besides, didn't it make sense to look as glamorous as possible when you were expecting, or at least hoping, to feature in the pages of French *Vogue*?

At the Gare du Nord she had parted with seven francs for the latest edition of the magazine. *Vogue* was celebrating the fiftieth anniversary of the Eiffel Tower and featured a startling photograph of a model named Lisa Fonssagrives wearing a Lucien Lelong dress, balancing on the tower's very summit, the city spread beneath her like a glorious map. Flipping through, Clara saw that the shadow of war had not been permitted to darken the magazine's pages. The chief international crisis of the day was the fact that Greta Garbo, Marlene Dietrich, and Joan Crawford were now being dressed by American designers. And a forthcoming movie called *Gone with the Wind* was to bring back the fashions of the American South. Was New York about to inherit Paris's crown? France was fighting back with a

Tyrolean style from Mainbocher and blue tulle veils from Jeanne Lanvin. The only inkling that anything more serious might be on the horizon was the news that Schiaparelli was calling her latest vivid shade Maginot Line blue.

Clara stuffed the magazine into her bag and made her way across town. It had been a long train journey, and the narrow bunk in the sleeping car had allowed only minimal rest, but she wanted to walk. She was longing for the brief respite from Berlin and the chance to savor a different city. She wanted to drink in the sight of ladies taking coffee at marble tables and peer through shutters the color of verdigris into courtyards with ivy-covered fountains. To hear the church bells, with their charming lack of synchronicity, sound out across the rooftops and wander into the shadowy medieval spaces, glimmering with candles and thick with incense. She wanted to absorb everything from the birds roosting on the windowsills to the sun piercing the wrought-iron balustrade of the Pont Alexandre III, lacing the pavement with a dark tracery of shadow.

THE RUE LÉOPOLD-ROBERT LAY in Paris's Fourteenth Arrondissement, between the Boulevard Raspail and the Boulevard du Montparnasse. The list of artists who frequented this district might have been especially composed to enrage the Führer. Picasso, Cocteau, Duchamp, Léger, Modigliani, and Dalí were locals, arguing all day in Le Dôme, La Rotonde, or La Coupole and carousing in the bars all night. Above the streets, rickety apartment buildings were packed with artists' studios, and beneath them lay the bone-stacked catacombs. It was as though Death stretched beneath the feet while Life danced above them.

She was early, so Clara stopped at a café called La Closerie des Lilas and sat inside, beside a dark wood and button-leather bar beneath a picture of Lenin. She ordered an apple tart, reveling in the rich, flaky pastry that melted in her mouth while observing the vignettes of Left Bank life all around. An elderly woman was passing with a baby carriage containing a minuscule dog with a ribbon in its hair. A flock of nuns, wimples lifting in the wind like somber gray wings, prayer books in hand, were on their way to mass. A toddler stretched out her hands at a falling leaf. Clara's eye was caught by a girl a few seats away who casually took out her compact and applied lip rouge from a pot with her little finger. It was a startling sight—no woman in Berlin would dare apply cosmetics in public.

Clara tried and failed to read a report in *Paris-Soir* about the imminent trial of Herschel Grynszpan, the young Jewish boy who had shot Ernst vom Rath, a German cultural attaché, in Paris the previous year, but it was hard to focus. Bit by bit, the tensions of life in Berlin fell away from her and she relaxed into the sensations of Paris. The French language, with its slick warp and weft and softly undulating vowels, flowed like silk around her.

She finished her coffee, paid, and walked the short distance to the Rue Léopold-Robert.

Number Eleven Rue Léopold-Robert was a dingy stucco, wooden-shuttered building with ornate balconies of latticed iron and a set of bells beside a peeling green door. Pushing the outer door open, Clara walked up three flights of a stone staircase with a twisted iron banister. The hall stank of urine and fish, and behind one of the doors a couple were carrying on a heated, uninhibited argument. When she reached apartment four, she found the door wide open, revealing a man half a head shorter than her, wearing a stained white shirt, horn-rimmed glasses, and red spotted cravat. He had a mass of gleaming dark hair, a beaky nose, and alert, intelligent eyes. He removed the Gitanes from his mouth long enough to say, "Mademoiselle Vine. I felt sure you would come. And so prompt. Would that all my models were so punctual."

Clara stepped into an atelier filled with pure northern light that poured through the long windows and glanced off the parquet floor. A few pieces of furniture were assembled randomly as in some avant-garde art show—a chaise longue, a table, various lamp stands, and a bed, beside which stood a glass ashtray overflowing with stubs. A white screen lit by four spotlights covered one wall. The others were filled with giant blow-ups of Epstein's work; bodies striped with light and bisected by operatic shadows and a life-size torso draped in wet silk. Through a doorway she glimpsed a bidet and a basin with nickel taps, on the side of which hung a single woman's stocking. A Siamese cat on the windowsill stared at her with indifferent grandeur.

Epstein opened the shutters with a rattle, prompting the cat to bolt, and switched abruptly from French to German.

"I hope you don't mind coming here. I could use the *Vogue* studios on the Champs-Élysées, but this place is miraculously cheap. A hundred francs a month, and the only catch is I vacate it between five and seven every day so the landlord can sublet for amorous purposes. Please. Sit down."

He gestured to the grubby chaise longue, and Clara sat uncertainly, still unsure what this meeting entailed. She knew Epstein would convey her message to Major Grand, but was the fashion feature in *Vogue* magazine genuine, or simply an elaborate façade?

"Are we actually going to do a photograph?"

"But of course! I love to shoot beautiful women. I live for elegance. It is a religion to me. The more elegance we have in the world, the less horror."

He picked up a length of silk and draped it experimentally over her face, then removed it, muttered to himself, and disappeared for a moment behind a Chinese screen, reappearing with a piece of material trailing dark ribbons.

"Here, Miss Vine, is your costume."

She gave a sharp intake of breath.

It was a corset. A piece of blush pink silk with inky black ribboned laces and stiff bones. The only corsets Clara had ever seen came from the Ufa costume department and were generally stained with old makeup and sweat from repeated use in historical epics, but this one was exquisitely stitched, like a piece of haute couture, and the silk shimmered in her hands.

"Just this?"

"Certainly. It will be subtle, of course. I like to strike a balance between modesty and eroticism. To both reveal and conceal. And this is not just any corset. Mainbocher showed it in this year's collections. Please."

He motioned Clara behind the Chinese screen, where she took off her dress, folded it carefully, and wriggled into the corset. It was a sensation she had never had before, to be so transformed by a single item of clothing, to feel the material enfold her, cool and liquid against her skin.

When she emerged, Epstein fussed about, leaving the top of the corset unlaced, and then positioned Clara with her back towards him, her face inclined slightly away.

"You mean you're going to take a picture of my back?"

"Precisely. We don't want to see your face, delightful though it is. We only want a glimpse, half in shadow and half in the light. That seems appropriate, doesn't it? In the circumstances? And please don't move. Hold that position. I want you emerging from that corset like a rose from its bud."

Not for the first time, Clara wondered how her sister had

ever managed a career as a fashion mannequin. Acting came instinctively to her, but modeling seemed so much less natural. She could practically feel her limbs seize up in self-conscious stiffness. Epstein fiddled with his camera and tripod, muttering to himself all the while, the cigarette perched permanently in the corner of his mouth, dropping ashes.

Yet while Clara's body was rigid, her mind was in perpetual motion. She had arrived here with an important message to convey. She was going to stay in Germany in the event of war. Yet Thomas Epstein seemed not the least bit curious. How long would it be before he got to the substance of their meeting, rather than merely requiring her to sit still and not fidget?

Epstein continued photographing, issuing terse instructions to turn slightly or raise her shoulder and occasionally darting out from behind the tripod to twirl at the corset's laces or reposition Clara's arm.

"The corset is a miraculous garment, don't you think? There is something so enticing about it. It implies at once revelation and concealment. Freedom and restraint."

Not to Joseph Goebbels, it wouldn't. God only knew what he would make of the photograph if he ever happened to see it. Being a Reich actress, the representative of the Reich Chamber of Culture, and posing for a French magazine dressed only in a corset could probably land her in jail. Only the previous year Goebbels had clamped down on actresses who portrayed themselves as "vamps." Women like that were a poison to the German nation. Goebbels's favorite costume for an actress was an apron.

Clara consoled herself with the thought that the picture was only a ruse. It would probably never appear in *Vogue* at all. After all, what had Leni Riefenstahl said? *The September issue!*

That's ambitious. Who knows what will be happening when September comes?

To divert herself, Clara asked, "You're a Berliner too, aren't you, Herr Epstein?"

"My accent, of course. That part of the identity is impossible to erase. You're right, I was born in Dahlem. A wonderful artistic family. They gave me my first camera at the age of ten—a nine-by-twelve with an ultrarapid anastigmatic lens, since you ask—and I began my career at sixteen working as an assistant to Yva. Have you heard of her?"

"Everyone's heard of Yva."

"She was a superb teacher. She encouraged me to follow my instincts, wherever they led me. Not to be crushed by the narrow morality of the brown plague. Unfortunately, that was almost my undoing."

"How so?"

"I had been working for seven years. I was a confident young man, almost cocky you might say, and I thought no subject was beyond me, no matter what the Nazis might say. I had taken a portrait of a milk-white woman embracing a black man. Very sexy, you know? But it came to the attention of some Nazi, and I received a very unpleasant visit. I would have to leave Germany. Fortunately a doctor friend of mine had a clinic in Paris and agreed to exhibit some of my pictures on his wall, with the result that I received a call from *Vogue*. So I joined the exodus. I hope for the sake of her future Yva will do the same."

He paused and peered around the camera, eyebrow raised. "But it's *your* future, Miss Vine, that concerns us now. Our friends tell me you have a decision to make."

"I've made it."

"In that case . . ."

He put down his camera and motioned Clara to dress.

"Have you finished? Did you get the photographs you want?"

"I did. Let's talk."

The flirtatious jollity had vanished, to be replaced with a deadly seriousness. Suddenly, Clara could see what made British intelligence trust a person like Epstein with its secrets.

"You are familiar with the terms *live* and *dead letter box*?"

She nodded. Live letter boxes were places agents met to pass on messages. Stations, cafés, and tourist traps were popular, because it was easier to meet in them without attracting undue attention. Dead letter boxes, on the other hand, were locations known to both parties where messages could be left.

"We have a number of dead letter boxes in Berlin, but in this instance you will use a live letter box. When you have something to communicate to us, you can take it there. Have you ever learned a book code?"

"Afraid not."

"Give me the name of a book you like."

"Any book?"

"Your favorite novel, perhaps. Anything. All that matters is that you must have a copy in your possession. And we must have one precisely the same."

For some reason Clara's mind went back to her first visit to the von Ribbentrops' home. Before their newfound loathing of the English, both von Ribbentrops had been ardent Anglophiles. They kept a large library of English books, and Frau von Ribbentrop had invited Clara to borrow one. Clara chose a John Buchan novel and somehow had never managed to return it.

"*The Thirty-Nine Steps*. It's a first edition. Published by Blackwood. In fact, it's in my bag right now."

"Good. Listen carefully. When you have a message to convey, find each word you want to use, select the page number, followed by the line, followed by the place that word occurs in the line. That way your message will be condensed into a set of figures, and the figures will operate as a code that can only be decrypted by someone using precisely the same book."

Clara murmured these instructions to herself the way she learned her lines.

"It should delay any attempt at decryption should our message fall into the wrong hands. It is fairly simplistic, but it's all we have time for right now."

"So where is this live letter box?"

"The Ritze."

He laughed at her puzzlement. "The *Berlin* Ritze. It's a bar in Mulackstrasse. In the Scheunenviertel. Do you know it?"

"I've been there once or twice."

"There's a bartender there. His name is Benno Kurtz."

"How will I recognize him?"

"He's in his sixties, has a gray mustache. He was a good-looking fellow in his time, and he still thinks a lot of himself. You'll understand when you see him." Epstein gave a wry smile. "Benno's very useful to us. When you find him, ask for a gin and tonic made in the English way."

"I'm not sure what that is."

"Something diabolical, no doubt, knowing you English and your drinks. But no matter. Benno will understand. In the meantime"—Epstein turned casually and hunted for something in a drawer—"Major Grand asked me to give you this."

It was a silver pistol, less than five inches long, gleaming treacherously in her hand as if it belonged there. The handle was made of smooth burled wood, its silver inlay decorated with elaborate swirls of engraving. It looked as beautiful as an elegant, finely worked piece of jewelry. Simply the feel of it made her shudder. How strange that something so deadly should possess such glamour.

"It's a derringer. We call it a stocking gun."

"It's tiny."

"It needs to be if you're going to conceal it. But the size means it can only be deadly at short range. There's no room for an automatic mechanism—that would only increase its weight—so you carry it loaded with the hammer at half cock. When you want to use it, you move the hammer back to full-cock position and pull the trigger. If you misfire, you can pull the hammer back and try again. But there's only the chance for two shots. You can only make one mistake."

Clara traced her fingers over the whorled wood and the cool swirls of silver engraving, trying to imagine what had gone through the mind of the man who fashioned it.

"That pistol has an illustrious history. It was a derringer that killed Abraham Lincoln."

"Not so illustrious then."

He laughed. "Here's the holster. I suppose you don't want me to show you how to attach it?"

She examined the piece of silky calfskin attached to an elastic garter.

"I think I can work it out. But, Herr Epstein . . . I don't need a gun. I can't imagine that I ever would."

The smile vanished from Epstein's eyes. "Only an amateur is unprepared. Keep it with you at all times."

He watched as she buried it in her bag.

"Our friend in London reminds you that time is pressing. He needs you to contact him within four weeks with whatever information you have obtained."

"Four weeks! That's far too soon."

"On the contrary. Let's hope it's not too late."

Epstein went over and leaned out of the window, watching the people in the café across the street.

"Look at them down there. Do they have any idea what's coming towards them? I hear the Germans are planning to mass their tanks on the Polish border by the beginning of September. But Hitler won't stop there. He will certainly look to the west. France has no chance against a rearmed Germany."

He lit another Gitanes and blew the smoke into the wind. "Have they any idea of the cruelty, the efficiency, of these Nazis? I have. I tried to leave the fear of it behind, but I suspect I haven't left it far enough. Perhaps it will never leave me. Perhaps it lives inside me."

"What will you do?"

"I'll be all right. I have my camera, and besides, I'm off to America very soon. I've had enough of *Vogue*. The editor, Michel de Brunhoff, swears he would not publish the magazine if the Nazis turn up, but most of the *Vogue* staff are frightful snobs. They're only interested in you if you have a title or a perversion. I suspect they'll be perfectly happy when a bunch of highborn Nazis arrive to occupy their city. Just so long as they're immaculately dressed."

"So you really believe that the Nazis will occupy Paris?"

"For sure. My concierge friend tells me that some German officers have already made reservations at the Ritz."

The Ritz. That cocoon of velvet opulence, where women still sat taking tea in Limoges china and choosing between mille-feuilles and éclairs. Where the Duke and Duchess of Windsor kept a suite and Noël Coward regularly dropped in. Clara thought of her brief visit to Coco Chanel's mirrored salon the previous year and wondered if the designer's powder-blue Rolls-Royce was still parked outside.

"Does Chanel still live there?"

He laughed. "She has room 302. Chanel may have liberated women's bodies from corsets, but she can't liberate herself from the damn Nazis. You know about her German boyfriend, of course."

Chanel's association with the Gestapo officer Spatz Dincklage was the talk of Paris.

"But surely . . . if it came to an occupation? A famous Frenchwoman like Chanel?"

"Nothing would change. Chanel says she doesn't believe in anything. She believes only in fashion."

He spun around, all traces of gloom vanished and his lively face transformed. "You're staying the night, I hope?"

"Just one night. I wish it was more."

"Then you must come to a party."

"What kind of party?"

"Does it matter? There are parties every night now. We're making the most of it. It's a reception at the Dingo Bar. There will be all kinds of faces there. Will you come?"

"Why not?"

"In that case, I have something for you."

He went behind the screen and returned again with an armful of shimmering silk, which he shook out to reveal a halterneck evening gown, a fluid drape of deep blue satin with a backless plunge that culminated in a bow and fell from the waist in sleek Grecian pleats. Clara's eyes widened.

"It's by Alix. Madame Grès. She dresses Marlene Dietrich and Greta Garbo. This frock is one of a kind. You won't find anyone else wearing it."

Clara couldn't stop herself from touching it, feeling the slippery flow of the satin between her fingers, marveling at its color, the profound blue of a deep summer sea.

"I'm sorry," she said decisively. "I can't take it."

"That's a shame. It's not my size." He grinned.

"I mean it's too generous."

"Miss Vine. You mistake my motivation. I'm off to New York any day now. Do you truly think I want to weigh myself down with ladies' gowns?"

Bundling the dress into a bag, he handed it to her with a smile and said, "Wear it tonight. I'll meet you there. The party will be fun, but be careful, please. Don't say anything that could compromise you. The Gestapo are already everywhere. They're deciding who to arrest when war comes."

IT WAS STRANGE TO stroll through the streets of Paris again. Everything about the city sharpened Clara's senses, making her surroundings appear in immense clarity, the details finely set like jewels. In St.-Germain, people in cafés were eating ice cream from little silver bowls, and the scent of frying onions wafting out of an upstairs window made her mouth water. Pungent herb fragrances floated from the door of a spice shop, and the intoxicating aroma of baking bread issuing from a boulangerie was so potent she could barely walk past. She passed galleries and shops brimming with bric-a-brac, elegant little bookstores, and a perfumier whose aromatic floral haze drifted seductively into the street.

Crossing the Seine, she reached the First Arrondissement, the heart of French fashion. The little streets around the Place Vendôme and the Rue Cambon were full of milliners and fashion salons and the perfect place for window shopping. On the ground floors were the mirrored cocoons of the haute couturiers, with their gilt fittings and silk drapes, while above them were ateliers of seamstresses patiently stitching the latest creations of Worth and Chanel and Balenciaga. For a moment

Clara dallied in front of a blue Schiaparelli jacket, with gold buttons and a rich scarlet lining, before turning away.

In the end she bought some Gauloises—good tobacco was like gold dust in Berlin, and people had resorted to stretching it with rose petals and grass—and several bars of Menier chocolate. Then she made her way to the Hotel d'Angleterre.

19

THE HOTEL D'ANGLETERRE IN THE RUE JACOB WAS A LONG way from the Ritz, in both geography and décor. The chandeliers in the gloomy hallway wore a slight coat of dust, the stone steps with their twisty wrought-iron banisters smelled of cleaning fluid, and the gilded chairs in the reception area were showing their age. But Clara's room, at the back, overlooking the courtyard, was clean enough, papered in faded toile de Jouy, with a heavy wooden armoire, a basin prettily tiled with flowered designs, and even a bar of soap. She picked it up and sniffed it greedily. It had a fragrance of lemon and cream, so unlike the soap at home, which was mostly a rank combination of animal fat and detergent. After a speculative moment, Clara tucked the little tablet away in her bag.

She traveled light—she always had—ever since her days in repertory theater in London, so there was not much to unpack. Once she had removed her clean underwear from the suitcase and hung her fresh blouse in the armoire, she washed, then pulled on dark stockings and a pair of lizard-skin T-straps with a peep toe, and reached for the Madame Grès evening dress.

It was beautiful enough laid out on the bed, but when she put it on it came alive. It fitted perfectly, and the material, far from being heavy, moved like gossamer. It looked timeless, as a classic dress should, and it possessed a kind of purity that meant it would never date. The glimmering satin clung to her body, flattering her curves at the bodice and flowing in Grecian folds from the waist.

Next she put on Steffi's pearl necklace, feeling its unfamiliar weight heavy against her neck, took out a bottle labeled SOIR DE PARIS, and touched a dab behind each of her ears. As the perfume, with its voluptuous notes of vanilla and violet, rose and mingled with the Paris air, it reminded her of Leo, who had loved it, and suddenly it was as though he was standing right there beside her.

She felt his presence so powerfully that she turned instinctively and stared around her. She felt his smile, his touch, his ironic humor. The shards of gold in his green eyes, the warmth of his arms around her. It was as though the whole of his personality had been distilled into an intense and visceral reality.

Was this Leo? Or had the force of her longing conjured a phantom out of empty air? Her mind went back to the precious weeks they had spent last year. For the first time, she realized it no longer mattered that she had refused his proposal of marriage. She didn't require any ring from him. Her commitment was deep inside. A band of longing that tightened round her heart when she thought of him. Despite everything she had been told, she held on to the belief she would see him again.

The Dingo Bar was at 10 Rue Delambre, a small street leading south from the Carrefour Vavin. The key to its success was the barman, Jimmy Charters, a onetime boxer from Liverpool, whose jovial presence drew a loyal crowd of wealthy American and British expatriates. Steps led down from the side of the bar to a nightclub crammed with people, as though all the tension and energy of the streets was somehow contained in this crowded arena full of smoke and heat. The dance floor was surrounded by tiny tables, and on the dais, a chanteuse was singing Cole Porter's "Night and Day." It was one of Clara's favorites, the rhythm tapped out like a heartbeat, its words coiled into her brain:

> *Whether near to me or far,*
> *It's no matter, darling, where you are,*
> *I think of you, night and day.*

It was almost impossible to move amid the crush of bodies. As her eyes adjusted to the dim light, Clara's gaze snagged on Thomas Epstein at the bar, drinking a Negroni. Beside him, the barman was pouring champagne into a glass containing a slice of peach, a sugar cube, and brandy. He offered the glass to a rangily beautiful woman with a clear brow and a loud laugh.

"Who's that?" Clara asked Epstein.

"Lee Miller. Another American. Paris is crammed with them."

A glance around the bar, at the Brooks Brothers suits and healthy tans, seemed to confirm it.

"Americans are always more optimistic than the rest of us. They won't let any war get in the way of their fun. There's a gossip columnist here, Elsa Maxwell, who has taken to replacing RSVP on her invitations with ICNW. It stands for In Case No War. Amusing, eh?"

"What about the British? Are they still coming to Paris?"

"Sure. They don't dare go to Berlin anymore, but Paris is just a hop across the Channel."

As if on cue, from behind them came a high English voice, strident with self-assurance and too much champagne. Clara turned to see a young woman, her body encased in a metallic silver-and-jet gown as tight as a bicycle inner tube. There was an empty bottle of champagne at her elbow, and she was haranguing an earnest young man, who was braced against the bar, unable to escape. He flinched as she waved her glass in his face.

"Don't tell me there's going to be a war, Jack! What a doom monger you are. Nothing will happen. France lost a million and a half men in the last war, can you imagine they will go through that again? For the French, simply having to drink chicory coffee constitutes a major sacrifice!"

"I recognize that woman," said Clara quietly. "It's Dolly Capel. She's a friend of our family."

The Capels were a wealthy landowning dynasty who had been generous donors to the Anglo-German Fellowship. Their support was heartfelt. They were said to keep a Meissen porcelain statuette of a Nazi storm trooper—a present from von Ribbentrop—on their mantelpiece.

As if sensing she was being watched, Dolly wheeled round. She enveloped Clara in a hot embrace, smelling of sweat and Guerlain's Mitsouko.

"Clara! Darling! Fancy finding you here! Where's Angela?"

"My sister? Certainly not here."

"Aren't you with her? I thought you were with her."

"She's not in Paris, as far as I know."

"Isn't she? Well, tell her to come. I'm having a simply glorious holiday. At least here people refuse to let this war talk cramp their style. There's a shop window near me where all the mannequins have gas masks over their shoulders with little colored bows on. Isn't that just like the French? So elegant. In London it's all Kirby grips and cardigans. The first hint of war and everyone gets out the sackcloth and ashes."

"Are you on holiday here?" asked Clara, mildly incredulous.

"Absolutely, darling. And I'm making the most of it. I was booked onto a slimming course at a spa, but the staff swore war was coming and we would all starve, so I thought why bother to do the Germans' work for them? Besides, everyone's here. D'you know the Mitfords? I saw Nancy just yesterday. She's been down in Perpignan in the south with that husband of hers, helping Spanish refugees. They're in camps there apparently, on the border, and Nancy had to drive a Ford van full of supplies. Can you imagine? I think it's tired her out because when I bumped into her in the elevator of my hotel she was frightfully short with me."

Sharing a lift with Dolly Capel would reduce anyone to silence, Clara thought.

"She said she's writing a new novel. The pursuit of something. I forget. What's Nancy pursuing, do you think?"

Peace, probably. But Dolly did not stop for an answer.

"Anyhow, I'd just been shopping and bought this adorable frock. I thought it was frightfully slimming, but Nancy said it made me look like I had been swallowed by a boa constrictor. What do you think?"

"It's very striking."

"Thank you, sweetie. Oh . . . ." As though in an afterthought, Dolly turned to the man beside her and said, "Have you met Jack? Perhaps I should introduce you two. Clara Vine, this is Jack Kennedy. His father's the American ambassador."

The young man standing before Clara was exceptionally thin, with a square-jawed, pale face and a broad smile that re-

vealed flawless American teeth. A row of dazzling ivory as regular as piano keys, the kind you never saw in European mouths,
so used to filtering black tea and rough tobacco. His expression,
too, had an earnest optimism about it that seemed unique to his
nation. The family of Joe Kennedy, the American ambassador
to London, had cut a swathe through English society, and Angela had frequently relayed how glamorous they were and how
good at tennis.

He looked at Clara gratefully, scenting escape.

"We haven't met," she said, taking his hand, "but you've
met my sister, Angela Mortimer."

His skinny frame belied his strength. His handshake was
strong enough to crack a safe.

"So you're Angela's sister! Are you just over from London
too?"

He pulled over a barstool, took out a pack of Gauloises,
leaned forward, and flipped a lighter. He was a true politician's
son—his manner immediately warm and engaged.

"Berlin actually."

"A tourist?"

"I live there."

He was instantly focused. "As it happens, I'm just back from
Danzig and Warsaw."

"What did you make of the situation there?"

"The Poles were dreading a Nazi attack, but I'm not sure.
And even if it came, would the Poles really fight over Danzig?"

"Everything's politics with Jack," said Dolly, bored already.
"Don't expect any chat, Clara. He's gorgeous, but he doesn't
make small talk." She turned to leave, doodling a finger on
Clara's shoulder. "If you do run into Angela, ask her to look me
up. I'm at the Montalembert."

As Dolly disappeared, Clara turned back to the young man

with the wide smile and quiet intensity. She guessed that as an ambassador's son, Jack Kennedy might be privy to more information than a regular tourist. Softly she said, "Yes. I think the Poles will fight. And they'll lose."

Kennedy sighed, rubbed his back, and ran a hand through his hair. Perhaps the complexities of what he had witnessed in his tour of Europe had taken a physical toll.

"You know, Miss Vine, at one time I genuinely believed that Fascism was right for Germany and Italy. The freeways were so impressive. The societies were orderly. I thought their evils were nothing compared with Communism. Now, I'm not so sure. I'm still trying to understand the fascination that surrounds Hitler. Do you understand it?"

Clara thought of the cheering birthday crowd that she had stood in so very recently, and the Führer shrine in the home of Lottie Franke. "A little."

Something about the expression on Kennedy's face, the earnestness in his eyes, roused in Clara a passionate desire to explain. Here was an American, the son of a very influential figure, who had, until recently, believed that Fascism was the right answer for Europe. Now he was asking her opinion. She needed to do everything in her power to let him know what the Nazi regime was really like. And yet . . . how much could she tell him, without giving herself away? Even here in Paris, even in the depths of a backstreet bar in Montparnasse, the Gestapo were entrenched. She recalled Epstein's warning. *Don't say anything that could compromise you here. The Gestapo are everywhere already. They're deciding who to arrest when war comes.*

She couldn't stop herself. "If you'd seen Hitler's birthday parade, you would know the extent of his ambitions. He's mobilized two million men. He won't hesitate to attack Poland if he thinks he can get away without the Soviet Union, Britain, or France intervening."

"But that's precisely what will stop him, isn't it? The Soviet Union."

"I'm not so sure. We're far too complacent about that. There's speculation about a pact between Germany and Russia."

"Coming from a family like mine that's always jawing about politics, I know that some people will speculate about anything. Doesn't mean it's going to happen."

"It might. And if it did, it would allow Hitler to continue his aggression towards the rest of Europe."

"The French seem very confident about their Maginot Line."

"Only because they underestimate the National Socialists. Don't let yourself do the same, Mr. Kennedy."

Her mind went back to the document she had seen the previous year. A document that gave firsthand evidence that the leader of Germany did not intend to stop at achieving further Lebensraum for his people. That revealed in unambiguous terms Hitler's ambitions to exterminate the entire Jewish race.

"Their plans for the Jews go beyond anything you can imagine."

She felt her voice rising in her effort to persuade him.

"Your father's so influential. Please, go back to London and beg him not to be deceived about the Nazis. Their ambitions are horrifying, and their efficiency is astonishing. It's a savage, monstrous regime, which poses a danger to the whole world."

She picked up a beer mat and scribbled a name on the underside. "There's an American journalist you must speak to. Her name is Mary Harker. She stays at the Adlon in Berlin. She interviewed Goering just the other day. She'll tell you how it is."

At that point both of Kennedy's arms were seized from behind and he was half lifted into the air. His captors were a pair of young women who dragged him from his barstool, laughing and beseeching him to join their table. Apologetically, Kennedy gave Clara a swift wave and disappeared.

"Bright lad." Epstein rematerialized at Clara's side. "His father uses him as an unofficial diplomat. Probably the only diplomatic thing ever found at the Dingo Bar."

Already Clara was cursing herself for having spoken out. "I hope I didn't talk too freely."

Epstein regarded her closely. "I'm sure he was listening, whatever you said."

"He seemed quite relieved to escape."

"He's probably a little wary of German actresses right now. His father's been having an affair for months with Marlene Dietrich at the Grand-Hôtel du Cap down on the Côte d'Azur. In fact, you're lucky you met the son and not the father. Joe's unstoppable. They say he sleeps with the friends of his daughters and the daughters of his friends, and just about every Hollywood starlet he can get his hands on."

Suddenly Clara felt dizzy with the music, the colors, and the press of people. Speaking English, not to mention speaking her mind, had been intoxicating. But ditching her normally cautious persona, even for a few minutes, had left her feeling exposed and disoriented. Bidding good night to Epstein, she made her way up the narrow stairs and went to collect her coat.

The coat-check girl had a sharp face, with kohl-lined eyes and heavily lacquered lips. She was wearing a modest little outfit with white collar and cuffs, but the modesty extended only as far as the briefest of skirts and a pair of fishnet stockings. As she handed over the coat, she gave Clara a conspiratorial wink. "You have an admirer, mademoiselle."

"I shouldn't think so."

After the talk of Joe Kennedy, Clara was in no mood for admirers.

"He was certainly very interested in you."

"Who was?"

The girl gave a slow, crimson smile.

"A gentleman. He left just now. You'll catch him if you hurry. If you want to catch him, that is."

"I'm pretty sure I don't."

"Shame. He looked nice."

Was this how all Parisiennes behaved? thought Clara. As though they were duty bound to establish an assignation? Sex, and the possibility of it, was never far from their thoughts. Perhaps that was the unspoken code of Paris.

The girl leaned over the counter with a surge of sweat and perfume. Her breath smelled of French tobacco and garlic. "I didn't hear him speak, but he was foreign, I think."

A sudden spark of excitement leapt in Clara. A foreign man had been looking at her. Could it possibly be Leo? Was that sense of him in the hotel a premonition? Some kind of subliminal awareness that he was near?

"If he didn't speak, how could you tell he was foreign?"

The girl pursed her lips into a magnificent pout at her expertise being called into question and gave a shrug that expressed her absolute conviction. "I know a Frenchman when I see one, and this man was certainly not French."

It had to be him! Surely this was why Major Grand had set up a meeting in Paris. He wanted to direct her to the place where Leo could be found.

"What did he look like?" Clara's heart was racing

"He was wearing a loden coat. No Frenchman wears a coat like that."

But Leo did.

"There was a look about him," the girl added. "He was interested in you. A woman can tell."

Trembling with excitement, Clara bundled on her jacket and dropped a *pourboire* into the saucer. "Which way did he go?"

"He turned left at the top of the stairs. Heading towards the Boulevard du Montparnasse. It was a few minutes ago. You'll have to hurry if you want to catch him."

As Clara emerged from the narrow stairway, the raw night air hit her face. She looked the length of the street, but there was no familiar figure of Leo waiting on the corner. Even from a distance, she felt sure she would recognize that brush of red-gold hair, that lean, sinewy frame, the hands, as always, plunged deep in his pockets. Decisively, she turned towards the Boulevard du Montparnasse and onto the Boulevard Raspail.

Paris at night, without a map to guide her and only the memory of a single previous visit to orient herself, was a chiaroscuro world. The City of Light was unrecognizable in darkness. Restaurants were beginning to close, and shadows piled on shadows, deepening like layers of indigo gauze. Lamps cast pools of light on the pavements, but between the high-sided buildings, narrow alleyways receded into blackness. Clara had memorized the route back to the Rue Jacob, but how, in this darkened city, amid unfamiliar streets, could she even begin to look for a single man in a loden coat? Should she turn left, or right? Her only thought was to head in the direction of her hotel. If Leo had found her at the bar, perhaps he also knew where she was staying.

In the Latin Quarter, faint traces of jazz leaked out of the basement bars and the bright neon of La Coupole hung in the still night air. She passed the vast shadows of the Luxembourg Gardens, scanning the streets constantly. The ghost of Leo was around every corner. Memory played tricks, so that several times she thought she saw a familiar building only to discover, when she came closer, that she had taken an entirely wrong turn.

At last she saw him. A figure in a loden coat and hat, striding swiftly, a hundred meters away. Too far to hear her if she called. But almost as soon as she had glimpsed him, he was swallowed behind a passing van. She hurried on, her heart bursting with excitement. It was odd to be the pursuer rather than the pursued. She was so accustomed to the idea of surveillance that she had thought herself often into the shadow's mind. How to hang back when approaching the quarry. Never get too close, yet never lose sight of the target. But this chase was different. The figure ahead of her seemed determined to evade her pursuit.

Towards St.-Germain, as the severe geometry of the mellow stone buildings gave way to a labyrinth of cobbled streets, following became trickier. Clara had lied when she told Goebbels that she didn't need spectacles. In truth, it was getting harder to see distant objects at night. In the darkness the faces of passersby loomed dim and indistinct, like figures in a painting by Edvard Munch. A drunk stumbled into a doorway. She turned her ankle on the cobbles—her heels were too high—and wished passionately that she had not chosen to wear the silk dress, now damp and flecked with dirt. Still she plowed on, turning back once or twice to reorient herself until, eventually, she drew to a halt beside the shuttered grille of a shop. It was plain that the man she was following was lost from sight, and what was more, she had no idea where she was. Despondently, she decided to retrace her steps to the nightclub. At the very least there she could find a taxi and return to the hotel in the Rue Jacob.

Just then, out of the corner of her eye, she caught it. The whisk of a coat around a corner. She glanced down a narrow alleyway, no wider than an arm's span, and saw him again, slipping like a blade of shadow until, at the end, the view opened up to the broad span of the Seine and the man before her had vanished.

He must have crossed the river. Clara walked swiftly across the Pont des Arts towards the classical façade of the Louvre and into the Cour Carrée, the magnificent cobbled courtyard in the western wing. Then, at last, she saw him. Leaning against the pillar, his exaggerated shadow lying diagonal along the ground, his coat now slung elegantly like a cloak over his shoulders. As he cupped his hand to light a cigarette, the flame leapt up to his face and she realized that it wasn't Leo at all.

"Fräulein Vine. What a surprise to see you here."

It was the handsome, sardonic face of Conrad Adler.

20

THE SURPRISE WAS ENOUGH TO STUN HER FOR A MOMENT. The breath tore at her lungs from the speed of her long pursuit, and the blood was still pounding in her ears. Shock and disappointment that the man she had pursued was so different from the one she longed to see robbed her of speech. For a second the image of Leo still imprinted itself on her vision, so that she had to shake her head to dismiss it before focusing on the man who genuinely stood in front of her.

Obersturmbannführer Conrad Adler. He was wearing a smart navy suit rather than his uniform, and the rigid perfection she had observed in him before seemed exaggerated in the lamplight, making the curve of his jaw and the ruthlessly carved planes of his face stand out in sharp relief. She slowed as she approached him. "What are you doing here?"

Even to her own ears it sounded curt. Although the urbane smile remained in place, she sensed that she had caught him unawares. Both of them were dissembling.

"I might ask the same of you. When we met you didn't mention that you were going to be in Paris. We could have shared the journey."

She ignored the invitation to explain herself.

"So why are you here?"

"I'm visiting the Louvre."

"It's closed at night."

He took a draw of his cigarette and exhaled a slow jet of smoke into the shadows.

"As a matter of fact, you're wrong. It appears to be open for business."

He pointed to a truck, its back doors open and a ramp leading up. An arc light illuminated a path where large wooden boxes were being wheeled. A team of workmen moved swiftly, silently, stacking a succession of crates. It was not hard to guess their contents. Under cover of darkness, the Louvre was removing its treasured paintings, steadily and methodically.

"Anyway, it's fortuitous that I should run into you just now." Adler's tone was conversational, as though they had bumped into each other on the Ku'damm rather than engaged in a close pursuit through a maze of Paris streets. "Because I've been finding out all about you. Researching you."

"Researching?" she repeated mildly, attempting to suppress her alarm. "I can't imagine why."

"But it was your idea. I was following your advice. You suggested I might be out of touch with popular culture, so I decided to watch all of your films. *Black Roses, The Pilot's Wife, Es leuchten die Sterne.* Now that I've seen everything you've appeared in, I feel I know you so much better."

"You actually watched my films?"

"Every one. Ask me anything. In fact"—he drew closer—"why don't we talk about it over dinner? You're certainly dressed for it." His eyes trawled the length of her blue silk gown. "I know a place that I think you might like."

In one way, there was nothing Clara wanted less than dinner with this Nazi official and his harsh, derisive sense of humor. Yet she hadn't eaten since the café that afternoon, and her senses sharpened treacherously at the thought of what would no doubt be a fine French restaurant. The words of Major Grand rang again in her ears. *Any way we have into the Foreign Office. It's urgent, I don't need to remind you.*

Conversation with a Foreign Office official, a man close to von Ribbentrop, who might be expected to know his mind and the chances of Nazi-Soviet negotiations, could be the opportunity she so desperately needed.

And yet . . . what did Adler want? Was it her company or something more? And if he had been watching her in Dingo Bar, had he overheard her incautious comments to Jack Kennedy?

She summoned a cheerful smile. "Well, I *am* awfully hungry. And it's not too late. Where's this place you know?"

"It's called Lapérouse. It's just across the river. Along the Quai des Grands-Augustins."

SHE HAD FULLY EXPECTED Adler to frequent the Ritz, Maxim's, or Fouquet's, one of the big-statement venues that Nazi officers favored, the kind of place that spelled out *Paris* in neon letters to the wide-eyed foreigner, with a trip afterwards to the Folies-Bergères. Yet Lapérouse was clearly a place for connoisseurs. The walls and ceiling were painted with eighteenth-century pastorals of gods and shepherds. Through a swing door Clara glimpsed a floor-to-ceiling rack of bottles, their dusty bottoms gleaming like blackberries. Ancient gas lamps hung over tables laid with starched napkins and packed with diners.

As if reading her thoughts, Adler leaned closer. "Most Germans who come to Paris make for the obvious destinations, but I like this place. It was created by a man named Lefèvre, who kept wines for Louis the Fourteenth. Flaubert, Zola, Victor Hugo, and George Sand all came here. Escoffier used to run the kitchen. In the back there are private rooms with couches where French aristocrats take their mistresses. A charming idea, don't you think?"

He helped her with her coat, lingering a fraction too long as he let his hand slip down the silk of her dress. When the waiter showed them to a table in a small alcove, she glanced at her reflection in an ancient, mottled mirror and adjusted the clip in her hair, then chided herself for her vanity. Why on earth was she bothering to look her best?

Although Adler spoke flawless French, he inspired the same chilly deference in restaurant staff that was directed at Germans throughout the city. Beneath a surface of unctuous servility, the familiar French superiority remained. The manager brought a bottle with a sepia label, and Adler gestured for him to pour it for Clara. She took a sip, astonished at the mellow warmth that slipped down her throat, redolent of chocolate and spice.

He smiled at her reaction.

"It's a good burgundy. See the way it has legs?" He pointed to the drip of wine, slowly funneling its way down the glass. "A single drop is probably worth more than a month of most people's salaries."

"Please don't spend money on my account."

"Why not? If it gives me pleasure."

She wondered how old Adler was. Mid-forties, she guessed. The steeliness of his Aryan looks and silvered hair marked him out from the more sallow French around him. His gray, metallic eyes reminded her of the surface of a lake, sometimes flat and impersonal, occasionally bottomless. He looked so different from the other Nazis she knew. Unlike Goebbels, with his endless sessions beneath the sunlamp, or Goering, whose efforts on an exercise machine were hopelessly futile, Adler glowed with health and self-assurance.

"That's a beautiful dress you're wearing. I hope the occasion was worth it."

"It was, thank you."

"It's my favorite color. Prussian blue."

"I didn't realize you were an expert on haute couture."

"I'm not. Prussian blue is famous. It was created by a Berlin chemist in 1706, and because we know the date, we can use it to authenticate paintings. There are numerous apparently genuine old masters that have been betrayed by the presence of Prussian blue on the canvas. Painters love it. Picasso could not have managed his Blue Period without it. You can see it in Van Gogh's *Starry Night*. As it happens, I can also see it in your eyes."

She couldn't help a wry smile at such obvious flirtation. Perhaps it was the fact that they were not in Germany, or the delicious aromas of the cooking rising around them, but she found herself relaxing.

"That's a first. No one has ever described my eyes as Prussian blue before."

"With a few flaws."

"You spoiled it."

"Not at all. Everything's more beautiful for having flaws."

The waiter appeared and Adler gestured towards Clara.

"Duck with olives. Or would you like lobster? I haven't had lobster for such a long time. The Führer hates to think of them suffering."

She shook her head. The scale of this hypocrisy seemed too great, just then, to merit comment.

Once he had ordered, he leaned back in his seat and surveyed her, deadpan. "I've been longing to know. What news of *Love Strictly Forbidden?*"

There was a curl of soft sarcasm in his voice. Despite herself, Clara was nettled. "Actually, I'm starting work on a new film with Leni Riefenstahl."

"Now that lady even I have heard of."

"It's about the Ahnenerbe."

His eyes widened at this information. "Himmler's organization?"

"Yes."

"I wouldn't have thought that was a fit subject for entertainment."

"Fräulein Riefenstahl thinks otherwise."

"And what do you think?"

Privately, Clara agreed with Adler. Memories of the rows of skulls and the fusty old books in the Ahnenerbe library came back to her. The preoccupations of the Ahnenerbe didn't seem at all the right subject to ignite the enthusiasm of a nation, let alone to showcase the dubious glories of Nazi Germany. But if anyone could make an epic out of them, it was Leni Riefenstahl. She had, after all, managed to transform the Nuremberg Party rally into two hours of compulsive viewing.

"I'm sure Fräulein Riefenstahl knows what she's doing."

He raised an eyebrow but said nothing further.

The food was astounding. It had been ages since Clara had tasted rich, creamy dishes that didn't have the telltale tang of gasoline about them. Between courses a sorbet was brought to cleanse the palate. She had to remind herself to stick to her task.

"You didn't explain. I mean really explain, what you're doing here," she said.

"Nor did you."

"That's easy. I was being photographed for *Vogue*."

Adler cupped his face in one hand, a cigarette poised between his fingers, and scrutinized her.

"Were you? I hope they've done you justice. It would be hard to capture a face like yours."

She laughed. "Actually, this photographer didn't want to photograph my face at all."

"Shame. Now I've watched your films I see how it responds to light. It changes entirely. I'm almost sorry they invented talking pictures. Your face would have done so well in silent films."

"Are you saying, Herr Adler, that I'd look better if I kept quiet?"

Now he laughed. "That applies to most women, but perhaps not you." He stroked a pensive finger down his wineglass. "I'd like to feel your face beneath my fingers. I would start there and proceed downwards."

The urbanity of his manner was entirely at odds with the audacity of the remark. Despite herself, her pulse quickened.

"Don't mistake me. All I mean is that beauty can't be fully appreciated through the eyes. It takes the other senses too—the sense of touch, taste, smell, to experience another person. And you have a particular glamour about you. A dangerous glamour."

"I don't see why glamour has to be dangerous."

He leaned forward. "Glamour is dangerous because it distracts the eye. It's like a jewel. It sparkles and dazzles and prevents us from seeing what is really there. Even the word itself has associations of enchantment and magic. *Glanz*. It means illusion. It implies radiance or luster, flashiness designed to distract. Ask Doktor Goebbels. He knows all about it. It's not by chance that his newspapers leaven every line of soldiers with pictures of actresses."

"If I did have any glamour, which I dispute, I'm sure you'd see through it."

"I would certainly hope so. I pride myself on seeing through things."

He reached over and touched the pearls at her throat with a fingertip. "These are good quality. I like women wearing pearls."

The unexpected contact caused Clara to flinch.

"A pearl has a character. It starts with a tiny piece of grit, deep in the heart of the oyster. The oyster is troubled by this, yet gradually it learns how to resist. It builds up its armor, layer upon layer, until at last, in the secret darkness, a pearl is produced. An object of total beauty, with a piece of grit at its heart. Perhaps that's what I like, the thought that beneath all that beauty lies a tough, unglamorous little piece of grit."

What was he saying? Clara ducked her head to avoid his eyes and watched the candlelight flickering in the bowl of her wineglass.

He asked, "Do you collect jewelry?"

She laughed. "Hardly."

"I'm surprised. Most women I know are dripping in jewels and furs."

"Then I'm obviously not like most women you know."

"That much is plain." His eyes swept over her with forensic precision, as though monitoring her for any further deviations from the norm.

"I think, perhaps, you remind me of a Vermeer painting. Vermeer loved women in pearls, though of course the pearls he painted weren't real at all. They were made of glass, because the price of pearls was too high."

"They look so convincing."

"That's because Vermeer understood light. As well as any Ufa cameraman. Better, no doubt. He saw how light falls on a face and the fold of a gown. How it sometimes sparkles, and sometimes glimmers or gleams. He was skilled at perspective, too. Some Vermeer canvases have tiny holes in them where he has stuck a pin so that he could attach strings to help the line of perspective."

"You seem to know a lot about him."

He refilled her glass and handed it to her, his fingertips skimming hers deliberately.

"He was my specialty. The subject of my doctorate. He left us only thirty-five paintings, yet such a great legacy. The Führer loves him too, above all others. He believes the tradition of Northern Renaissance realism will be the building block of our new Germanic empire. He has already bought Vermeer's *The Art of Painting* for his museum in Linz, and he paid more for it than he has paid for any painting ever."

Adler paused as the waiter brought a dish of desserts, and he pushed them towards her. It was an *assiette*—a miniature version of every dessert on the menu—wild strawberries sprinkled with white wine, tiny diamonds of marzipan shaped into jewel-like petit fours, and fruit tarts with scalloped edges. Clara picked a truffle and felt her head swim as the unaccustomed rich chocolate swirled in her mouth.

"You were saying . . . what you're really doing in Paris?"

"I'm advising on a collection."

That was no surprise. All Germans were collectors now. From Himmler's grisly skulls to the cigarette cards passionately collected by the children and the jars of coffee hoarded by the housewives. Their collections were like flimsy bulwarks, shored up against the fear of what was to come.

"Paintings?"

"Various things."

His eyes flickered with amusement at the cautious tango of their conversation. The wine was dancing in her veins, and it occurred to Clara that perhaps she had misjudged Conrad Adler. Perhaps he was nothing more than he said—an art lover who found himself co-opted into the Foreign Ministry, a man bored with the daily detail of politics.

He called for the bill and stood while the waiter helped her on with her coat.

But as they walked outside, he gripped her arm. "Walk with me awhile. It's a full moon, and they say that's how Paris is meant to be seen."

He slung his coat over his shoulder, and she felt the warmth of his arm through his jacket. Moonlight slid over the cobblestones and turned the Seine beside them into a flat metallic gleam.

"If war comes, that river will be a guide for bombers," she commented.

"I wouldn't worry. Hitler will never bomb Paris."

"You sound very sure."

"The Führer says that Paris is his favorite city in the world, despite the fact that he's never even seen it."

"How can he know?"

"Because he has studied every architectural monument,

every building, every map and street. He spends his evenings poring over pictures and street plans. You have no idea of Hitler's attention to detail."

Clara did. And she was beginning to understand it enough to know that when Hitler paid attention, others should watch out.

"How do you know all this?" she asked.

"I was present once when he wanted advice on a matter of architectural history."

They walked on for a while in silence. Clara found herself relaxing, even enjoying their meandering path, and she had to force herself to return to Major Grand's request.

"Do you miss the Foreign Ministry? It must be annoying to leave at such a busy time."

"Busy?"

"I mean with the diplomatic moves being made. Danzig and everything." She hesitated, then added, "I've heard talk that von Ribbentrop is making moves towards Russia."

He looked at her sharply. "And where would you hear talk like that, I wonder."

"People at the studios were discussing it."

"And there I was thinking that actresses spent their time talking about makeup and partying. But now I see that between scenes in *Love Strictly Forbidden* the cast is fiercely debating the intricacies of foreign diplomacy."

Clara could not help the flush rising to her face. Without thinking, she said, "Your prejudices about people you have never met astonish me."

He stopped and looked down at her, a slow smile spreading across his face. "I'm glad I astonish you. It wouldn't do to be dull."

His gaze was unflinching, and she was certain she had never been so closely scrutinized by anyone. For a second, she experienced a sharp, reciprocal tug of attraction. The closeness of Adler, the clean, fresh smell of him, undercut with hot, masculine musk, and that smile, as though the two of them shared some private knowledge . . . He was attractive, there was no denying it, and she averted her eyes so that he would not divine it.

He leaned even closer, cupping her head as if to kiss her, but instead he bent and whispered in her ear. "There's something wild about you, Clara Vine. Something secret. Which I intend to uncover."

She jerked away. The arrogance, the sheer presumption of that remark! Evidently Adler thought all his flaws, his vanity and sense of superiority, were in fact strengths.

"I doubt you'll get the chance."

He laughed. "Let's wait and see."

"You'll be waiting a long time."

"I'm a patient man."

They walked for a little longer, until Clara forced herself to return to the matter at hand.

"So we're wrong, are we? About Russia?"

A weariness entered his tone. "As I said, I haven't been into the Foreign Office recently. As a matter of fact, I'm glad to be out of it."

"What did you actually do for von Ribbentrop in London?"

He shrugged. "The usual diplomatic rounds. I met people. Eased the diplomatic channels."

"Did you like Britain?"

"Immensely. I enjoyed London society, but I admired British culture even more. The museums, the concerts, the theater. The National Gallery was two minutes from my office at Carlton House Terrace, and I used to go in my lunch hour and spend an hour looking at the paintings. It was such a pleasure. Unfortunately, art doesn't seem enough for most people. They seem to need drums, flag-waving parades. Films. Cheap sentimentality."

She decided to ignore the slight. "And did you enjoy the work?"

He grunted. "Unfortunately, working closely with our foreign minister was not so civilized. Von Ribbentrop sees conspiracies everywhere. He's convinced Goering and Goebbels are plotting to have him assassinated, or that they're hand in glove with British intelligence. The embassy was bristling with concealed listening devices. We used to amuse ourselves by holding conversations for his benefit. *Do you think von Ribbentrop is as great as Bismarck? No, I think he's greater.* Schoolboy stuff, but a sense of humor was essential in that place."

Clara steeled herself not to look around, to check who might be listening. She was astonished at the freedom with which he was speaking his mind in the open, yet the last thing she wanted was for Adler to stop talking.

"Von Ribbentrop has a lot to answer for," he continued. "The man's a buffoon. He has convinced the Führer that the British are ruled by a decayed and privileged clique who will never allow their country to go to war. His wife's even worse. She may be a stickler for correct behavior, but she hated curtsying to royalty. Her influence on Hitler is strong, and believe me"—he glanced at her thoughtfully—"she utterly detests the British."

"I heard."

"It was being in London that did it. When the Führer came to power, he favored a partnership with the British—he saw the British empire as a template for his own plans for expansion. But they laughed at Frau von Ribbentrop, and now she has a very different agenda. In fact, if she has her way . . ."

He stopped to guide Clara across the road to the ancient

white Pont Neuf, arching over the Seine to the Île de la Cité, with the looming medieval bulk of Notre Dame beyond. The pale stone was punctuated by iron lamps that cast pools of soft light in the darkness, and Adler paused in one of the alcoves, leaning on the balustrade, gazing into the ink-black water below.

Clara asked, "How is it you're so familiar with Frau von Ribbentrop's thoughts?"

"She took rather a shine to me."

"Can't think why."

Adler acknowledged her implication with a dip of his head. "True. I was a single man, away from home, with no ties. Extremely rich and of more than adequate social rank. Annelies is infinitely more intelligent than that husband of hers, and besides, she was bitterly jealous that he was sending carnations to Wallis Simpson at the time. And, of course, we shared a passion."

He laughed at Clara's puzzlement. "Nothing as exciting as you imagine. Annelies studied art history in Munich. She liked to swap professional expertise with me. I think she felt it might lead to something more, but I preferred to keep to the subject of painting. She owns several important pieces herself— Courbet and Manet and even a Madonna by Fra Angelico. She brought it to London with her and rigged it up to a burglar alarm. Unfortunately, the alarm kept going off, causing a complete evacuation of the embassy every time."

Clara laughed. The earlier tensions of her chase through the streets had dissipated. There were far worse situations than to be here in Paris, enclosed in an ivory circle of lamplight, with only the comforting rumble of the city around them, the occasional hoot of traffic, and the laughing murmur of a cluster of men walking beneath them on the banks of the Seine.

"Did you work in the art world professionally? Before going into politics?"

"For years. I lectured first, then did a little dealing, and advised on authenticity. Funnily enough, Art was not my first love. Philosophy was. When I was a student, I thought I might make a future in that, but eventually I chose Art. Philosophy is a stricter mistress. It requires a mind that is as hard as diamond. That's what I admire the Jews for. They cherish the intellect. You should appreciate that, Clara," he added casually, "being Jewish yourself."

His words went through her like a knife. The relaxation she had felt until that moment, the pleasure in his company, evaporated instantly. The warmth of his manner, the conversation about Art, had encouraged her foolishly to relax and recklessly to let down her guard, yet here was a senior Nazi officer casually dismissing her carefully constructed persona. At once the sounds of the city, the murmur of traffic, fell away, and it was just herself and Adler, looking at each other eye to eye.

"That's not true," she protested, quietly.

"Isn't it? Let's see your documents then."

Everyone in Germany was used to showing their ID. In Berlin it happened all the time, and both of Clara's documents had always passed scrutiny. She kept them together, in a small calfskin wallet in her bag. The Deutsches Reich Kennkarte, the compulsory gray identity card complete with photograph and fingerprints, and the red cardboard document with an eagle on the cover containing an Aryan certificate, the *Ariernachweis*, confirming that Fräulein Clara Vine was a member of the German race, possessing birth and baptismal records of her parents and grandparents and a genealogy table going back to 1850. It was the document required for all members of the Reich Chamber of Culture, and it had been procured for her by Leo

Quinn, the Jewish ancestry of her mother and grandmother expertly replaced with Christian blood. For a second she contemplated telling Adler that she had come out without her papers, but no German would risk being without them, even in a foreign country. Even here in Paris.

She handed them to him.

Adler took a brief look. "Impressive."

"What do you mean?" Another chill went through her.

"Obvious forgeries."

"Don't joke."

"You forget, my dear, in my business I have plenty of experience in spotting fakes. And these are fakes. They're quite good ones, I admit, but they have certain elements that betray them instantly to the trained eye. The color of the eagle—that imperial purple—is not quite precise, for example."

Clara was rooted to the spot, despite her urge to flee. What was she to make of his nonchalant dismissal of the documents that had served her so well for the past six years?

"I don't know what you're talking about."

"Don't you?" he asked, sounding bored and lighting a cigarette, her papers in one hand. "I'm surprised. You seem such an intelligent woman."

Clara repressed a shudder. What else did Adler know about her, that she so confidently believed was concealed?

He scrutinized the cards more closely, squinting in the lamplight. "A specialist, you see, is trained to tell the genuine article through the minutest scrape in the paint or the pattern of brushstrokes. I can see a forgery in a patch the size of a thumbnail. My eye is honed to authenticity in the same way a piano tuner's ear can tell if an instrument is tuned. I know all about provenance. So I know yours."

Clara did not trust herself to speak. This man held her entire future, her work as a member of the Reich Chamber of Culture, her credibility with the senior Nazis, her freedom itself, in the palm of his hand.

"You should get a new one made. Tell your man to pay more attention to color. And the bleeding of the ink at the edge of the stamp. Just there. That kind of definition can be hard to replicate with cork stamps."

"Please give them back to me."

He was enjoying himself.

"In a minute. You see, it's interesting to mark how they've made the forgery. This stamp here . . ."

"Give them to me. Now!"

Clara reached to snatch the documents from his hand, but as she did, he lifted them out of her reach and she stumbled and collided with his chest. He put out an arm instinctively to steady her, clasping her to him, and in the process lost hold of the cards. They spiraled into the air, then pirouetted lazily down behind them into the river twenty meters below. Instantly, they both reached over the balustrade and stared as Clara's pale cards flashed a second on the surface before being engulfed in the vast, swirling water of the Seine.

"Forgive me . . ."

At that moment the rumble of a well-tuned engine caused them to turn. A black Mercedes, shiny as a jackboot, pulled up on the bridge alongside them. The man who climbed out of the back was in his forties, balding and thuggish, dressed in a clearly expensive evening suit, and he leaned against the car regarding them, lazily snapping a pair of calfskin gloves. In an instant Adler's deportment changed.

"Herr Adler. I've been looking for you. But as so often, you've found yourself a more appealing diversion."

Adler stiffened. His eyes became flinty and unreadable. His

face was formal again, sculpted into official disinterest. He was transformed into the sober Obersturmbannführer. "I'm afraid I must leave you, Fraülein Vine."

Clara was still too dumbstruck by the loss of her precious documents to make a proper reply. She gazed at him in desperation.

"Please don't let me hurry you, Herr Adler." The man had a lascivious gleam in his eye. "I wouldn't want to interfere with private . . . *affairs*. But if you have finished with this young lady, I would remind you that we do have some pressing matters."

Adler bowed and gave Clara a swift hand kiss, leaving her only with the rough brush of his cheek against her skin and a sense of utter desolation as he turned abruptly and climbed into the car.

HEDWIG LOVED THE LIBRARY AT THE AHNENERBE. It was her secret domain. Other people assumed she enjoyed her workplace because it was in an upmarket part of the city, amid leafy, pine-scented streets where expensive cars stood in the driveways, but it wasn't anything to do with that. When she was in here, outside life dissolved away, and she was alone in an exotic realm, smelling of floor wax and the concentrated must of ancient wisdom. She loved the idea of History, that things had been going on for thousands of years and would continue long after they were all gone. Everyone kept telling her they were living in historic times, by which they meant the Führer's birthday and the expansion of the Reich, but that wasn't the kind of history Hedwig liked. For her, History was about an ancient world, and most of all it was about books. At home they hardly had any books—only a couple of children's fairy stories and Goebbels's autobiography, *From the Kaiserhof to the Reich Chancellery*. And a big picture book called *The*

Growth, Struggle, and Victory of the NSDAP, which came in
the form of a family album, for which her parents had collected
coupons in their cigarette packets and exchanged for real snap-
shots of the Führer. But the books here were different.

The books at the Ahnenerbe were fragile manuscripts with
strange scents of spice and leather. Some were so old their pages
furled up like tobacco leaves and their ink was clotted and dark,
as if they had been written in blood. She imagined them preserved on their shelves like fossils, their wisdom gradually so-
lidifying, compressed between the pages like dirt transforming
into diamonds. Some books contained photographs of natives
looking into the camera with alien, thousand-yard stares. When
Lottie used to come and visit—no one ever minded Lottie
visiting—Hedwig would guide her friend proudly around the
library and Herr Doktor Kraus would join in, explaining how
the Tibetans and Mongolians, with their exotic faces like crin-
kled autumn leaves, were really part of the Aryan tribe. "Why
do they want to be Aryans?" Lottie demanded. "Why couldn't
they stay being themselves?" Secretly, Hedwig agreed. It was
hard to believe that all those flat-faced tribesmen could possibly come from the same Aryan family as she did. Then again, it
was often hard to believe that her own parents came from the
same family as she did.

HER MOTHER HAD STARTED again last night.

"I hope you haven't been seeing that boy."

They were in the kitchen, preparing dinner on the scarred
oak table. The kitchen, with its dark brown papered walls, was
the warmest room in the apartment, courtesy of the coke stove,
from which clouds of steam were uncoiling. The damp, urinous
smell of boiling laundry mingled with a bone broth on the

stove. Kurt was perched in a high chair for Hedwig to feed him, looking around with a bright excitement as if everything they did was a splendid game.

Trussed in an apron, chopping potatoes, Mutti looked hot and fat. Six babies may have earned her a silver Mother's Cross, made of blue enamel with the motto DER DEUTSCHEN MUTTER displayed proudly in a frame on the parlor wall, but six pregnancies had left layers of flesh around her middle like the rings around a tree.

"Jochen's not a boy. He's twenty-one," Hedwig protested, not actually denying their meeting. She offered a spoonful of porridge to Kurt, but he turned his head just before it reached his mouth, so the spoon collided with his cheek and he laughed.

Mutti tossed the potatoes into her stew and gave it a savage poke.

"He looks like a Bolshevik." Then she began decapitating the green fronds from the carrots.

Hedwig knew for a fact that Mutti didn't know what a Bolshevik looked like. Reiner and Wolfgang came in and started wrestling on the floor, tumbling like puppies until their mother smacked them on the backs of their heads. Kurt observed the proceedings with a lordly air.

"How could he possibly be a Bolshevik when he spends all day painting the Führer? You liked that painting he gave you."

Mutti allowed the truth of this with a grudging tilt of her head. She began peeling carrots, and Kurt reached out for the festive ribbons that curled onto the tabletop.

"He wasn't in the HJ though."

"So what? He'll still be called up if there's a war."

"There's something about him I don't trust."

"There's nothing wrong with him!"

Mutti turned and nodded savagely towards Kurt. "So if he's

going to be called up, why throw yourself away, Hedwig? You want to be a widow before the age of twenty-two stuck with some screaming brat in an apartment in the bad end of Pankow?"

Oblivious to the bad press he was getting, Kurt slapped his hands into the bowl, spattering porridge everywhere, then wiped them on his hair. Hedwig often wondered if Kurt owed his existence to the enticing prospect of the silver Mother's Cross, which qualified her mother for all sorts of privileges and better treatment on public transport. No one with a silver Mother's Cross would ever find herself standing on a tram or at the back of the bread queue. Then she chided herself. Mutti loved children, even if it didn't seem like it most of the time, and perhaps Kurt's difficult birth, or his playfulness, accounted for the fact that she never seemed to show him much affection. Secretly Hedwig had vowed to make up for that. As she took a cloth to his chubby face, Kurt chuckled and reached his sticky fingers out to catch her braids.

"You met Vati when you were eighteen."

Mentioning that was a mistake. It was no doubt her own experience that led Frau Holz to warn her daughter against hasty decisions. That was why Hedwig was at the Faith and Beauty school, trying to be something her mother was not.

"Vati's not a Communist."

"Nor is Jochen."

"What is he then?"

"He's an artist."

Mutti started on a turnip, slicing off its sprout with surgical precision and reducing it to dice.

"You'll waste everything, Hedwig. Everything your parents have given you. All your heritage."

Heritage. That word again. The word that seemed to obsess

everyone. The word that she heard every day at the Ahnenerbe. *Your Aryan Heritage.* As though everything in life was about pretending you were a certain kind of person—pure and uncomplicated—when in fact everyone, not just Hedwig, was a glorious mixture of contradictions. Who cared who her grand-parents were, that Jochen's mother was Polish or that Jochen's grandfather had been a farm laborer?

"Did you meet him through Lottie?"

Hedwig glared at her mother. Lottie might have been re-sponsible for many things, but Jochen was not one of them.

"No."

Why couldn't Mutti see Jochen for what he really was? She knew in her heart that her mother's true disappointment was in her own life and her chief hope was that her only daughter would do better for herself. Valiantly, Hedwig tried a rap-prochement. "Irna Wolter's wedding is this Saturday."

Irna Wolter was the Faith and Beauty group's big success story. Not only was she marrying an SS officer but her future husband was being trained for high office in the SS leadership school.

"It's going to be a classy affair," she added, laying out the details like a peace offering, to allay the focus on her own, un-satisfactory romance. "It's at a castle that belongs to the SS."

"That sounds lovely."

The glow in her mother's eyes was almost enough to make up for her previous disappointment. But not quite.

"So where were you then, yesterday evening? If not seeing that boy?"

"I was visiting Frau Franke."

It was true. Udo Franke was still drowning his sorrows at the *kneipe* bar down the street, so Marlene was all alone in the stuffy apartment. Hedwig had forced herself to stay an hour, trying to breathe through her mouth so as not to inhale the stink of fried onions and enduring, repeated, sweaty hugs from Marlene, who clutched Hedwig to her pillowy bosom as though for a few moments she was able to retrieve her own child. Marlene was so different from her elegant daughter. Lottie had been cool as ice cream, but Marlene was blowsy and bulging out of her apron, her face a blotchy mess. She wanted to talk endlessly about the girls' childhood, their first day at school, their holidays in the little cottage by the lake, and Hedwig didn't mind that—she wanted to talk about Lottie, too—but it was hard when there was so much that Frau Franke must not know.

"Poor soul," said Mutti, wiping her hands on her apron and coming over to scoop Hedwig into her arms. "You were good to go."

Her eyes were bright with tears. Her only daughter might be involved with a Bolshevik, but at least she wasn't dead.

Hedwig's visit had not, however, been one of sheer compassion. She might have made a promise to Lottie, but Lottie was dead now and past caring, so after enduring Marlene's odorous hugs, she had asked to visit Lottie's bedroom. *Just to be alone with her.*

The bedroom had been preserved exactly as Lottie left it. Utterly tidy, unlike the rest of the apartment, and decorated with the kinds of quirky personal touches that gave it style. Her collection of antique perfume bottles on the mantelpiece. A gemstone necklace hanging from the mirror. Five peacock feathers they had found on Pfaueninsel in a jar. In some ways, the room was like a shrine to Lottie, with her notebook laid out on the desk at the page of her last completed sketch. Hedwig ran her hand along the bookshelf, rummaged in a stack of fashion magazines, then felt beneath the mattress and behind the headboard. She leafed through Lottie's notebook and investigated the drawers of the desk. But it was useless. She found nothing.

NOW, STANDING IN THE Ahnenerbe library, she came to a decision.

If you remember anything else, just call me.

She didn't need to remember anything because there was not a second when the matter was not running through her mind like some dreadful newsreel devoted to a single subject. Several times she had taken out the page from Clara Vine's leather notebook and looked at the autograph—a tendril of black ink with loops like the petals of a flower—before folding it carefully up again.

She had made Lottie a solemn promise. But Lottie was dead now, so what did it matter? Clara Vine was the only person who had ever shown the slightest interest in her feelings about Lottie's death, so perhaps she deserved to know. Hedwig decided to call her.

22

For a second, as Clara awoke and stretched out luxuriously on Ursula's white linen sheets, the day ahead lay sunlit and full of possibilities. Outside, it was an exquisite morning. Wild birds were calling, pale columns of birch trees shimmered around the languorous expanse of the Griebnitzsee, and clumps of reeds rose like slender green blades from its depths. Then she remembered. She was a Jew, in Nazi Germany, without an ID.

THE TRAIN JOURNEY BACK from the Gare du Nord had been fraught with anxiety. The possibility of being caught without her documents, not to mention the gun in her suitcase, almost paralyzed her with fear, but she had needed to maintain a careful synchronicity of movement between carriages to avoid the scrutiny of the guards. Shortly after the train left Paris, she'd informed the other passengers that she had a bad headache, necessitating several trips to the corridor for "fresh air." It had worked well, until they crossed the border into Germany, when she had been obliged to lock herself in the lavatory as a pair of guards came through. But she had underestimated their thoroughness and emerged only to run right into the second of the guards, who was systematically checking the passengers in the final compartment. He was young, not much more than nineteen she reckoned, with a complexion that didn't need shaving and fair hair cut savagely short. Yet his youth was an advantage, Clara realized at once. He was flustered by their un-intended physical contact, and he flushed.

"Documents," he snapped, automatically, then looked up with a flash of awed recognition in his eyes. Perhaps he had sat through romantic comedies under pressure from a girlfriend, or maybe he had seen Clara's war film, *The Pilot's Wife*, in which she had been married to a lost Luftwaffe pilot, played by the real-life air ace Ernst Udet. Whichever it was, finding him-self face-to-face with an actress from the big screen was over-whelming for the young man. For the first time in her career, Clara was relieved to be recognized.

"My apologies, F-F-Fräulein." He had a stammer. "Is it . . . ?"

"Clara Vine, yes."

"So sorry. Your identity documents, please?"

She smiled sweetly, glad that she had just reapplied her lip-stick in the train's narrow mirror and was wearing Steffi's pearls.

"I'm afraid I've left them in my compartment. And it's all the way back down the corridor."

"I'll need to see them," he insisted, in a starstruck mumble.

She tilted her head, coquettishly. "Do you? Really? Even if I promise I am who I say I am?"

The guard gave a nervous laugh, which turned into a cough. Far ahead in the corridor, his colleague shouted at him to hurry up.

"You could come back with me to my compartment. It's quite a way"—

The young man cast an anxious glance at his companion, who was making impatient gestures in the distance. God forbid the older man should return to help his colleague out. Clara moved fractionally closer. Lowering her voice to a seductive whisper, she suggested, "Perhaps you want to search me instead? Is that what you'd prefer?"

The boy leapt away as if electrified, a puce blush suffusing his entire complexion. "Fräulein, forgive me! Not at all. It's just we have to . . ."

"How about I give you an autograph instead? That should prove my identity. Do you have a pen?"

Hastily the guard reached for his top pocket and brought out a pen and notebook.

"I've seen your movies," he stammered, confirming her suspicions.

"Do you have a favorite?"

"The Pilot's Wife."

"I guessed you'd say that!"

"With Ernst Udet."

Everyone loved Ernst Udet. The fact that Clara had starred alongside him was as good as a golden Party badge in most people's eyes.

"Well, it's lovely to meet you, Herr . . ."

"Herr Wolmann. Ludwig Wolmann."

"To Ludwig . . ."

Clara scrawled her name, hoping that he would not notice the tremble in her hand, gave him her most dazzling smile, and tucked the book back in his top pocket. Then she strolled down the corridor as slowly as her legs could manage and tried to quell the wave of terror that threatened to engulf her.

It had taken hours for the shock of the encounter to wear off, and she had sat staring out of the window, barely able to focus on the countryside as it passed. Rooks sat like musical notes on the power lines, and in between the fields gun emplacements had sprung up on city borders. But there were no more requests to inspect her papers, and as the train entered the Anhalter Bahnhof, she had felt the tension that had been holding her body rigid suddenly ease, her shoulders slumping like a puppet whose strings have been released.

While she may have escaped inspection of her papers, however, Clara's inspection of herself was merciless. As she lay in bed, the questions came at her like gunshots. How could she have been so careless with Conrad Adler in Paris? Why had she relaxed her guard? What impulse had made her try to snatch the documents from his hand, with the result that they ended up in the Seine? The answer, she knew, was that she had allowed Paris to get under her skin. The atmosphere, the food, the alcohol, and the sheer foreign beauty of the place had intoxicated her. And perhaps the jousting conversation and bitter, ironic humor of Conrad Adler, too.

Yet the questions about Adler, the ones she needed to answer, remained. Why was he watching her in the Dingo Bar? And what did he want with her? Above all, how had he known she was not all she seemed?

Climbing out of bed, she pulled a wrap around her, entered the bathroom, looked into the lightbulb-fringed mirror, and switched on the wireless to drown out the fears crowding her head.

The smooth voice of the announcer came on. "And now, it is with great pleasure that we bring you the Hamburg City Orchestra with Franz Schubert's *Winter Journey* song cycle."

The Hamburg City Orchestra. Where her mother had once played as a concert pianist. If life had been different—if the dashing Ronald Vine had not sat in that audience and fallen in love with the young Helene Neumann as she played a Brahms concerto, and she had not followed him back to England—then it might have been her mother on the radio that day. Except, of course, it wouldn't, because, as the daughter of a Jew, Helene would have been banned from any orchestra in the Reich. She would have been excluded from the Reich Chamber of Culture because she could not show an *Ariernachweis*. And now her daughter was facing precisely the same terrifying predicament.

After applying a light coat of Elizabeth Arden foundation, Clara finished her makeup with a dusting of powder, sprinkled a little salt on her toothbrush in lieu of tooth powder, and pondered her options.

Archie Dyson, her contact at the British embassy, had been relocated to Rome, a plum promotion that must have thrilled his ambitious wife, but left Clara without any direct contact with British intelligence in Berlin. Even if she got a message to Major Grand through Benno Kurtz of the Ritze bar, and he was able to organize another ID for her, how long would that take? For a second she considered asking Mary Harker if she had any contacts, but such a request could compromise Mary, too, and that was a risk Clara refused to contemplate.

A memory flickered. Something Steffi Schaeffer had said.

We have a young man who produces passports and identity papers for us. He turns his hand to anything … His work is superb.

She felt a rush of pure relief, like sun streaking across the lake, and her heart lightened. She made a quick cup of coffee, pulled on a jacket, and took up her bag. She needed to find Steffi without delay.

WITHIN AN HOUR SHE was on a bus, heading down the Königsallee. Fortunately, Berlin's big cream buses, like London's scarlet Routemasters, had open platforms at the back, making it easy to get on and off in a hurry. Clara sat, as always, at the back, which meant that she could observe whoever got on from behind. The bus reeked of stale clothes and unwashed bodies. The windows were mottled with condensation. Beside her, at eye level, the standard notice had been fixed: THE FARE DODGER'S PROFIT IS THE BERLINERS' LOSS. Underneath was a line instructing readers to report anyone not paying the twenty-pfennig fare to the authorities.

The bus was held up periodically by workmen installing the new air-raid shelters. A vast honeycomb of tunnels and shelters was being created beneath Berlin, a dark mirror to the new city rising above it. A rabbit warren of tunnels, cellars, and giant concrete vaults with soundproof walls several meters thick as though, if bombing happened, there was the faintest chance people would be able to sleep through it.

CLARA FOUND STEFFI SITTING in the back room of Herr Fromm's shop with pince-nez perched on her nose, almost buried behind a length of field-gray serge.

"Hold on a moment. I'm just finishing the buttonhole," Steffi said in greeting. She unwound a length of thread expertly from the spool and matched it to the material, then continued sewing, her fingers slipping, dipping, tucking, and weaving, marrying needle and cloth in a balletic rhythm that was soothing to watch.

"The Wehrmacht is extremely particular about its buttonholes. They insist they're hand-stitched a certain way, and they always check. The stitches need to be a certain length and made from the correct thread. There are very precise regulations. Herr Fromm says no one knows as much about the details of a Wehrmacht uniform as I do."

"So you're as particular with your Wehrmacht uniforms as you are with your Chanel frocks?" Clara smiled.

Steffi would run up exquisite copies of designer outfits at prices even actresses could afford. Chanel, Worth, Lanvin, Patou; there was nothing she would not turn her hand to. She studied the originals and reproduced them down to the finest details so that it was impossible to tell the difference between Steffi's creations and the real things.

Now she frowned and bit off a length of thread. "More, if possible. I've done so many now, it's become my new specialty."

"Some specialty."

Steffi looked up at Clara over her pince-nez. Her face was alive with suppressed meaning.

"Oh, but it is, Clara," she said softly. "Did you know there are more than thirty SS cuff bands and sleeve diamonds? Could you tell me what color stitching to use for a death's-head collar tab and how that differs from the silver flat wire on the SS Gruppenführer's collar tab? How the diamond insignia on an SS Obersturmbannführer's collar tab should line up relative to the tresse? There may come a day when that kind of knowledge proves very useful."

She returned to her stitching.

"Fortunately for me, most officers have their uniforms tailor-made, so I've had plenty of time to learn."

Clara felt in her bag for the bars of Menier chocolate. "I brought these for Esther. How is she?"

"Not here, I'm afraid."

Catching Clara's alarm, Steffi took off her spectacles and lowered her voice. "We had to move her."

"Where?"

"There's a *Konditorei*—the Konditorei Herschel, do you know it?"

"Of course. It's in Winterfeldtplatz. At the end of my street. I've been there with my godson several times."

It was a typical Berlin place with a finely scrolled ceiling and delicately tiled floor filled with a fluctuating population of women chatting and men looking for a quiet moment of relaxation with a newspaper. Its cakes, displayed proudly beneath a glass counter at the front of the shop, were true works of art. Turks' heads; sweet, flaky pigs' ears; towering piles of profiteroles, *Spritzkuchen,* and *Nusstörtchen*. Soft sponge that melted in the mouth and pastries oozing cream and cherries. Even if the flour was low-grade and the butter was whale blubber, the nation's sweet tooth demanded cakes.

"That explains something."

Clara had noticed that certain visitors would enter the café and linger at the glass case, chatting to Frau Herschel, glancing around at the clientele happily consuming their coffee, and then leaving without buying anything. For a close observer like Clara, it wasn't hard to deduce that Frau Herschel's *Konditorei* had a second, more secretive, line of business.

Steffi stood up and stretched, rubbing the ache in her lower back. "The proprietor there, Frau Herschel, has helped us in the past. She's a good woman, but we can't rely on her for long. We still need to get Esther to England."

Clara glanced behind to check the door was closed and said: "As a matter of fact, I didn't just come to bring the chocolate. There's something I need to ask you. You mentioned you knew someone who could do documents."

A wary glance. "Who is this for?"

"Me."

"You?"

"I need a new *Kennkarte*. And an *Ariernachweis*. Mine have been destroyed and . . . I don't think it would be possible to get new ones."

"Why's that?"

"The genealogy records would be lacking. Do you think your man could help me?"

Clara was used to Steffi's sharp scrutiny. The dispassionate look that came over her face whenever Clara tried on a new dress, arms crossed, lips pursed, eyes raking ruthlessly up and down, taking in all her defects and not sparing honest comment if a line didn't flatter or a style made her hips look too large. But this was one aspect of Clara that Steffi had never seen or suspected. Jewish blood.

Nonetheless, she absorbed it swiftly.

"Go to the zoo. Next Thursday lunchtime. Bring two photographs of yourself."

"Thursday! That's six days away. I have no identity documents at all. What if I'm stopped before then?"

"I'm sorry. It's the soonest our friend can manage. Go precisely at one o'clock and you will see a man there."

"Where? The zoo's a big place. How will I recognize him?"

"He'll recognize you. When he sees you, he will leave immediately and you must follow him. He will lead you a few streets away. When he enters a building, wait, then knock on the door twice. If anyone but him answers, say you were looking for a Herr Vogel."

"Herr Vogel? Is that his name?"

"That's no one. If our friend is alone, and certain that you were not followed, he will let you in."

"Is it safe in daylight? Shouldn't we meet later?"

"Our man believes he is far less conspicuous in daytime. Innocent people don't go scurrying around at night. And, Clara . . ."

There was the clang of the bell, and from behind the velvet curtain came the sound of someone entering the shop followed by the unctuous, indistinct tone of Herr Fromm's voice and the curt male bark of a customer.

Both women stiffened.

"You should leave," said Steffi. "But wait a moment, I have something for you."

She crossed the room and reached into a wardrobe, bringing out a slate blue jacket on a hanger. It was three-quarter length, with gold buttons and a rich scarlet lining. Clara recognized it at once. It was the same jacket she had seen hanging in the window of the Paris store.

"A Schiaparelli jacket!"

"I saw it in *Vogue* and I had to try it."

"But where did you get the materials?"

"That's the thing. You can't get the textiles, but I thought, that shade is awfully familiar, and I realized it was close to Luftwaffe blue. And there was a bolt here that we had to reject on the grounds that it was not precisely the right shade. It wouldn't pass inspection. The Luftwaffe is very strict like that."

"You shouldn't have!"

"Perhaps. But if war comes, clothes are sure to be rationed, and you won't be able to get hold of a thing. Try it on."

Clara pulled the jacket on, sank her hands into the deep pockets, and did a little twirl. Steffi stood back, arms crossed.

"Well, I'll say this for you. You certainly *look* like the real thing."

23

S CHWANECKE'S WINE BAR ON RANKESTRASSE WAS A popular hangout for actresses and theatrical types. In the old days photographers would gather outside, hoping to catch a shot of Marlene Dietrich as she emerged and the actress would favor them with one of her trademark hundred-watt smiles, but Marlene Dietrich was an ocean away now, beaming at Hollywood photographers, and the press had other things than actresses on their minds.

There was a sign on the counter.

DO NOT ASK FOR COFFEE.
WE HATE TO DISAPPOINT.

Clara was nursing a cup of watery tea. She had, as always, paid up front so that she could leave quickly if necessary. From her position at the back of the café, she could see every customer by profile, as well as keep an eye on potential observation points across the street as she leafed through a copy of the *B.Z. am Mittag*.

Already the euphoria of the Führer's birthday had faded and the paper had returned to its customary fail-safe formula of propaganda, threats, and atrocities. In the top right-hand corner was a list of people who had refused to contribute to the Winter Relief fund. Naming and shaming was a way of life in Germany. Anything from homosexual love affairs to hoarding food, reading banned books, or the catchall crime of holding "attitudes negative to National Socialism." Often the only way to escape denunciation was to denounce the accuser. Recently, however, police had begun to buckle under the weight of accusations coming in, with the result that a fresh incentive had been dreamed up. Now you could win a reward for denouncing anyone making false denunciations.

That day's center pages, however, did contain something fresh. A double-page spread devoted to the scale model of the Welthauptstadt, the new world capital that Albert Speer had created for the Führer's recent birthday. It was a marvel of its kind—far more impressive than the models Clara used to buy for Erich from Märklin's toy shop in Charlottenburg. Every house in Speer's city was rendered in bone-colored balsa wood, windows glinting, streets gleaming, the great dome of an enormous Volkshalle like an upturned ostrich egg and the replica cathedral cleansed of its grimy façade. It was a pearl-white paradise, delicate and shimmering as a heavenly city—except this was a city that existed only in Hitler's mind. Clara imagined his fingers dawdling along the façades, poking into doors and windows, marching down Unter den Linden, caressing the curve of the giant dome. Every detail was perfect and exact, except for the fact that there were no people. It was as if the world had been tipped and all the untidy, inconvenient inhabitants had slid off the edge.

Someone has been saying some very unkind things about you.

For days, Magda Goebbels's comment had been sounding at the back of Clara's mind. What had she meant? Was it just the usual whispers that swirled around actresses, who were always the targets of gossip and innuendo? Or was it another scrap of the feverish speculation that obtained in the upper circles of the Nazi Party? Was Clara genuinely being watched? With filming on *Love Strictly Forbidden* ended and work on *Germania* yet to begin, there was a hiatus. So that morning, she decided to find out.

All spies, Leo told her, must learn to read. Not newspapers but voices, body language, faces. She watched as a man entered the café and came to sit beside her and thought of the first rule on Leo's list. *Look out for the unobtrusive.* Beneath the fedora the man had a worn, creased face and a hangdog expression, and this anonymity, as well as the fact that he made no eye contact and gave no subtle acknowledgment of her, instantly aroused her suspicions. That was until his roll and hot tea arrived and he began to wolf it down with feverish haste. She realized instinctively that the man must be a non-Aryan, no longer allowed in cafés or restaurants, and that he was desperate for a pleasure that he might not experience again.

A speech came on the radio, and the owner reached over to turn it up. As the jackal's bark of Joseph Goebbels rang out, all conversation hushed immediately—it was the law—and most people even stopped chewing, as if eating and drinking were disrespectful when the propaganda minister was holding forth. They weren't far wrong. No element of normal life was too trifling to avoid Goebbels's scrutiny, and this issue had, in fact, been covered in a recent pamphlet, "Instructions to the Catering Trade on Restaurant Etiquette in the Case of Political Pronouncements." Clara, like everyone else, lowered her cup and allowed her face to go blank. In more zealous districts, customers would stand and salute the radio, but in this upmarket area silence was thought to suffice. It was not an easy listen. Hitler's shriek was bad enough—it must hurt his throat as much as it hurt the listeners' ears, Clara thought—but there was nothing seductive about Joseph Goebbels. Yet his voice reminded her of something he had said. *You look totally unrecognizable with those spectacles.* By chance the spectacles she wore for her film part were still in her bag. Fishing them out, she waited for the speech to finish, then left the café.

SHE WALKED DOWN THE great stuccoed apartment blocks of the Kurfürstendamm, now decorated with antiaircraft guns pointing into the porcelain-blue sky. Stopping at Harry Lehmann's perfume store, she spent a few minutes testing her favorite scents—tulip, violet, and rose. Sunlight created iridescent reflections on the flasks of perfume, which were ranked along a shelf with a mirror at their back. A leisurely show of sniffing, dabbing, and testing enabled her to keep an eye on the street outside, but no figure shuffled to a stop, or loitered against the green Litfass advertising column to light a cigarette.

After leaving the perfumery, she turned in to Fasanenstrasse and passed the remains of the synagogue, burned to the ground the previous November. When the fire was at its height, the synagogue cantor had appealed to the fire crews who drew up outside to save it, but the firemen explained they had come only to protect the neighboring buildings.

Clara's eyes scanned the road. It was the least likely people you watched for. The elderly gentleman in gray homburg, kid gloves, shiny boots and spats, an umbrella over his arm, proceeding at a leisurely pace along the other side of the road. The woman queuing outside the fishmonger's for a fresh consignment of herring. The newspaper seller, calling out a friendly greeting from his cast-iron kiosk.

There was one man she noticed, with a sallow, forgettable face, proceeding at a steady pace behind her. She stopped where a salesgirl was rattling a Winter Relief box and fumbled for her purse. As she hunted for coins, the girl winked and said, "For guns." Cynicism was everywhere on the streets, like a black-market brandy that passed from one person to another and warmed the secret places of the soul. It was what made Goebbels's joke maker such an inspired idea. Clara deliberately dropped a few coins on the ground, but when she dipped to the pavement to collect them, the sallow man overtook her and vanished from sight.

All the same, she descended into the U-Bahn, past the sign that said Jews and dogs were barred from the escalator, and let the first train leave without her. When the next train arrived, she waited until every other passenger had boarded before slipping on just as the doors closed. Two stops later she got off and caught a train in the opposite direction, then left the U-Bahn and jumped on a big cream bus as it was moving off.

Eventually she came to the Marienkirche. The thirteenth-century church, with its red bricks and its green spire, could not seem more of a contrast to the granite monumentalism of Albert Speer. Although churchgoing was frowned on now, and most places of worship were deserted, a visit to the Marienkirche counted as a cultural outing because of its most famous artifact—the *Totentanz*, the dance of death.

The fresco had been lost for centuries until it was glimpsed under a layer of whitewash and painstakingly brought back into the light. How like life that was, Clara thought. Death hovered out of the corner of the eye until it came suddenly, drastically into view. The theme was a German tradition. Death danced, holding the hands of cardinals and popes, saints, kings, and fools. Looking at the saints, with their eroded features, softened by time and devotion, Clara wondered: Would Hitler's own features one day become dulled and worn away with familiarity, until, like that of a monstrous king, the sight of him no longer had the power to surprise?

Coming out into the bright sunshine, she ran straight into Hugh Lindsey.

"How lovely to see you," he remarked, as though they had bumped into each other on Oxford Street, or at a cocktail party in Mayfair. "I was miles away."

She almost laughed with relief. In his Burberry coat, tie slightly askew, and hat pushed back on his head, Hugh was like a great breath of Englishness. It was just the way she had felt on the bus in the King's Road, surrounded by the staid, understated citizens. Everything about him made her feel safe.

"Were you, Hugh? What were you thinking about?"

"You don't want to know."

"I do."

"All right. I was thinking about England's batting averages. At the last count . . ."

Clara held up a hand and laughed. "You're right. I don't want to know. I know absolutely nothing about cricket, and I'm not sure I'll ever learn."

"As a matter of fact I was heading back to the Adlon. Care to walk with me?"

The two of them progressed companionably through Alexanderplatz, past the circular lawn in one corner of the square.

"You know, in 1918 there was shooting going on in this square. Fighting between the Reds and the Freikorps," remarked Hugh. "But even though crossing this lawn was the shortest distance through the square, and the obvious way to escape the bullets, Berliners still refused to walk on the grass. Isn't that extraordinary? Lenin said he realized at that moment that the revolution was lost. He said you can't hold a revolution in a city where people obey the Keep Off the Grass signs."

In the Schlossplatz, arcs of water spurting from the Neptune Fountain turned into rainbows in the air, and Hugh brought out a packet of cigarettes. He lit one, then almost immediately chucked it into the water.

"I can't smoke these things! I've run out of Benson and Hedges, but these are like a hand grenade going off in your chest."

"Have one of mine."

"A Gauloise? Lucky girl."

"I got them the other day, in Paris."

"Paris? What were you doing there?"

"A fashion shoot for *Vogue* magazine."

"How refreshing to find a British girl who loves fashion. Most women I know don't give a hoot about it. Their favorite shade is porridge, and they like their tweeds hard as a board."

It was a relief to be with Hugh. He had a way of speaking that was midway between joking and serious. Englishmen were often like that. It helped them cope with feelings—that was what Rupert Allingham used to tell her. Irony was the first lesson Englishmen learned at school. Even Hugh's manner, and his way of swiping away his forelock, reminded her of her brother, Kenneth, and his friends, who were just as obsessed with the fortunes of the English cricket team.

He inhaled the Gauloise greedily. "You need these things to take the edge off the appetite. Don't you find yourself getting frightfully hungry nowadays? I have a recurring dream that I'm at Rules, on one of the back banquettes, being served smoked salmon, potted shrimps, Dover sole, and jugged hare. Followed by crumpets and buttered anchovy toast."

He hesitated. "I'm not making you feel sick, am I?"

Being with Hugh, talking about England, had brought on a compelling urge to confide.

"I think I'm being followed."

"Is that all? I shouldn't worry. Mary says we're all being followed. I imagine my chap is having a jolly dull time of it."

"Not like that. That's just the regulation minders from the Propaganda Ministry. I think this is something different."

His smile dropped, and he regarded her more seriously. "Could it possibly be to do with that man we saw the other evening? Herr Adler?"

"I'm not sure . . ."

"I don't mind telling you, there's something about him I didn't like, Clara. I think you should keep away from him."

"I will. I can't imagine I would see Adler again. But it's nothing to do with him."

"Do you know what? I think I can guess what's really bothering you." His eyes were kindly, with an Englishman's repressed emotion. "It's that business about the Faith and Beauty girl. You knew her, didn't you? And you said you were living close to where it happened."

"Yes."

"The whole affair must have been a tremendous shock."

"It was, but . . ."

"They think the man's still around, don't they?"

"Apparently."

"That decides it then. I'm giving you a lift home. My car's

right outside the Adlon. It's a Mercedes Sport Roadster. Burgundy red and a real thoroughbred. Runs like a dream. I'm pathetically proud of it."

"Thank you, I'd like that."

ONCE THEY WERE IN the car, and driving towards the west of the city, he lifted a silver Dunhill hip flask from the side pocket and tipped it towards her.

"Can I tempt you? I always keep a little something, and since I've managed to get hold of a half-decent bottle of Glenmorangie, it would be a shame not to share it."

Clara sipped, grateful for the Scotch's slow, reviving fire.

As they entered the fringes of Griebnitzsee, they passed a couple of police cars. Since the murder, there'd been police cars all around the area. The newspapers claimed there was to be "no expense spared" to catch the killer. It was as if Lottie Franke had come to symbolize everything that was good and pure about German womanhood, and her hideous murder was an outrage that threatened to sully the whole of the Aryan race.

Hugh parked his car outside Ursula's home and peered enviously through the screen of trees. He gave a low whistle of admiration. "Some place."

"It's only temporary."

"Bet it looks right out on the lake."

"It does."

"Want me to come in? See you're all right?"

She knew she should invite him in. Hugh had, after all, gone out of his way to drive her home in his smart new car. The very least she could do was to brew up some of Ursula's stash of coffee. But she knew she would not be good company.

"Really, I'm fine. Another time?"

"Absolutely." He gave a dazzling smile and steered away.

The sight of the police had brought Lottie Franke to the forefront of Clara's thoughts. She had promised the girl's parents that she would see if there was anything she could discover about their daughter's death. That had been weeks ago, and in that time the tearful hysteria of Marlene Franke and the quiet desperation of her husband had tugged constantly at her heart, yet Clara had been far too busy to give it any attention. But the previous day something had happened that renewed her resolve to find out what she could. Hedwig Holz had left a message at the studio, asking if she would mind stopping by the Faith and Beauty home. Clara had been certain there was something Hedwig was not telling her, and no matter how trivial, it could be the information that helped the Frankes in their heartbreak.

She had made a promise to them and she would do her best to keep it. She decided to visit the next day.

24

I T WAS UPSCALE, AS ALL THE VILLAS WERE OUT IN THE affluent suburbs west of Berlin; Schlatchtensee, Niko-lassee, Wannsee, Griebnitzsee. Groups of large, turn-of-the-century villas with gravel drives and high gates that allowed only a glimpse of a world framed by curly wrought iron, of sunlit lawns screened by abundant pines. This was the heartland of Berlin's aristocracy. Back in their heyday, in the 1900s, there would have been carriages in the drives and families photographed on the front steps, plump men in swallowtail coats and ladies in wide hats, flanked by their servants. There would have been dances that went on until dawn, with fairy lights strung in the trees and views across the lakes. All the big house owners were rich industrialists, law-yers, and bankers; patriarchs with wide mustaches who were the very picture of confident prosperity. Many of them were Jewish, and they had plenty of good taste to go with their money. They hung their halls with fine art, and their gardens were filled with statuary. But in 1933 everything changed. Most of the owners were moved out of their villas in as little time as it took to pack a suitcase. Some of the new residents reported finding the coffeepots still warm.

The Faith and Beauty home was an ornately decorated house whose builder had, in common with many around here, regarded the Austrian Tyrol as the apogee of architectural sophistication. Stained-glass windows and Jugendstil decoration were garnished with a pair of antlers affixed above the doorway. Little gables and cross timbers gave it the air of a hunting lodge plucked from the Bavarian countryside and transported intact to the plush district that edged up against the Grunewald's dark heart.

Inside, sun swirled up to the icing-sugar cornices of the high ceiling, filling the room with a wash of pale gold. An early bee butted softly against the window, like a bomber failing to reach its target. An opened window carried the smell of grass on the breeze, and as she waited for Hedwig, Clara glimpsed a group of girls practicing gymnastics on the lawn, shiny braids swaying in unison. From somewhere in the distance came the sound of clear girls' voices singing a marching hymn to the Führer.

> *Unsere Fahne flattert uns voran,*
> *Unsere Fahne ist die neue Zeit.*
> *Und die Fahne führt uns in die Ewigkeit!*
> *Ja, die Fahne ist mehr als der Tod.*

> *Our banner flutters before us,*
> *Our banner represents the new time,*
> *Our banner leads us to eternity!*
> *Yes, our banner means more to us than death.*

Their singing unfurled into the air, rising and falling in un-certain counterpoint, a tapestry of sound that occasionally achieved harmony but then frayed and fell apart. Every now and then it was interrupted by the bark of the singing instruc-tor. "Enough! Again. I remind you, ladies, the Führer requires *perfection*!"

Clara had deliberately arrived a few minutes early to allow for a look around. As she stood in the hall, she felt the glances of passing girls sweep over her, as prickling and hostile as sting-ing nettles, as though her intrusion in their domain was some kind of threat. But a threat to what? To their privacy, their to-getherness, their beliefs? Or was it merely the natural distrust that any stranger inspired after the violent trauma that had recently taken place in their midst?

Hedwig Holz hurried down the stairs, apologizing as she came. She had changed since the last time Clara saw her. The girl's face was taut with misery and her eyes were ringed with fatigue. She stood before Clara, pushing the sleeves of her smock up and then tugging them down again.

"Shall we go in the garden?" Clara suggested.

They navigated the path past the gymnasts towards a bed where a display of tulips stood to attention at the end of the lawn. Even the grass was of a higher quality here, soft and springy, its fragrance floating in the air. The sunlight was stud-ded with pollen, and glinting insects were coasting on the warm spring currents, dipping past the blood-red petals into the tu-lips' molten hearts. A group of girls had spread a rug beneath a tree, and as the two women passed, the crunch of their feet on the gravel turned curious probing eyes on them.

"Thank you for your message, Hedwig. Can I call you Hed-wig?"

"Please." A quick smile lifted the girl's features. "Though I hate my name actually. There's only one person who doesn't call me Hedwig, and he calls me Hedy."

"I've just been in France. There they would call you Edwige."

"Would they? That sounds so much better. *Edwige*. It's beautiful. I'd love to visit France. Lottie promised that if we joined the Faith and Beauty we would end up visiting all sorts of foreign places."

"Was that why she wanted you to join?"

"I suppose. She said she wasn't going to be some old hausfrau, shuffling around in slippers with a load of brats at her ankles. She was going to travel. She wanted to live somewhere glamorous. She had expectations."

Hedwig used this word reverently, as if it conjured all the magic of foreign places, of haute couture and a life where she would never again wear her hair in braids or sit around with a hundred identical girls sharing the greasy contents of an *Eintopf* stew.

They walked past the flower beds and through an arch of budding roses, towards the dapple of sun and blur of shadow at the end of the lawn. Beyond it lay the fringe of forest separating the order of the garden from the wild and unknown. Conrad Adler's comment came into Clara's head. *There's a narrow boundary that separates the savage from the civilized.* Here, in this temple to female purity, that boundary had grown thin and permeable and savagery had seeped in.

"That's where they found her."

At the edge of the trees Clara could see a flutter of tape marking off an area of the ground.

"We're not allowed to go near," Hedwig told her.

Clara wanted more details, and thought about asking Hedwig outright, but she seemed like the kind of girl who would clam up at a direct question. She was the kind who let her twisting hands and involuntary glances do the talking.

"Did Lottie often go into the woods?" Clara asked instead.

Hedwig was kicking at the gravel, scuffing it and turning over the stones.

"She used to say that solitude was essential for the development of character. She was quite a private person." Clara remembered the composed and secretive smile that Lottie gave. "She said that was what was wrong with our country—I'm sorry, Fräulein Vine—that people were never alone. She felt it was impossible to be a creative person if you didn't have solitude."

"But why could she not be alone?"

"You don't know what it's like here, Fräulein Vine. All the women in one group stay together throughout their membership. In that time we're encouraged to share everything—we eat together and learn together and sing together. It's hard to feel different. They don't want you to. But other people don't realize that."

Clara did. She had felt it standing there in the hall. She could feel the emotion in the place pressing up against the walls, all eyes alert, hearts beating as one, the sense that everyone there was part of something bigger than themselves. That was a powerful emotion. It was the emotion that the Third Reich relied on. It was the kind of emotion that could move mountains.

"Most of the people here have known each other since they were little girls anyway. All their parents know each other too. Lottie and I were the only ones who came from the east of Berlin. That's good, I suppose. They always used to point Lottie out to visitors, to prove that there was nothing stopping a girl from an ordinary background being special in the Reich."

Hedwig and Clara stared together into the blurred shadows.

"So, was there a reason that you asked to see me?" Clara nudged.

"I should have told you this before. I think . . ." Hedwig cast an instinctive glance behind her. "I might have a thought about why Lottie was killed."

Her voice had layers of secrecy in it. She was concealing something.

"You said there was a boyfriend, and that she was frightened of him?" Clara prompted.

"That's true. But it's about something that happened, just before she died. It was a Saturday like this, and Lottie came into the house. She had makeup on, but her face was dirty and you could see the tearstains on her cheeks. She laughed a little when she saw me—she always laughed—but I could see something was wrong. She was late to the art class, and I know she had spent the night with him. She was all flustered, which was so unlike her, Lottie was always perfectly turned out. Anyway, after the art class was finished, she came out here and told me a secret. She said she had stolen something."

Hedwig's words seemed to hang in the air, glinting with meaning.

"I had to promise not to tell anyone else about it. She was very aggressive. She frightened me. She made me swear on my life."

"What was it that she stole?"

"I don't know."

"And where is it now?"

"I'm not sure . . ."

"Didn't you ask her?"

"I would have. But that was the last time I saw her. The next thing I knew, they found her body." Hedwig swallowed, reliving the horror of the moment. "I've tried so hard to think what she stole and where it might be. I visited her parents and went into her bedroom, saying I wanted to spend a last moment alone with Lottie, and I searched everywhere, but there was no sign of anything."

As they walked back to the house, the high, clear voices of the girls were finally rising in harmony, coming together in clear, pleasing unison in their hymn to the Führer.

"The only thing she said was, 'It's precious, Hedwig. It's more precious than you can imagine. There are a lot of big people in Germany who would kill for this.'"

Clara had a sudden, spiky sense of dread. Was it possible the murder of Lottie Franke was not, after all, the random act of a lone madman? Could it have roots that went deeper? Roots that stretched and touched and entangled others, and ultimately reached out to the darkest places of the Reich?

"I'M AFRAID I'M NOT TO BE TRUSTED, CLARA."

Conrad Adler was holding the reins of a dappled gray horse, saddled up and ready for a ride. He was dressed in a finely tailored riding jacket, breeches, and high boots, his slick hair shining and a sharp edge of amusement in his eyes. To his side stood a groom with a larger chestnut horse, already snuffing the air impatiently and tossing his head against the reins.

The Reitclub Grunewald, the city's smartest riding stables, enjoyed an idyllic location next to the Grunewaldsee. Though the water and the woodland gave it the feel of deep countryside, the club was near enough to the S-Bahn that one could travel from Ku'damm to stable door in twenty minutes flat. Berliners loved horses, and the city was full of bronzed beasts, sculptures of horses rearing in battle, their manes blowing in the wind. Even the famously unsporty Hitler liked to carry a riding whip in his hand. But there was no substitute for the real thing.

That morning the place was humming with activity, grooms polishing harnesses, cleaning out stables, and loading wheelbarrows with old straw, darting in and out of the tack room and hanging saddles on the doors. And two dozen shining, well-fed horses were clattering their hooves on the cobbles, thumping against the stable doors as they waited for their rides or being rubbed down, their coats steaming in the morning air.

"Why can't I trust you?"

"I told you I wanted you to accompany me to the cinema. But now it comes to it, I can think of nothing worse than wasting an evening with you watching drivel. I would far prefer to take a ride and talk to you. And we're lucky to have countryside like this so close to the heart of the Reich."

Clara had found Adler's postcard when she returned home the previous day. Vermeer's *A Young Woman Seated at a Virginal*. A sweet-faced girl in a blue dress, dreamily poised with her fingers on the keys, the sunlight dazzling off the blue of her silk gown, a lustrous choker of pearls around her neck. She had snatched up the card with apprehension, wondering how Adler had managed to find her address, before turning it over and reading his invitation.

THE REITCLUB GRUNEWALD.
12:00 P.M. TOMORROW?

The invitation had thrown her into an agony of indecision. Since that evening in Paris, Adler had a terrifying hold over her. He knew the truth about her, yet she had no idea what he intended to do with it.

The horse assigned to Clara tossed his head fretfully and she soothed him, rubbing his velvety nose.

"He's gorgeous."

Adler eased a place where the bridle was tight.

"D'you think you can handle him? Perhaps he's too large for you."

"I used to have a horse back in England. Inkerman. This one's about the same size."

"Then this will remind you of happy times."

She took the reins from Adler and swung herself up into the saddle as Adler's groom helped him onto his own horse.

"Thank you, Karl," he said.

They made their way along the bridle path, out of the sunshine and into a tunnel of shadow. Here the density of the darkness was layered with the low gurgle of wood pigeons. Once or twice the flash of a coppery squirrel crossed their path. The horses picked their way expertly along a route they knew by heart, their hooves padding softly on the leaf mold. It was just as Adler had said. The sight of the chestnut-brown horse in front of her and the rising scents of warm horsehair, oiled harness, and burnished leather provoked in Clara a sharp stab of nostalgia. In truth, Adler was right—the horse was larger than she was used to—but he seemed calm, and she loved the sensation of him moving beneath her, the instinctive communication between animal and rider. It had been years since Clara had been on horseback, and then it was down lanes in the Surrey countryside, fringed by hawthorn hedgerows. Here in the Grunewald, the air was fresher, with an edge of pine, and unlike the deciduous English woodland, the densely packed pine trees were dark and impenetrable.

Apart from the occasional command to his horse, or a suggestion of right or left, Adler progressed without speaking, following a route deeper into the wood. From time to time Clara glanced across, but she could tell nothing of his thoughts other than that he was apparently absorbed in his ride. Leaning down to slap his horse's neck, he asked, "What do you think of Flieger? He has the most wonderful pedigree, but I don't care about any of that. I bought him because he is such an intelligent animal. The moment I saw him I had to have him."

There was a tenderness in his voice she had not heard before, and Clara's heart warmed to him in response. She had never met a man who loved horses the way she did. The men she knew liked a hard, competitive gallop, or a morning's hunting on the south downs.

"Karl looks after him wonderfully. I've told him to make the most of it while he can."

"Why's that?"

"He's a Jew," Adler answered, matter-of-factly. "The Führer will soon ban Jews from caring for animals. So Karl won't be able to work at the stables anymore. He's going to be looking around for a new occupation."

After a while they emerged from the forest trail to a clearing where a timbered *Biergarten* stood, complete with a cobbled yard dotted with scarlet geraniums, where drinkers were sitting in the sun. A man in lederhosen and a short Bavarian hat was playing Mozart on the violin, and sparrows hopped and pecked between the tables. A stag's head hung above the door, and glancing into the dim interior, Clara saw a collection of other animals—birds, badgers, and pine martens—in glass cases. Foxes' heads snarled at each other across the room, and a molting hare, inexpertly stuffed, cocked a glassy eye. At the entrance a stuffed bear with the fur rubbed away at the snout stood, paw extended, like a maître d' welcoming new customers.

"This place has been here for centuries. Shall we stop?" Adler asked.

They sat in the dappled shade, and he ordered beer for both of them.

"So. Did the ride bring pleasant memories back?"

"I'd almost forgotten how much I love it," Clara told him. "I haven't ridden for so long. It reminded me of being a child."

"What were you like as a child?"

His question brought her up short. Her childhood seemed a vanished dream of gardens and lessons, of intense, intimate adventures with Angela and Kenneth. Yet also, she realized with hindsight, childhood had been a time of secrets. Of concealed diaries, repressed feelings, and hidden emotion.

"I suppose I was a typical middle child. Self-reliant. Reserved."

"Yes." His keen eyes seemed to penetrate her. "I can see that. Though from my time in London I would say that's something of a national trait. The English are very skilled at concealing their emotions."

She smiled briefly but did not trust herself to reply. Since Adler's discovery of her forged documents, she was determined to guard every detail. She had no idea of his intentions towards her, or what he planned to do with her secret.

"So why were you reserved, Clara? Were your parents unhappy?"

He could not have been more accurate. Towards the end of her mother's life, Clara had found herself going between her parents like a double agent, translating and embroidering their comments for each other, patching up the glaring cracks in their façade of family life. Her father retreated to his study with its bay window overlooking the rose garden and her mother to hours of practice on the grand piano.

"I think they were mismatched. They had a whirlwind

romance—I suppose that's what you'd call it—and once it died down, they discovered they were very different."

"There's nothing worse than a romance that has gone sour. It's why I have always preferred my solitude. What was your first memory?"

"The *Titanic* sinking. I remember my parents sitting at the breakfast table—our breakfast room had high walls with a pattern of dark green leaves like wreaths, and I was counting them. My father was reading the newspaper, and he said, 'All those people dead,' and I tried to allot a wreath in my mind to each dead person. It filled me with fear."

"Why? It wasn't your tragedy."

"The idea that death could come quite suddenly, out of nowhere. And then of course it did. My mother died when I was sixteen. I thought as time went by I would miss her less, but in fact I miss her more."

"What was her name?"

"Helene. Helene Neumann."

Not the name on the gravestone in the churchyard of St. Michael and All Angels, softly eroding as the rain dripped down its runnels. But her mother's absence was chiseled into Clara's life in a way that could not be erased. It had brought home to her the telescoping of time. Time that felt tangible, curdled, the minutes growing thick. Gradually running out.

"I miss my sister too. We were so close at one time, you would never believe. We just grew apart."

"Do you see her much?"

Clara had a sudden, passionate desire to talk about Angela. It had been so long since anyone had asked her questions like this. Yet she refused to let herself relax.

"Not really. And I haven't seen my father for years."

"Would you like to?"

"I suppose."

"Why stay in Germany then?"

"For my work."

"Can your work be so important?"

"I think so."

She took a deep draft of the beer. It was a Berlin *Weiss*, with a shot of fruit syrup—unexpectedly refreshing. Adler's barrage of questions disconcerted her. She shifted beneath his dissecting gaze and said, "Enough of me. What about you. Were you born in Berlin?"

"My family comes from Weimar." He looked away, smoothing a lock of hair from his eyes. "I'm a count, actually. Von Adler. The decoration was bought a few generations back. I'm not proud of it, that's just how things are. I had every blessing I could ask. A perfect heritage, a bloodline, money, and land in the finest city in Germany."

"I've never been to Weimar."

"It's the home of the Reformation, and of Goethe, of course. You should take a trip there. Have you read *Faust*?"

"I don't think I have."

"You must know the story. The man who made a pact with the devil."

"He sold his soul in return for anything he wanted on earth."

"That's the one. Don't go reading anything into that, though."

He took a sip of foamy beer, and the sun caught his glass and made it sparkle.

"I often think of my life back in Weimar. The place was enormous. You can't imagine the upkeep, but as a boy one never thought of those things. We had horses, of course, stables of our own, magnificent gardens. A lake and a chapel. Even an ice palace. My mother was much younger than my father, and neither of them had the slightest idea about how to care for children. I was the only one they had, and they treated me as a type of miniature adult. Or rather . . ."

He paused, as though this was the first time he had ever considered it "Like a dinner guest. They were always utterly courteous. Polite. They talked about politics, or history, or art, as though I would understand, which of course, being intelligent, I did."

Clara looked into Adler's impenetrable eyes and tried to see in him the young boy, polite and awkward. Isolated.

"In the winter we would go hunting. There's a hare there that learns to camouflage itself perfectly against the land. It has a deep gray coat, but in winter it undergoes a molt and turns entirely white. I admire that. The skill of camouflage. You can't be a good hunter unless you've studied camouflage. This little hare turns white so expertly that only the best hunters can see it against the snow."

"Sounds like you miss it."

"I do. I often wish I had made my life back there, managing the estate, living quietly. Keeping out of politics."

"So why?" She tried to keep her voice to a whisper, but her words flared with passion. "Why get involved in all this . . . brutality? If you didn't have to?"

A cool shrug. "It was necessary to join the Party if I was to pursue my work as an art specialist. Once the Reich Chamber of Culture was instated, it was mandatory."

"You didn't have to enter politics."

"I didn't think of it as politics. When von Ribbentrop was made ambassador to England, he invited me along as his aide, and I liked the idea. I've always enjoyed foreign travel. I would have liked it a lot more if it hadn't been for the attentions of his wife. She never let me alone."

"Why?"

"Annelies liked me. Or rather she liked my wealth. My aristocratic heritage. Probably the same reasons you like me."

"Who said I like you?"

He laughed, delightedly. "But of course. You came here this morning solely for the exercise. And you accepted my dinner invitation in Paris out of a desire to discuss international affairs."

She fought the urge to tell him how accurate he was. "Talking of Paris, I was wondering. Who was that man you met?"

Adler's face shuttered instantly, the way it had on the bridge. "It doesn't matter."

"Is it something I shouldn't know?"

He sighed. "His name is Alfred Rosenberg. You've heard of him, I take it?"

Alfred Rosenberg was the mad philosopher-seer of the Nazi Party, one of the earliest members to demonize Jews, Freemasons, and Communists.

"Rosenberg has been put in charge of overseeing the acquisition of art. There are a lot of Jews selling their stuff right now, in an effort to raise money to leave the country, and there's desperate competition for it, from the highest places. It's a joke really. Rosenberg likes art about as much as he likes Jews. To have a man like that in charge of art is quite ridiculous."

"So he's on the lookout for paintings being sold?"

"Not just that." A dry laugh. "He's masterminding the cultural audit of Paris."

"What does that mean?"

"All these questions, Clara Vine. Your curiosity is extraordinary."

"I'm interested."

"Fair enough. I'll tell you. We're bureaucrats, we Nazis, you see. That's where we excel. Some of the best works in the world are in Jewish hands—all the rich families, the Rothschilds, the Wildensteins, the Seligmanns. Rosenberg's scouts are finding where the Jews live and marking down their addresses. Paris is crawling with art experts, art restorers, art packers, catalogers. It's the same all round Europe. Inventories are being made of every important object of artistic and cultural value. Not just paintings but sculptures, furniture, tapestries, bronzes, carpets, antiques, jewels."

"Jewels?"

He's been cheated out of a jewel. He's looking for it high and low, and God help anyone who gets in his way.

Adler shrugged. "Everything. It will all be noted and entered in a ledger just in case the Reich needs to acquire it."

"Just in case."

"As you say. Just in case."

"So the people at the Louvre . . . ?"

"The French are working overtime sending all their museum works to châteaus and other places in the countryside. They think they can hide things, but they'll never outwit Rosenberg. His spies know precisely where the valuable things can be found."

Clara could scarcely believe she was hearing this. She tried valiantly not to look around her, to see if they were being overheard, until she realized that these comfortable burghers, with their great steins of frothing beer and their plates of heaven and earth—clouds of mashed potato with black pudding—probably agreed with Adler. The riches of a foreign country would sit far better in the Reich.

"So France will be relieved of her art if the country is invaded."

Adler gave a casual shrug. "Is it any different from what

Napoleon did? He was the greatest art thief in history. And what about your Elgin Marbles? The glories of the Parthenon carried off to London. Beautiful objects will always be desired by the powerful. They will be well treated, appreciated. Loved even."

"And you're one of Rosenberg's spies."

"God, no!"

"He seemed to want to speak to you pretty urgently that night."

"As I told you, I was advising on a collection . . . On which subject . . ." Adler had recovered his composure and his eyes were mellow again, dancing with amusement as though everything that passed between them was a game. "I mentioned I was in Paris to see beautiful things, and as it happens"—he reached to his side—"I did come across something beautiful."

He brought a minute parcel from his pocket. It was a burgundy leather box, with the name Cartier tooled in gold. Adler flicked the little catch to display its glinting contents sitting snugly on snow-white linen and pushed the box across the table towards her. Two sparkling diamond studs set in bright, buttery gold. A shaft of sun lit the stones like a lick of flames at their core.

"Like fire behind ice. They reminded me of you."

"I can't possibly."

He swept a nonchalant hand. "I was inspired by those pearls you wore the other evening. You seemed a woman who suits fine jewelry."

"I couldn't accept them."

"I hoped you might see them as by way of apology. For inconveniencing you. On the bridge."

Quietly, she said, "I don't think diamonds are the answer to that."

"It's a gift, but if you find it inappropriate, then really, no matter."

"I'm sorry." She slid the box back across the table.

"As you wish." He picked it up and replaced it in his pocket.

She felt a surge of panic. Had her rebuff angered him? Knowing what he did about her, she would be mad to provoke him.

"Shall we go?" He was rising from the table and reaching for his crop. "There's something I'd like to show you."

Adler strode ahead of her out of the *Biergarten*, remounted, and led the way farther into the wood.

It was darker here. The pale sky was lanced with branches, and in the complicated shadows, deer skittered away through the brushwood. They continued as the bridleway narrowed, forcing them to duck beneath low-hanging trees with fists of fungus protruding from their trunks. The air tasted of dusk and decay. Dark-dappled birds flashed out of the boughs in a rustle and shiver of leaves, and in the claustrophobic gloom, all you could sense was the dank aroma of moss and soft, rotten mulch underfoot. Clara could not help thinking of Lottie Franke and how, just a few miles from here, her body had been found.

Suddenly, the trees cleared and an expanse of lake lay ahead. On the far bank it was possible to see a large white villa, modeled in old Tyrolean style with red roofs and formal, well-cultivated gardens. Adler dismounted and tethered his horse to a low branch. Clara followed suit.

"That's my home."

"It's beautiful. And very isolated."

"There's no one there apart from my housekeeper and my dogs."

"Were you ever married?"

"More questions, Clara."

"You're quite happy to question me."

"No, then. Never married."

"Don't you get lonely?"

"I like it that way."

He turned towards her and reached out. "Perhaps you'd like to see it someday."

He leaned to kiss her, but she averted her face so that his lips merely brushed her cheek. Undeterred, he put his hands round her waist, pulled her roughly towards him, and tipped her face up to his.

"Don't tell me some part of you doesn't desire this."

Shock made her laugh, but she could hear the bubble of fear beneath.

"I can't imagine why you would think that."

"Can't you? I thought you were different from the others, Clara. Do you want me to play some complicated game, to court you with flowers and violins?"

"Not at all."

"Good. Because I'm not like that. If something pleases me, if it gives me pleasure to look at, then I say so. If I like it, I make that clear. I may be much older than you, but I sense we're both realists. We're both capable of taking what we want."

"This is not what I want."

He frowned, as if her refusal was some ancient philosophical problem that he was determined to solve.

"There must be someone else then. But he's not in evidence. Let me think. He must be married to another woman. Are you one of those actresses who have to make do with the scraps of a married man's attention? Or delude themselves that he will ever leave his Frau and his *kleinen Kindern*. Who live out their lives waiting for the telephone to ring, losing out on their own hopes of happiness? Take a lesson from Frau Goebbels. You've heard the gossip. A woman is capable of making her own romantic decisions."

"This man isn't married."

"But he's not here, is he?"

"No."

"Nor, I assume, is he married to you?"

Clara passionately did not want to tell him any more. She had been crazy to give away any details about her personal life. Any scrap of information was enough for the Gestapo to work on. Like a single drop of blood to a hungry predator, the smallest detail was enough for them.

He was staring down at her, arms crossed, eyes drilling into hers. "I'm not sure I believe in this phantom lover of yours. I don't believe in ghosts."

"He does exist."

"What's his name then?"

Leo. His name leapt into her mouth, but Clara could not give it breath. Instead she said, "It doesn't matter."

"You don't swallow all that nonsense about there only being one person, one soulmate, do you? It's a delusion, you know."

"Not to me."

"You're far too intelligent to fall for all the nonsense about love. That kind of thing is only fit for the script of *Love Strictly Forbidden.* You know as well as I do that's not for adults. Human emotions are entirely untrustworthy. I, for one, have never been in love and I don't intend to start now."

He was smiling, yet she could see from the bruised eyes and the way his fingers flicked that her refusal had bothered him.

He paused, as if struck by a sudden thought. "Perhaps I

could think of a bargain," he said lightly, taking her hand. "If you become my mistress, no one would need to know that you were Jewish."

Instantly all Clara's fear was turned to a scalding fury. Any attraction he had ever roused in her evaporated. She wrenched her hand away. "If that's what you think I am, why would you want a Jewish mistress?"

He looked at her impatiently. "I told you. I don't care about race. Pedigree. I thought you realized."

"What would that relationship be worth, if you bought it at a price?"

"Everything comes at a price. Even the greatest art is traded in the marketplace like bread or eggs."

"And you think human beings have a price?"

"Don't be a fool, Clara. Of course they do. I'm proposing a bargain. We all make bargains in our lives. I'm not a savage. I don't want to force you into something against your will. That would be beneath my dignity."

"So is making threats against me!"

He lifted a hand to touch her cheek, and she jerked away.

"You can't want a woman under these circumstances. What about love, or affection?"

He shrugged. "Just words."

An image flickered through her mind. Something she had not thought of for years. Her brother Kenneth's collection of butterflies. Ken had been obsessed with butterflies. He'd collected them throughout one summer—red admiral, cabbage white, purple emperor—and once they had expired he stuck them with pins into a frame. As a girl she had shuddered to see those tiny fragments of beauty, designed to be seen only in a transitory flutter, fixed forever, the dust on their scalloped, intricately patterned wings offered up to the most analytic gaze. That was what she meant to the bored, cultured Conrad Adler. A pretty specimen to be studied and admired, but imprisoned by compromise and circumstance.

Ducking out of his arms, she sprang back onto her horse, turned his head sharply, and spurred him to a canter. The horse responded willingly, flying much too fast through the difficult forest terrain until a bird whirring up from the brushwood caused him to startle and he shied forcefully to one side, wrenching her loose from the saddle. There was a blur of brambles and a sharp scratch of thorns before the jolt of collision sent pain splintering down her shoulder and arm and a shower of dank earth in her face.

Instantly Adler was at her side. As he hauled her up with one hand, the sardonic, jousting manner was gone.

"Are you all right?" His eyes were serious and concerned.

"Yes. I think so."

He caught her horse's reins and slung them across a branch, then squatted beside her.

"Rest a minute. Lean against my arm. Take a while to recover."

The shock of the fall had momentarily dazed her. She leaned back against him, grateful for his reassuring solidity, and when he touched a tentative hand to her forehead, she did not resist. A minute passed as the blood returned to her head and her heart slowed. The quiet of the forest surged around them, birds scuffled in the undergrowth and dust and leaf mold spangled the sunlight where it filtered through the high trees.

He had slender hands, the hands of a pianist or an artist or a surgeon. Hardly the hands of a member of Himmler's elite. But then, what were the hands of an Obersturmbannführer supposed to look like? Delicately he traced a lock of her hair away from her brow and with infinite gentleness turned her face towards him. Yet already the old, sardonic smile was back in place.

"You should think about it, Clara. After all, I'm not a ghost. I have the great advantage of being flesh and blood."

CHAPTER

26

SHE HAD LIVED ALL HER LIFE IN BERLIN, YET HEDWIG had never set foot in the Admiralspalast, even though it was everything she loved. With its scrolly Expressionist façade, it was the biggest and brashest of the fantasy palaces that lit up Friedrichstrasse's theater district. The Admiralspalast was a great baroque barn of a place, seating twenty thousand people for a repertoire that included dance acts, operetta, magicians, and every aspect of light entertainment. It was probably the last place on earth that Jochen would want to visit, so it was with a mixture of astonishment and delight that she heard he had tickets for the Saturday evening show.

That night an eager queue wound along the street. Theater attendance was up this season. Everyone was trying to escape the worries of the present—the continual daily niggles of what the next meal might resemble and, when they'd eaten it, how to look presentable enough to go out. And once they'd gotten there, whether the gaudy signs and blinking neon billboards of the theater might be plunged into darkness if war arrived in a few months. Just then, all anyone wanted was to get lost in a few hours of romantic nonsense, and that evening's variety performance perfectly fitted the bill.

Standing beneath the pillared entrance, her face dappled emerald and ruby in the flashing lights, Hedwig shuffled her feet and hoped Jochen would not be much longer. Her legs ached. All day the Faith and Beauty girls had been practicing waltzes for the Goerings' ball. Their own ball dresses—white taffeta and silk with blue sashes—were not yet finished, so they were wearing gym uniforms, which only seemed to make the waltz practice more ridiculous, and the routine was being supervised by Fräulein von Essen, whose hefty form was more at home on an alpine hike than pirouetting around a dance floor.

Waltzes were what the Führer loved best, due to his Austrian heritage, and not only would the Führer actually be present at the ball but there was a chance that one of the Faith and Beauty girls would be asked to dance with him. Even the thought of that made Hedwig rigid with horror. If the Führer's gaze fell on her, would she have the courage to go through with it, or would her legs simply give way beneath her? She consoled herself with the knowledge that Fräulein von Essen would regard the partnering of Hedwig and Hitler with precisely the same horror, and would ensure that if there was any line of female partners for the Führer, Hedwig would be at the back of it.

Especially after that morning's practice. Hedwig had been partnering Hilde, one of the prettiest and most graceful of the Faith and Beauty girls, with a doll's delicate, creamy complexion and a glossy crown of braids. It was bad enough that Hedwig had two left feet, but Hilde's skill made everything worse. A couple of Kripo detectives, part of the investigation team for Lottie's murder, had loitered at the doorway ogling and making ribald remarks, but the sensation of the policemen's eyes on her had made Hedwig trip on Hilde's feet, and even from the other side of the room she could hear the detectives' snorts of laughter.

She gazed anxiously up the street. Friedrichstrasse was thronged with people. The crowds flowed seamlessly between those returning from work and others setting out for an evening's entertainment. Trams screeched, people jostled, and neon dazzled all around them. The show was due to start in less than five minutes, and Jochen was nowhere to be seen.

I was going to ask you something.

Every night since he had said that, she had lain awake, puzzling over it, cherishing it like some delicious secret, wondering what it might be. Or, more precisely, what her decision would be, because she had guessed already what Jochen was going to ask.

He was planning for them to elope. The idea sent a thrill through her, even as she mentally shied away from the daring it would entail. How would she pluck up the courage to leave the home she had known all her life? There would be more work for her mother without help in the kitchen, let alone with all the boys. Yet also there would be one less mouth to feed, and with the apartment so crowded, they could use the extra space. But how could she leave the children? How would darling Kurt, with his sleepy smile and milky breath, cope without her? Kurt was more like her own child than her brother. What would it do to him if she suddenly disappeared?

Despite these dilemmas, Jochen's proposition had come as a welcome distraction. It was the only thing diverting her from endless brooding about Lottie's death.

"Sorry I'm late, Hedy. Work."

He broke into her dreams with a gust of cold air and a rough kiss on the cheek. He had his briefcase in one hand, and with the other he took hers and tugged her through the throng. "We have precisely two minutes."

They edged their way in and settled in a row at the front of the stalls, waiting for the luxurious swags of purple velvet to rise and reveal the stage.

"What have you been doing?" he whispered.

"Practicing for Reichminister Goering's ball."

"Sounds interesting."

He was being polite. That was another change. Jochen had been in a difficult mood lately, and much as Hedwig tended to attribute all problems to her own deficiencies, she knew it was more likely the stress of work. His company had been working overtime making anniversary editions of *Mein Kampf*, and Jochen was an important part of that process, crafting the elaborate medieval-style frontispiece for each edition in Gothic writing, replete with swirls of black ink, oak leaf swags, and fat little cherubs at the margins.

"It's not just dancing. We're having to practice conversation. They say it's important that the Prince of Yugoslavia gets a good impression of Germany."

Most girls could barely lift their thoughts above their families and their favorite movies, but Faith and Beauty girls needed to understand the currents that motivated world affairs.

"Apparently Russia holds a Bolshevik dagger at Germany's throat but Prince Paul can help the Führer restore balance to Europe."

"And how exactly will he manage that?"

"I can't remember."

Hedwig was sketchy on the details because she had lost all ability to concentrate. Every visit to the Faith and Beauty home these days filled her with apprehension. Everything had changed. The place was buzzing with policemen, shouldering their way through the corridors, building a picture of Lottie's last hours. A pair of detectives had even come into the art class and hauled Herr Fritzl out for questioning. Hedwig couldn't help thinking that his face, chalky with fright, had resembled one of the pieces of Degenerate art he was so eager to condemn.

"They read a speech from Reichsführer Himmler. He says he wants us to be *hohe Frauen*, sublime women. We're going to be trained in several languages, as well as debating and chess."

"So I'm taking out a sublime woman, eh? I don't need Heini Himmler to tell me that."

She could feel the undercurrent of laughter in his voice. Not derisive mockery, like the Kripo men, but affectionate amusement.

The lights darkened, and she shuffled down in her seat as the chorus line came on. A variety show always started with the chorus. The orchestra struck up *"Dein ist mein ganzes Herz,"* the song that Richard Tauber had sung to Marlene Dietrich in *The Land of Smiles*. "You Are My Heart's Delight." It could hardly be more perfect. Hedwig reached across to Jochen and felt his warm fingers stroke the back of her hand.

Even though they were dressed in feathers and tulle, the girls performed with as much military discipline as any storm trooper in the Führer's birthday parade. When they goose-stepped, turned, bent, and regarded the audience through their parted legs, Hedwig expected to feel Jochen stiffen with distaste, but instead he was transfixed. It was a revelation to her that he might like dancing. She hoped he never wanted to dance with her.

The girls changed costumes and returned dressed as red Indians with strategically placed feathers preserving what little modesty they possessed. Watching Jochen more closely out of the corner of her eye, Hedwig realized that, despite their shapely legs and high kicks, it was not the dancers who had captured Jochen's attention but the orchestra. And in particular, one member of the orchestra. Following his gaze, she saw a stunningly lovely brunette playing lead violin, her instrument clenched beneath her chin and her bow sawing the air with febrile energy. She must have been in her early twenties, her thick hair bundled up like a ballerina's from a face that acted as a mirror to the passions of the music, by turns grave and joyful. Jochen was studying the girl with intensity; it was as though all the dancers, musicians, the theater audience, and even Hedwig herself did not exist.

A blind surge of jealousy erupted in Hedwig. Early in their relationship she had coaxed out of Jochen the dismaying news that he preferred brunettes to blondes, except in her case. Now, she knew, he was reverting to type.

WHEN THEY EMERGED FROM the theater two hours later, Friedrichstrasse was glinting with a thin sheen of water, the puddles rippling with speckled light. People jostled for cabs and flung up their umbrellas. Others huddled into their fur collars and turned down the brims of their hats. To her surprise Jochen seized her hand and ushered her around the corner into the dank alley to the theater's stage door.

"I just need to see someone for a moment. Don't mind, do you? It's work."

"Work?"

His face was shuttered in the way that brooked no argument. "I'll be out in a moment."

Hedwig stood mutely beneath the misty light of the stage

door, trying to keep out of the rain and to prevent herself being engulfed in a wave of misery and outrage. How could Jochen bring her to the theater if his true interest was some brunette who played the violin? Did he imagine she wouldn't notice? Or did he think she was the kind of doormat who would tolerate some amorous adventure when he was supposed to be on a date with her? She heard her mother's voice again, with its knowing, cynical ring.

There's something about him I don't trust.

Less than two minutes later he was back, briefcase under one arm.

Hedwig walked stiffly, trying to transmit her unhappiness through silence, but Jochen actually preferred walking without conversation, so eventually she said, "What was all that about?"

"All what?"

His mouth was a tight line, and his jaw was set like rock. As they dodged the crowds pouring out of theaters and cinemas into the evening's drizzle, he increased his stride.

"The girl in the orchestra. I saw you watching her. Then you went to meet her, didn't you?"

"You're not jealous, surely." He gave a little humorless laugh.

He was walking fast. Hedwig had to do a little skip to keep up.

"Why did you see her?"

There was an even longer silence, so that she feared he was furious. Part of her longed to abandon the matter entirely, although another part insisted that she discover everything. After a while he said, fiercely, "You don't want to ask these questions. You won't like the answers."

"Just tell me!"

They had proceeded as far as the Gendarmenmarkt, where

the gray stone Concert House was flanked by two matching cathedrals, the French and the German. The plinth where the bust of Schiller, Germany's Shakespeare, had stood for generations was still empty, the sculpture having been removed a few years previously on account of his newfound degenerate status.

Still Jochen stared ahead, saying nothing. Something intense and dangerous loomed between them. Hedwig didn't care anymore about the rain that blurred her spectacles and mingled with her tears. She didn't know where they were heading, or why the man she loved was behaving in this cruel and unfamiliar fashion. Her voice choked in her throat.

"Jochen?"

Eventually he replied. "Are you sure you want to hear?"

She nodded weakly. She didn't trust herself to talk.

"All right. I'll tell you. Her name is Sofie. We meet every Tuesday."

"Do you love her?" she asked, in a small, stricken voice.

"Sofie has nothing to do with you and me."

"I asked if you loved her."

"I admire her, certainly."

"How long have you known her?"

"Some time."

"And where do you meet?"

"Her father has a villa in Dahlem."

It was everything Hedwig feared. Her beloved Jochen was in love with a clever, rich, beautiful woman. A woman whose family lived in Dahlem, which was so far from Moabit in its social status it might as well have been Timbuktu. No social graces Hedwig could ever learn at the Faith and Beauty school—no amount of ballroom dancing, or flower arranging or chess—could match the social status of a girl named Sofie who lived in a villa in Dahlem.

"And does she take you there?"

"Yes. For dinner. Her family know all kinds of artists, politicians, and priests. Important people. They talk about literature—Brecht, Schiller. Other people I've not heard of."

A conflict of emotions warred in his face. "A lot of them are aristocrats, bohemians. Not my sort. But their hearts are in the right place. And the main thing is . . ."

He stopped, turned to her, and moved his face very close. "They all hate the Nazis."

His words floated quietly on the night air, like a hiss.

"Some of them hate National Socialist politics, but others just consider the Nazis ill-bred. Rich people think like that, you know, but being smart works in these people's favor. No one believes a family like Sofie's could have money and still belong to the KPD."

The KPD. The banned German Communist Party. Hedwig's heart sank like lead. Mutti had been right.

"Are you a Communist?" she whispered.

It was not a word she ever used. It felt as bitter in her mouth as a lump of shrapnel. Communists were never mentioned at home, except as a curse. Bolsheviks were Germany's worst fate, it said on the radio. The Jew devil.

"No. I'm a good German. But we do have Communists. And Conservatives, Social Democrats, Catholics, Lutherans, Jews. Doctors, officers, academics. One of them is a playwright who works in the Propaganda Ministry. There's a guy named Helmut who's the official dentist to the Ufa studios. He does all the stars' teeth. He gets us typewriter ribbons and ink for our newspaper."

"Why would he do that?"

"Same reason as any of us."

Hedwig was floundering. Grappling with her coordinates

the way she tried to work her compass in the forest. Trying to reset everything she had believed with this new information.

"They're not all smart types. There's a waiter at the Kaiserhof who reads all the foreign newspapers for us, everything—French, English, Danish, Dutch, Russian—so we get an idea of opinion beyond Goebbels's lies."

Her whole world was shifting on its axis. Everything she knew had turned cruelly upside down, as though an enormous wrecking ball had taken aim and was reducing her life to rubble.

"But why? What do you want to do, Jochen?"

"I wanted some way of resisting what was going on, and it wasn't going to be killing Hitler. I was never going to be able to manage something like that."

Killing Hitler? Hedwig's knees almost buckled beneath her, and she craned her head round in the quick, instinctive glance that was known as *der deutsche Blick.* The German look.

"How did you . . . how did you meet these people then?"

"Through a friend. He thought I would be useful because I'm a graphic artist, but he still screened me first, to check my leanings. He gave me a cigarette packet, and when I opened it I found a message asking me to make a flyer denouncing the occupation of the Sudetenland."

The Sudetenland. Then this must have been last year, Hedwig thought, desperately making mental calculations and trying her hardest to recall the current affairs that generally passed her by. "And did you? Do what he asked?"

"I did. I designed the pamphlet and someone else in the group printed them. Then another member, who is a Persil washing powder distributor, packed them in Persil boxes and covered them with detergent."

"What happened to them after that?"

"I don't know. The idea is that we don't know too much. So we can't reveal anything if we're caught."

The frankness with which he alluded to this terrifying possibility astonished her. Yet although alarm and horror were churning through her, there remained a residual sense of jealousy.

"And that girl at the theater? Sofie. What about her?"

"Sofie's a professional musician. She's extremely talented. She studied under a student of Mendelssohn's."

"Oh." This information did nothing to alleviate Hedwig's jealousy.

"At the moment she performs in the orchestra at the Admiralspalast every night, then after the show she takes our pamphlets out in her sheet music portfolio. No one ever suspects sheet music."

It was dark now that all the streetlamps had been dimmed to save money, and they had reached the point in Französischerstrasse where an arch supported by giant caryatids flung a pool of deeper shadow. Jochen stopped and drew her towards him.

"What we do is important, Hedy. One of our members has a brother in the army who supplies him with details of Jews who are scheduled for arrest, so we can warn them in time."

"Are these friends of yours Jews?" The word almost choked in her throat. Whenever Hedwig thought of Jews, she imagined the leering figures you saw on the front of *Der Stürmer*, like crooked shadows with their long black coats and yellow eyes.

"Some are. Some have been in camps, but we have to be extra careful with those because sometimes people are only released from camps on the condition that they find their former friends and lead the Gestapo to them. They call the people we help U-boats. Submarines. You must have heard of them."

Now that he was speaking, it was as though he couldn't stop. But Hedwig wanted to stick her fingers in her ears. The delightful evening had taken a terrible wrong direction. She wanted everything she had heard to disappear.

"Why are you telling me all this?"

"You asked me."

"I had no choice."

"And now, my darling, you do have a choice." His eyes burned into her like acid, so fierce she almost flinched. "You can denounce me, or you can help me. If you denounce me then I will be hauled off to be shot and maybe you too. Perhaps even your dear Mutti and Vati will come under suspicion."

Her tears began to stream, and Jochen took her in his arms.

"Don't cry. I can't bear that. I never intended to involve you. I had every intention of keeping you out of this. But you're going to need to choose. Just like we all have."

"I could never denounce you." She wept.

He kissed her. A tender, lingering kiss.

"I knew that, Hedy. We'll meet next Thursday, shall we, like always? At the usual place?"

27

A LONE HAWK HUNG IN THE SKY. CLARA WATCHED as it hovered, then dropped like a stone and slammed through the mist into the leather glove of the falconer below. Beyond it lay the horizon of the Westphalian plain bisected by the river Alme, damp and gray as a photograph slightly out of focus. Stone houses and dairy farms hunkered beneath a low drizzle that was rolling across the sky. On a hill above them all stood a hulking castle, as brooding, implacable, and ominous as anything from the Ufa studio's own horror movies.

Wewelsburg. The spiritual heart of the SS.

Himmler had discovered the derelict castle of Wewelsburg in 1933, close to the site where an ancient Germanic chief had defeated the Roman army of occupation. With a provenance like that, it couldn't appeal more to the Gestapo chief. Without hesitation he bought the lease and set about establishing a Reichsführerschule to train the elite ranks of his SS. Yet although Wewelsburg combined German prehistory and mystical significance in one implacable, blank-walled monument, the castle was far more than an officers' leadership school. It was to be Himmler's Camelot, the place where he would raise up a new order of Teutonic knights, a blood brotherhood of the racially pure.

For that reason, much to Clara's relief, no women would ever be permitted to stay the night.

They had traveled in Leni Riefenstahl's Mercedes convertible, past undulating fields plowed in corduroy rows with a film of green hovering over the turned earth and isolated half-timbered houses with casement windows and geraniums at the sills. South of Paderborn they passed a gang of ragged workers, who, judging from their stubbled faces, starved frames, and striped uniforms, must have been drafted in from a concentration camp. Some were digging trenches in the earth, and others were hacking at piles of rocks, cleaving them into smaller pieces. None turned to sneak a glance at the sleek maroon car, with its gleaming brunette at the wheel. Were they afraid, or were they simply used to processions of shiny vehicles whose passengers seemed to look out at them and yet look through them at the same time?

"What are those workers doing?"

"They're building an SS village," said Leni. "Himmler has bought up a lot of the land around here to provide homes for the wives and children of SS men. Those workers come from a camp."

"I didn't know there was a camp near here."

"There wasn't. Himmler built one, especially for the building work. The only problem is, they keep unearthing old pottery beakers and cup handles, and every time they find a fragment Himmler orders a halt on account of it being part of our ancient Germanic heritage." She gave a gravelly laugh. "It will take them years at this rate."

She turned off the road at a small timbered lodge with a carved wooden exterior and a sharp triangular gable called Ottens Hof.

"Let's stop. I don't think I can manage this without a drink."

But one glimpse inside Ottens Hof, and it almost required a stiff schnapps to get over the threshold. The tavern might have been plucked straight out of the sixteenth century, complete with hunting gear, harnesses, and medieval torture implements fixed to the walls. Axes, spears, and animal traps were suspended beneath a high timbered ceiling, from where candles in elaborate wrought-iron holders only dimly pierced the gloom. Sturdy oak tables, set for dinner, stretched the length of the hall, yet at this time of the day, the place was almost deserted, with only a single barmaid mopping the floor. She straightened up as they entered and resumed her place behind the bar.

"This is Himmler's private dining club," Leni told Clara. "All the senior SS men come here to relax after summits at the castle. Look at the benches."

Peering down, Clara saw strange symbols carved into the wood. Looking closer, she saw that the intricate letters were runes, worked all around the seats and along the legs of the tables. Identical markings appeared on a frieze at the top of the wall, and carved into jutting timbers between the alcoves. Although the wording was indecipherable, the message from the emblazoned SS symbol was all too clear. No place was too obscure to escape the influence of Himmler's enthusiasms.

Leni returned with two glasses of beer, pounced on Clara's French cigarettes, and leaned back against the death's-head skull carved on the pew.

"What a journey! Why does Himmler have to choose Westphalia of all places? Wewelsburg may be the center of the world, but it would help if it was a little more . . . *central*."

"In what way is *this* the center of the world?"

"Oh, it has ancestral energy, apparently. Himmler says it will be the center of the rebirth of the Germanic nation. You know how he is about superstitions. Some astrologer told him an old Westphalian legend says an army from the East will on this very spot be beaten by an army of the West. He adores that kind of thing. You've met him, haven't you?"

"Once. Last year."

At five foot eleven, nearsighted, flat-chested, and with surprisingly delicate fingers, Himmler represented the precise opposite of his Nordic ideal. To look at, he might have been an accountant or a lawyer or a clerk, anything rather than the head of a fifty-thousand-strong terror organization. Though he probably knew more about the atrocities being visited on people in the Reich than even Hitler himself, Himmler was an ardent family man, devoted to his daughter, Puppi, and his scrub-faced wife, Marga—a dour woman seven years his senior who obstinately refused the siren call of Berlin and all its glamour, preferring to stay home on their rural farm. Though Clara hoped passionately that Himmler would not remember her, it was said he never forgot a face. He himself barely needed the rotating file index of fifty thousand names that had been installed at Gestapo headquarters in Berlin.

"The way he's behaving you'd think the castle was under siege already. His office has been impossible about the filming. I told him I needed a crew of a hundred and he said no more than thirty. What's more, we won't be able to film inside anywhere except a single room where a wedding consecration is taking place. Himmler loves weddings."

A sardonic grimace.

"He's going to allow outstanding SS men to marry two wives. He calls it a reward for heroes. Apparently there was some custom in the early Germanic tribes, where men of elevated social position were exempted from monogamy."

"It's not that ancient. I know plenty of men who think the same," Clara remarked.

Leni grinned. "I've met those men too. So we'll start with you, up on the battlements, the wind in your hair, symbolizing the legion of German ancestors who have repelled the enemy from the East. A tight shot on your face, then we pan out to reveal the entire landscape of Germania spread before you. You saw the costume?"

Leni's costume idea for the Spirit of Germania translated to a modified dirndl, a deep green dress with a laced bodice and square neckline, but fortunately without the frill of lace or the spill of cleavage that the true Bavarian costume would demand.

Clara nodded.

"Lovely," said Leni, stubbing out her cigarette and rising to her feet. "Shall we get on with it then?"

UP CLOSE, WEWELSBURG LOOKED more like a prison than a castle. Its ranks of narrow windows gazed blankly out across the valley, and its turrets were stark silhouettes against the lowering sky. It had a striking triangular design, with massive stone walls oriented in a north-south axis and twin domes garnished with the fluttering black and white lightning-flash flag of the SS.

As they crossed the drawbridge, Clara realized she was trembling. She kept her hands folded in her lap and her gaze fixed, but her stomach was as clenched as a fist, and she could barely swallow. This was the moment of truth. It was inconceivable that she would be allowed to enter Himmler's most precious domain without an identity check. Her plan was to say that her identity document was "lost"—a situation that counted as a misdemeanor in itself.

At the gatehouse there was the sound of dogs barking and a harsh command of silence as two soldiers with helmets and rifles, wearing waterproof capes against the first spattering of rain, approached the car.

"Don't look so gloomy, Clara! It's a tremendous privilege to be here. Himmler is obsessed with secrecy. A big part of him doesn't want anyone to know that this place even exists—but he recognized that our film would be incomplete without it." Her face lit up with a slow, crimson smile. "Well, hello, young man."

The guard's chiseled features and hard eyes broke into a grin of surprise when he recognized her. His expression said it all. The Führer's film director! So that was who all the cameramen and lighting operators and production crew were waiting for.

"Fräulein Riefenstahl. Welcome to Wewelsburg!"

"I'm honored." Her voice was huskily seductive. "I hear you don't often get female visitors."

"Only for wedding consecrations. Today is a special day."

"Then we shall have to make the most of it."

The guard peered closer into the car, towards the passenger seat. Beside him, his dog was broad and muscular, with dense black fur like the canine equivalent of an SS dress uniform. Clara focused on its flat, uncomprehending eyes.

"And your companion?"

Of course the soldier would want to know who she was. Wewelsburg of all places in the Reich would employ dedicated guards with the most scrupulous attention to duty. How could she possibly have hoped that her lack of identity documents would be overlooked?

"My star, you mean?"

"Of course!" He registered half recognition, but not enough to deter him from his duty. "I wonder if . . ."

At that moment there was an almighty crash, the sound of splintering glass, and a volley of shouts arose from across the courtyard. Furious voices called for help. The guard glanced behind him in confusion and waved them through. Leni drove the Mercedes into the courtyard and the gate clanged behind them. Clara closed her eyes for a second, weak with relief.

Inside, the forbidding, medieval-style exterior gave way to a triangular courtyard, which contained an unexpected bustle of activity. The crash they had heard was a steel ladder falling from a truck containing lighting equipment being unloaded down a ramp into one door of the castle. It appeared the ladder had only narrowly avoided decapitating a camera operator. Other production staff scurried around, trailing wires and carrying megaphones. Standing arc lights, lenses, and a number of aluminum boxes were being ferried into the building. Against an opposite wall, the drivers leaned, killing time with a cigarette break. A couple of SS officers in leather coats skirted the truck with unmistakable irritation at the intrusion of the film world on their private domain, but Clara was glad for these tokens of normality. Wewelsburg castle was under siege that day, and she didn't give a damn if the movie world laid waste to it.

Leni parked, adjusted the rearview mirror, touched up her mascara, and gave herself a quick dab of powder. "If this is the only time women are allowed to set foot in the castle," she told Clara, "a girl has to be her best. I'm not looking bedraggled with the cream of SS honor guards standing around me."

Yet again Clara was astonished at Leni's coquettishness. She was the greatest female film director in the world, she counted numerous distinguished figures among her lovers, and she had the ear of Hitler himself—yet still she cared about her complexion in front of a bunch of SS leadership trainees.

Leni stowed the makeup away and grabbed her bag. "The crew have had plenty of time to set up. I need you in position right away. You're up on the north tower. We open with a leaflet fluttering along the battlements. Its headline says GERMANIA. The camera will pan up to your face. You look towards the east. You are solemn, but transfixed. Your face glows with optimism for the future and faith in the Führer. And remember, you represent your country."

It was chilly on the battlements, and needles of rain were carried on a sharp wind. Clara spent an hour gazing into the distance with Leni and a cameraman lying on a trolleyboard at her feet. Though she tried her best to summon a look of optimism for the future, the sight of an SS guard mustering in the courtyard beneath with parade ground precision made it quite a challenge.

After five takes Leni was satisfied and the crew began to dismantle their equipment.

"It's the wedding next." A sardonic grimace. "Irna Wolter's special day. We don't need you in this scene, Clara, but you're welcome to watch."

Clara followed her down the stone steps.

For a wedding, it would be hard to imagine a venue more funereal. With spartan brick floor, exposed timbers, and windowless walls, the consecration hall was an oppressively gloomy space barely penetrated by the greasy light of a gas lamp hanging from a wrought-iron fitting. At the front, a wooden table was furnished with a pair of *völkische* candlesticks and oak leaves, and as a gesture to the essentially joyful nature of the occasion, a picture of their host, Himmler. The groom was in

place already, fiddling with his belt and cap and trying valiantly to ignore the bevy of lighting men, sound men, and camera operatives around him, not to mention the figure of Leni
Riefenstahl, crouching at knee level. All around, black uni-
formed officers engaged in the same awkward chat that occupies any wedding party, as they awaited the entrance of the
bride.

Irna Wolter looked younger than her twenty years. She had
procured a long white dress and had been furnished with an
armful of creamy roses, whose weak fragrance wavered faintly
across the chilly space. Her face was pale and strained, as well
it might be, considering the amount of preparation she had
devoted to this moment in the previous six weeks. Apart from
her time at Bride School, essential to gain the document of
marriage consent, Irna must have compiled a sheaf of further
certificates—proof of her ancestry and physical health, of the
measurement of her facial features and her blood type, not to
mention medical certificates to ensure that no one in her family
suffered from any mental or congenital illness. There was more
paperwork in a Third Reich wedding than any amount of confetti.

The officiating officer began his talk—a brief drone center-
ing on the responsibilities of SS marriage, including having at
least four children and entering their names in the clan bible of
the SS Sippenbuch—and after overseeing the exchange of silver rings engraved with runes, and gifts of bread and salt, he
presented the happy couple with a copy of *Mein Kampf*.

Either the oppressive air of the wedding chamber or the
ever-present fear of meeting Himmler was suddenly more than
Clara could bear. The tension was making it hard to breathe.
Turning tail, she slipped softly out of the door and headed

down the corridor, trying to remember the way back to the north tower.

It was more complicated than she had imagined. After two wrong turns she found herself in a long brick corridor studded with doors that appeared to be offices. The passage was narrow and badly lit, and the icy walls themselves seemed to exude a sense of menace. She hesitated, wondering whether to turn back, when from the far end of the corridor came the crunch of boots and she hurried on, taking the next available turn and descending a flight of treacherous steps into depthless darkness.

It was a crypt of sorts, about fifteen meters wide, with spears of light lancing down through the narrow apertures onto twelve seats set into the walls. Each had a wall niche above it, and on the ceiling, a swastika extended its crooked arms. In a circular depression in the center of the room, an eternal flame flickered. She guessed at once that the twelve seats represented the twelve knights of King Arthur and the Round Table. A devotion to Wagner was compulsory among the Nazi elite. Hitler would stand on the balcony of the Berghof with the prelude to *Parsifal* playing on his gramophone. Goering had concocted his own Wagnerian fantasy in the shape of his hunting lodge, Carinhall. Even Goebbels claimed to love the composer and devotedly attended the annual Bayreuth festival. Himmler—intent on surrounding himself with a band of racially pure blood brothers, had chosen Wagner's Camelot as his personal obsession, but the future occupants of these seats would be no knights in shining armor.

Scanning the crypt, Clara detected at the opposite side a gap in the wall. It led to a spiral staircase of damp stone, and she made her way up countless winding steps until she felt the first breath of fresh air on her face and saw a glimmer of daylight ahead. By her calculation she was close to the battlements once more, but as she reached the top she was distracted by the sound of voices. She froze.

Leni Riefenstahl was standing with the falconer they had seen on their arrival. The hawk was hooded now, with a bell tied to its leg, and the falconer was running his finger down the bird's glinting plumage, tenderly stroking the feathers of its neck, as Leni engaged in a lively argument with two men. The men had their backs to Clara, but even from behind, the shaved skull, wide breeches, and black cap of the nearest would be unmistakable to any citizen of the Reich.

SS Reichsführer Heinrich Himmler.

Clara shrank back against the wall of the staircase as their conversation carried on the wind.

"I thought you understood, Fräulein Riefenstahl. Animals are prohibited in Reich filmmaking. Surely you of all people should know that?"

"I wasn't aware that birds were covered by that edict," said Leni, with a sweetly furious smile.

"Of course, birds. I, of all people, understand the intelligence of birds. I ran a chicken farm for years. No German under my command will mistreat animals or birds or inflict any unnecessary suffering. I hope I can ensure that you will abide by these restrictions for the remainder of your stay."

"Whatever you say, Herr SS Reichsführer."

With a curt gesture to the man beside him, Himmler turned on his heel.

Clara found Leni cursing softly.

"Damn."

"What was all that about?"

"I had a beautiful shot lined up with that hawk. It was to be the final image of the entire film. The brooding ancient walls, the sheer perfection of the lines of young men, then I pull focus to find a single hawk climbing upwards, eastwards, until it disappears into a rent in the clouds. The hawk symbolizes ambition, the future, the eternal quest of the Reich. But Himmler, of course, disapproves. He understands nothing about art. He says filming his wretched hawk constitutes illegal exploitation of animals."

"Who was that man with him?"

"Oh, his masseur." Leni rolled her eyes, good humor partially restored. "I know. Hard to imagine, isn't it?"

More than hard. The image of a prone Himmler, relaxing for a tender muscle rub, was inconceivable.

"Himmler was unbearable because he was in constant pain and no one could help him. His staff were beside themselves, until eventually someone discovered this man, Felix Kersten, who had studied Tibetan skills under a lama. Himmler was persuaded to try it, and fortunately for Herr Kersten, the treatment actually worked. Himmler was an instant convert, but the thing is, Kersten has to stay a big secret. That's why Himmler meets him here. He does everything he can to keep Kersten out of sight."

"Why? Is he embarrassed?"

"Are you joking? Nothing could embarrass Himmler. No, he's terrified that Heydrich will find out and get hold of his medical details."

"But Heydrich's his own deputy."

"That means nothing. In Heydrich's mind, information is power. He has a locked safe that he refers to as his 'poison cabinet,' where he keeps all his files on the senior men."

Seeing Clara's face, Leni laughed and added: "Sounds crazy, doesn't it? But the fact is, all the top men are at each other's throats. Their true war is with each other. Goering hates Goebbels far more than he could possibly hate Poland, and you know how much the Goebbelses despise Himmler. Himmler is rivals with all of them. I never told you why I chose you for this part, did I?"

"You said I had the right face."

"Of course, darling." A smile of malicious pleasure. "But I could have chosen any number of actresses. It's not a difficult part, after all. And I knew Goebbels would not be too happy with the idea. But the reason I chose you was to annoy Himmler."

The wind was battering their words away, so there was no danger of being overheard, but all the same Clara lowered her voice. "Why on earth would choosing me annoy Himmler?"

Leni chuckled like a girl revealing a conjuring trick. "Oh, he was terribly interested in you. I've overheard him asking about you, and I was curious because Himmler doesn't go for actresses, as you know. That's Goebbels's specialty. And despite all his windbaggery about Wagner, Himmler doesn't really have a cultural bone in his body. I despise him, actually."

Clara looked down the battlements to the field below. The hawk was swooping again, rising high, then coming in like an arrow onto its prey. "And . . . you said it would annoy him if I had the part?"

"I certainly hope so."

"Why? What was he saying, when you overheard him?"

"Just inquiring about the rumors."

"Rumors?"

A moment of pity softened Leni's sardonic features. As if explaining to a child, she said, "That you were in some way non-Aryan."

Clara was frozen with shock. It explained everything. Magda's remark. *Someone has been saying some very unkind things about you.*

"I wouldn't worry too much, Clara. There's nothing new about it. They're always discovering that someone might have Jewish roots. Goebbels started that smear about me, too, only he reckoned without my blessed Führer. He made his photographer, Hoffman, take a photo shoot of Goebbels and me walking together in my garden to scotch the rumors." Leni's face brightened at the memory. "Anyway, the fact is I can't stand Himmler or his wretched Ahnenerbe, so choosing you was ideal. It's mischievous of me really, but I thought what a laugh it would be to cast Clara Vine as the symbol of Germany. Himmler couldn't object because the Führer has given me absolutely free rein, and besides . . ."

"Besides what?"

"They have nothing on you, do they? They must have gone over your background with a fine-tooth comb. If there was a drop of Jewish blood in you it would have leaked out by now."

Tension was holding Clara's limbs together like steel cords, tighter than the most expert masseur could relax. She asked, "When you overheard him discussing me, who was he talking to?"

"It was at Prinz-Albrecht-Strasse. I try to keep away from that place, but I was called in a while ago so that Himmler could discuss this film with me. We were in Heydrich's office and Himmler and Heydrich were talking together and there was someone else there—that Ubersturmbannführer, Conrad Adler."

"Adler?"

"D'you know him? Frightfully good-looking, but a bit of a

mystery. I can't get on with him, to tell the truth, though they say he's a loyal member of the Party and he's worked for the Foreign Ministry for years."

"He's at the Propaganda Ministry now."

"With Goebbels? No. Adler's been assigned to Heydrich. That's why he was there. He's working on some special project. I've got no idea what it is, but it's terrifically hush-hush. I shouldn't even have mentioned it."

TWO HOURS LATER THEY had loaded up the trucks and Leni's Mercedes was making its way down the cobbled road out of Wewelsburg. The effort of trying to appear normal as she processed Leni's revelation was almost beyond Clara. Conrad Adler, the man who had approached her, who had asked such tender questions about her childhood, had taken her riding and propositioned her, was an acolyte of the head of the SD security service. Reinhard Heydrich, with his long equine face and hair shaved a savage three inches above his ears, was a sadist, pure and simple. Clara racked her brain to recall what Adler had specifically told her about his assignment and realized that, in fact, she had simply assumed he was working for Goebbels. *I'm on loan. Like a painting in a museum.* But if Adler was working for Heydrich, what was his interest in her?

The drive back would be long, but Leni was in high good humor. She leaned her arm out of the window, trailing a thin scarf of cigarette smoke in her wake.

"I've just had a message from the Führer. He's told me that Albert Speer is to set aside thirty thousand square yards in the new capital for the Riefenstahl Studios. All funded by the state! He's going to announce it next week. In fact . . ." She glanced across, beaming. "He's invited me to a film evening at the

Chancellery. I have to go, so you might as well come with me. I'll put your name on the guest list. It's next week. Brace yourself, though. Goebbels may well be there, along with that ghastly wife of his. But the event will be useful. While we're there I can think about how to shoot the Führer."

Clara gasped, and Leni glanced at her curiously.

"On film, of course."

28

Berlin was alive with rumors. The British prime minister had resigned. The Poles were about to attack. An illegal radio network called the Freedom Station had sprung up, moving its transmitter around Berlin to avoid detection. An atmosphere of nervous anticipation stalked the city like a living thing. The proximity of war made every goodbye more intimate, every kiss more intense, every friendship more important. At tram stops, in the bread queues, and amid the momentary knots of customers that coalesced round coffee stalls, conversation flowed between strangers. Yet while the talk was of foreboding, there was also excitement in the air. It eddied down the quiet residential streets of Schöneberg, rippled through the smart boulevards of Wilmersdorf and Charlottenburg, swirled round the dank tenements of Moabit and Wedding and Prenzlauer Berg. People felt part of something, even if it was not something they desired.

———

THURSDAY DAWNED HEAVY, the sky stippled with cloud. There was no call for filming that day, so ostensibly Clara had the day free. By ten to one she was standing on Budapester Strasse outside the outlandish, spectacular Elephant Gate of Berlin Zoo. The gate, with its green turrets, red and gold arch, and kneeling sandstone elephants, could not be more of a contrast to the somber street architecture around it. It stood freakishly proud, a splash of Oriental color that jarred against the orderly grays and browns. It suggested that merely by entering, citizens could escape the gloom of Berlin for a more joyful, exotic world.

Clara felt it, too; the zoo was special to her. It was the place that Leo had first taken her to teach her the art of espionage, when she was a nervous ingenue and he a brusque passport control officer. And conflicted, as he later confided, that he was inducting a naïve young actress into peril she could scarcely comprehend. Since then she had visited numerous times with Erich, who would always head for the Gross Raubtiere Haus, eager to see the elegantly pacing lions and tigers, to marvel at the sleek jaguars and panthers. That was until he announced that he couldn't bear to see such magnificent animals caged and would never go again.

She bought a ticket and made her way along the meticulously planted beds of begonias and roses towards the animal enclosures. The zoo was a haven of peace in the city's heart, and just now it was at its most beautiful. The traffic fumes were replaced by a sweet mingled aroma of straw and dung. Two boys in lederhosen flashed past on scooters, threatening to scrape the shins of anyone foolish enough to get too close. A dog in a little overcoat waddled importantly along. A pair of excitable matrons were being hoisted onto an elephant, idly coiling his trunk as he waited to give his hourly ride. Clara threaded through the crowds wondering what would happen to these animals if bombing came. Were shelters being built for them, too?

He will find you.

Clara hadn't questioned Steffi's suggestion at the time, but now it seemed absurdly ambitious. Even on a weekday at lunchtime, the zoo was busy, and the visitor numbers were further swelled by the arrival of a gargantuan sea lion named Roland, whose appearance on the Ufa Tonwoche newsreel had granted him celebrity status. How could she begin to find a complete stranger here, especially if he was purposefully anonymous?

Her first thought was to head for one of the more distant animal houses. Surely the elephant house on the farthest edge, or the elegant ostrich enclosure, styled like an Egyptian temple, would be better suited to an assignation. And yet, if he had been seeking privacy, why had the man she was to meet chosen such a public place? Was it, perhaps, precisely because of the crowds? After a moment's deliberation she gravitated towards the milling throng that had gathered to watch the sea lion being fed.

It was a spectacle of high entertainment. Every time the keeper, armed with a bucket of sprats, dangled a tiny, silvery shimmer above the water, the sleek gray mass would rise abruptly, water sheeting from his sides, to a volley of delighted shrieks. The sea lion would then heave his three-ton bulk onto a rock and open his mouth. Predictably he had already been nicknamed Goering.

As Clara focused on the feeding ritual, wondering what to do, a flicker of movement wrenched her eyes upwards. A man leaning with his elbows on the far side of the rail, dressed in wide-legged trousers and a nondescript checked jacket, had glanced in her direction and adjusted his hat. He had a sharp-edged face, but the trilby's deep brim shaded his eyes as he stared, apparently absorbed, into the enclosure below.

At the back of her mind a memory stirred. There was something about that half-shaded profile she had seen before, but where? The image remained frustratingly unknown, floating free, without context, evoking only an uncomfortable frisson of unease.

Then she looked again, and recognition electrified her.

When she was a child she had adored puzzle books. Each Christmas her parents would give her a story album that was interspersed with games, crosswords, and picture puzzles. As she grew, she progressed to entire books of them, and one of her favorites was called *Spot the Difference*. It featured pairs of scenes with tiny changes that forced the eye to focus on fine detail. "A Sunny Day," "On the Beach," "At the Fair." Two versions of Trafalgar Square but in one a man was carrying an umbrella and in the other he was empty-handed. Two identical jungles with a missing monkey in one of them. You knew if you looked closely, really closely, you would uncover aspects that had not at first revealed themselves. Comparing the man at the railing over and over with the image in her mind, Clara realized, with a jolt of horror, what was bothering her. That lean face, the eyes that deliberately avoided hers. It was the man she had found standing in the lobby of her apartment in Winterfeldtstrasse. The man who, she was convinced, was not sheltering from the rain.

Hovering at the back of the crowd, she fought the urge to walk away as fast as possible. Was this the man she was supposed to meet? If so, either the Gestapo had somehow discovered their plans and replaced Steffi's accomplice with their own person or the figure before her was genuine, and her assumption about him was wrong.

Even as she hesitated the man threw his cigarette stub down on the ground and peeled languidly away, as if motivated by nothing more than a casual desire for lunch. As he moved slowly towards the gate, Clara made up her mind to follow him.

Immediately outside, he headed towards a dark green bicycle leaned against the railing, mounted it, and proceeded slowly eastwards, along Budapester Strasse and across the Landwehrkanal, turning right towards Lützowplatz. Almost immediately he turned right again into Keithstrasse. Although the bicycle was proceeding slowly, Clara was forced to walk as fast as she could to keep up, and by the time he stopped outside a tall, brick-faced residential block, she was gasping for breath.

She lingered on a porch on the opposite side of the road, assessing the situation. The building was the type of multiuse block that could be found all over Berlin. An office on the ground floor, apartments above. A location with a floating population that afforded a certain amount of privacy from prying eyes, and where unfamiliar visitors would raise no eyebrows. The man dismounted and disappeared inside.

Clara glanced around her. The street was empty and there were no parked cars close by. A burst of laughter spattered out of an upper window; a radio buzzed farther off. Eventually, she knocked twice, preparing to ask for Herr Vogel if any other face answered the door. But it was the same man.

"You took your time. I was beginning to give up on you."

He was young, now she saw him close up, and spoke with a rough accent, but his demeanor was shrewd and intelligent.

"It's hard following a cyclist."

"It's safer than buses or trams. No one looking you up and down. You'd better come in."

He led her down a dim tiled corridor through a door to a back room, containing only a couple of cheap wooden chairs and a table.

Clara looked around her.

"You know what I'm here for?" she asked.

"A *Kennkarte* and an *Ariernachweis*."

"My documents fell into the Seine in Paris."

He gave a dry laugh. "Use that as an excuse and it might get you points for originality."

"It's true, as it happens."

"It's of no concern to me, Fräulein, where you lost them. I'm here to replace them. I've already got the cards ready. All I need are photographs of you."

She fished in her bag for the contact sheet shots that had been taken for the publicity for *Love Strictly Forbidden*. He surveyed them critically.

"Ideally we'd want one with no smile."

"It's the best I can do."

"They're not too bad."

She recalled Leni's words. *Your face has a useful quality. It's a blank canvas. It's like I can project anything I want on it.*

The young man switched on the desk lamp and bent over a piece of card: an *Ariernachweis*, on which Clara's details had already been filled in. He took the photograph and placed it in the corner of the card, then fixed it to the pass with brass eyelets.

"It took ages to get these looking right. Eventually I found a cobbler who supplied me with the tool he uses to fix eyelets for bootlaces. It was perfect."

He reached for a fine brush and a jar of purple dye and began painting on a separate piece of card.

"There are twelve long and twenty-four short feathers on

the German imperial eagle, did you know that? The hardest thing is to get the correct color and shape."

He continued working intently. His movements were as tender and delicate as if he were creating a Renaissance Madonna and Child, rather than an eagle and swastika. His face was closed, intent, inscrutable in the dim light. When he had copied the eagle, he took a piece of newspaper, dampened it with spittle, and pressed it down on the newly painted symbol, creating a mirror image on the newspaper. He then took the paper and pressed it onto the photograph of Clara.

"The stamp needs to project across the photograph. Now we'll have to give it a few minutes to dry."

He sat motionless, as if expecting that she, too, would sit in silence beside him. But Clara had too many questions.

"Where do you get the passes to copy?"

"One of our supporters is a church pastor. Some of his congregation drop their expired ID passes into the collection box instead of money. They know how valuable they'll be. I've had all kinds, even Wehrmacht passes. The equipment I get from work. There's no shortage of brushes or paint there."

"You make it sound simple."

"That's only the beginning. Once we've given someone a new identity, we advise them to join a lending library and get a card with their new name on it. As many extra pieces of ID as possible."

"So you can make anyone into anything?"

"Not at all. You need to match the face with the occupation. If I have a card which gives the occupation as kitchen cleaner, I can't hand that out to some smart lady whose husband owns a department store."

"Are you busy?"

"It's constant. But time's running out. People are going to need more than ID documents. Jews here are trapped in a net. They need places to hide."

"Or they need to leave Berlin."

"No." He said it adamantly. "Berlin's the best place to hide. Did you know almost half of the city is underground? There are a thousand bunkers in Berlin. Speer has built a tunnel running all the way from Mitte to Tempelhof so Goering can ride the whole four miles in his car. The customers of the Adlon hotel have their own shelter under Pariser Platz. Not so grand for the rest, of course. We'll mostly be using the U-Bahns. They've just finished a new shelter at Alexanderplatz."

"I was there only the other day. I didn't see anything."

"You wouldn't. It's entirely inconspicuous. You walk along the tunnel to the U5 line and you pass a green steel door. You'd miss it if you didn't know it was there."

So that was where they would huddle. Waiting for the bombs to drop. Listening to the muffled explosions and imagining the lick of flames.

The young man stabbed out his half-smoked cigarette and tucked the stump in his pocket.

"The Nazis may be driving people underground now, but one day soon they'll be driven underground themselves."

He jumped up and checked the card. "There. You're no longer a Jew. But don't go dropping it into any French rivers again. And don't allow it to get wet at all. Even a drop of rain might dissolve the watercolor."

She placed the identity in her bag, then looked at him soberly.

"Thank you. I'm sorry. I don't even know your name."

"I'd be a fool to tell you. If anyone thought this was a forgery, they'd ask where it came from and who forged it. There aren't many people who can resist answering when they're having a chat with the Gestapo."

"Passport forgery is punishable by death, isn't it?"

"You ask a lot of questions, Fräulein. Most of my clients are too frightened to do anything but sit in silence."

"Just because I ask questions, doesn't mean I'm not frightened too . . . I do have another question, though. When I first saw you, I knew I'd seen you before. In the lobby of my apartment in Winterfeldtstrasse. You remember, don't you?"

"You're an observant lady."

"What were you doing there?"

He smiled, a quick smile that utterly transformed his features. "As a matter of fact I had just posted a flyer on the wall opposite. I had my leaflets and the paste bottle in a suitcase. But a policeman appeared and I needed to hide in a hurry."

CLARA LEFT THE APARTMENT as swiftly as she could and got on the first bus she found. As she traveled, the bus rocking under her, she thought how her whole life was like the young man's painstaking work. The least inconsistency, the tiniest slip, and her entire, carefully fabricated existence would unravel, like the silk spooling from a beautiful gown. Yet in a few days the existence that she had crafted for herself over the past six years was facing its greatest test. And whatever happened, she would not be the same person afterwards.

29

THEIR MEETING PLACE WAS THE BRIDGE OVER THE SPREE just before Museum Island. It was, according to their heritage studies teacher, the place where the first settlers in Berlin, who were fishermen, had erected their wooden huts. Hedwig leaned for a moment, watching the canal as it glittered in bright rings beneath the setting sun, stirred into lazy arrows by the coal-heaped barges making their slow progress westwards. Above, the sky was as luminous and mottled as an oyster shell, and faint traces of linden blossom were carried on the breeze. It was a lovely spring evening, but Hedwig was sick with nerves.

She had barely slept since the evening of Jochen's revelations. Tonight was their regular meeting, but she had no idea what they might do or where they would go. Everything had changed now. She had hurried home after work and pulled on a flowered dress that Lottie had sewed up from one of her own designs. It clung to her curves a little too obviously for her taste, and Hedwig was only wearing it because Jochen had once remarked casually that he liked girls in flowered dresses. And because the memory of the beautiful brunette Sofie, whom Jochen admired, burned in her mind.

A hand on her shoulder made her jump, but the sight of him brought the reflex rush of excitement.

"So where are we going?"

"Somewhere interesting. Up west."

"Where exactly?"

"I'll tell you when we get there."

"Is it . . . to do with what you told me? The other night?"

He grinned. "Patience, Hedy! It's a secret."

On the tram Jochen seemed lost in contemplation, so she stared out of the window at the glimmering shop windows and the commuters in their office outfits hurrying home from work. How foolish she had been to assume that Jochen was planning to propose! Perhaps it was for the best. She thought of her mother savagely scrubbing, her father looking her up and down in that way he had. They already thought badly enough of Jochen; God knows what they would think if they knew what he was really doing. Since Lottie's murder her life seemed to be spooling out of control, with one terrible surprise following another. She desperately hoped that this evening would not be the next.

She waited until the tram had reached the smart boulevards of Wilmersdorf, and they had disembarked, before she spoke again. Jochen moved fast, hands jammed in his pockets, as if propelled by some urgent inner force.

"I still don't know where we're going."

"We're going to see a fortune-teller."

Hedwig so wanted to believe him. It was such a wonderful,

imaginative idea, and it might have been planned expressly to delight her. Numerous friends had visited fortune-tellers to investigate their romantic futures. Palm reading and tarot cards were all the rage. Irna Wolter had visited a psychic with her fiancé before they married and had learned they would enjoy a long, happy marriage, blessed with five children. Hedwig had not consulted a psychic herself before, but she never missed her horoscope and she kept a Winterhilfswerk donation pin in the shape of her star sign—Pisces—in her lapel. She had bought one for Jochen, too—Aries—but she had never seen him wear it.

"I thought you didn't believe in fortune-tellers."

She couldn't keep the excitement out of her voice. Her stars in that month's edition of *Der Zenit* promised dramatic developments in her love life.

"I believe in this one. Her forecasts are impressively accurate."

After a few minutes they reached a building in Pariser Strasse, the kind that Hedwig sometimes fantasized about inhabiting but had never set foot in. It was a five-story stucco block with fancy scrollwork round a doorframe. A lot of smart houses were having swastikas set into their lintels, but here the plaster was molded into a pretty confection of leaves and squirrels. Next to it a buffed brass plaque read, PSYCHIC CONSULTATIONS. FIRST FLOOR.

The door was opened by a maid, who ushered them into a front room with a vaguely Eastern air, bestowed by drawn tasseled curtains, fringed red lamps, and rich Turkish carpets. Around the room, low tables were clustered with the accessories of the trade—crystal balls, tarot cards, and a china phrenological head segmented into areas with labels like CAUTION, SE-

CRECY, ELOQUENCE, and ARTISTRY. A pungent odor hung in the air. Hedwig was quite used to homes that smelled strongly, but unlike the cabbage intercut with rancid fat that perfumed her family's apartment, this scent was exotic and mysterious. Nutmeg, cinnamon, and frankincense, perhaps. Like the incense in a Catholic church or the ancient smells that emanated from the library at the Ahnenerbe.

The door opened, and a short, commanding figure swept in, wearing a cerise kimono-style silk jacket and a beaded cap. She must have been in her late sixties, with a crooked nose and kinked hair, her dark caramel eyes heavily lined in kohl, and her makeup thickly applied. Exactly like a fortune-teller was supposed to look, thought Hedwig, enthralled.

"This is Hedwig," said Jochen brusquely. "Hedwig, this is Frau Annie Krauss."

The Annie Krauss! Everyone had heard of her. All the top people—film actors and singers and sports people—were said to consult Annie Krauss. There had been a feature on her work in *Der Zenit*—"Madame Krauss Prognosticates," with a picture of her craning over a crystal ball wearing a fringed headband, and reports of some of her predictions, mostly picking winners at the Hoppegarten racecourse. It was impossible to get an appointment without booking months in advance.

Frau Krauss approached Hedwig and seized her hand. There was an unexpected strength in her stringy claw, and Hedwig wondered if the old lady could discern her future merely from the faint impressions of lines on her palm. Frau Krauss squinted up at Hedwig, as if reading the secrets of her soul.

"Good evening, my dear. I've heard about you. I'm so glad to meet you."

A beady glance up and down. Yet again Hedwig regretted wearing the clingy dress.

"I'm honored to meet you too, Frau Krauss. I've always wanted to."

"Hmm." The old woman turned away slightly, allowing Hedwig to whisper to Jochen, "Is this about telling our futures?"

He shrugged, enigmatically. "In a manner of speaking."

30

FROM THE PAVEMENT TABLES OF THE CAFÉ KRANZLER IT was possible to see a line of people stretching most of the way round Pariser Platz to the doors of the American embassy. The queue for visas began before dawn and would still be there at dusk. Not that there was anything interesting about a queue in Berlin. Waiting was a way of life. Along with the ordinary queues for bread and meat and vegetables, there were long, snaking queues for train tickets and visas, and foreigners crammed the stations like walkers desperate to get home before the first drops of a storm arrived. A pair of hard-faced soldiers had been deputed to guard the American embassy queue, but no one seemed remotely likely to step out of line. Disorder was not something they could afford. Occasionally a secretary bearing a tray of tea and sandwiches moved along, pouring cups and asking people if they required sugar. Their faces registered astonishment at the young American's query. It had been so long since they were considered not just

names and numbers but humans, with preferences and opin-
ions, even about how much sugar they took in their tea.

A few hundred yards away, Clara was waiting for Mary
Harker. She had no idea why Mary had asked to meet, but she
was glad of the diversion. The previous evening she had
reached into the jar of Melitta coffee beans in Ursula's kitchen
and retrieved the derringer, wrapped in a piece of cloth. She
had held it for a moment, turning it over and over, wondering
if this tiny object would be capable of such a momentous act.
Even now she could feel the shiny menace of the pistol imprinted on her palm. Seeing Mary, if only for a few hours,
would distract her from the task she was about to undertake.

Mary arrived late, wrenching off her battered felt hat and
running her hand through her hair so that bits of it stood up
vertically in a tangle of straw.

"I'm trying to calm down." She threw herself dramatically
on a seat, lit a cigarette, and inhaled furiously. "I've just been
expelled from a press conference."

"Not another one."

"I know. There are two press conferences a day now, so I
have twice as much opportunity to get ejected. I wouldn't
bother, but with everything moving so fast, you can't afford to
miss one in case they let slip anything important."

"And did they?"

"No such luck. It was 'Good News About Employment.' The
usual mixture of boasts and lies. They said full employment
has finally been achieved in Germany."

"I'm guessing that's not true."

"I felt obliged to point out that if there was full employment, it was only because all the workers are now producing
armaments. Before I knew it, two thugs had frog-marched me
out of the door."

"And you let this upset you?" asked Clara incredulously.

"Don't be silly. I've been thrown out of more press confer-ences than I've had hot wurst. No, that's not why I wanted to see you. It's about your Faith and Beauty girl. Take a look at this."

She pushed across the table the latest edition of the *Völkischer Beobachter*, the ultraloyal Nazi newspaper. Clara glanced at the headline: INVESTIGATION CONTINUES INTO SLAIN GIRL. There was nothing new in the report except that it was accompanied by a fresh photograph of Lottie Franke. All the previous shots had shown her wearing her regulation Faith and Beauty outfit, but this was a large, glamorous image of Lottie dressed in a provocatively low-cut dress, eyes smoldering at the camera, one leg propped vampishly on a chair. In the upper right-hand cor-ner was the photographer credit: *Yva.*

"What does this photograph say?" demanded Mary.

"That she modeled her own designs. She was artistic."

"Nope." Mary thrust the paper away, as if disgusted.

"A picture's worth a thousand words, right? And I know how newspaper picture desks work. If they have a choice of photo-graphs to illustrate a piece—and there seem to have been a hundred pictures of Lottie Franke—then they'll choose the one that transmits the correct message. Most of the *Völkischer Beobachter* might have been dictated by Goebbels himself, and this photograph is not an accident. It says Lottie was *not* the archetypal German maiden. She was not the pure Faith and Beauty girl everyone imagines. She was different, original, a little out of the ordinary. In other words, this girl got what was coming to her."

"She deserved to die?" Clara was appalled.

"Pretty much."

"But why?"

Mary frowned. "That's what I don't understand. For some reason the investigation is changing course. Did I mention that they have a suspect now?"

Clara clattered her cup back into the saucer. "Mary! You left it until now to tell me?"

"When I was leaving the Propaganda Ministry this afternoon I bumped into one of the few sane press deputies. He told me they've arrested a man. They're announcing it tomorrow."

"That changes everything."

"No it doesn't. Because it's a Pole. If you believe the police department—which of course I don't—Poles have been responsible for most of the crimes in the Reich for the past three months. Whoever this man is, he didn't do it. But it shows that they're tired of the story now. The police are no longer trying to solve the murder. If they can't tar Lottie as a promiscuous eccentric, then they'll pin her murder on a Pole. I'm afraid, Clara, it means they can no longer be bothered to find the right man."

"Or they don't want to."

Clara felt again that intuition that had dawned at the Faith and Beauty home: that Lottie's murder was not the act of a lone madman. That it had roots in something far beyond the opportunistic sexual murder of a girl in the wrong place at the wrong time. But it was impossible to explain, and besides, Mary was rushing impatiently on.

"Also, Clara, I wanted to say goodbye. I'm leaving town for a while."

"Just because you were expelled from a press conference?"

"Much better reason than that." Mary grinned. "I'm making a trip to England because I've had the strangest request.

Jack Kennedy, the son of the American ambassador in London, wants to meet me. He thinks I might be able to give his father a better idea of what the Nazis are like up close."

Clara smiled. "I bumped into Jack Kennedy when I was in Paris. But I never thought he'd ask you to lecture his father."

Mary reached over and gripped her arm. "I might have guessed it was you. Thank you, Clara. It's an incredible opportunity. And believe me, I won't hold back. I owe you."

Clara hesitated . . . "In that case, there is something you can do for me. There's a girl, Esther Goldblatt. She's fourteen. Jewish. She reminds me of myself at that age. She desperately needs to get out of Germany, and she has a visa for America, but it will take years before her number comes up. She could get an exit visa to travel to England, but only if she has a sponsor there who is prepared to adopt her."

"That's quite a hurdle."

"I think I know the right person."

Clara reached for her notebook. "Here's her address and telephone number."

Mary looked down at the paper. "Angela Mortimer? Are you serious? I would have thought your sister was the last person on earth to contemplate adopting a little Jewish girl!"

"That was my first instinct, but there's more to Angela than you think. Her views may be reprehensible, but she's a decent person at heart. She was very motherly to me when I was a truculent teenager. And she has no children to mother, so it's perfect. Tell her I'll write and explain but she needs to register as a sponsor as soon as possible. She must contact Bloomsbury House in Great Russell Street. It's the headquarters of the Jewish Refugees Committee. Oh, and something else." Clara reached up to her neck and unclasped Steffi's pearls. "Take these, sell them for the best price you can, and give Angela the money. Tell her it's for Esther."

She watched as Mary stowed the pearls carefully in her bag.

"Good luck."

"Thanks."

But Clara knew if anyone was going to need luck, it would be her.

31

THE KAISERHOF HOTEL WAS A DINGY BUILDING THE COLOR of bad teeth. It stood out in the Wilhelmstrasse because all the other buildings in the government area had undergone makeovers of impressive expense. The new Reich Chancellery, directly across the street, had been finally completed that January, a quarter of a mile of yellow stucco and gray stone stretching down Voss Strasse, its monumental proportions designed to quash any lingering concessions to the human scale. Goebbels's Propaganda Ministry, originally housed in an old Empire-style palace across the way, had been given a total revamp, with an extension that was architecturally severe and modern, in line with Goebbels's modernist taste. The Kaiserhof, however, Hitler's first home in Berlin, lingered on like a widow in dowdy lace, steadfastly resisting cosmetic enhancement.

Clara had arrived early and installed herself in the bar of the hotel. What the Kaiserhof's proprietors had saved on exterior renovation they put towards securing the best of the city's available food, making it one of the finest places to eat, but today Clara had no interest in food. She had brought her copy of *The Thirty-Nine Steps* to distract herself and sat with it open in front of her, the sour, gritty taste of fear washing round her mouth like grains of ersatz coffee. Occasionally she stole glances across the road to where security police known as Schupos, in their green uniforms and black leather hats, manned the Chancellery gates.

If the opportunity arose, we would not want you, Miss Vine, to be hindered by fears of "unsportsmanlike" behavior.

All day she had questioned herself. Would she ever have the courage to do it? Could she shoot Hitler? Sitting in the garden at Griebnitzsee that afternoon, with her eyes closed and the sun flaring scarlet against her eyelids, she felt so intensely alive. Her limbs tingled with vitality, every fiber of her body wanting to live, even if her lover was missing and her family estranged.

Never before had she come so close to Hitler, yet it would also be the closest she had come to death herself. Shooting Hitler would, almost certainly, mean death, but without him Germany would be free. There would be no fighting, and thousands of young men would no longer be required to go to war. Erich would be safe.

Yet all the time, seductive counterarguments whispered sweetly. What if war didn't have to happen? If there could be a way to negotiate? What right did she have to kill another human being? What if the derringer failed to fire? And even when the questions receded, the hideous images remained. What special tortures would be reserved for the assassin of the Führer?

When she looked back on her life, she could see that so much of what she had done had been impulsive, actions taken on the spur of the moment. Her decision to become an actress had been motivated by the disapproval of her parents. She'd moved to Berlin to escape an unwanted fiancé. She began spying at the request of Leo Quinn. She had put herself at the service of others—people whose motives she strongly believed in—but never at her own instigation. This time it was different. This audacious, deadly plan was hers alone. Its execution owed nothing to anyone except herself. It required her to summon every ounce of moral courage and to quash every doubt. She remembered what a Luftwaffe officer had once told her—that being a truly successful pilot meant losing the last shred of fear. Then she thought of all the people she had known in her six years in Berlin, the brave men and women who had tried to resist the Nazis. They had all made their own choices, but this decision, so hard, was hers alone.

Eventually, the murmuring arguments died down and Clara felt the fear inside her harden into resolve.

In the afternoon she had returned to Winterfeldtstrasse to go through the belongings in her old apartment. Rudi, the warden, who carried out his duties from a chair in the corner of the hall, seemed almost pleased to see her. Despite his advanced age and crooked spine, he sprang up to block her path. He had always been a staunch Nazi, and it surprised Clara that it had taken him so many years to cultivate the little postage stamp mustache that he now sported proudly in emulation of his hero.

"Heil Hitler, Fräulein Vine! Are you back for good?"

It was almost as though he'd been missing her, though the old fraud had never shown an iota of fond feeling in his life. More likely, he was calculating how the landlord might raise the rent if she chose to end her lease.

"Not sure yet, Rudi. How's everything?"

"Busy. We're converting the cellar into a shelter. We have directives from the Air Protection League."

"Of course."

She tried to scurry away up the stairs, but Rudi was well practiced in forestalling escapes. Edging forward, he barricaded her way as effectively as a squad of riot police. His breath smelled of the kind of alcohol not found in high-end Berlin clubs.

"A gentleman was calling for you yesterday."

"What kind of gentleman?"

"Ah, that's not for me to say, Fräulein. I'm a simple man. I can't judge. Perhaps it was a fan."

"I doubt it."

It was almost certainly a collector. Barely an hour went by some days without a charity official knocking on the door and rattling a tin, demanding funds for the Hitler Youth or the BDM. For the orphans or the poor or the Luftwaffe or the rebuilding of Berlin.

Rudi gave a smile of greasy complicity. "I told him I had no idea where you were. That was right, wasn't it?"

"Yes. Thank you, Rudi."

"I know you actresses need protection. That's what I'm here for."

Sidestepping him, she fled up the stairs and shut the apartment door securely behind her. Then she made a rapid inventory. If she was arrested she needed to ensure that there was no trace of Erich. No books with his name in them, no photographs or school reports, none of the birthday cards he had given her. God forbid that his name should be linked with hers. She dreaded the thought of the Gestapo raiding the tenement in Neukölln, shaking the bewildered old Frau Schmidt out of her bed and hustling Erich to some frightening basement, where he would be questioned about the woman he had known since he was a child until his tired mind made a mistake and he somehow incriminated himself, too.

She wandered round the apartment, touching her possessions. She pulled the fur coat that her mother had left her out of the wardrobe and buried her face in it, inhaling the ghost of violets that she once wore. The fur was chill in her hands, but when she pulled the coat on, its warmth enveloped her. Finally, she picked up a book of Latin verse Leo had given her and kissed it, the way Italians might kiss a prayer book, the way she wanted to kiss him. She thought of that sensation she'd had in the Paris hotel room and tried to bring it back, but she felt nothing.

TOWARDS EVENING, THE ADRENALINE began to exhaust her. She had dressed methodically, assessing every item with careful scrutiny. Around the top of her thigh she fastened the calfskin holder with the stocking gun inside. It fitted snugly against her leg, and she marched up and down the room to ensure it did not slip as she walked. When she donned the Madame Grès dress, it was exactly as she had guessed, the flowing Grecian folds giving no hint of the metallic bulge beneath. The dress also went perfectly with her new Schiaparelli jacket. She brushed her hair until it gleamed and fastened a diamanté clip in it, rejecting her Elizabeth Arden Velvet Red in favor of a lipstick that was almost nude. The Führer had been known to confront lipstick-wearing women and subject them to a rant on how cosmetics were made of human waste and poisoned the health of German womanhood.

Her leather jewelry box was battered now, its oval mirror spotted and cloudy, like a blurred portal into the past. She touched the silver locket her mother had given to her when she was sixteen, with pictures of them both inside, but after a moment's reflection, she picked a diamond brooch in the shape of

a swastika. It came from Jaeger's jewelers off Unter den Linden and had been given to her six years previously by Joseph
Goebbels himself. She remembered him pinning it to her dress
at a fashion show in full view of the press—a deliberate act to
mark her out and compromise her in everyone's eyes. Back then
Goebbels had trusted her as his go-between—a secret weapon
in the ongoing war with his wife—but now, who knew what he
thought?

Her hand hovered over her perfume bottles until she chose
one called Scent of Secrets. It was sweet and floral—jasmine,
Turkish rose, and violet iris, with a darker heart of musk,
woodsmoke, and leather. The scent reminded her of her childhood garden in England and her mother's favorite rose, the am-
nesia rose, with its unusual blooms, which looked almost gray
at first, before shading into lilac. She inhaled the scent deeply,
as if for strength. If the evening was to end as she feared, she
wanted the memory of her mother to accompany her.

THE FÜHRER'S FILM EVENING at the Reich Chancellery was
the hottest ticket in town. It was the invitation everyone wanted
and no one expected to enjoy. Each night when he was in Berlin, Hitler would invite a select group of high-ranking Nazis
and actors for a private screening in the Chancellery Music
Room. The advantage was that visitors got to see films denied
to ordinary Germans. Goebbels's latest blacklist of sixty American actors did not extend to the Führer's private parties, and
all the latest Hollywood releases—Tarzan movies, *Tip-Off
Girls, The Lives of a Bengal Lancer, Captains Courageous* with
Spencer Tracy—were firm favorites. Walt Disney was held in
special esteem, thanks to his public reception of Leni Riefenstahl the previous year, when other Hollywood producers had

pointedly turned her down. The disadvantages of the evening were self-evident. Everyone was on their best behavior, no one could smoke, and it was impossible to relax. Relaxation, like coffee, eggs, and chocolate, was now a luxury that not even VIPs could afford.

The reception hall of the Reich Chancellery was done out in contrasting colored marble like an ugly cathedral. The walls were black slabs splintered with quartz, interset with veined, bloody red Saalburger stone, and there was yet more marble underfoot. As she followed an SS orderly dressed in the short white jacket that all Hitler's domestic staff wore, Clara was overwhelmingly conscious of the gun against her thigh. She had guessed that no one on Hitler's guest list would be subjected to the indignity of a body search, yet she was intensely aware that she must not slip on the highly polished surface and send the gun skittering beneath her. The floor was as treacherous as a skating rink, deliberately waxed to a dazzling shine. It was a private joke for Hitler, who refused all requests to lay a carpet because diplomats needed practice moving on a slippery surface.

At the far end of the hall, a door was flanked by two of the Leibstandarte, Hitler's personal bodyguards. Selected for their above average height and unquestioned fidelity to the Führer, they formed an invincible barricade against his enemies, but at Clara's approach they moved simultaneously sideways, opening the doors as though to Aladdin's cave to reveal a dazzle of sound and light.

The party was already in full swing and studded with VIPs, most of them stars of stage and screen. Leni Riefenstahl and Heinz Rühmann were talking to Gustaf Gründgens, another favorite actor of the regime. The actress Jenny Jugo, in magnolia satin, was air-kissing Zarah Leander. The good-looking celebrities were a festive sprinkling to leaven the dark mass of politicians. Rudolf Hess and his wife. The Goebbelses and the Speers. Youth Leader Baldur von Schirach and Reich Labor Minister Robert Ley. Everyone was there. The entire upper echelon of the Third Reich was assembled to watch Mickey Mouse.

To Clara's relief, Hitler had not arrived. She was desperate not to meet him. She had heard of the effect he had; *Führer Kontakt* it was called, an intense magnetic hold that made the person with him believe, just for that moment, that he or she was the only one in the room. A hypnotic force that dazzled, empowered, and enslaved.

Instead, one of the first faces she saw was Conrad Adler. He was standing in the corner nearest the door, inclining his head close to Henriette von Schirach, the youth leader's pretty blond wife. Her face was turned adoringly up towards him, and she was smiling merrily. Although he barely turned his head, Clara knew Adler had seen her, and she registered a spark of alarm in his eyes. She sensed that he was about to break off and approach her until something deterred him, and, turning, she saw Joseph Goebbels looming behind.

"Fräulein Vine. What a surprise. And may I say what a charming choice of brooch. For a charming woman."

He reached out to brush the spot where it was pinned, letting his fingers trail her breast, and then, for the first time in their acquaintance, he moved to kiss her. As his hand traveled round her waist and downwards, Clara's flesh turned to ice. If he strayed any further, he could not miss the stocking gun attached to her left thigh. Her entire body was rigid with alarm, yet even as she froze, she realized her reaction would arouse no suspicion at all. Goebbels must be well used to women flinching at his touch. Barely suppressed distaste was the natural response to the propaganda minister. How else should any woman react to a man who had persecuted so many and sent thousands to their deaths? Whose bigotry had goaded an entire nation into a spiral of coruscating hatred?

"I've not seen you here before. Remind me who invited you?"

"Leni Riefenstahl," said Clara, stepping backwards and looking hastily around. "She thought I might enjoy it, so she put my name on the guest list."

"She's like that. She likes to take liberties with other people's invitations. Still. It's always a pleasure. The last time I was here was with your English friend, Unity Mitford. We watched *Cavalcade*."

"She mentioned that." According to Unity, Hitler had declared Noël Coward's film about three generations of an upper-class British family his favorite movie.

"I thought it very poor," said Goebbels.

"It won Best Picture, didn't it?"

A snort. "Perhaps in one sense that film is what Britain does best. An extended wallow in a rose-tinted version of her past. We in Germany prefer to focus on our future. But then——"

He broke off midsentence, and Clara became aware of an intense, hostile glare. She looked round to see Magda Goebbels approaching, causing her husband to move swiftly in the opposite direction, like one in a pair of repelling magnets. Magda was dressed in high-necked, monkish black and wore the tragic expression of one invited to her own funeral.

"Don't let me interrupt. I can see you and my husband were deep in conversation," she snapped.

"Not really. We were discussing films."

"That's what he always calls it. Discussing films. You take me for a fool, Fräulein Vine. Especially considering the way you're sporting his brooch."

Clara cursed herself for choosing Goebbels's swastika. She had thought of it as a useful accessory, part of her disguise. Instead, it had parachuted her into unforeseen difficulties.

"I have one exactly like it," Magda continued. "But then, so do half the women in Berlin. He has his jeweler make them. Some men—Goering, for example—take a real interest in jewelry, but my husband lacks that imagination. Joseph orders precisely the same trinket every time. Usually when he wants to reward an actress for 'discussing films.'"

What misfortune to encounter a paranoid Magda Goebbels on a night like this. Clara was just summoning conciliatory words when the minister's wife lifted a glass from a passing tray and shrugged. "Don't bother to deny it. I don't care anyway. I just want this evening to be over. Let's hope the Führer's tired."

"Why's that?"

"Because when he's not he watches two films, back to back. I've been here so many times, and it's always the same routine. Cartoon first, then a newsreel, then the movie. Or two. Then he stays up talking until four in the morning, and it's always the same subjects. Vegetarianism, Wagner, history, dogs. I'm praying it's not a two-movie evening."

Clara glimpsed her escape in the adjacent room, where a vast marble table was piled with diverse objects, like a grand church jumble sale.

"Are those the Führer's birthday gifts?"

"Haven't you seen them yet? You should. You wouldn't believe some of the junk the poor man has been given. In my opinion most of it should go straight to the Winterhilfswerk."

Magda was right. The display was exactly like something one might find at a wedding, only far larger and more vulgar. Instead of wineglasses, fish knives, and toasters, the Führer's beloved nation had produced an extravagant and frankly kitsch selection of gifts. A bust of Goethe rubbed shoulders with an ivory hunting horn. Dull landscapes were propped against oils of ancient military figures. A garish gold model of the Führer's art gallery in Munich, the Haus der Deutschen Kunst, jostled for the bad taste prize with a handcrafted castle studded with precious stones. One citizen with a vivid imagination had supplied a pair of baby bootees and a knitted bonnet, which had been deftly concealed behind a vase of striking ugliness filled with dried flowers.

Clara stared at the gifts without seeing them, focusing on what the next hour would bring. She wanted to choreograph her movements precisely, minute by minute. She saw herself as if from above, unstoppable, like a character in a film, except that no rehearsal could prepare her for an attempt like this. No prompt could help her. There was no possibility of a retake. This task had to be carried out perfectly, and she had only one chance.

"Aren't they wonderful? The people love their Führer very much."

The speaker was a young woman in her twenties with frizzy, dark hair and a deferential expression. Compared to those of the Nazi wives, her clothes were dowdy and her manner restrained. She extended a polite hand.

"I'm Christa Schroeder, the Führer's secretary."

"Clara Vine."

"Yes. I mean, I recognize you, Fräulein Vine. I know who you are. I was admiring your dress. Is it French?"

It was a mistake to wear Parisian fashion in Hitler's presence. Not only did he hate the French, but he believed the slender Gallic silhouette was the last thing likely to encourage the fecundity he wanted for his Reich.

"It was a gift," Clara replied noncommittally.

"Such a lovely one. And look at all the Führer's gifts! We've been working round the clock to catalog them. People have been so generous. He's had a Titian portrait, and the most marvelous Meissen porcelain, and a sailing ship made entirely from flowers. Captain Bauer, his pilot, gave him a model Condor airplane. Just over there. And Herr Porsche gave him a model car as well as a real one." A little confidential smile. "To tell the truth, it's the models the Führer loves best. He's like a kid with them."

The secretary sighed fondly. "But the birthday was so tiring for our poor boss. All those receptions went on for days . . . I'm sorry, Fräulein, are you cold in here?"

"No." Clara rubbed the goosebumps on her arms. "I'm fine."

"It's nerves, isn't it?"

"Nerves?" Clara said evenly.

"Please forgive me saying, but it's quite normal. That's how everyone is when they meet the Führer. If only they knew how important the film evenings are to him. He loves being with people, and being entertained. He used to adore going to operettas and variety shows at the Wintergarten or the Admiralspalast, but he can't go anymore because his presence disrupts the performance. So he sends his steward instead, and the man brings a program back for the chief to look at. But that's no substitute. It's sad really. This is the nearest he gets to an evening of pleasure."

Suddenly, from the room behind them, the click of heels rang out like pistol shots, followed by a volley of Heil Hitlers and a large dog, fur plush and shiny and claws skittering on the marble floor, padded into the Music Room. As it stood with its long, pink tongue hanging out, absorbing the gazes of the guests, it was as if, for a freakish moment, the dog itself was the object of their adulation. Then, a heartbeat later, its master arrived.

When Hitler entered, it was as though all the air had been emptied out of the room and replaced with something sharper and more electric. Every eye was drawn to him as if on a wire, every expression one of bright, jewellike intensity. Here was the face that had launched a thousand placards and posters, that hung in every shop window and featured on almost every stamp. The face that appeared to some women in their dreams and others in their nightmares.

Hitler's eyes were very dark blue. His hair had a stark side parting, and one lock, like a scribble of charcoal, sliced diagonally across his brow. He was wearing a plain gray suit, and under it a white shirt and spotted tie. His expression, which generally looked long-suffering and aggrieved, as though it was enduring some intolerable injustice, was now relaxed, and he was smiling broadly. After all, aside from military maneuvers, movies were his favorite thing.

Several rows of red plush seats had been arranged in front of the screen, much like the gilt chairs Clara had shunned in the VIP enclosure at the birthday parade, and as soon as Hitler arrived, there was an undignified jostling for position, as if the whole company were engaged in a party game of musical chairs, and if they didn't hurry they might find themselves with nowhere to sit. Clara looked around in confusion. She had not anticipated this. For a second, as the seats filled up, she hoped she might be reprieved—perhaps she would find nowhere to sit, and like a child at a party be forced to leave the game—until Christa Schroeder came to her aid. She had taken two seats in the row directly behind the Führer.

"Won't you sit by me, Fräulein?"

The chairs were arranged so that viewers could see between

the heads of the people in front. Clara's chair was behind and
to the right of Hitler, out of his peripheral vision and close
enough to see the bull neck with the beginnings of a roll of fat
above the collar and the comb marks in his oiled hair, tightly
shaven at the back and sides. Everything appeared in extraordinary clarity, as through binoculars. Clara saw the patch of stubble on the pallid skin that the razor had missed, and the place
where a boil was forming on one side of his neck. She heard the
snuffle and grunt of the dog lying, head on paws, at its master's
feet.

She let her hand drop to her thigh and felt again the apprehension she remembered as a child during a sermon at church,
worrying that she might lose all power of inhibition and shout
Major Grand's words out loud.

*I hope if you were ever in the same room as him, you would
have no qualms.*

Now she *was* in the same room as him. She was sitting no
more than two feet behind him. She could even detect the edge
of his famous halitosis, mingled with Kölnissch Wasser, his favorite scent, and see him chewing a fingernail. She removed
her jacket and laid it over her lap, then she let her hand cover
the shape of the derringer beneath her dress. Its warm steel
burned against her thigh. She practiced the movement in her
imagination. Her previous nerves vanished, and she felt
strangely calm.

As the lights dimmed, Hitler fished out the pair of gold
spectacles that he hated people to see him wearing, and Christa
Schroeder leaned back with a sigh. This must surely be the
most pleasurable part of her job.

It would be best to wait until after the newsreel.

*It's always the same routine. Cartoon first, then a newsreel,
then the movie.*

It made sense to act when all attention was immersed in the action onscreen. How long would the cartoon last? Ten minutes perhaps? Ufa Tonwoche newsreels were longer—typically up to twenty minutes. That meant half an hour, at the outside, before the main feature, and then another ten minutes until the opening credits had rolled and the story properly begun. Forty minutes then. She couldn't stop herself glancing at the Leibstandarte, the ones who would shortly arrest her, standing impassively at the door. Then at the shadowy form of Conrad Adler, to her left on the end of the first row, sandwiched between Goebbels and the pretty Frau von Schirach. Adler did not glance back, but the fixity of his posture told her he was well aware of her. She felt intensely alert, her head throbbing with tension. Everyone flinched as the projector issued a high-pitched squeal and then, with a splash of frenzied Technicolor, *Mickey Mouse and the Society Dog Show* burst onto the screen.

The softness and warmth of the cartoon shapes could not have been more out of place in the Reich Chancellery's marble tomb. As Mickey's falsetto, dubbed into German, chattered brightly through the action, Clara tried to keep her eyes rigidly ahead. It seemed that Pluto had been entered into a ritzy dog show, but despite being buffed and perfumed, pulled like an elastic band and squashed like a doughnut, he and Mickey were hopelessly outclassed. Everything about the cartoon's vibrant jollity and rubbery invincibility was dramatically at odds with the chill formality of the assembled audience. The dog-loving Hitler gave himself up to loud, delighted laughter, but the reactions of the others were less fulsome. Robert Ley yawned. Goebbels wore a little sneering grin and his wife a stony glare. Rudolf Hess's face was a study in blank incomprehension.

The cartoon lasted nine minutes. Slightly shorter than her estimate. It was followed seamlessly by the trumpet fanfare and black and white spinning globe of the newsreel. The Ufa Ton-woche would contain, by Clara's reckoning, at least five items. It was narrated in the usual tone of high-pitched, hectoring excitability—both pessimism and reflection were frowned on in news reports—and began with footage of military exercises taking place near the Polish border. Row on row of marching men and tanks were followed by a camera panning towards a stack of newspapers pegged to a kiosk. WARSAW THREATENS BOMBARDMENT OF DANZIG. THREE GERMAN PASSENGER PLANES SHOT AT BY POLES. GERMAN FAMILIES FLEE POLISH MONSTERS. WHY IS GERMANY WAITING? The customary mob appeared, cheering and saluting. A country coaxing itself into a frenzy of adrenaline.

The next item was about the Ahnenerbe. Men in civilian dress were seen loading equipment into large trunks, and the screen filled with a map of the world, marked by arrows stab-bing towards South America. Following the Ahnenerbe's suc-cess in Tibet, another, even more expensive, jaunt was under way to Bolivia, on the assumption that Nordic colonists sailed there a million years earlier. The face of Doktor Kraus loomed onscreen, explaining that through a series of expeditions, ex-plorers would probe every corner of the earth to uncover music, folktales, even paintings, that testified to the ancient preemi-nence of the German race. Hitler removed his glasses and took out a handkerchief to clean them. Others shifted in their seats. The adventures of the Ahnenerbe might have captured Him-mler's imagination, but nobody else was quite so enthralled.

Eight minutes into the newsreel. Clara's hand beneath her jacket edged up the side of her dress. Her fingers eased the der-ringer from its holster and slipped it into her palm. It was small enough to remain entirely hidden beneath her hand. *When you want to use it, you move the hammer back to full-cock position and pull the trigger. If you misfire, you can pull the hammer back and try again. But there's only the chance for two shots. You can only make one mistake.*

Another twelve minutes to go.

The compilers of the newsreel always liked to mix in trivial items with the heavy news. It was a journalistic technique, Clara knew, called light and shade. The next item concerned a Hitler Youth marching band in Bremen that had won a national competition. The players were toting their instruments like rifles, notes clashing like swords in the air. The youngest were still in the Pimpf and could not have been more than ten years old. At the sight of the smooth, clean faces, shining with ardent pride, Hitler replaced his glasses and peered closely. Clara thought of Erich. What would he say to see her here, so close to his beloved Führer? And what would he think of her tomorrow? Would he ever forgive her?

A glance at her watch. Fifteen minutes in. Hitler belched and not a head turned.

The final item concerned Stalin reviewing his troops in Moscow. He stood on the viewing dais on the top of the Lenin Mausoleum alongside a row of Soviet top brass, Molotov, Andreyev, and the rest of the Politburo, breath frosting as they inspected a march in Red Square. Every cinemagoer in Germany was accustomed to regular news of Russia. And even those who never visited the cinema could not escape it in newspapers and endless political speeches. The Russians were Bolsheviks. Slavs dominated by Jew devils. Stalin was controlled by the Jewish world parasite. This report, however, was different. Startlingly different. The script was conspicuously neutral. The usual snide remarks were absent, and the cameras, usually angled to portray the podgy Stalin's least flattering aspect, provided a more appealing perspective. The smiling Soviet leader with his bristling mustache appeared reasonable, if not benevolent. Strong but fair.

In front of her, Hitler shifted in the gloom. He smoothed his hair with the side of his hand and leaned forward. Instinctively Clara tightened her grip on the gun beneath her palm, and slid her finger into the trigger. Hitler was speaking—far too softly for most to hear—but she caught his words.

"That man has a good face. One should be able to negotiate with him."

Then he rose abruptly and marched away without warning, prompting a scrape of chairs and a scramble of officers to their feet, a hurried clicking of heels and a raising of right arms as the Leibstandarte seamlessly opened the door and Hitler left the room.

For a second, a startled silence reigned. Then loud chatter broke out. The relaxation at being out of the Führer's presence, mingled with relief at being spared another film, sparked a feverish jollity. The lights went up. People pushed back their chairs and began to mingle. Others pulled out cigarettes and lit up greedily, the film forgotten.

Only Clara sat in silence. The significance of what she had just heard was dawning in her mind, drowning out the shock of her assassination attempt, so narrowly averted.

One should be able to negotiate with him.

Why was Hitler talking about negotiating with Stalin unless the rumors of a Nazi-Soviet pact were not rumors at all? Unless an alliance between the Third Reich and Stalin was already under way?

In which case Major Grand was wrong and British intelligence needed to know without delay.

CHAPTER

32

I T WAS NOW NINE FIFTEEN. DROPPING THE GUN INTO HER beaded evening bag, Clara slipped discreetly out of the Music Room and retraced her steps through the reception hall of the Reich Chancellery, across the road to the Kaiserhof Hotel. She headed towards one of the polished telephone cubicles at the back of the lobby, its bottom half enclosed and the top half glassed, closed the door, and pulled out the copy of *The Thirty-Nine Steps*, repeating to herself Thomas Epstein's instructions. Her heart was hammering and her breath coming in shallow gasps.

When you have a message to convey, find the words you want to use, select the page number, followed by the line, followed by the place that those words occur in the line.

She bent over the telephone directories as though searching for a number. Then, tearing out a page from her gilt-edged notebook and leafing quickly through the novel, she transcribed the words she needed.

Russia—page four, line seven and seven words along
Germany—page four, line seven, nine words along
Alliance—page four, line five, six words along
Very—page three, line three, two words along
Soon—page eight, line nine, first word along
    477, 479, 456, 332, 891
Russia Germany Alliance Very Soon

SHE ROLLED THE SCRAP of paper up to the size of a matchstick, inserting it horizontally deep in the bottom seam of her
jacket pocket. Then she bundled the novel back into her bag,
left the hotel, and turned right, to make her way quickly along
the Wilhelmstrasse.

BERLIN AT NIGHT WAS the photographic negative of Albert
Speer's pearl-white city. The pavements were drowned in a cre-
puscular gloom, interspersed with pools of dense shadow.
Barely any light issued from the office blocks that ran the
length of the government sector. The Air Ministry was a looming cliff of darkness, and blackout gauze had already been
erected on the Propaganda Ministry's windows. A few lights,
however, were still visible in von Ribbentrop's Foreign Ministry. Clearly its staff was working overtime.

Clara progressed north up Luisenstrasse, past the jagged
shadow of the Charité hospital, where Erich's grandmother
worked. In the courtyard she noticed one of the metal collection points—a pile of twisted saucepans and old tin cans destined for the Luftwaffe—and propping one foot against the
wall she snatched off the calfskin holster. She tossed it and the
derringer into the collection bin.

She hurried on as swiftly and inconspicuously as possible until a right turn along Torstrasse brought her to the Scheunenviertel, the Jewish quarter.

Fingering the matchstick of paper containing her code, she wondered if she would recognize Benno Kurtz when she saw him. *He's in his sixties, has a gray mustache. He was a good-looking fellow in his time, and he still thinks a lot of himself.* She would ask for a gin and tonic made in the English way—presumably nine tenths gin to one tenth tonic—and pay him with a banknote, the paper concealed beneath.

As she went she tried to remember what she could about the Ritze bar. It was, from what she could recall, as far from its Paris namesake as was possible to imagine. Its wallpaper, lit by a series of gas sconces, was mottled and peeling, and its hospitality extended to cheap chairs grouped round deal tables on a scuffed wooden floor. Yet the place was a Berlin institution, famed for its ancestry and the diversity of its celebrity clientele.

You didn't need to be rich to drink there—the glass "hunger tower" on the bar contained only humble delicacies like meat in aspic, bread dumplings, salted eggs, gherkins, and pickled herrings—yet it attracted celebrities as diverse as Bertolt Brecht and the cabaret singer Clara Waldoff, and the far less salubrious stars of the Berlin underworld. Its reputation had been formed in the Weimar era, when Berlin was a sexual Wild West, and that spirit lingered on in a variety of humorous signs taped behind the bar.

PROSTITUTION IS STRICTLY FORBIDDEN.
AT LEAST ACCORDING TO THE POLICE!

With a customer base like the Ritze had, no wonder it stayed open most of the night.

Five minutes later she turned in to Mulackstrasse and glimpsed the hanging iron lantern at the far end of the street illuminating the entrance of number 15. But as she did, she became aware of a car behind her, its headlamps glittering on the cobbles.

Listen for a car that moves either too fast or too slow.

There was no other vehicle in the street. No jam up ahead. No parked cars to overtake. Yet the car behind her was moving at walking speed. When she slowed slightly, to allow it to over-take her, the car slowed, too. She quickened her pace, and as in some devilish ballroom dance, it matched her. By now, Clara was just yards away from the hanging lantern of the bar. She guessed there were another twenty steps to go. Giving in to the urge to glance behind her, she saw the car come to a halt at the curb. It was a black Mercedes 260D with low-visibility head-lights. Regulation Gestapo transport. She began to move faster, the rapid thud of her feet on the paving echoing the accelerat-ing beat of her own heart. Three feet from the door of the Ritze she moved across the pavement to allow a man coming from the opposite direction to pass. Then, with a slow horror that seemed to freeze time, she sensed two people approach from behind, and the man in front of her came to a stop, clos-ing ranks to form a trio that surrounded her entirely. Fear winded her like a fist in the stomach.

The two officers behind slipped their arms through hers, as politely as if they had been rivals competing for a waltz, and led her towards the waiting car.

"I HOPE YOU WON'T MIND IF I DON'T ACCOMPANY YOU." Annie Krauss gestured slightly towards the velvet-covered table. "I am expecting a customer."

Baffled, Hedwig looked at Jochen. But he was already moving towards the far end of the house. He had obviously been here before, because he led the way through a kitchen to a door and then down a flight of narrow steps to a low-ceilinged cellar with bare walls. A single weak bulb illuminated a table holding a machine, several jars, and stacks of paper.

"What's going on? I thought we were going to have our fortunes told," Hedwig said.

He was sorting through a pile of papers on the table with his back to her. "I think mine's already decided."

Reality was dawning on Hedwig. Hard, unhappy reality. "This is about the people you were talking about, isn't it, Jochen? Are you going to tell me who they are?"

"I can't. None of us must know too much. They tell us to think of a stone thrown into a lake. The stone causes circles and then more circles that ripple out to the edges of the lake. We are in one of those circles."

We? How happy she would have been a week ago, whenever she heard Jochen use that word. How she longed to go back to that time, when her only worry was whether he preferred brunettes or blondes.

"And is Frau Krauss part of this?" she demanded, incredulously.

"Annie is a very valuable member of our group. She's well respected in her profession."

"Everyone knows that."

"Precisely."

His eyes were shining. "Everyone knows Annie Krauss, and that includes a lot of military men. Hard to believe, isn't it? But the fact is, they flock to her. They like to think Germany's destiny is dictated by the planets. Remember that quote from Shakespeare? They do teach you Shakespeare at that place?"

She nodded dumbly.

" 'The fault, dear Brutus, is not in our stars, but in ourselves.' These military men prefer to believe the fault for the Fatherland's problems lies in the stars rather than in themselves. Or in that ugly dictator in Wilhelmstrasse. Well, I'll tell you something. Recently they've been consulting Annie about Hitler's plans. They say he's fully intending to invade Poland. They ask, what should they do?"

Hedwig fought the impulse to turn tail and run up the stairs out of the house. "And what does she tell them?" she asked faintly.

"She tells them an invasion is a bad idea. The heavens are against them. But she doesn't say too much. She wants them to keep coming back. Every snippet of military detail they give away gets straight back to us."

Hedwig picked up one of the leaflets on the table. It took the form of a newspaper front page except that it was much smaller, six inches by ten, and printed on rough, mimeographed paper. A headline read, GERMANY AWAKE! WE ARE SLEEPWALKING INTO WAR! RESIST HITLER! and underneath was the subheading: WORKING FOR A NEW FREE GERMANY.

"Where do you leave these?"

"Public places: phone books, cafés, doctors' waiting rooms. We deliver them at night. We make flyers too. And documents. One of our people has a daughter in the Bund Deutscher Mädel. She takes them around wearing her uniform. It just looks like she's delivering copies of the BDM newspaper."

He gestured at the mantelpiece, where a bottle of cleaning fluid stood alongside a box of matches. "We keep these ready so we can burn them at a moment's notice if we get an unannounced visit."

Hedwig's mind was a blur, the words collapsing before her eyes into tiny heaps of soot.

GERMANY AWAKE! WE ARE SLEEPWALKING INTO WAR!

"So why did you bring me here?"

"I was coming to that."

He put the stack of papers down and perched on the edge of the table, arms folded, eyes locked on hers.

"That ball you're going to."

"The dance for the prince?"

"The whole idea of the evening is to persuade the Prince of Yugoslavia to just stand by while Hitler carves up Europe. There will be guests there from all over the world. Influential people from every country. They need to know that there's some kind of resistance in Germany—that we're not all on Hitler's side—and that if he's given carte blanche to invade

Poland, he won't stop there. The ball is a perfect chance. I have a friend there."

The way he said "friend" told her everything. There was an undercurrent of admiration. A whisper of enchantment.

"It's Sofie, isn't it? From the orchestra?"

"She plays in a string quartet that has been hired to perform at the ball. She will distribute the pamphlets."

"So what does that have to do with me?"

"You need do nothing more than take the pamphlets in. I'd do it myself, but there's no way they'd let me into the Schloss Bellevue."

Hoping against hope, she raised a protest. "What's the point? What good can reading a pamphlet do? It's just a piece of paper."

He was suddenly excited, impassioned. "Quite the opposite. Reading is everything—Goebbels knows that. It's why he controls what we Germans can read. He burns books and censors the newspapers, so people can't find any voices except his. We Germans have always been great readers. Literature is our life-blood. But Goebbels would rather people sat and watched variety shows or romantic films than lost themselves in books. He knows that if you control what a nation reads, you control their souls."

A terrible realization came upon Hedwig. Had Jochen only met her, had he only ever told her he loved her, because of what she might do for him? Had everything, from their first kiss onwards, been leading up to this?

She stared at him, a bright sheen of tears in her eyes, and summoned all her courage.

"Tell me truthfully. Is this why you were interested in me?"

He ducked his head to evade her gaze, running his finger up

and down the table as if the grain of the wood might spell out an answer. Then he stood up fully and put his hands on her shoulders. His gaze was frank and unflinching.

"It's true. Robert wanted me to get to know you."

"Robert Schultz?"

Her childhood friend. A local boy who would scuffle in the schoolyard with a football and whose tawny hair and good looks had sometimes earned him an admiring glance from Lottie Franke.

"Robert thought you might be useful to us."

"In that case . . ." Misery and hurt pride welled in her throat, but Jochen pressed his hands into her shoulders so hard it hurt and shook her a little.

"Stop. That may be why he introduced us, but that doesn't change how I feel. I love you, Hedy."

She felt a sudden ferocity, a churning mixture of anger and fear. She had always been the one longing for his affection, cravenly seeking his love, but now a new strength, born of bitterness, rose in her.

"If you loved me, you wouldn't ask me to do something as dangerous as this."

"I used to think that. But now I think it's *because* I love you that I want you to do it."

Was this what love meant? Being brave, taking risks? Living in fear? Hedwig remembered Lottie's face the last time she had seen her. Lottie was in love, and love had made her frightened, too.

"Have you gone mad, Jochen?"

"No. I think we're the only ones who are sane."

34

The Barminstrasse women's prison in Friedrichshain was generally crammed to the rafters, but following an amnesty to celebrate the Führer's birthday a large number of prisoners had been released in a spirit of joyful reconciliation, with the result that the place was emptier than usual and Clara had a cell to herself. The single bulb was kept on at all times, presumably for the purpose of sleep deprivation, but the light was failing miserably at its job, stuttering and blinking fitfully and casting only a purgatorial gloom around the narrow space. The window looked out onto a courtyard ten feet below. Previous prisoners had left their marks on the brickwork, a selection of clumsily scratched initials all that remained of their individual identities. Attached to one wall was a single wooden bench worn smooth. How many women had sat there before her, wondering what came next?

If the prison guards were surprised at the sight of a woman wearing a couture evening gown and diamond swastika arriving in their cells, they did not betray it. Nor had the men who arrested her been rough, but instead icily polite. There was no shoving or wrenching of hair, yet her wrists had been cuffed, making it impossible to remove the code paper from her pocket, and as soon as she arrived both jacket and bag had been taken away.

Clara was desperately tired. Her eyes were gritty, and exhaustion seeped upwards in her limbs, like a draft of sedative. Although she did everything she could to keep her mind alert, it was hard. From time to time she drifted into a light sleep, but she was jarred awake when her head hit the wall or by shouts and crying from the other cells. Most of the time she was shivering with cold. The window had no glass in it, only bars, and the flimsy silk evening gown was no protection against the freezing night air. A deep, unflagging terror settled in her guts, yet still she tried to focus through the fog of shock that engulfed her. She dropped her head to her knees, hoping that the blood coursing round her brain would help her to concentrate. It was as though she was solving some dreadful cryptic crossword puzzle, whose clues and half-formed suppositions spun around, split apart, and refused to come together in her brain.

How long had she been followed?

She knew now that the young man in the lobby of Winterfeldtstrasse was not a police tail but an illegal flyer poster, who also forged documents for Steffi's resistance group. Yet the instinct that she was under surveillance had continued for weeks, even on the day she had spent walking through the city. Had the Gestapo been shadowing her all this time? Had they followed her to Paris? And if so, what exactly did they suspect?

Somebody has been saying some very unkind things about you.

Leni Riefenstahl had told her Himmler had suspicions about

Clara's Aryan status. That meant right now they would be scrutinizing her identity documents. Despite the forger's skill, who was to say that the fake *Ariernachweis* would not be just as easily spotted as the one Conrad Adler had so expertly deconstructed? After all, the Gestapo had a string of fine arts specialists on their books, precisely for the task of examining documents. And yet . . .

Being apprehended for false identity was so much less grave than being arrested as a spy. The penalty for false identity was imprisonment, a camp perhaps. Please God that they suspected her only of being a Jew. Because to be convicted as a spy was far worse. But nothing so bad as if they suspected her of an attempt to kill the Führer. There was only one penalty for that.

She turned the problem over and over in her head, examining it like a jewel of many facets. Questions revolved in a dizzy, sickening whir. Would they have found the tiny scrap of paper that she had so carefully concealed deep in her jacket pocket? She remembered Steffi telling her that the Gestapo had become adept at ripping the linings of coats and jackets, running their fingers along the seams in the hunt for hidden valuables. If they found the paper, what importance might they place on it? Would they suspect Benno Kurtz? She was glad she had not actually had the chance to contact him before they took her away; if he was anything like as resourceful as he sounded, he would be able to bluff his way out. But what would it mean for Erich, and his hopes of SS leadership school, if his godmother was arrested as a spy? Tears stung her eyes. How betrayed he would feel!

Eventually, she gave up and ran through the store of images that, like a series of glittering stones, lit the path back to her own childhood. Her early theatrical career, the films she had acted in, coming to Berlin and meeting Helga Schmidt and

Erich. Loving Leo. In her head she played the adagio of Mozart's Clarinet Concerto, the one that Leo so cherished. He said it was the closest that music came to prayer. She teased out each note in her memory, forcing her limbs to relax into its yearning. She thought of the first time she had seen Erich, on an outing to the amusement park at Luna Park, and the following years, his voice breaking, his shoulders broadening, his life opening out before him.

Everything hung in the balance now. Her whole existence might soon be unstrung, like a necklace snipped and its pearls sent spiraling over the ground.

THE TABLE IN THE interrogation room was pocked with burns, sending the ominous message that the interrogators were far from cautious about where they stubbed out their cigarettes. A low cloud of tobacco smoke, acrid in the mouth like gasoline, hung in the air, barely troubled by the draft from an open window. The officer slouched in a chair with his legs crossed had an unhealthy, jaundiced look, as though he spent his life in the artificial glare of a Gestapo spotlight. His face might have been plucked straight from one of the cabinets at Himmler's Ahnenerbe, with skin stretched taut over the cadaverous cheekbones, pale scalp beneath his freshly shaved skull, and a yellowish tint of ivory to the eyes.

He rocked back in the chair when he saw her, and twisted his cigarette to join the others in the ashtray on his desk.

"Sit down, Fräulein Vine."

She wondered how senior he was. Not very, or he would have been at home asleep, rather than doing an interrogation night shift. The look of brute malice in his eyes seemed to confirm that.

"My name is Kriminalsekretär Riesbach."

Her guess was correct. He was relatively low-ranking, which made it all the more important that she gauge her responses carefully. There had been a rash of Ufa performers arrested recently, hauled in for questioning about activities detrimental to National Socialism. Their brash, actorly manner, their name dropping and threats, had only served to irritate the rank-and-file policemen, who treated them more harshly as a result.

"Perhaps you can explain why I'm here," she said quietly.

"I was rather hoping that you would explain that to me, Fraülein. But maybe you will need some encouragement."

"Could you tell me why I was arrested?"

Riesbach made a clumsy play of reasonableness, as though he had decided that because she was an actress, a degree of playacting was appropriate. He spread his hands. "Why not? A loyal patriot advised us that we should keep a watch on you, Fräulein Vine. From your file I see it's not the first time you have come to the attention of the authorities."

"That was a mistake. I was released immediately and without charge."

A frown descended on Riesbach's brutish features. He was pretending puzzlement. "Have you ever heard of the saying 'No smoke without fire'?"

"Yes. It's a common cliché."

"So what are we to make of this? Another arrest. Another patriot who believes you are engaged in actions against the well-being of the Reich."

"Actions?"

"Espionage, woman!" His face flushed, and his voice rose to an angry bark. "This patriot believes you may not be loyal to the Reich. That you may in fact be an English spy."

Stay calm. Don't react instinctively.

"That's an outrageous accusation."

Indignation and fear was the only correct response. The response of the innocent.

"I'm glad you see it like that. I feel the same. But then we found this."

With a flourish, he reached beneath the desk and pulled out a book, which Clara recognized as her copy of *The Thirty-Nine Steps*. She bit her lips to keep the color in them, in case they should have blanched with fear.

Riesbach opened the book carefully at the frontispiece, as though examining some precious, ancient manuscript.

"You can imagine my colleagues' excitement when they found an English novel which appears to belong to the library of the foreign minister. Unfortunately, when they telephoned the Herr Minister's home, only Frau von Ribbentrop could be found, and she was not pleased to be contacted in the middle of the night."

The figure of Frau von Ribbentrop in a dressing gown, summoned to the telephone to explain why an actress should be carrying one of her husband's books, would indeed be formidable. Clara could only imagine her response.

"My men decided to postpone their questions, for the time being at least."

So she had been saved. Saved by the foul temper of Annelies von Ribbentrop.

"But please don't think that our inquiries have ended there."

A twist of pure pleasure spread across Riesbach's face as, like an amateur magician, he produced an envelope and tipped it out on the table. It was Clara's tiny matchstick of paper, carefully unrolled to reveal the line of numbers. How foolish she had been even to hope it might escape them, or ever to underestimate their efficiency.

He poked at the paper with an extended finger. "I wonder what this might be?"

"I have no idea."

"Strange, when it was found in the pocket of your own jacket."

"I'm sorry. I'm very tired. I can't remember."

This was inadequate, but it was the only answer Clara could summon while her brain moved at lightning speed to explain away the code.

"A list of numbers. What should we deduce from that?"

"It's probably a telephone number. Fans pass me their numbers all the time. They push notes into my pockets."

"Good try, Fräulein. We called it already. Or tried to. That doesn't work."

"Then, I'm afraid . . ."

"Perhaps you need to take a closer look?"

As Clara bent to examine it, Riesbach moved abruptly forward, reached over, and swatted her upwards, across the face. The impact of the ring on his knuckle sliced the skin on her cheek. The blow took her by surprise, and she reeled backwards.

"Perhaps that will refresh your memory."

She straightened, her hand to her cheek, and replied curtly, "It hasn't."

"You're an actress, Fräulein. You're supposed to remember things. Another one might help."

A second blow, this time against her temple, making her ear ring and forcing her to clench her teeth.

"What innocent person walks around with a list of numbers in their pocket?" Riesbach demanded.

Clara decided to keep her head very still, as though facing an aggressive dog, in an attempt to forestall another attack. They had taken away her watch, but the clock on the wall opposite told her it was nearly 5:00 a.m.

"As I said, Inspector, people put things in my pockets all the time."

The door clanged, and another man entered the room. Although Clara did not turn, she could tell that he was senior by the way that Riesbach half rose, and out of the corner of her eye she saw the newcomer jerk his head abruptly and lean against the wall, arms folded.

"Carry on, Dieter."

Riesbach's tone modified, marginally, and took on an air of aggrieved bureaucracy. "I was asking the prisoner the significance of a list of numbers found on a piece of paper in her jacket. I felt——" The newcomer interrupted.

"The charges before you are extremely serious, Fräulein."

From what she could see the senior man had a hard face and a toothbrush mustache. His voice was more educated than Riesbach's, exuding the deep tedium of the early hours.

"Charges?"

"Allegations, precisely. The charges will come later. You need to talk to us. One way or another, we are going to require some answers."

Clara continued staring rigidly at the clock. In her sleeveless evening dress her flesh rose in goosebumps, but shivering would look like fear. She wrapped her arms round her in an attempt to keep warm.

"Not cooperating is not going to help you, Fräulein Vine." The senior man's tone said he was bored, his civility in short supply.

"Playing dumb might work at the Ufa studios, but it won't work here."

"I have cooperated in every way."

"Fine." He scraped a chair by its legs across the room and brought it right next to her, his face so close that she could feel his breath on her cheek. He smelled of tobacco and good aftershave.

"Perhaps you think I'm a little stupid."

"Not at all."

"Only, as Kriminalsekretär Riesbach says, we are puzzled by this piece of paper that was found in the pocket of your evening jacket. Dieter, can you fetch the jacket?"

"No need. The paper's right there."

"I said fetch the Fräulein's jacket."

Sullenly, Riesbach got to his feet and left the room. As he did, the tall officer rose swiftly and moved to the door. He pulled it shut, brought a chair up to Clara, and put his face even closer to hers. Forcing herself to look at him, she saw two different eyes. One brown, one blue.

Such a distinguishing feature would make undercover work impossible.

That was what she had thought when she passed a man in the corridor of Section D in London. Could it be that the same man, with his narrow, tawny mustache and mismatched eyes, was standing right in front of her? Could a man trained in the depths of British intelligence have been transplanted to the Gestapo in Berlin?

As if to confirm it, he spoke in English, very quietly.

"I'm going to get you out of this. Go quickly. Find somewhere to stay out of sight. If my senior officials object, there's every chance you will be picked up again."

Clara couldn't move. She was paralyzed with fear. "Who informed on me?"

His voice was so low she could barely catch it. "It must have been someone close to you. I heard Dieter say it was the last person he would have suspected. Now *go*."

As she rose, the door clanged open and Riesbach returned, Clara's jacket suspended like a rag from his fist. Springing to his feet, the senior officer snatched it from him, tossed it across the desk to her, and turned to his colleague with an expression of barely suppressed fury.

"For Christ's sake, Dieter! All your talk of codes. One look at this and I can tell the lady is plainly innocent. Did you even bother to examine this nonsense?" He picked up the paper and held it tauntingly in front of his baffled colleague before screwing it into a ball and tossing it out of the window.

"Have you never seen a line of Reichslotterie numbers in your life?"

35

DAWN HAD BROKEN. A SHEET OF CLOUDS WAS PULLED across the sky, lanced with sunlight that left them pearlescent and marbled as mother-of-pearl. Early workers were beginning to arrive at the textile factories and whistles were sounding. A horse-drawn milk cart was making its rounds, awaited by hausfraus toting capacious blue cans for their deliveries, and the first queues for bread and groceries were beginning to form. Here in the east, Albert Speer's construction work was well under way. Blocks of houses were being razed, the dust blooming into the air. Twisted metal and hunks of mortar lay alongside pathetic domestic debris: a stray kitchen sink, a banister, a wardrobe mirror, a cot. Everywhere, it seemed, life had been turned inside out. What was previously concealed was now on full display.

Clara wiped the wound on her cheek where Riesbach had hit her and tasted metallic blood on her finger, but she barely registered the injury. Her mind was racing. Who had betrayed her?

I heard Dieter say it was the last person he would have suspected.

Was that because the informant was the wife of a senior government minister? Had Magda Goebbels reported her, out of a mistaken paranoia that Clara had slept with her husband? Or, more likely, had Conrad Adler decided to punish her, merely because she refused to become his mistress?

Although the Gestapo officer had warned her to stay out of sight, she had no idea where to go. She had no desire to return to Griebnitzsee, nor would she dream of seeking shelter with Erich and his grandmother in Neukölln. For a moment she contemplated visiting the Adlon and finding refuge in Mary's room before remembering that Mary would be on her way to London by now. And that she badly needed a change of clothes. Clara decided to return to her old apartment in Winterfeldtstrasse and seek at least temporary sanctuary while she worked out what to do next.

In Nollendorfplatz, early-morning commuters were already streaming into the station with its high glass dome, the red and yellow trains clanking along the elevated section. Clara walked swiftly along Potsdamer Strasse, but as she turned the corner into Winterfeldtstrasse, a figure stepped out of the shadow of a recessed doorway.

"Do you have a death wish?"

Conrad Adler was still in the suit he had worn the previous evening at the Führer's film night. His coat was draped over his shoulders, and by the look of it, he had not slept all night. His face was shadowed with stubble and his eyes bloodshot.

He gripped her roughly by the arm and pushed her back into the porch, away from the road.

"You're a damn fool, coming back here."

Anger rose in her. Fury at the treacherous sexual attraction she had felt for this man who, if her suspicions were correct, was prepared at a moment's notice to consign her to a horrible fate.

"I'm a fool ever to have listened to a word you said. I expect you're wondering why I'm walking the street, considering you handed my name to the Gestapo. You were hoping I'd be sitting in Prinz-Albrecht-Strasse by now."

As if on cue a car proceeded slowly up the street and pulled to a stop farther along the road opposite Clara's apartment. The engine died, but no one got out. Adler pulled Clara closer into his arms. In their evening clothes they resembled a pair of lovers who couldn't bring themselves to separate after dancing until dawn. His face was just inches from hers, and she detected his shock at the purpling slash on her cheek.

"You don't know what you're talking about."

"I was informed on and arrested. I know the informer was you."

"That's absurd. Why would I have you arrested?"

"There's no telling what someone like you would do."

"Someone like me?"

"Magda Goebbels told me someone was spreading rumors about me. You must think I'm naïve. Listening to your talk, having dinner with you, riding with you, when all the time you're working for Heydrich."

"What makes you say that?"

"Leni Riefenstahl overheard you and Heydrich discussing me."

Adler's grip on Clara loosened slightly. Outwardly, he was composed, but his eyes were alive, calculating.

"I can't deny that I have undertaken some work for Heydrich. But I promise you, Clara, for what it's worth, I have not informed on you. I knew nothing whatever about you until we met on the night of the Führer's birthday."

"So how did you know where to find me now?"

"Goebbels insisted I attend that goddamn film evening. He had the nerve to suggest I might find it educational. When you left the Chancellery in a hurry, I followed you. I saw you being picked up. Later I inquired at the police station and was surprised to discover you had been released. I guessed you might head for your old apartment."

"And how did you know this address?"

"I'm a bureaucrat, Clara, remember? I told you I did my research."

He reached his coat round so that it draped over both their shoulders, and arm in arm they turned back down the street.

"My car is parked round the corner. From the looks of it, you might need a change of plan."

ADLER'S LAKESIDE VILLA WAS the epitome of good taste. Its shutters were painted a buttery yellow and it was framed by magnificent *Blutbuchen*—blood-red beech trees that flamed against the sky. At eight in the morning the air was fresh and still. As she climbed out of Adler's car, Clara would not have been surprised to find a servant at the porticoed entrance, but it was Adler himself who pushed open the door and ushered her inside.

Even from the outside, she could never have guessed at the sumptuousness revealed within. Everything spoke of long, deeply established wealth. The thick carpet and the carved, mahogany banister. The walls lined with ivory silk and the table bearing a bowl of white roses and a platter of fruit. Even the light felt expensive in this room, pale, lemony sun gilding the burnished wood, glancing off the oak paneling, and illuminating the paintings, row on row of them, hung in frames of clotted gold.

A dog came to greet them, a silvery Weimaraner with a coat like polished steel, his body highly sprung, lithe and muscular like the precise canine equivalent of his owner. The dog's eyes were piercingly pale and amber-colored, his spine undulating beneath the pelt. When he came to a stop next to his master, the tendons on his legs stood out like strings on a bow, and Adler placed a tender, proprietorial hand on him.

"Most hunting dogs have an unrivaled instinct for prey, but this one is an exception. He doesn't like to run with the pack. He's a very individual animal. He goes where he pleases."

As if in demonstration, the dog trotted off again.

"Wait here," Adler commanded.

He disappeared down a corridor and Clara heard the distant clink of china. In his absence she looked around her. There was a rolltop desk in the corner on which stood an SS-issue Olympia typewriter, specially fitted with its double lightning flash key. There was a stack of official looking papers beside it, a tortoiseshell inkstand, and a brass reading lamp. A glass paperweight like a teardrop, inside which a flower was imprisoned. And the tooled Cartier box containing the diamond earrings she had refused.

She drifted across to the paintings, gleaming like gems in their polished settings, their pigments almost alive. They were portraits mostly, ordinary seventeenth-century citizens gazing out at the viewer with inscrutable eyes, enclosed in a soft glow of shining domesticity. The men were playing cards or the lute, and the women were immersed in the simplest of tasks— stitching, pouring milk, reading letters.

"The Dutch Golden Age," said Adler, over her shoulder. She turned. He was carrying a tray bearing coffee, rolls, and a bottle of cognac. He proceeded to pour a glass and handed it to her.

"Northern European realism is my greatest love. It was a time when artists moved away from religious painting to the detail of their own lives. Vermeer, of course, is the master."

He swirled the cognac around in his glass, then swallowed it.

"It troubles me that Hitler should love Vermeer. Does it devalue the art, do you think, when evil people love it?"

Clara looked up sharply. She had no idea where this was heading.

"Perhaps Hitler approves of seeing women in a domestic setting," he mused. "Maybe he thinks the paintings express some time-honored concept of Germanic tradition. Whatever his notion, he obviously has no real idea of what Vermeer is about. Nor have any of them."

He continued to fix her with an odd, speculative look.

"I ask myself, is Wagner's music less ravishing because it is adored by a sadist like Himmler? Is a Vivaldi concerto as beautiful when it is played by a psychopath like Heydrich? Does a vicious thug like Goering sully the Titians and Rubenses he professes to adore?"

Adler's eyes were intently on her own, as though his life depended on her answer. "What do you think? Tell me, Clara. It's a question that torments me."

"Of course not. An object can't be accountable for who loves it, any more than a person can."

"I'm glad you think that. Because that's their crime as far as I'm concerned. It matters far more to me than their politics or their ambitions. I'm not a political man. In my opinion Germany is the greatest nation on earth, and she deserves her empire. No empire is achieved without the spilling of blood. But these men have committed a crime against civilization. They have no respect for Art, no true understanding of it. Art is a commodity to them, like iron or steel. The masterpieces they squabble over are pearls before swine. Goering, that fat sentimentalist, may profess some scintilla of cultivation, but he's no better than a greedy child running his fingers through a jewelry box, picking out the biggest, most glittering stones. Hitler is a peasant, and has a peasant's appreciation of Art. Goebbels may have the wit to perceive, dimly, the value of some work, but he has become a vandal. You heard about the bonfire? Four thousand artworks? Irreplaceable. All in an attempt to impress the Führer."

"And how do you propose to stop them? By advising Rosenberg on which works are the most valuable?"

If this barb struck home, Adler barely flinched. He seemed distracted, as if some long-suppressed confidence was now tumbling unstoppably out of him. He refilled her glass.

"I've never spoken about this before. Or only once, and that was during my stay in London. I was with a man from British intelligence, as it happens."

A tremor went through her, and she hoped that his sharp eyes had not detected it.

"Why would you meet with British intelligence?"

"It wasn't my idea. A colleague named Erich Kordt, one of von Ribbentrop's entourage, had put feelers out. Kordt's an Oxford man and a convinced Anglophile, and he engineered a meeting. The fellow I met seemed to think I would want to work with them. He told me I was too intelligent not to."

"And what did you say?"

"He was right, of course, about my intelligence. It's impossible to avoid the fact that the National Socialists are by and large a group of ignorant thugs. There's no real intellect among them. Cunning perhaps, in the case of Goebbels, but a notable lack of brain cells elsewhere. That's why Frau von Ribbentrop is so dangerous. Annelies has all the intelligence her husband lacks. I often wonder what she suspects of me."

It was very still in the villa. Only the distant ripple of bird-song pierced the air.

"So . . . did you accept his offer?"

"Of course not."

The anguish left his face, and he gave a dazzling smile. "What a suggestion, Clara! Can you imagine the penalties for that kind of thing? In fact, Kordt must be a quivering wreck now, imagining that I will report him, but so far I haven't felt the need to tell anyone."

He cast his evening jacket aside and wrenched off his tie.

"Eat something, won't you?"

She took a roll, helping herself to the thick pat of butter and wondering where it came from.

He scrutinized her as she ate. "Are you tired?"

"I think nerves are keeping me awake."

He came in front of her, touched the abrasion on her cheek left by Riesbach's ring, and turned over her wrists to reveal where the handcuffs had left sore red bracelets of skin. Then, to her astonishment, he bent and kissed them.

"I can't imagine what they did to you in that prison. I would like to kill the brutes who put their clumsy hands on you. Do you want to sleep?"

"I'm not sure if I could."

"In that case, we'll have to decide what to do with you."

She gazed at him directly. The air between them seemed to shimmer with expectation.

"Do with me? What do you mean?"

A small smile lifted up the corners of his mouth. "There's something you should see."

He pulled her towards a door. Inside was a small window-less, wood-paneled room, like the chapter house of some medieval castle. The burnished walls were hung floor to ceiling with paintings, every surface covered and canvases stacked two or three deep. Yet it was not the number of canvases that surprised her but the paintings themselves. They were portraits mostly, almost all of them women. An ocher nude of a woman reclining in a posture of luxuriant abandon. Another woman, her neck sharply turned away, skin pale and luminous as a pearl. A couple, clinging to each other in the wreckage of a world, unsettled and utterly alone, both fascinating and repelling. The figures were spiky and angry and their quality intense and stunning, unlike anything she had seen before. Adler's personality flared out of them savagely, in bold brushstrokes and angular lines.

"I come in here when I need to escape. Whenever I have attended meetings with Heydrich or wasted my time with von Ribbentrop, I know that I can return here and shut myself away. I find it useful to immerse myself in Art. It cuts me off from the ugliness of everyday existence."

In one portrait she recognized something. A pose from her film *The Pilot's Wife*. The girl in the picture was Clara, but as she had never seen herself, caught in a few deft strokes, a figure whose stark lines and angular intensity reminded her of Egon Schiele.

"Why keep these pictures secret?"

"Isn't it obvious? Mine's a dangerous art. It's what those barbarians would call Degenerate. Hitler fears us, and I understand why. Modernists are angry and self-loathing. We paint

our own crisis of spirit. Our work emits the scent of our uncon-
scious. The Nazis want art that's full of sunlight and pure
maidens, whereas we see man the way he is—flawed, miserable, ignoble, compromised."

"You didn't tell me you were an artist."

"I was at the Berlin School of Arts when the Gestapo moved
in in 'thirty-three. I remember staring out of an upper window
when they took all the Modernist work down to the courtyard
and destroyed it. I knew then I had a choice—I could be like
Emil Nolde; change my style, stick to insipid watercolors and
pastorals. I could be like Otto Dix and agree to paint family
portraits of the von Ribbentrops and their fat children. Or I
could hide in plain sight. I think that's what they call it. I could
wear their colors, like that little hare I told you about in the
fields back home. I would focus on the old masters and allow
everyone to believe I had abandoned my own work."

"There was another alternative."

He frowned. "And what would that be?"

"You didn't have to become involved with these barbarians.
Nobody forced you to advise them on which masterpieces to
steal."

"I told you: I'm not political."

"You didn't have to work with them. To stand by while they
ride roughshod over every law and civil right. While they arrest
and murder thousands of their own citizens. You could have left
the country."

"You think I should have run away?"

"You're already running away. You're hiding from everything the Nazis represent. You shut yourself in here and pretend the world outside doesn't exist. That you don't bear some
responsibility for it."

"But my dear Clara, it was my responsibilities that kept me

here. There was the estate to look after. That's my patrimony, you understand. The von Adlers have lived in Weimar for generations. It was unthinkable. No, I knew my passion must be concealed. You see"—he gave a quick, sharp glance at Clara, brimming with meaning—"concealed passions are nothing new for me."

He moved towards her, easing his fingers through her hair, pulling it away from her head so that it kindled against the light and revealing the side of her neck.

"I love the place where the skin is translucent and you see the blood beneath," he murmured. "It's like seeing through you."

She felt desire quicken in him, his breath hot on her skin. She said: "You don't want me, Conrad."

He drew back, his perfect face clouded with incomprehension. "Why not? That would be particularly irrational, and whatever else you know about me, you know I am a rational man. Besides, I like you."

"You said human emotions were entirely untrustworthy."

"Perhaps I'm coming round to them."

There was barely any room to move in the contained space. Running his hands down her shoulders, he eased the straps of the evening dress from her shoulders, so that it fell from her and lay in a puddle of silk at her feet. Then he drew her towards him and kissed her.

Just for a moment she gave in to him, then she pulled herself free. He laughed and spread his hands. "Very well then. First things first. I also want to paint you."

SHE SAT FOR HIM in the drawing room beside a wall of Delft tiles, bathed in the pure light coming in from the lake. As his hands moved across the paper, Clara felt his eyes sweep over her, taking in every detail of her coloring and complexion, right down to the dusting of freckles on her nose and the flecks of darker blue in the irises of her eyes. It was the type of close attention that would serve a policeman well, but in Adler the appraisal seemed entirely nonjudgmental, as though he was simply evaluating her living flesh, assessing her proportions.

"I still want to know. Why were you in Paris, if you were not following me?"

A distracted shrug. "I told you. I was advising on a collection."

"For Goering or for Hitler?"

"Clara Vine, this persistent line of questioning does not suit you. Especially when you should be grateful to me."

"Grateful to *you*? Why?"

He sighed, and threw down his pencil. "All right. I'll tell you."

Reaching behind him he found an old shirt, daubed with paint, which he tossed towards her. Instantly, she covered herself up.

"It's true, Goering and Hitler are engaged in a race. Their intention is to carry off every piece of art they desire to the Reich. But my business in Paris was something quite different. You see, when I first met you I recognized your name."

"That's not entirely unusual for me, though it might be hard for you to understand."

"Be patient, woman. Let me explain. When you asked me what I was doing in Paris, I told you I was advising on a collection. I have allowed you to think that collection was one of paintings. But it wasn't. It was names. And when I first met you, it wasn't your Christian name I recognized."

"You'd heard of my father? That's no surprise."

"Perhaps I should explain what I was advising on and why. Shortly after I returned from England, Reinhard Heydrich contacted me. To say it was a surprise is an understatement. A call from Heydrich is not the kind of invitation you put on the mantelpiece. But I went along to his office in Prinz-Albrecht-Strasse and saw to my dismay that he had my file open before him on the desk. Always a bad sign."

What had Leni Riefenstahl said? *In Heydrich's mind, information is power. He has a locked safe that he refers to as his "poison cabinet," where he keeps all his files on the senior men.*

"But contrary to my expectations, he began to compliment me on my memory."

"Do you have a good memory?"

"Exceptional, actually. I'm a freak of Nature. When I was a child it was called an eidetic memory because I could recall images and objects with high precision. Even the minutest details. It's declined a little with age, but it is a talent all the same, and it was that talent Heydrich wanted. He knew I'd spent two years mingling with British society, reading British newspapers, meeting British aristocrats, politicians, and writers. He pointed out that my enthusiasm for that country was flagged in my file as a warning. There had been fears that I intended to make London my home. Suggestions I preferred the British way to life in the Reich." A gruff chuckle. "I was able to reassure him on that score."

He glanced out of the window at the splendor of the gardens beyond. "Who would forsake somewhere like this in a hurry?"

"So what did Heydrich want?" Clara prompted.

"He told me something in deep confidence. It wasn't a confidence I wanted, but once I had it, I was bound by it. Heydrich knew he had me captive simply by telling me his plans. Isn't that how it works with secrets? Once you know them, you're trapped.

"Heydrich is creating what he calls his Black Book. A collection of all the most significant enemies of National Socialism in Great Britain."

"You mean, in case of invasion?"

"Should his plans go ahead. Ultimately his deputy, Walter Schellenberg, will be in charge of this operation. Schellenberg is chief of Amt VI—that's the foreign intelligence branch of the SD, but in the meantime Heydrich wanted my advice. I'd spent two years immersed in British society, so I was perfectly placed."

His gaze was distant, as though he was seeing far beyond the boundaries of the Reich to England, and all the people and parties and places he had once enjoyed.

"Take your film about the Ahnenerbe, Clara. Germans traveling the globe, studying different societies. Well, what Heydrich wanted from me wasn't so different. He has compiled a picture of British society, made up of not old bones and skulls but names. On that day in his office he gave me his Black Book. He asked me to provide notes on which of the names inside it were friendly to the National Socialist government and who might prove hostile."

"How many names?"

"Two thousand, eight hundred, to be precise. Both British subjects and European exiles, who are to be arrested or taken into protective custody in the event of a successful German invasion. The people deemed enemies will be arrested immediately. Churchill. Eden. Duff Cooper. They'll be seized within days. Churchill will be placed in the hands of Foreign Intelli-

gence. The rest will be turned over to the Gestapo for imprisonment. The others, lower down, will merely be put on trial."

"Who are they?"

"I recognized most of them immediately. H. G. Wells, Vir-
ginia Woolf, Noël Coward, E. M. Forster, Aldous Huxley, Ste-
phen Spender, Sigmund Freud, Rebecca West. And when I
heard your name, I recognized it too."

"But . . . my father has been a fervent supporter of the National Socialists for years. It's well known. He was a Nazi sym-
pathizer right from the beginning. It would be absurd to arrest
my father!"

"I'm not talking about your father."

Adler walked across to the rolltop desk and felt in the top
drawer. He retrieved a photograph of a woman, cut from the
pages of a magazine—*The Tatler* it looked like. She was in evening clothes with a mink stole around her shoulders. Her hair
was neatly pinned in a chignon, her eyebrows lifting slightly, as
if in surprise.

"This is your sister, I believe."

Angela.

CHAPTER

36

"I HEARD YOUR SISTER WAS IN PARIS, SO I MADE A QUICK visit. That was why I was there that night at the Dingo Bar. I was eager to see if what I had been told about her was true."

Clara gave a sharp laugh of disgust.

"If Heydrich has my sister's name in his Black Book, then that's proof he has absolutely no idea about English society. My sister was a founding member of the Anglo-German Fellowship. She and my father held the earliest meetings at our family home. Her entire life is devoted to fundraising in support of closer ties between Germany and Britain. You couldn't find a more devoted admirer of the Nazi cause than Angela."

"Or a more deceptive one."

She stared at him. Tiny fragments of thought were glinting in her mind, like diamonds in rubble. The image of the maid at the door of Elizabeth Street. *She's visiting her sister.* Dolly Capel in Dingo's bar. *I thought you were with her.* What reason could her sister have for visiting Paris? Unless it was true that Angela concealed as great a secret as Clara herself.

Turning to the rolltop desk again, Adler took a piece of paper from a sheaf and read aloud.

"My inquiries in London, and later, confirm my view that Angela Vine is an agent of the British intelligence service, working undercover to infiltrate German-sympathizing factions within the British establishment."

"That's impossible."

He continued reading. "She has held these views from the early days of the Reich. She reports on the activities of Nazi sympathizers to the British government. More recently she has been liaising with agents in Paris to assist resistance in the event of a German invasion."

"But I . . ."

"You what? You never suspected that your sister had a talent to deceive?"

"If it's true, why did I never guess?"

"Presumably that's the idea."

"I should have, though. I've known her all my life."

"That's probably the point. You were too close. You could never get perspective."

"I can't believe you would give my sister's name to the Gestapo."

"I didn't produce these names. I was merely asked for my opinion. What these men and women stand for. Who they are and what they believe in."

"Your opinion will be their death warrant."

"They are known opponents of the Reich, and in the event of invasion their fate is unavoidable."

"So you'd happily line them up for a firing squad!"

"Not happily."

He walked over to the window and surveyed the patterned box hedges dividing the flower garden and the crystalline purity of the lake beyond. A man was raking the lawn, and Clara saw that it was Karl, the groom from the Reitclub Grunewald.

"Happiness is not something I expect, Clara. I never have. I always assumed that one needs to learn happiness early, like a foreign language. If it comes too late, you can never properly be fluent. You'll never understand its inflections. I don't think I'll ever know what it is to be happy."

He turned round. "Does he make you happy? This unmarried man who is so intriguingly absent from your life?"

"Yes."

"Is he coming back to you?"

"I choose to believe so."

"So Love gives you faith, does it? Faith's a pretty poor substitute for real life, Clara. Look at that picture there." He pointed to a portrait of Venus being pursued by Adonis, prettily depicted in glinting oils. "They're imprisoned like that forever. They never fade, but they never kiss. They exist in an eternity of yearning. Is that what you want?"

"Who cares what I want? What does it matter?"

"You're right, of course. But it matters to me because I have a proposition for you."

"I already said . . ."

"Hush." He put his fingers to her lips, then smoothed the hair from her temples and rubbed a strand of it between his fingers, as though it was silk. The way he was looking at her had changed now. He was no longer the painter, examining his subject, but a man savoring something precious, like a jewel.

"War is coming soon between our two countries. Hitler has already breached the terms of the Munich treaty. I've read documents demonstrating the enormous superiority of Germany's air force over those of Britain and France. I've played a small part in the preparations myself, so I can scarcely claim innocence. But you, Clara, will be in a difficult position. A woman who is half English, and hiding her Jewish identity. You've just spent the night in a prison cell. What could be safer than marriage to a senior member of the Party?"

"Marriage?"

"You'd have to go through the selection procedure, of course, for marrying into the SS. There's a questionnaire, with preposterous queries about whether you like cosmetics and perfume. Whether you smoke."

"As you've already noticed, I would hardly pass the Aryanization tests."

"I'm sure that can be arranged. You have blue eyes, which is good, even if they're flawed with something darker. And besides, we Nazis are not the only ones who are good at faking our identity. If we can invent a cultural heritage, why shouldn't you?"

Still, she was staring at him in astonishment.

"Don't look at me like that. It's as though no one has ever asked you to marry them before."

"And you look like no one's ever refused you. I don't love you, Conrad. That must be obvious."

"I'm not asking you to love me. I wouldn't presume to think that affection was involved. On your side at least. I merely suggest it as a strategy you might find useful. An alliance if you like, between interested parties."

"You deserve more."

"I'll be the judge of what I deserve."

He turned his attention to a Dutch interior on the wall. It was of a young girl sewing, with a dreamy look on her face and light from a window filtering through the glossy web of her hair.

"Vermeer's wife was Catholic, did you know? That was illegal in seventeenth-century Holland. So by marrying her Vermeer was making a secretive alliance. I like the idea of that. Making our own alliance. You would be safe under my protection, and I wouldn't deny you your freedom. You could come and go as you choose, but I would suggest that, at least for a while, we move to my estate at Weimar. It is, my darling, one of the loveliest parts of Germany. Not only the home of Goethe and Schiller, but it also boasts the most beautiful woodland, the lovely forest of Ettersberg."

The way he was discussing it, it was as though she had already agreed. For a moment, the exhaustion of a night without sleep overcame her and Clara allowed herself to contemplate his proposal. Would it be so bad, this loveless marriage? Reporting for her *Rasse Merkmale*, her racial characteristics assessment, where she would be examined, weighed, and have her upper lip measured? It would need only be a temporary measure. It would mean she could stay in Germany with a safe cover for her work. More important, she could stay close to Erich.

Adler watched these thoughts travel across her face, and his voice dipped.

"Don't you ever get lonely, in that house out at Griebnitzsee, eating your solitary dinner? Don't you ever long for some intellectual companionship as barbarity descends?"

"Are you seriously suggesting that you would marry me just to keep me from arrest?"

"That wouldn't be my only motivation, but it might be yours."

"So a short-term marriage of convenience?"

"I think that's the phrase. That's one thing I've always admired the French for—their approach to affairs of the heart. They have none of the dull Protestant rigidity that afflicts us Germans, and the British too. The French understand that human passions come in many forms."

She shook her head. "It would be living a lie."

"Aren't we all living a lie? You have, I assume, sworn an oath to the Führer as a condition of your employment at Ufa?"

He was right. Whatever Goebbels said about big lies being needed to convince people, life in Nazi Germany was full of little, everyday lies. What would one more matter?

Adler smiled down at her, a rare trace of tenderness softening the perfect lines of his face as if he were a statue momentarily blurred by rain. "Besides, there would be honesty between us. Sometimes the most unlikely partners come together for mutually beneficial reasons. That's an idea being actively propounded in my old Foreign Office workplace just now."

She was instantly alert. "You're talking about the Soviet Union."

"An alliance between Germany and Russia is coming any day."

"How do you know?"

"You'd shown such an interest that I took the opportunity to catch up with Frau von Ribbentrop. She loves to confide in me. Perhaps she thinks, because I share her interest in old masters, I must share her other views. I raised the subject with her."

"And she told you?"

"Something she shouldn't have. But she couldn't resist. She knew I would understand why. It's a personal triumph for her, you see, although the world will never realize it. All those years of hostility, that long-nurtured hatred of the English, has finally born fruit. What is that saying? *Hell hath no fury like a woman scorned.* The way they laughed at her in London. Mocked her pretensions. Ridiculed her husband's infatuations. It hurts, being laughed at. It leaves a lasting legacy. Now Britain will reap the consequences. Annelies showed me something actually. Perhaps you'd like to take a look."

He picked out a piece of paper and handed it to her casually. At the top it bore the eagle and swastika, the official stamp of the Foreign Ministry, and beneath it von Ribbentrop's personal seal, featuring his family coat of arms. Clara scanned it, trying to accustom her eyes to the dense Gothic script.

Reich Ministry for Foreign Affairs: Top Secret

OPERATION WHITE
OPERATIONAL ORDERS FOR
THE INVASION OF POLAND

Issued by German Military High Command

"Von Ribbentrop is shortly to fly to Moscow to negotiate a nonaggression pact," said Adler. "The Soviet Union and Germany will join arms and carve up Poland between them."

Clara's eyes raced to the final paragraph of the directive.

PREPARATIONS MUST BE MADE IN SUCH A WAY
THAT THE OPERATION CAN BE CARRIED OUT AT ANY
TIME FROM 1ST SEPTEMBER 1939 ONWARDS.
BY COMMAND OF THE FÜHRER.

Heil Hitler!

Adler watched as she absorbed it. Musingly he said, "Curious, isn't it, how important a scrap of paper can be? We Germans place such childish faith in what is written. We surround ourselves with minutes, directives, cultural audits, requisition orders. Invasion plans. We document everything. It's as though, once something is committed to paper, everything that follows is legitimate."

"September first? So they've set a date."

"And now you're wondering when you can alert your sister." He plucked the paper from her hands. "But you mustn't. If they find out that I've shown you this, they'll take a very dim view of me. Showing top secret ministry documents to actresses is probably worse than showing them my portraits."

Clara looked up at him soberly. "If I married you, would you take Angela's name off your list?"

"Yes."

"How can I trust you?"

He was entirely unmoving, his face tense and still, his eyes shining with some unexpressed emotion.

"You can't. None of us can trust each other. That's the message of this murderous brigade. They show us the true face of humanity. They may try to stamp out reality by destroying paintings, but who needs paintings when we have ourselves to look at? Besides, if you want to understand human nature, we still have the old masters. Brueghel's a good start. I recommend him."

He drew her towards him, and she felt the fight go out of her. His body felt hard and solid, like a pillar, and she was so tired.

"I need time to think . . ."

"Time, I'm afraid, is one thing we don't have. Let me explain. While I was in Paris, I met an American. That's not unusual; Paris right now is crammed with Americans trawling for any booty on offer, but this man was different. He offered me a job at the Metropolitan Museum of Art. It would be a dream of a job. I would be an expert by day and a painter by night. You mentioned the idea of running away, and I admit I am coming round to it. I'm forty-four, Clara. I'm the last of my line. I have no parents, no wife, no children. Nothing to lose. In a couple of weeks the doors will slam shut and my chances of leaving will be gone. So I need your answer quite soon."

He wrenched her face up by the chin and kissed her, a thick, greedy kiss.

"Accept me, Clara. You'd be insane not to."

Still that arrogance, that patrician confidence, the disbelief that he might be refused.

She almost loved him for it.

"THEY BUILT THIS PLACE WHEN WE HAD OUR FIRST colonies. The plan was to collect exotic plants from German territories all over the world and bring them back to Berlin. Think about that. The entire German empire in a garden."

They were walking along a gravel path through the lush borders of the Botanical Garden, a short ride on the S-Bahn to the southwestern borough of Steglitz. The garden was the city's green jewel, an oasis of greenhouses, intersected by streams crossed by small bridges and stepping-stones, with meadow areas and formally laid parterres set behind high, unprepossessing walls. It was a favorite outing for Berliners, and even more for Hedwig and Jochen because it was where they first met.

It was more than a year ago, on a rare Saturday when Hedwig was not in classes at the Faith and Beauty school. She had taken a book with her to the Botanical Garden, but the book was only a prop because what she actually wanted was to sit beside the decorative lake beneath a monkey puzzle tree and imagine that she lived there. She loved the garden, partly because it was situated as far from Moabit as was possible in Berlin, and partly because being there allowed her to indulge her fantasy of being a Hohenzollern princess living in elegant splendor, rather than in a dank tenement with washing hanging in the courtyard.

But that day her fantasy was interrupted by Robert Schultz, an old school friend who, it turned out, was carrying out his *Arbeitsdienst* year as a gardener. He had a friend with him, a wiry, fierce-eyed young man who showed great interest in the book she wasn't reading. Shortly afterwards, Robert left, and she and Jochen spent an hour in intense conversation before he leaned over in the shadow of the monkey puzzle tree and—to her astonishment—kissed her.

They had come here often since then, although their approaches to the outing were entirely different. While Jochen was obsessively interested in botanical detail and would frequently squat down and scrutinize the plants and their Latin names, Hedwig was happy simply to gaze around her. She liked Nature to be orderly, and the sorting of plants into their appropriate categories—the Japanese garden, the Italian garden, the rose arbor, and so on—appealed to her sense of tidiness.

Today, however, the garden's tranquillity was shattered by the racket of drills. A band of workers at the far end of the garden were constructing yet more air-raid tunnels. A digger was biting straight lines into the ground, slicing through the grass and leaving a frill of earth behind.

"Those tunnels are going to house all the SS files and personnel," commented Jochen quietly. "They've decided it's one of the safest places in the city when the air raids come."

"How would you know a thing like that?"

He didn't answer. Apart from his comments about the colonies, he had scarcely said a word since they met at the S-Bahn and made their way here. There was nothing new about that—Jochen never saw the point of small talk and Hedwig was quite used to his moods—but that day his jaw was clenched more rigidly than ever and his tension, like that of some hunted wild animal, alarmed her. The horror of the past few weeks—of Lottie's murder and Jochen's revelations—had filled her with a constant, tremulous anxiety. But the task he had asked of her now—to smuggle illegal pamphlets into the following week's ball—made her feel physically sick. She had barely eaten for days. Even Mutti was casting suspicious glances at her.

They came to the biggest greenhouse, the Great Pavilion, an Art Nouveau triumph of glass and steel that towered at the garden's center like a glittering crystalline castle. As they passed from the clear air to the sweltering, damp atmosphere inside, the humidity clung to Hedwig's skin and the lush, dense plants seemed to pulse with their own life. This was another world, an enclosed, mossy universe, surprisingly noisy with the screeches of birds in the rafters and the rushing of artfully constructed waterfalls into koi ponds. Giant vines and bamboos stretched to the highest parts of the roof, and glossy leaves, as big as elephants' ears, waved all around. Between the delicate fronds, orchids dangled from hairy vines thick as babies' arms, and at their feet, the ubiquitous Berlin sparrows pecked at a tangle of ferns.

Hedwig and Jochen followed the winding path to the deepest part of the glass house. This area was reserved for the flesh eaters: the flytraps, with their suggestive lobes and stamens thrusting frankly up from reddened petals. Vivid tubes that persuaded insects to crawl into their pendulous prisons. Hedwig had always hated carnivorous plants. The whole idea of plants eating flesh seemed a dreadful inversion of the natural order.

Jochen sat down on a bench that had been painted yellow to indicate that it was for Jews. Since November, Jews were no longer allowed in the Botanical Garden, so the yellow benches had reverted to Aryan use, but they still bore the instruction *Nur für Juden*, and despite the fact that they were unobserved, Hedwig felt uneasy about disobeying an order. Beside them cacti, cobwebbed with flimsy silk, reared up, their spikes tipped with flowers like hanging drops of blood. She realized Jochen had chosen this spot because the trickle of a stream into a stone grotto behind them drowned out their conversation.

He reached into his bag and brought out a book wrapped in plastic: *The Proper Care of Cactuses.*

"Good, isn't it? I made it up at work. Never judge a book by its cover."

He took off the wrapping and opened it. Between the stiff boards was a wedge of what Hedwig immediately recognized as *Flugblätter*, a wad of pamphlets tightly packed together. She didn't want to look at them.

"You remember everything I told you?"

"Yes." Just the thought of it made her feel even sicker.

"When you have the afternoon rehearsal at the Schloss Bellevue, go to the women's washrooms. They're on the ground floor, to one side of the reception hall. You'll have the book with you. Leave it in the cistern of the cubicle on the far end."

"And Sofie will pick it up?"

"That's all you need do."

"Why can't she take them herself?"

"The guards check their instrument cases and everything. The orchestra doesn't arrive until an hour before the ball begins, but the Faith and Beauty girls will be practicing all afternoon."

"What if someone sees me?"

"They won't. Put it away in your bag now."

"What if the pamphlets drop out of the book?"

"It's simple enough!" he snapped. "Just do it, Hedy!"

He was sitting with his elbows on his knees, staring ahead.

After a moment's silence she said, "Why are you being like this?"

Jochen took out cigarette paper and tobacco, rolled it, and lit up, even though smoking was not permitted in the pavilion.

"Something's wrong." His voice was gentler but grim. "I think my number's up."

Her insides churned. "Why? What happened?"

"There was a woman, the other day. Part Jewish. I was making an identity document for her. Everything seemed straightforward. I did the cards and we waited a while for them to dry. She left quickly and I waited a few minutes before leaving. But when I came out on the street, I realized she was being followed."

"That's her problem, surely."

"No. Don't you see? I have no idea how long she had been shadowed. If the man was watching her before we met, he would have tailed her all the way to the house, and then he would have seen me too. The house can't be used anymore. And they may be onto me too."

"Oh, Jochen." Instinctively she looked around her to check for eavesdroppers, but it seemed they had the jungle to themselves. "What did you do?"

"I evaded him at once. Jumped on a tram, doubled back. There was no sign that he was after me."

"So you're safe?"

"No. I'm blown, Hedy. I'm sure of it. I've already moved out."

"What did you tell your family?"

"I said I'd been sent away. I'd been specially requested by a manuscript factory in Dresden. They won't find out for a while."

"But if you're stopped?"

"I'm changing my identity."

"What about your job?"

She had a sinking feeling of desperation, as though they were in trouble with no path back, like a butterfly that has crawled into a flytrap and finds its frail wings stuck to the treacherous nectar. Insofar as there was no way out.

He flicked his cigarette into the leaves, where it fizzled out in the damp vegetation, then turned to face her.

"I'll have to leave it and lie low for a while. There's no alternative. I need to disappear completely. There are people who can help me. There's a pastor in the Westend who's offered me a place for a while, so please don't worry about me."

"How do you expect me not to worry about you?" Her voice was harsh with anxiety.

"If you need to contact me, leave a message with Robert. You know where he lives, don't you? You can trust him."

Panic was starting to overwhelm Hedwig, and she began looking wildly around her. "Of course I'll need to contact you. I need to see you—"

"And you will. I promise. We'll be together after all this is over."

"Take me with you!"

He took her face in his hands as if he was trying to stamp the image of it in his mind.

"Do you mean that, Hedy? You'd leave your family and all

those little brothers, would you? You'd leave the Faith and Beauty? Because you couldn't go back, if you went underground with me."

She thought of everything she had been told her life would be: all the painting and dancing and chess. Then she thought of her real life: Mutti's tired face, the boys jousting and squabbling. She heard Kurt's laugh. Love was supposed to be uplifting. Love was a balm that made your life complete, not a knife slicing your heart into ribbons. Not a constant stream of questions about who you wanted to be. Hedwig or Hedy? Ordinary or exceptional?

She blinked back her tears and forced herself to focus.

"Yes. Yes I would."

He smiled. "Perhaps then. But first, there's one more thing you can do for me."

She clutched his hand tightly, as though he was proposing to vanish right there and then.

"What? What is it now?"

"I need you to find me a gun."

38

*R*ULE SEVEN: STICK TO PUBLIC PLACES.

The spot in the Alte Nationalgalerie where the Titian had hung bore a small label:

**ON PERMANENT LOAN TO THE COLLECTION
OF HERMANN GOERING.**

The Alte Nationalgalerie was one of the first places Clara had ever visited with Leo, and in the years since then it had become a regular outing for Clara and Erich. Increasingly, however, the more famous of the artworks were notable by their absence. Goering had led the way, favoring paintings of naked women, the more voluptuous the better. Then Goebbels had taken his pick, on the pretext of creating a home of sufficient grandeur for his ministerial rank, and Hess and von Ribbentrop had followed suit. Soon the walls were pockmarked with labels alerting the citizens to the fact that the gallery's paintings were serving a more important function in the private homes of the Nazis' senior men.

That day the gallery was thronged with summer tourists. A crocodile of Bund Deutscher Mädel girls were being shepherded through a gallery of Austro-Bavarian realism—the type of folksy landscapes the Führer adored, replete with jolly monks and tavern scenes. Art came well below sprinting and long jump in the BDM curriculum, yet the occasional tour round the duller parts of the city galleries, avoiding nudes or foreign painters, was offered for those who showed an interest. And, judging by the giggling, even those with no interest at all. Clara drifted in the girls' wake, pretending to eavesdrop on the lecture, but all she could hear was a date.

September 1. Just weeks away. The date for the invasion. The date for war.

She had stolen back to Winterfeldtstrasse that morning for a change of clothes. She'd made her way up the familiar stone steps, so worn away by the tread of thousands of feet that they caved in the middle, shut the door, and leaned against it, trying to absorb everything that had happened. The suggestion that her own sister was liaising with anti-Nazis in France was astonishing, but whether it was true or not, Angela's name featured in Heydrich's Black Book, and accepting Conrad Adler's proposal was the price for her sister's safety.

Clara longed to barricade herself inside, to sit amid her own belongings, brew coffee, to linger and reflect. Yet what if her apartment was no longer a sanctuary but a place of danger? She had no idea if her release had been approved, or whether a Gestapo car would appear in the street outside, ready to pick her up. There was no point in waiting to find out. She donned a pair of sunglasses, covered up the gash on her cheek as best she could with foundation, and closed the door behind her.

Walking through the ground floor of the gallery—Neoclassical and Romantic—she focused on the people around her, checking for repeating faces, or anything that suggested anomaly. An art gallery was the perfect place to disappear. One could linger, staring not at the pictures but the reflections in the glass, wandering this way and that as taste dictated. Clara found herself gazing blindly at still lifes of dead game, spoiled fruit, and rotten, blown flowers. The bloodied fur of a rabbit posed beside a dying rose. Until a soft voice came in her ear.

"Did you know that the Führer originally wanted to be a painter? He was turned down by the Vienna Academy of Fine Arts twice. I wonder if they're regretting that now."

She turned, astonished. The speaker was a man of middling height with solemn brown eyes and a fedora, which he doffed with an air of old-fashioned gallantry.

"Forgive me. You are, I think, Fräulein Vine?"

Strangely she felt no alarm. There was something benign in the man's expression and his vaguely beseeching air. He looked more like a salesman than a policeman. Besides, what choice did she have?

"That's right."

"I wonder if I could have a word?"

"Should I know you?"

The man glanced round the gallery, with his gray felt hat clasped in front of him, as if he too was unsure why he was there.

"Not at all. We've never met before. But you might know my brother. My name, you see, is Goering. Albert Goering."

With his slender frame, thin mustache, and sideburns, Albert Goering could not look less like his older brother, Hermann. His high, arched eyebrows gave him a startled air, and he was dressed with dapper Viennese charm, from the hand-

kerchief sprouting at his jacket pocket to a fat gold watch suspended by a chain across his waistcoat. He looked more like an
assistant in a high-class gentleman's outfitters than a member of Nazi royalty. Instantly Clara recalled Emmy Goering's
words.

It was Hermann's brother who wanted you to come, actually.

"I have tried to contact you a couple of times. I even visited
your apartment. I hoped to find somewhere discreet, but it
seems Fate has intervened. Shall we visit the Postimpression-
ists?"

Clara shot a glance around her, searching for any police or
security services, but there was nothing unusual. Besides, who
was going to arrest her with the brother of Hermann Goering?
He was employed at the film company Tobis-Sascha, Emmy
had said. Perhaps he wanted to talk to her about a part.

"Why not?"

The Postimpressionist gallery was predictably deserted. The
exhibits that had not been filched or deemed Degenerate were
of dubious quality and mostly French. No schoolchild in Germany was going to waste time learning about French artists.
Although there was little to detain them, Clara and Albert
Goering strolled slowly along the undistinguished walls.

"Are you here for the ball, Herr Goering?"

"I had a little business to attend to first."

"Film business?"

"No." He fished out his handkerchief and gave a quick, fas-
tidious dab at his mustache. "It was to do with some Jewish
friends. I needed a word with my brother about them."

He acknowledged her astonishment.

"It is a little sideline of mine. I escort them personally to the
border and provide them with currency."

"And your brother knows about this?"

"Of course." He gave a quick, nervous laugh. "Hermann says he will decide who's Jewish. He tells me he can get anyone he likes redesignated as Aryan. Occasionally it works the other way. It was Hermann who called me about Henny Porten. The actress. You've heard of her, I'm sure."

Henny Porten had been a legend of the silent movie era, but with the arrival of the Nazis, her star had faded. Although she was Aryan herself, her husband was Jewish, and she had no inclination to divorce him.

"I met her a couple of times."

"It was Emmy, I think, who got Hermann to contact me. I was able to secure a contract for Miss Porten at my company, so she moved to Vienna."

There was no way to know how to react to this. That Hermann Goering, a man capable of such extreme viciousness, who had inflicted so much misery throughout the Reich, who had personally dreamed up the plan to fine Germany's Jews a billion marks for the damage inflicted on Kristallnacht, should bother himself with sorting out the affairs of an aging actress and her Jewish husband.

His brother gave a pained grimace.

"You look surprised. But Hermann wouldn't be the first to be flexible in his approach to Jewish affairs. Goebbels was once engaged to a half-Jewish girl, I believe, and his wife was involved with a Zionist. I can't pretend I have anything but abhorrence for Hermann's behavior. My brother's actions horrify me, Fraülein, but I do what I can to atone for it. It's a very little part, but the Jews have a saying. 'He who saves a single person, saves the whole world.' It comforts me."

"So what exactly did you want with me?"

"It's a bit of a story." Albert Goering looked around him, but the room remained as deserted as a church. Not a soul had entered or left in the time they were there. All the same, he lowered his voice.

"A few months ago, a friend of mine, Gustav, a former employee of Tobis-Sascha who I had helped escape to England, got in contact with me. He is now working for British intelligence services, and he said there was someone coming to Vienna that he wanted me to meet. Gustav said the man would be waiting at six o'clock in the musicians' section of the Zentralfriedhof—the big cemetery, you know. He would stand by the Mozart memorial."

Mozart. The closest that music comes to prayer.

"I went to the cemetery, and sure enough, the chap was there."

Her throat constricted. "Leo."

"Yes. Mr. Quinn knew I was in the habit of making regular trips to Berlin, and he begged me to get in contact with you. He gave me your address and made me promise to find you. He said he had needed to leave very suddenly and that you would be worried about him. But you must not be. Does that make sense to you?"

"Yes. Yes, it does!" She was laughing, half mad with delight. In her joy she barely registered that Albert Goering remained somber. "Thank you, Herr Goering. Please, tell me, where is he now?"

His kindly eyes dipped. "That, my dear Fräulein, is the part of the story I am less happy to tell. We arranged to meet the following day at the same time and place. But when I arrived, there was no sign of him."

"So he missed the meeting. There must have been a hitch. Or some misunderstanding. Surely you went back?"

"I did. I returned the following day. And the next. And I asked around, as much as I could."

Clara reached forward and gripped his wrist unintentionally hard. "You must have contacts. Couldn't you ask them?"

"Of course. That's exactly what I did. And what I discovered was most unfortunate. A policeman I knew reported that a suspected enemy agent had that day been denounced to the Gestapo. I'm afraid the man who betrayed his predecessor must have betrayed Mr. Quinn too."

"But you don't know."

"I fear the worst, dear lady. I'm very much afraid that he's gone."

Gone. The word hit Clara like a piece of shrapnel. It ripped inside and hollowed everything out.

Albert Goering rested a hand on her arm, then replaced his hat and made to leave.

"I'm sorry to bring you this news, Fräulein Vine. If you are ever in Vienna, please come and visit me at the Tobis-Sascha studio. I would be happy to see you again."

After he had left she stood for a while, clenching and unclenching her fists. She needed to move, yet stood as if transfixed. Was it true then, as Conrad Adler said, that she was in love with a ghost? Did she face years of private mourning, or never being able to tell another soul what Leo had meant to her? Would she become one of those women she had known in childhood, who lost their fiancés in the war and were dogged with disappointment and silent grief?

There was a painting in front of her. It was of a naked girl washing. With a shock she realized that she recognized it as one that Leo had pointed out to her when they visited the gallery together, all that time ago. It was a small pastel by Manet of a woman in a tin bath, the water silvering her back, looking up at the painter with a frank and open gaze. It had a kind of purity about it. The model was not ashamed of her sexuality, nor was there anything salacious about it. Instead the connection between the woman and the painter seemed to contain a deep, unspoken conversation. She wondered how this portrait had remained in place without being removed. How it had been spared Goering's wholesale pilfering and Alfred Rosenberg's strictures on degeneracy. How it had escaped the attention of Robert Ley, the labor minister, famous for his salacious tastes. Perhaps being inconspicuous, or simple, or foreign was what it took to survive.

It was then that she made a deal. A pact with whichever deity might be listening. If Leo was alive she would do whatever he wanted. Go back to England, abandon her work, leave Berlin entirely. Become the woman he wanted her to be. If only he was alive. Let him be alive.

IN THE COURTYARD OF THE SCHLOSS BELLEVUE, A FOUNTAIN shot a shower of diamonds into the night air. High above, fireworks blistered the sky, and inside everything was candlelit—china, crystal, and flowers, all captured in an antique, golden glow. It could have been a tableau from another era as butlers dressed in knee breeches and powdered wigs welcomed men in eighteenth-century frock coats and women barnacled with jewels in long, sweeping gowns. The great hall was hung with art treasures and perfumed by elaborate sheaths of hothouse orchids, roses, and white lilacs. But despite the historical décor, nobody was giving much thought to the past. Not when the future hung so perilously in the balance.

A flurry of attention signaled the arrival of Goering's car, a distinctive aviation-blue Mercedes 540K cabriolet, dubbed the Blue Goose. Because he liked to drive himself, the vehicle had been modified not only with the standard bulletproof glass and armored walls but with a specially engineered seat broad enough to squeeze the corpulent minister behind the wheel.

Whatever his wife might claim, Hermann Goering's diet did not appear to have been much of a success. The minister's fat fingers were manacled with emeralds, and gems of sweat were already glinting as his gargantuan paunch preceded him out of the car and into the reception hall. His outfit of embroidered mauve frock coat, frilly cravat, and tight silk breeches did little to flatter him, nor did the floor-length white fur coat conceal his curves. Emmy, at his side, looked almost svelte in a low-cut eighteenth-century gown, the neckline drawn aside like a pair of theatrical curtains to reveal her powdered bust.

An extensive cast of diplomats, aristocrats, politicians, hangers-on, and members of the film and theater world had been assembled to greet the Yugoslav royals. Tonight was the summit of the state visit and the culmination of Hitler's attempts to flatter and intimidate Yugoslavia into remaining neutral in case of war. Yet alongside this important agenda, a range of lesser ambitions were on display. Joseph Goebbels, in white uniform and medals, was purposefully late. Magda lagged a deliberate few steps behind her husband with a dyspeptic glare. And von Ribbentrop had opted to accessorize his full Foreign Ministry fig with the magnificent diamond-studded Collar of the Annunziata, expressly to annoy his host.

Once the guests were gathered, a string quartet struck up a waltz and a host of Faith and Beauty girls, arrayed in taffeta dresses white as clouds, began to dance.

Clara skirted the edges of the packed reception, the reds and blues and golds unfurling and mingling before her eyes. The sparkle and glitter of the evening reminded her of the line from *Paradise Lost* about "barbaric pearl and gold," yet it was impossible to concentrate fully on the scene when her mind was still in tumult. She was in possession of a secret more valuable than diamonds—the date for war—but there was nothing she could do with it. She could barely focus on anything, with the thought of Leo drumming in her mind. After the meeting with Albert Goering, she had gone to the Ufa studios in a daze and spent the afternoon buried in the costume department, selecting a dress for the evening ahead.

"You know what they're all gossiping about."

The voice was icily familiar. Syrup undercut with steel. Clara turned to find Annelies von Ribbentrop, sheathed in gray lamé as tight as an aircraft fuselage, standing uncomfortably close.

"I don't, I'm afraid."

"Oh, but I'm sure you do," Annelies insisted, lips puckering into a smile. "All anyone's talking about is the pact."

The pact. Could it really be this simple? Was the alliance so far advanced that it was already a topic of casual party conversation?

"Don't tell me you haven't heard?" The malice in Frau von Ribbentrop's face glittered like the gemstones at her neck. "I thought someone who likes gossip as much as you would be bound to know before the rest of us. You always seem to have your ear to the ground."

"Not in this case."

She shook her head sorrowfully. "It's the pact between the Goebbelses. Joseph has signed a document with Magda agreeing to a year's good behavior, and Hitler has offered to act as guarantor. It's the only peace treaty Hitler has ever put his name to."

Clara looked over at Magda Goebbels. Though she towered like a chessboard queen over her husband's pawn, she had evidently succumbed to checkmate. The pact might have been a small victory in her marital war, but she had plainly been obliged to attend the ball, and to add to her humiliation she was at that moment being introduced to Veit Harlan and his wife, Kristina Söderbaum, the director and star of *Die Reise nach Tilsit*, the film that Goebbels intended to commit his affair to romantic posterity.

"You wonder why Goering has to invite all these actors. I mean, I know our hostess feels more comfortable surrounded by fellow performers, but really, there must be the entire staff of Ufa here tonight. Was there some kind of round-robin invitation?"

"I was asked because the minister wanted some English speakers."

"Oh. Of course." A tight smile. "The English are all very well, I suppose, but must they endlessly try to butt in on our business? Threatening war over the return of a city like Danzig, which is German already. And when the Poles provoke us in the extreme. Hitler has been in love with England for years, but I tell him, it's unrequited. All these years he has paid court to England, admired her empire, entertained her aristocrats. And what does he get for it? My husband says all we ask of the English is that they recognize the Germans are also a great nation, with our own special sphere."

Clara was saved from continuing this conversation by the announcement that dinner was to be served. Annelies von Ribbentrop disappeared to take her place at the top table, and Clara drifted towards the grand dining room, where a feast of clear soup, goose with potatoes, and lettuce, cheese, fruit, coffee, and pastries was waiting. Not to mention the kilo of Russian caviar that had been delivered that morning from the Soviet embassy.

They were only on the first course—*crabe royale à la mayonnaise* with asparagus—when there was a muffled cry and a shout, which caused heads to turn up to the balcony. The cry came from a beautiful young woman whom Clara recognized as the violinist from the string quartet. She was leaning over the balcony, screaming something and pulling from her lace-edged yellow jacket a flutter of paper, white and colored, that came drifting down onto the crowd below. The guests ducked and cowered, as if bombs, rather than leaflets, were being rained on their heads. One drifted to the table beside Clara, and the man next to her, a Dutch diplomat, picked it up and studied the headline: HITLER MEANS WAR! Then he dropped it again, as if he had received an electric shock.

Most of the guests politely averted their eyes from the girl on the balcony, but Clara watched, her heart in her mouth. For an instant the girl stood poised, as if she was planning to fly down to join them, before three soldiers arrived and seized her roughly, stretching her arms outwards like those of a crucified saint. The light shone a gold halo on her head, and the tendons stood out on her slender neck as her terror transmitted itself through the air. When they wrested her away, the girl's face was drained of color, but her expression was calm and trans-fixed. She submitted quickly, walking with dignity between the men, her upright bearing failing entirely to disguise her terror.

At the table, waiters leapt forward instantly, sweeping up stray leaflets like embarrassingly spilled milk. Goering's face was puce with fury, but for the first time that evening, Goebbels gave a thin, colorless smile.

Conversation started up again, and the clatter of cutlery re-sumed, but Clara's appetite had deserted her. It was impossible to eat with the memory of the girl's bloodless face in her mind and the thought of what she might now be enduring. She looked so young. The fact that she must have known the penalty for such a public protest was no consolation. Suddenly, it was as though all the colors in the room were vibrating and blurring into each other, the candlelight off the chandelier splintering into a thousand stars.

"Please excuse me," she told the Dutch diplomat. "I feel a little dizzy."

She escaped to the balcony overlooking the magnificent garden, which was lit that evening by a hundred lanterns, and waited for her head to clear. From the shadows beside her, a figure appeared.

"Hello, Clara. I thought it was you."

The Russian actress Olga Chekhova was wearing a low-cut strapless gown with a full-skirted froth of gray tulle, studded with roses at the hem.

"Are you all right?"

"I needed some air."

"I'm not surprised. That poor girl. One dreads to think . . . Breathe deeply, darling, and drink more champagne. It'll settle you."

Olga came up and leaned her arms against the stone parapet with a sigh.

"I had to get away from Goebbels. Do you know, he uses me as an alibi? When he's been seeing that woman, Lida, he tells Magda that *I've* invited him for dinner. He does drop by my apartment, but he only stays a few minutes and then he leaves. So every time I see Magda she glares like a witch who has put a curse on me. Tell me. Is she watching now? Don't make it obvious."

Clara peered back into the ballroom. "I can't see her."

"Good. I wish I'd never come. I only came because the Yugoslav princess is half Russian and she's a fan apparently, but Goering hasn't even bothered to introduce me. He's been utterly boorish towards me, in fact. Quite rude."

There might be no better opportunity than this, in the quiet gloom of the garden, for Clara to tell Olga what she knew.

"Actually, I think I know why."

A sharp, interrogative look. "You do?"

"Frau Goering mentioned it to me and I haven't had the chance to tell you. The fact is, Olga, Goering suspects you of spying."

In the darkness, the actress's expression was impossible to read, but she coolly opened her velvet evening bag and drew out a cigarette, lighting up before replying.

"Well, I can't say I'm surprised. Why should he be any different? *Everyone* suspects me of spying. You have no idea what a nightmare it is for me, Clara. I'm both German and Russian. In Moscow, they suspect me because I live in Germany; and here, people assume I will be leaking secrets to my brother, Lev, because he's close to the Russian government. And I can't say a word. How could I ever denounce Stalin while my relations are living in Moscow?"

"It must be hard."

"Oh, don't worry about me. The truth is, Clara, it's you I'm worried about."

The older woman inclined her head. The blithe precision of a Viennese waltz danced out of the open doors behind them, and a hundred pairs of gleaming shoes shuffled on the shining floor.

"The other day in the Adlon, you were talking to a man."

"I thought you didn't see me. I called and you didn't reply."

"Forgive me, my darling, I did see you. But I pretended not to hear. The fact was, I couldn't disappear fast enough. You see,

I knew that man. The one you were with. He's a friend of my brother Lev."

Clara looked out into the darkness. Her fingers were so tight around the stem of her glass that she almost crushed it.

"The man you were talking to is a senior officer in the Soviet secret service, the NKVD. I would recognize him anywhere, but I hardly expected to find him standing in the bar of the Hotel Adlon."

In the second before Clara completely understood, it was as though she was standing in the shadows of the soundstage, looking into the dazzle of the set, trying to see a face against the light. Waiting for the face to take shape as her eyes adjusted.

And then she knew.

"Be careful, won't you?" Olga Chekhova touched Clara's shoulder lightly and walked away.

40

I T WAS LATE BY THE TIME HER TAXI REACHED GRIEBNITZSEE. A lustrous moon made the shadows denser, the darkness blacker. Firs crowded in across the narrow road. Silence came sifting down like snow, and a fine sheen of rain puckered the glistening surface of the lake.

Clara guessed now who it was that had given her name to the Gestapo, and the knowledge had made the world change shape and close in around her. Her adrenaline was firing like an electrical charge, sparking through her body, yet her mind remained focused and determined, rinsed clear.

The big villas with their gates and long drives were draped in darkness. Shutters were closed and curtains drawn. Either the owners were away or they weren't bothering to light the street for the benefit of a rare late-night passerby. Yet again Clara regretted moving to this isolated spot. In the city there would be noise and nosiness, but in Griebnitzsee there was only indifferent silence.

As she approached the house, she remembered another point on Leo's list. *Listen for what you don't hear.* Pay attention to anything unfamiliar, to the gaps in the surroundings. A whisper of anything that lies beneath the natural stirrings of the forest and the waves in the lake thudding against the jetty. She stopped for a moment, ears strained for any change in the texture of the silence. Anything that might make her senses prickle, the way they did when danger was near.

And it was there. The rattle of the front gate, which had been left unlatched. The gate that Clara always closed. Like a bat squeak of menace, it sounded a high note of alarm in her ears.

But it was not until her key turned in the lock that she realized he would be waiting for her.

HUGH LINDSEY WAS STANDING in the drawing room holding the postcard of the Vermeer painting that Clara had propped on the mantelpiece. The lamps were unlit, but the flood of moonlight washing in through the long windows accentuated his face in unfamiliar chiarascuro.

"I like this one. *Young Lady Seated at a Virginal.* It's from the National Gallery, isn't it?"

"What are you talking about, Hugh?"

He continued as though she had not spoken. "Vermeer's ladies look so pure and innocent, don't they? But who's to say they are really? Isn't that what appeals to us about them? The suggestion of corruption underneath? This one here—this little musician—we know that she may have more than music on her mind, because there are erotic paintings behind her. There's Cupid and a procuress."

Clara snapped the light on, causing him to blink.

"What are you doing in my house?"

"I've been here a couple of times actually, since I drove you that evening. I wish you'd invited me in then, but there was obviously something on your mind. I've been thinking about you. I've watched you."

"You *watched* me?"

"Don't take it personally, Clara. I like you a lot. I know your family. But ideology means more than pure sentiment."

"You mean Bolshevik ideology."

"If you like."

She remained where she was standing, by the door. Her legs were trembling too much to move.

"You probably don't know, but your dear Bolsheviks are planning to team up with the Nazis. There's a pact under way right now. What does that say about them that they're prepared to ditch their principles at a moment's notice?"

He smiled. "Principles are a luxury that other people pay for. Besides, this pact you're talking about—*if* it happens—will ultimately advance the cause of Bolshevism."

"And how is helping Hitler going to advance your cause?"

"I'm no admirer of the Nazis, as you well know. But Stalin needs to protect the world from the expansion of British imperialism."

"Protect the world? The English are the only ones who will oppose Nazism."

"Oh, Clara, the English are hopeless. They have no idea of the Nazis' methods or intentions." He looked around him, restlessly. "I suppose you don't have any more of those Gauloises with you?"

She reached in her bag and withdrew the packet, tossing it to him.

"Thank you."

He pulled out his silver lighter and inhaled languidly.

"There's something about us English which makes us think that because we all go to the same schools and belong to the same clubs, White's or Brooks's, or the Athenaeum, or at a stretch the Reform, and because we share the same tailors, that we must also share the same mind. King, Country, Class, and Club, that's our religion. The effortless English gentleman. Born to rule the waves. The only rules being not to sleep with a colleague's wife and not to light one's cigar before the third glass of port. Our highest test of character is to be a good cricket umpire and play by the rules. Ideological dispute is the stuff of university common rooms. Well, I've never been part of that pompous, self-satisfied tribe."

"So it was better to become a spy?"

He gave a gravelly, cigarette-choked laugh. "My dear, isn't that rather a case of the pot calling the kettle black? It takes one to know one."

If Hugh Lindsey knew about her, what others might he be aware of? Despite his outward languor, she felt their two minds matching each other, calculating, intensely alert. Trying to compute which of them was the more dangerous.

"As soon as I realized what you were up to, I informed my friendly local Gestapo. But for some reason they allowed you to slip the net."

Clara had heard that in extreme situations, fear would turn to anger, and now she felt fury, pure and hot, coursing like fuel through her veins. It was so difficult to equate the handsome, cultured, smiling being before her with the threat he posed.

"Why not have the courage of your convictions and join the Russians outright?"

"Perhaps. But how much more satisfying to destroy the citadel from within. It's rather a thrill, outwitting others. Hugh St. John Lindsey. Just the sort of chap they expect to mingle with them, attending their grand dinners at the Grosvenor House and the Dorchester and Claridge's, listening to their deeply misguided speeches."

Claridge's.

"It was you, wasn't it? You were the man Lottie Franke met in London. The one she fell in love with."

"There was a hotel dinner. The Faith and Beauty girls were being paraded like Hitler's little princesses. The pearls of the Reich. Well, a couple of nights in the company of the lovely Lottie was enough to settle that question. Lottie was like one of Vermeer's girls. An exquisite face and morals of the gutter. Did you see that photograph of her in the paper the other day—the one by Yva? It captured her perfectly, I thought."

"But to kill her, Hugh? Why would you need to do that?"

"She was threatening me, I'm afraid. In the most extortionate way. She wasn't a nice person, Clara. She'd stolen from me."

"I know all about that. She stole a jewel."

"A jewel? No."

For a moment he looked baffled, and his bloodshot eyes blinked as though Clara was speaking a foreign language. Then he smiled.

"Ah. That's what Gurlitt called it. A jewel. Because it is, in its way. One of the great gems of Western culture. It was a book."

"A book? That can't be true."

"But it is. I had come by a rather lovely manuscript. I knew what it was because, without being immodest, Roman literature of that era is my specialty. And this was a copy of the Tacitus *Germania*."

"You're lying. I met an expert at the Ahnenerbe who told me it was in Italy."

"As indeed it was. The Codex Aesinas. Hitler's dearest wish. The one manuscript above all others he would like to possess. But there was another codex. It had spent hundreds of years at a monastery in Austria until it came into the hands of an antiquarian dealer there. Who was unfortunate enough to have his collection thieved by Nazi louts and sent back to Berlin. I'd heard of it years ago, in Vienna, and once my contact described it, I knew exactly what it was. I just had to have it. I went to Austria to find it, but no luck. It had already been carted off back to Berlin. So I followed it, and once I arrived here I discovered I had come in the nick of time. The stash was being held in a warehouse in Kopernikusstrasse under the auspices of a dealer called Hildebrand Gurlitt. The riches there were mouthwatering. Paintings, silver candlesticks, porcelain, all sorts. But most importantly the *Germania*."

The fragments that had been spinning around Clara's mind began to pair and come together.

"So that was what Goering wanted."

"Goering wanted it passionately because the Führer wanted it too. The competition between them is pitiful. Goering was a regular visitor to the warehouse, and when he heard about the *Germania* he was determined to have it. He's engaged in some kind of race with the Führer, and knowing how much the Führer desired the Tacitus made it all the more desirable to him. I managed to buy it the day before he arrived. It was better in my hands than theirs, I reckoned."

Clara felt a choking emotion. Pure rage that this man had dispensed with a life so casually.

"So Lottie had to die for that? Just that?"

"She stole my codex, and unfortunately she refused to hand

it over when asked. I didn't want her to die. I wanted her scared. That's what I told the man. But he was a local Communist hoodlum, and he killed her in an excess of patriotism."

"Is that what you call murder?"

"The chap assumed she was an enemy of the Soviet Union. Indeed she probably was."

"And where is this precious codex now? The one that's worth a woman's life?"

"That's my greatest regret. It's lost. I'm afraid it will have to remain a casualty of war. It's a shame. I must be one of the very few people in the world who could recognize that codex right off for what it was. I was a Greats scholar at Oxford, you know. There was only one man above me. He took the Newdigate Prize. Just pipped me to it. And it still rankles, if I'm honest."

Hugh had entered a kind of reverie. The whites of his eyes were cracked and yellowish, like the glaze on an old painting. Clara realized he must have been drinking all evening. He leaned against the mantelpiece and turned the photograph of Clara's mother around to face him.

"I suppose whether one likes Stalin or England, Fascism or Communism, it's all a question of taste, isn't it? Like the difference between Vermeer and Klimt . . ."

He took a swig of whiskey from a bottle on the mantelpiece, then replaced it with the deliberation of the profoundly drunk.

"I'm not proud of this, Clara. I've been a faithful servant of the Soviet Union since my twenties, and if Stalin wants me to dispose of British agents, that is what I must do. No matter how much I might personally like or admire them. I do like you, very much."

He reached downwards, and she saw the sudden glint of metal in his hand.

"But I suppose betrayal is one of those things we English do so well. Like garden parties and well-made gentlemen's shoes."

"You wouldn't shoot me, Hugh. Think how easily you'd be traced."

"As a matter of fact everyone imagines I'm in Prague. I was obliged to leave my car in the care of the Adlon, and I'll be heading off tonight."

She looked down at the pistol. It was bigger than the tiny derringer she had possessed. As Hugh moved the muzzle a fraction, pointing it more directly at her chest, a cold fear clutched at her. She looked over at the pictures of Erich and her mother on the mantelpiece and wished passionately that she had kept a photograph of Leo after all. Yet it was still Leo's face in her mind as the shot rang out.

THE NOISE FILLED the room and blasted out into the darkness. Hugh Lindsey staggered, as if surprised, a dark trickle of blood beginning to stain his suit. As his body jerked sideways and backwards, and then crumpled to the floor, Clara looked around. The shooter's arm was shaking so much that the muzzle of the gun was a blur. The room smelled of gunpowder and perfume.

"I never thought I could shoot someone."

Hedwig's voice was slightly trembly, but she lifted her chin resolutely. "All those lessons must have counted for something."

Clara forced herself to remain calm. She wondered if Hugh might die, and how quickly, but looking at him sprawled awkwardly on his back, she saw that his skin was already becoming chalky, and his eyes were open and motionless, as if he were surprised. She moved swiftly to the front window and looked out.

"Don't worry," said Hedwig. "They're always hearing shots round here. They'll think it's the Faith and Beauty girls having pistol practice in the forest. Either that or someone shooting geese."

Clasping her arms around her chest, as if to protect herself from the trauma, Clara walked off into the kitchen. She felt a violent nausea at the sight of Hugh Lindsey lying there, and her own surprise at not being dead.

Something he had said, a comment she'd barely registered in the fear of the moment, now resounded.

I was a Greats scholar at Oxford, you know. There was only one man above me. He took the Newdigate Prize. Just pipped me to it. And it still rankles, if I'm honest.

The Newdigate Prize was Oxford's great honor for poetry. John Buchan had won it in his time, and Matthew Arnold and Oscar Wilde. And, more recently, it had been awarded to another gifted student: Leo Quinn.

Hugh Lindsey must have fostered a grudge against Leo. A grudge that had stretched all the way from the golden stone cloisters of Oxford to the other side of Europe. And finally, decades later, he had found a way to take his long-desired revenge.

CLARA TURNED ON the tap with trembling fingers and poured herself a glass of water, then turned to face Hedwig.

"Why are you here?"

"I had to get a gun for my boyfriend. He's in trouble."

"I thought you were going to the ball?"

"I was. I went to the afternoon practice, but I was terribly nervous. I made quite a hash of it. I kept getting out of time. At the end of it, Fräulein von Essen took me aside and said I stood out too much. I didn't stay in line. If I took part in the dance I would let down not just myself but the entire Faith and Beauty movement and probably the Führer himself. She had been considering making the whole group withdraw because of my laziness, but instead she had decided that I should suffer the shame alone. I would not be able to come to the ball and should just stay quietly at home."

"So you came here."

"I went to the Faith and Beauty home. I knew it would be deserted, and it was the ideal opportunity to collect my pistol."

Clara's head was still spinning, trying to piece together everything that had happened.

"Why does your boyfriend need a pistol?"

"He works as a forger. He makes documents for Jews in hiding. Identity documents. Recently he undertook a job and he thinks he was followed. He was providing a document for a lady . . ."

"A forger you say?"

"Yes. He had a job, and when this lady left, he could tell she was being watched."

"How could he tell?"

"He saw she was being shadowed."

Fragments of information were colliding in Clara's head, like shards of a broken vase forming together into a whole.

"But that's not the point," continued Hedwig. "If this lady was being tailed, then it's likely that they saw Jochen too, so he's worried now that the Gestapo are on to him too. He's already left his job. And he wanted me to get him a pistol."

"But why come here? To my house?"

"I was on my way back to the S-Bahn and I saw a man ahead of me. I recognized him at once."

"Because you'd met him in London."

"Lottie was obsessed with him. I told you. They'd become

lovers. As soon as I saw him again I realized it must have been him that Lottie had been meeting. That was the man she was terrified of. The man who must have killed her. But I still don't know why."

A sudden, sharp clarity possessed Clara.

"I do. You were right about the jewel, Hedwig. He killed her for it. And I think I can tell you where it might be."

ELSA NEULÄNDER-SIMON'S PHOTOGRAPHY STUDIO WAS in a tall stucco building in Schlüterstrasse, just off the Ku'damm in the west end of the city. For years, Studio Yva had been the most successful studio in Germany until the Nazi regime blacklisted the photographer and obliged her to carry out all her work under the supervision of an Aryan studio manager. It would take more than that to stop Yva working, however, and every part of the house, from its pillared entrance to its grand balconies and winding staircases, continued to be used as backdrop to her dramatic, sensual art. The door was opened by a fey young man in a sleeveless sweater and bow tie, who ushered Hedwig into a parquet hall and yelled, "Yva! Ein Fräulein to see you."

A reply floated down from several floors above. "If it's another one of those girls collecting for the Winterhilfswerk, tell them we don't want to buy any more tanks."

The young man gave a camp little shrug and said, "Follow me."

The studio, a sparsely furnished, open space running the length of the house, had a vacant, abandoned air. It contained only two chairs, a cabinet, and a pile of dust sheets. In the middle a slight woman was kneeling on the floor dismantling a cumbersome tripod.

"You'll have to wait."

Awestruck, Hedwig looked around. The girls whose portraits hung on these walls were entirely different from the images of womanhood she had seen anywhere else in Germany. Here were no hearty, fresh-faced mothers, none of the wholesome members of the Faith and Beauty Society or the League of German Girls, but glacial blond goddesses who emitted a cool artifice that seemed to say although they might be advertising cosmetics, shoes, or jewelry, their bodies remained their own. Their limbs were hard as marble, their eyes heavy-lidded, and they had a smoldering erotic charge.

One picture in particular caught her attention. It was a young woman, platinum hair rippling in tight waves, fur coat flicked aside to reveal a slash of ivory flesh from the top of her stockinged leg to the snow of her exposed breast. The composition was all geometric lines and oblique perspectives, like an old silent movie, its dramatic lighting and edgy glamour breathing a sense of violence and danger. The expression on the girl's face, the poise of her body, and the cigarette dangling from one hand were at once decadent and rigidly controlled. It was as though all the sex that had been suppressed in Germany was distilled in a single photograph.

The subject was Lottie Franke.

"Everyone loves that one. It was taken by my apprentice, Helmut Newton. He loved big blond girls in high heels," said Yva, getting to her feet. "Especially naked ones. He's left me now, unfortunately. He could have been quite a talent, but he would insist on emigrating. Perhaps he was right. I had an offer from *Life* magazine to go to New York, but I turned it down."

"Why didn't you go?"

"My husband hated the idea. Only now that he has lost his job and been given a new occupation as a street sweeper, he's regretting his decision. But there we are."

Yva finished folding away the tripod and began meticulously dismantling the camera. Her angular, intelligent face, framed by dark brows, looked in no mood to expend any niceties on Hedwig.

"I'm sorry to disappoint you, but this studio is officially closed. They've given me a new job too, as it happens. A technician in the Jewish hospital, working with X-ray cameras. Is that a joke, do you think?"

"I think they have no sense of humor."

"You're probably right. Anyhow, if it's photography you're after, I'm unavailable."

"That's not what I came for."

"Then . . ." The eyebrows lifted slightly.

Hedwig nodded towards the photograph on the wall. "Did you know her well? Lottie Franke?"

Yva's voiced hardened with suspicion. "Who are you exactly?"

"My name is Hedwig Holz. I was her best friend."

"Ah." Yva abandoned her business with the tripod and rose. She made her way to the solitary cabinet. "In that case, perhaps you'll share a drink with me."

She poured two large whiskeys into cloudy tumblers and handed one to Hedwig, who gulped it like lemonade, the unfamiliar burn causing her to choke. Yva perched on one of the chairs, extended a long, fishnet-stockinged leg, and stroked it thoughtfully.

"I first met your friend Lottie a year ago. Perhaps she mentioned it."

Hedwig nodded silently.

"She came to me with some sketches for clothes and wondered if I would photograph the finished products. Perhaps I would speed her progress as a designer. But though they were good, it wasn't only the clothes I was interested in. I could see your friend had quite another talent. I said I would only photograph the clothes if she modeled them, and she agreed immediately. She had drive, that girl, and a hard ambition. I recognized something of myself in her. I was one of nine children—my mother was a milliner—so I knew what it was to work hard and graft. To use everything God gives you to succeed. Lottie was not ashamed of using her body if it helped her. Helmut Newton loved her. He said Lottie was his ideal woman. But then, with a body like that, I daresay she was a lot of men's ideal woman. Even the Führer's."

Her needle-sharp glance grazed Hedwig's own legs, causing her to blush fiercely. But Hedwig persisted. "The last time you saw Lottie, did she seem distracted by anything?"

"If she was, I wouldn't have known it. She was far too professional."

"The fact is . . . the day before she died she told me about something she had. And I wondered if perhaps she left it here."

Yva continued to scrutinize Hedwig for a moment, as if trying to decide whether she was worth trusting. Then she nodded.

"She asked me to look after it. Just for a few days. She wouldn't say what it was, or why she wanted me to take it, and my first instinct was to refuse. You don't hide other people's possessions without a very good reason nowadays. But your friend had the face of an angel, and I was not about to lose a model that good. Unfortunately, the next time I saw that face it was on the front page of the *Berliner Tageblatt*."

Quietly, so quietly that her voice barely traveled across the narrow distance between them, Hedwig asked, "Where is it now?"

Yva remained motionless for a moment, then she stubbed her cigarette on the floor, ground out its embers with the toe of her shoe, and rose decisively. She crossed to the cupboard where she had found the whiskey bottle and rummaged behind rows of satin dresses until she retrieved it.

It was a light tan leather briefcase, expensive-looking but slightly scratched and worn at the corner, with brass fittings and the gilt letters H S L indented on the front. A smaller monogram on the clasp said ASPREY OF LONDON. Hedwig's fingers trembled as she unlatched it. The air that escaped smelled of burning, the mustiness of an old fireplace, the ancient molecules of another era. And vacancy.

"There's nothing here."

"What were you looking for?"

"A book. A manuscript."

"Oh, that. I disposed of it."

To one accustomed to handling the manuscripts in the Ahnenerbe with white cotton gloves, Yva's casual comment was devastating.

"You can't have any idea what it was!"

"On the contrary, my dear. I knew exactly what it was. No good German can fail to be aware of the importance of the *Germania*. To me, it is the world's most dangerous book."

"But where is it?"

"As I think I mentioned before, I'm a Jew, Fräulein. I reasoned that the book belonged somewhere far away from the hands of those who would use it for their own purposes. Last

Saturday I was taking a picnic out by Krumme Lanke. We go there to sunbathe and swim, though it is still not quite warm enough for my tastes. Anyhow, at one point I made my excuses and went into the woods. Your manuscript is there, somewhere. Don't ask me where. I forget."

In that instant, her shock evaporated, and Hedwig almost laughed at the little woman's ingenuity. She was right; it couldn't be more appropriate. The *Germania*. The work that meant so much to Doktor Kraus and SS Reichsführer Himmler and everyone at the Faith and Beauty Society. The key to the German people's past. How fitting that old Roman Tacitus would have thought it, that his work on the ancient forest tribe should remain where it started, deep beneath the must and moldering leaves of the Grunewald.

Berlin Mitte might have been washed in blood. It was ablaze with crimson pennants, marching troops, and the clatter of drums and brass. There was a greasy swirl of gasoline on the wind, and a sea of eagle-topped banners, glinting in the sun, recalled the triumphal march of a Roman emperor. Percussion shivered in the air, and the thump of snare drums made the ground quiver. An excited crowd of sightseers had gathered to watch, and every so often the monstrous operetta of boots and belts and guns caused them to break into frenzied applause. If something was that good to look at, who cared if it was fake?

The filming of *Germania*, like every other project in the Reich, was proceeding at an extraordinary pace. No obstacle would be allowed to get in the way; every barrier, no matter how great, would be conquered. Not that many people dared put up obstacles to Leni Riefenstahl, even when her work required commandeering half of Unter den Linden and the whole of Pariser Platz and filling it with cameramen, lighting crew, still photographers, and a squad of fifty Faith and Beauty girls.

Several detachments of soldiers from the nearby Lichter-felde barracks had been co-opted—some to march up and down for as long as the director required and others to string up banners, halt traffic, erect barricades, and clear the way for cameramen on roller skates who were filming the troops from street level. The guards participated enthusiastically, agog at the girls, assiduously preventing ordinary citizens from crossing the square lest they collide with extras dressed as ordinary citizens crossing the square. It made a pleasant change from their usual occupation of practicing military maneuvers and endlessly cleaning and reloading their guns.

Leni herself had spent much of the day winched on a minute wooden platform up a ten-meter-high flagpole next to the Brandenburg Gate, squinting up the new East-West Axis with a viewing device and defying the inelegance of the situation with a pair of Dior trousers and her glossy hair bundled tightly beneath a director's cap. Around midday the Führer had dropped by for a viewing, accompanied by Goebbels, who was unable to resist the opportunity for an impromptu speech. "Whoever has seen and experienced the face of the Führer in *Triumph of the Will* will never forget it. It will haunt him through days and dreams and will, like a quiet flame, burn itself into his soul." Leni, dressed in her trademark white greatcoat, stood by smiling, though everyone knew that inwardly she was seething at the waste of precious time.

The previous day Clara had left Griebnitzsee for good. It was impossible to stay in the place where a death had happened, where she had lugged a man's body down the garden like a sack of rotten cabbages and watched it slip, without a trace, into the dark water of the lake. Since then she had scarcely slept and was grateful for the quantities of Pan-Cake makeup stipulated by Leni to achieve the masklike visage of the Spirit of Germania.

By midafternoon her scenes were finished, and Clara changed into her own clothes to watch the final shot of the day. It was the scene everyone was waiting for, the technically dazzling feat that would showcase Leni Riefenstahl's trademark choreography. Leni had already explained her plans. The shot would form the opening sequence of the film. Accompanied by a soundtrack of Wagner's *Lohengrin*, a Luftwaffe plane piloted by the Führer's favorite aviatrix, Hanna Reitsch, would approach and dip down like a divine messenger from the skies. The onboard camera would record the clouds parting to reveal the whole, glorious city of Berlin laid out and, right in the center, a swastika. As the plane drew closer, the swastika would be revealed as a troupe of perfect Faith and Beauty girls massed in the Tiergarten. In an uninterrupted tracking shot, the camera's eye would come right down to ground level, until the focus was resting on the face of a single girl.

Word of the stunt had spread. Sightseers had been collecting at the west side of the Brandenburg Gate for the past hour, their gaze oscillating between the celebrity director herself and the film of low cloud covering the sky. Soldiers linked arms to control the crowds. From a perch on a viewing platform beside the gate, Clara joined them, looking out at the sea of entranced faces below.

They didn't have long to wait. It was just a sound at first, a low rumble from the distance, growing to a roar as the Junkers appeared, a gray gleam in the air, the swastikas on the underside of its wings clearly visible. The faint buffeting breeze strengthened to a wash of air that flattened the leaves on the trees as the plane descended, like some monstrous bird of prey, wings tilting slightly on the currents. Every face was excited, expectant, enthralled as a crowd of children at a conjurer's trick. Every face was turned upwards.

Every face except one.

She couldn't see his features, because his hat was tilted down over his eyes, but he stood immobile, hands in pockets, pressed into the crowd, staring right at her. Even as she saw him Clara noticed something else—the only moving figures in the throng, two men shouldering their way fast in his direction. They were wearing long, belted raincoats, the unofficial uniform of the Gestapo, and were making a direct line for him. When Clara looked back at the place he had been standing, he had disappeared.

As swiftly as she could, Clara darted through the dense press of onlookers in the direction of the man she had glimpsed. But it was useless. With so much practice waiting in queues, Berliners had gotten used to standing their ground. They moved as slowly and obstinately as cattle. No one was giving way, certainly not to anyone without official ID. Once Clara had fought her way through to the spot where the man had been standing, he was nowhere to be seen. She stood looking around in frustration.

Was it Leo? Or a figment of her imagination? And if it was Leo, where would he go?

To the west of the gate lay the Tiergarten, the largest park in Berlin, dense with trees that could provide cover, but at that moment staked out with cameras and arc lights, as the Faith and Beauty troupe held their gymnastic pose in the open ground. To the left was Potsdamer Platz; behind stretched Unter den Linden. Anyone being pursued would surely be more likely to make his way towards the busiest center of population, where streets and crowds and buildings offered potential escape. Clara turned and pushed her way back through the stolid crowds to Pariser Platz.

Past Wilhelmstrasse she came to the Soviet embassy, a handsome building with high brass lanterns, and she stopped and changed her bag to her other shoulder, giving her the opportunity to glance casually behind her before scanning the street ahead. It was filled with pavement cafés and ambling shoppers, but there was no sign of Leo. If he had headed this way, both he and the men following him had already been swallowed up in the crowd.

On the corner of Friedrichstrasse two policemen were standing, their eyes traveling over the passing pedestrians with more than usual scrutiny. Were they a second patrol on the lookout for Leo? And if so, how many others had been posted to join the hunt?

A couple of minutes later she had the answer. Towards the Lustgarten and crossing the bridge, a ribbon of lights on the dancing waters of the Spree, she noticed a car moving slowly, two men in the front seat, their faces sweeping left and right, scanning the crowds on the pavement as they trudged home from work.

At the same moment, she caught sight of him. A vague shadow, far ahead, moving swiftly, dipping in and out of the throng. A flash of red-gold hair. He turned sharp left, up the Museum Island, along the side of the canal where it was impossible for a car to follow, heading for the maze of streets around Hackesche Höfe. Clara turned too, but once she had reached the elevated S-Bahn arches, she lost him again.

In this area, Albert Speer's redevelopment of Berlin was at its most advanced. In some places entire streets had been flattened, and elsewhere half-demolished homes stood like broken teeth, their debris coated with dust. Cranes and trucks were parked for the evening. She hastened along Spandauer Strasse, past a restaurant whose glass front was shattered and a board hammered diagonally across the door. Inside tables and chairs were overturned, cups and plates abandoned on the tables. A paper was taped to the cracked door.

CLOSED FOR FURTHER NOTICE. BY ORDER OF POLICE

A zealous official had added a handwritten explanation.

I CHARGED EXTORTIONATE PRICES AND THAT IS WHY I AM NOW IN A CONCENTRATION CAMP.

Blood drumming in her ears, Clara looked around her, wondering if she had been wrong, trying to guess where in the maze of streets Leo might go. The streets in this part of the city were narrower, older, more winding than the broad boulevards elsewhere in Berlin. She remembered that Leo had once had an apartment near here, in Oranienburgerstrasse, close to the enormous, gold-domed Neues Synagogue. That meant he knew the local streets well and he knew where best to vanish.

Amid the jangle of trams, a high-pitched, angry shout rang out, and faces turned. The police car that Clara had seen earlier had rejoined the street two hundred meters behind at Dirckenstrasse and was coming in her direction, one man's head craning from the passenger window. Ahead of her, the figure of Leo darted across the road. The occupants of the car had seen him too.

At that moment the air was riven by a clanging bell. A siren wailed like a mournful wraith, and a plume of smoke mushroomed into the street, obscuring the houses on each side. Traffic drew to a halt. Klaxons sounded, and people on the street looked hesitantly around until they saw a patch of waste ground where a row of HJ boys was assembled in a line facing their corps leader, a grown man in shorts with a whistle, issuing staccato instructions through a megaphone. Almost immediately surprise mutated into mild irritation. Everyone knew what this was about.

Air-raid drill.

Practices for the bombing raids were happening every day now, and they always involved the Hitler Jugend. The HJ, Erich had told her, would play a vital part in air-raid precautions. It would be their job to assist in the cleanup, to get casualties to first aid points, and to help relocate bombed-out civilians. Some would act as air-raid wardens and others would help put out fires. The really lucky ones, Erich said, would get to help operate the flak guns.

Amid the swirling smoke, a host of boys with Red Cross armbands dashed forward with stretchers. Others threw themselves enthusiastically on the ground, issuing loud, theatrical groans, enacting the aftermath of a bombing. Further recruits spilled from a nearby building. Others, outfitted in gas masks and fireproof suits, proceeded to spray the ground with water, dragging wheeled canisters behind them as if removing traces of poison gas.

Immediately a traffic jam formed. Trams slammed on their brakes. Cars bunched up. A cream bus shuddered to a halt, its passengers looking out incuriously. Most pedestrians vanished down side streets, unwilling to be detained by a performance they had seen numerous times before. Behind the bus, the police car revved in frustration and sounded its horn. Inside, the driver banged the steering wheel hard in frustration, but the HJ leader was blocking the road, arms outstretched officiously as his troupe carried their pretend casualties on stretchers into an adjacent block decorated with a large red cross. Another boy stood by with a placard that read 2 DEAD. No one was allowed to interrupt an air-raid drill. The police car reversed with a screech of gears.

Up ahead Leo was making a U-turn, heading east in the direction of the city palace, the Schloss.

Clara hurried on breathlessly, pain tearing at her chest, desperate to slow down, yet terrified she would lose sight of him. She could barely believe the direction he was taking. Of all the places a fugitive might go, why would anyone being hunted by the police head for Alexanderplatz?

The windswept square, intersected with yellow trams, was the home of the Polizeipräsidium, the central police station. The building known as the Alex rose with its towering dome on one side of the square, lit up in the dusk like a great ocean liner, with several hundred policemen inside.

Standing at the center of the square, Clara made a 360-degree turn. Leiser's shoe shop—the biggest in Berlin. The Mokka Fix Café. A Ufa movie theater that she saw, with a shock, featured her name on a billboard in a poster for *Love Strictly Forbidden*, due to be released in a fortnight. The effect of it was somehow more than any unexpected, unflattering glance in a mirror. The lighthearted smile, calculated to deceive, the head thrown back in joyful abandon, told no truth about her except one. That her life was one long façade of playing a role.

Of Leo there was no sign. As she scanned her surroundings, Clara's gaze snagged on the tall limestone arch that announced the entrance to Alexanderplatz U-Bahn:

ALMOST HALF OF BERLIN LIES UNDERGROUND.

Then she understood.

———

BERLIN'S U-BAHN STATIONS WERE the envy of the world. The work of the architect Alfred Grenander, they were little palaces of elegant design with their finely wrought iron fittings, Art Nouveau lamps, and mosaic inlays. Alexanderplatz was no exception, sleek with green-glazed tiles and elegant iron banisters, serving both the U5 and U8 lines. Clara dashed through the entrance hall and bought a ticket. She hunted fruitlessly for the figure of Leo among the flow of commuters, then at random she followed the signs to the U5 line and arrived amid the green steel arches on a platform smelling of dust and stale air. A train appeared, emptied its passengers, and moved off.

She was torn between leaving immediately and remaining where she was. The U-Bahn was the obvious place to disappear, but if Leo was being pursued, surely he would have taken the train rather than stay where he was.

Unless he knew that she had followed him.

She looked into the darkness of the tunnel. The rails lit up with a dim gleam, and the tracks hummed in anticipation of the next train, heading east for Lichtenberg, Frankfurter Tor, and Friedrichsfelde. In the flicker before it arrived, the crowd on the opposite platform parted, and she glimpsed a figure on a bench, hat pulled down over his face. The train passed before her eyes—the driver in his cabin, face set, and the passengers, exhausted by work and soothed by the jolting motion, blinking sleepily at the seats opposite—but once it had disgorged its set of passengers and moved on, the opposite platform was vacant. Only empty benches remained beneath a poster, HARIBO MAKES CHILDREN HAPPY!

Clara stood frozen with indecision. Another train burst into the station with an upwash of warm air. The crowds swelled and cleared and the train departed. At that point, a hundred yards away at the end of the platform she occupied, a figure appeared. This time she could see his face. It was not the face of a phantom but a living breathing man.

CHAPTER

43

AT PRECISELY THE SAME MOMENT, THE POLICE SHE
had seen before arrived on the opposite platform, looked
across, and shouted.

Springing up, Clara signaled to Leo that he should
follow her. She ran back up the steps the way she had
come, along the exit tunnel, trying to recall what Jochen
had told her.

Almost half of Berlin lies underground.

She knew now why she had chosen the U5 line. It
was not a random choice but a subconscious memory.

The green door to the air-raid shelter was entirely
inconspicuous, just as he had said. A blank sheet of steel
studded with iron rivets and a vast handle, newly set
into the wall. She pulled it, and to her relief, it was un-
locked. Seconds later, Leo caught up and they slipped
through the arched entrance into the darkness, pulled
the door closed, and flattened themselves against the
damp brick.

Inside, the air was dank and claustrophobic, but a

glimmer of light revealed luminous paint outlining doorways and exits, and a long corridor punctuated by thick steel doors. There were signs for washing rooms and lavatories. Bedrooms. And immediately before them an immense, shadowy space like a station waiting room fitted with wooden benches. An entire underworld hotel with accommodation for hundreds.

Leo looked different in the phosphorescent shadow, at once strange and familiar. The light emphasized his finely cut features. He had grown a mustache, which made him seem older, and a triangle of tanned skin showed at his throat. He leaned against her, enfolding her entirely in his arms, and she felt his heart slamming against his chest. She pressed harder into his body—the body she knew by heart—inhaling the warm, familiar musk, feeling the pull of yearning for him, even now, and the answering surge within him. There was not an inch of air between them. His cheek was rough with stubble as they kissed.

They tensed themselves for the tramp of feet in the corridor outside, listening for the stamp of heavy police boots, the hurrying footsteps to halt outside the door. But amid the regular flow of travelers, nothing stood out.

She whispered in his ear. "How many are following?"

"Three teams, I think. Two on foot and another one in a car. By now, there could be more." His breath was hot against her ear, his entire body tense and alert. "I had to come back and find you. I needed to make sure you were safe. I couldn't return to England without knowing."

"You're going to England?"

In the darkness she gripped his hand as if to lock him to her, the questions tumbling through her mind.

"My name's a priority on the Gestapo watch list."

"If you're on a watch list, they would have stopped you at the border . . ."

"They spotted me at Tempelhof. They could have picked me up there, but they chose not to. I assume they wanted to see who I was meeting. I've put you in grave danger, my darling. We need to keep moving. We have to get out of the underground."

THE S7 LINE TRAIN was full of commuters traveling home to the western suburbs. Past the Zoo, Charlottenburg, Grunewald, Nikolassee, bodies rocked companionably on the wooden benches to the soothing rhythm of the train. The clattering of the tracks, the stops and starts, the squeal of brakes, and the station announcements. Leo insisted that they not sit or speak together, so she chose a spot three rows away and tried to keep herself from looking at him. The tension of being unable to hold or touch him was excruciating. It wasn't until the train approached its final stop that he rose, and she followed him up the steps and out into the prettily gabled station of Berlin-Wannsee.

Wannsee station, with its Gothic signs and arched windows, might have been straight out of a woodcut of a fantasy Germanic past. Even the air was different here, pure and green, infused with the watery scent of the Havel River, which lay to one side, pocked with sailing boats making their slow, scenic way in the summer dusk. On the opposite bank, a path meandered through dense woodland all the way to Potsdam. On Sundays the route was thronged with hikers, cyclists, and families out for a lakeside walk, but now, on a weekday evening, only the occasional dog walker could be seen along the leaf-strewn path.

They crossed the bridge, but it wasn't until they reached the cover of woodland that Leo allowed himself to speak. They walked, clasped close to each other, the filigree of branches above them framing a darkening sky.

"The night I received that call they told me that two of our agents had disappeared in Vienna. All we knew was that they had arranged a meeting in the Café Louvre, at the corner of Wipplingerstrasse and Renngasse, with a pair of German officers who were thought to be anti-Nazis."

"I know the Café Louvre. I made a film in Vienna three years ago. We used to go there." Clara recalled the pale spring light streaming through the generous windows, the violin-backed chairs, and booths finished in dark brocade along one wall. The schnitzel and creamy Kaffee mit Schlagobers.

"I went straightaway. I became a regular and made friends with the barman. A nice chap. Georg."

Clara pictured Leo faux-drunk, boozily intimate, leaning against the bar late into the evening.

"Sure enough, Georg told me what had happened. He saw the agents arrive and sit at a table with two other men. And it must have been a trap. Because within minutes the door slammed open, there was shouting, and the Gestapo came in with guns and dogs."

Clara imagined the dogs slavering, pulling against their leads.

"Our men were taken away, almost certainly to be tortured and shot." Leo swallowed and paused.

"But Georg had noticed something curious. There was another customer in the bar, not a regular, and he was there as the arrest took place. Georg said to me, 'Something like this happens, everyone tries to hide their face, but they're looking all the same. They can't help themselves. But this man, he didn't turn a hair. Just kept reading his book.'"

"What does that prove?"

"That he knew the arrest was going to happen. That he was part of the trap. And Georg was doubly curious because the book this man was reading was in a foreign language. It wasn't English, he insisted, or French, or Hungarian, any other language he recognized. All he could say was that it was the language you found on tombstones."

"Latin?"

"Exactly." Leo stopped and turned to Clara, urgently.

"And there was only one person I could think of who would sit in a café, reading a book in Latin. As soon as I realized, I knew you were in danger. I had to get to you before he did."

It was her turn to astonish him.

"Hugh Lindsey is dead, Leo."

Jaggedly, she explained about Hugh, and the young woman he had had murdered, and about how he had tried to kill her too. As she spoke, Leo laced his fingers through hers and gripped her tightly, as if attempting some retroactive protection.

"I should have known," he said bitterly. "I should have seen through Hugh much earlier. Good old Hugh. Everyone's best friend. Always the life and soul of the party, even if he did like one too many and was always the last to leave. If anyone had looked more closely, they might have sensed a vacancy in him. There was a kind of emptiness, which he filled with drink and liaisons with other people's wives. But nobody did look closely."

"Why was that?"

"Because Hugh had the most lethal of all qualities. Charm. Charm deflects inquiry. We're taught about those types in training. They're dominant. They imagine they can calculate risks and manage them better than anyone else."

"You knew him at Oxford, didn't you?"

"I liked him a lot actually, though we were intellectual rivals. We had some of the same friends, but we lost touch afterwards. Hugh lived a peripatetic existence. After Christ Church he traveled to Vienna, then went back to England and took up a job as a journalist. At the same time he began working for the Intelligence Services."

"Like you."

"Only, in Hugh's case, it was a cover for his work for the Soviet Union. He'd formed Marxist sympathies in Austria and began to spy for the NKVD. They managed to infiltrate him into D Section, and that gave him knowledge of our entire European network. Hugh knew I was in Vienna, and he let the police know too. I disappeared just in time."

Leo pulled Clara to him, resting his chin on her head and kissing her hair.

"There was a day, when I was on the run, that I slipped into a cinema and saw a film of yours, and I felt you were right there, in my arms. It was so real, I could almost taste your skin and smell that perfume you wear. It was like . . . a vision. I knew I'd been wrong to enforce that vow of silence on you. I had a plan, Clara. I thought I knew best. But things don't always turn out the way you plan them. All I know now is that I want you with me in England. Safe. There's no telling when war could break out."

"There is. Von Ribbentrop is flying to Moscow imminently to finalize a nonaggression pact. The Soviet Union will stand by when Hitler invades Poland. I've seen the memorandum. It's code-named Operation White. And they've set a date. September first."

"Have you told anyone this?"

"Only you."

It was darker now, the surroundings becoming monochrome. They had emerged at the spot where the elegant gray-green steel arches of the Glienicker bridge spanned the Havel. To the north the land rose up in densely wooded slopes to the land-scaped park and fairy-tale turrets of the Schloss Babelsberg. To the east, a few fragile points of light signaled the outlying streets of Potsdam. Leo gestured to a car parked on the far end of the bridge, its engine idling.

"There was a man I knew in the German Foreign Office. I'd met him years ago in London, and I thought he might be sympathetic to us. He was unwilling to cooperate, though I sensed that he was not an ardent Nazi. So I took a chance and called him earlier today. He agreed to drive me across the border to-night."

"Are you leaving?"

"No. You are. If we try to leave together, we risk attracting attention. You will take my place in the car. I'll follow."

"How can you follow? You're on a Gestapo watch list. How long could you evade them?"

"I'm not leaving you here."

"You don't have a hope of escaping them, Leo. This is your best chance."

He squared his shoulders, wrapped his arms round her waist, and looked at her. The movement of his body against hers aroused the old, familiar feelings, the urgency of desire, the recognition that loving each other had become a part of them—the best part perhaps—and that what they possessed was solid and incorruptible. Clara yearned to stay suspended in that mo-ment, for the earth to halt in its orbit and the stars above them to slow.

He said, "I've spent so much of my life in the shadows. Pre-tending. Deceiving people. That's the job, I know, but I don't want to live like that anymore. I want the most important part of my life to be open, public, dull even. I used to crave excitement and novelty, but now I want my life to be normal, or as normal as it could be alongside the loveliest woman in the world. I want a row of children with your eyes. As many as you like. I want to be able to say 'Look, everyone, this is Clara Vine, who is not only the most beautiful woman you have met, but is also my wife.' "

She glanced away, down to the river below, remembering her pact with the deity, that she would do whatever Leo wanted if only he was alive. That she would be the woman he wanted her to be.

"What good would it do if you were dead? How could we marry then?"

He carried on, almost as if she had not spoken. "There's a poem, by Martial, a Roman poet. He says we should not 'miss the rich life within our reach.' You're my rich life. Take my place, Clara."

He looked at her, as if trying to compress a lifetime's conversation into a single glance. As though his life depended on her answer.

"I'll come as fast as I can. But I can't leave Germany without saying goodbye to Erich."

"Erich will understand." The light in his eyes pierced as sharply as the first time she had met him. That same level gaze, whose intensity almost made her shiver.

"There are three surveillance teams looking for you. No one's looking for me. I can take the first train out of Berlin. I can leave Germany tomorrow."

"No."

"When war comes Erich will be called up, and I might never see him again. I have to see him before I leave. You must trust me, Leo. You do trust me, don't you? There's no point in anything if you don't."

He cupped her face. Although his face remained controlled, a tremor in his hands betrayed the depth of his emotion.

"I do."

"And you believe I'm capable?"

"That's one thing about you that I have never doubted."

She linked her fingers into his, as tightly as if they had been parachute jumpers, planning to launch themselves together into the cold unknown.

"Go then."

He walked along the bridge. She could see the soft glow of the car's gauges and the gleam of the leather inside. But whether Conrad Adler saw her, as the door opened and Leo got inside, it was impossible to tell. She stood watching, until the car's lights dimmed into the distance and finally faded from sight.

N̲O EVENT WAS MORE CENTRAL TO THE OUTBREAK OF WORLD War II than the Nazi-Soviet Nonaggression Pact. Signed on August 23, 1939, it was an enormous coup for Hitler, turning Germany's greatest foe into an ally overnight and avoiding the danger of a war along the eastern borders of the Reich. Leni Riefenstahl records how she was present at the film evening at the Chancellery when Hitler's remarks about Stalin gave the first inkling of his intentions.

The *Sonderfahndungsliste G.B., The Gestapo Handbook for the Invasion of Britain*—was designed to be given to every soldier. It was a who's who of the British establishment, listing more than two thousand people, complete with photographs, home addresses, and private hobbies. It also probed every facet of British life, from political parties, police forces, and secret services to newspapers, radio stations, and trade unions.

The Rote Kapelle, the Red Orchestra, was a network of seven resistance groups with more than 150 members, including the fortune-teller Annie Krauss. They sheltered Jews and Communists and provided forged papers for those attempting to flee.

More than 120 members of the Berlin group were arrested in 1942 and sentenced to death.

Alois, the half brother of Adolf Hitler, ran a restaurant at 3 Wittenbergplatz for many years. He was approached anonymously by the Rote Kapelle with an invitation to join them and circulate a typed flyer denouncing the Nazis' culture of lies. Instead he handed the note over to the Gestapo, and the leaders were ultimately arrested and executed.

Albert Goering, brother of Hermann Goering, took a different approach. The SS kept a file on him, and he was declared a "Public Enemy of the Reich," but Hermann rescinded the arrest warrant. When he was arrested at the end of the war, Albert secured a speedy release by producing a list of thirty-four key figures who would testify to the numerous people he had helped. He refused to change his name after the war and died impoverished.

Magda Goebbels's affair with Karl Hanke came to an end when he volunteered for military service. *The Journey to Tilsit* was launched in November 1939 in Berlin. Magda Goebbels ostentatiously walked out of the premiere.

A large amount of the "Degenerate art" seized by the Nazis went missing. A celebrated haul was discovered in 2012 in the Munich flat of Cornelius Gurlitt, whose father, Hildebrand Gurlitt, had amassed 1,406 works by painters including Matisse, Chagall, Beckmann, Nolde, and Picasso while working for the Nazis.

Elsa Neuländer-Simon, also known as Yva, was a celebrated fashion photographer in Berlin and gave Helmut Newton his first apprenticeship. She and her husband were deported to the Majdanek concentration camp and murdered in 1942.

Leni Riefenstahl abandoned her film *Germania* on the outbreak of war.

ACKNOWLEDGMENTS

I T TAKES SO MANY PEOPLE TO MAKE A BOOK, AND THERE HAVE BEEN some particularly brilliant people who have contributed their talents to this one. I am grateful for the editing expertise and generous enthusiasm of the legendary Kate Miciak, as well as the support of Julia Maguire, Christine Mykityshyn, and all those on the Ballantine team. Huge thanks to Nina Pronovost, and to Zoe Maslow, Adria Iwasutiak, and everyone at Penguin Random House Canada.

To my agent, Caradoc King, for believing in Clara Vine from the time she was just a twenty-six-year-old actress fresh off the train to Berlin, and to fellow writers Elizabeth Buchan, Liz Jensen, Amanda Craig, Kate Saunders, and Anne Sebba for cheering her along.

My special thanks go the wonderful Joanna Coles, whose gift for friendship has been unrivaled since the day we met on a Fleet Street newspaper diary column. To John Carey, whose encouragement and enthusiasm have been a constant inspiration, and to my children, William, Charlie, and Naomi, who patiently steer conversation away from World War II to the more important topics of social life, travel arrangements, and food in the fridge.

I never imagined, when Clara Vine first stepped off that

train in the Friedrichstrasse station, that I would follow her so far. But her destiny piqued questions in me that demanded answers about how she would come to terms with her past, what war would bring, and what her future might be. It has been wonderful to continue her story, and I hope you enjoy it.

The
PURSUIT
of
PEARLS

JANE THYNNE

A
READER'S
GUIDE

THE REAL HOUSEWIVES
OF NAZI GERMANY

WHEN I FIRST THOUGHT OF SETTING A SERIES OF NOVELS in prewar Berlin, I knew a few things. I knew that my heroine was going to be Anglo-German and an actress. I decided that she would be a spy who gains a valuable glimpse of the Nazi elite through the women around her. Yet while I understood a fair bit about the men and the politics of the Third Reich, I realized that I knew far less about the lives of the women in that regime. And increasingly, as I delved deep into the lives of women through their letters and journals, I became fascinated by what I came to think of as the Real Housewives of Nazi Germany.

Under Hitler, every aspect of a woman's life was tightly controlled, from child-bearing, marriage, and social life, right down to her daily appearance. The ideal woman didn't pluck her eyebrows, paint her nails, or dye her hair. Nor did she smoke. In the early days of the Reich, bars and restaurants throughout Germany were plastered with signs saying GERMAN WOMEN DON'T SMOKE, and storm troopers who saw a woman smoking in public were advised to dash the cigarette from her lips.

But the control over women's appearance didn't stop at cigarettes and cosmetics. One of the first things Hitler did when he came to power in 1933 was to establish a Reich Fashion Bureau. He realized that fashion carries a potent political message and he knew exactly what image he wanted German women to project to the world. The female look should celebrate tradition, so the Bureau promoted dirndls, bodices, and Tyrolean jackets. Women should only wear clothes made by German designers, with German materials. By "German," Hitler meant Aryan, which posed an immediate problem because the fashion industry and the textile trade of the time were dominated by Jewish companies. Hitler also frowned on Parisian couture, both because he disliked the French, and also because designers like Coco Chanel encouraged an unnaturally slender silhouette. A nation of women striving for slim hips and boyish bodies was certainly not ideal if Hitler was to achieve one of his major objectives—to encourage prolific child-bearing.

In one of the many bizarre hypocrisies of the Third Reich, the woman chosen to preside over this Fashion Bureau was Magda Goebbels, the wife of the Propaganda Minister. Like many other aspects of Nazi Germany, Magda Goebbels's participation was rife with contradictions, and Magda herself was the living, breathing opposite of everything the Bureau promoted. Famed for her love of couture, she changed several times a day, slathered on Elizabeth Arden cosmetics, chain smoked, and wore hand-made Ferragamo shoes. Her favorite fashion designers, Paul Kuhnen, Richard Goetz, Max Becker, and Fritz Grünfeld, were all Jewish.

Yet there was a far greater contradiction in Magda Goebbels's life than her fashion sense. Before she married, she had a passionate involvement with a leading Zionist called Victor

Arlosoroff, who returned to Berlin in 1933 aghast at his for-mer girlfriend's choice of husband. To me, the idea that the wife of the arch persecutor of the Jews, Joseph Goebbels, should have had an affair with an important Jewish agitator seemed astonishing. But it was typical of the ironies that reigned in that terrible, turbulent regime.

One question always at the back of my mind while I was researching the lives of Nazi women was the extent to which they themselves had exerted a political influence on their husbands. Did any of them act as the power behind the throne? In some cases, the answer was yes. Annelies von Rib-bentrop and Lina Heydrich were both considered more ar-dent Nazis than their husbands. Yet others, like Emmy Goering, actively interceded with their husbands on an oc-casional basis to save friends. Henriette, the wife of the Hit-ler Youth leader Baldur von Schirach, was the only one who actually remonstrated with Hitler when she confronted him over dinner at the Berghof about the treatment of Jews in Holland. She was never invited again.

Women are so often the untold half of history and their perspectives are frequently ignored. I think it's impossible to visualize the Nazi leaders as people without getting a glimpse of their private lives and their most important relationships.

For me, understanding the Real Housewives of Nazi Ger-many, from the wives of the elite to the ordinary women in the street, was the key to making history and, I hope, my novels come alive.

QUESTIONS AND TOPICS
FOR DISCUSSION

1.   Despite their seemingly different political inclinations, Clara visits her sister when she is upset by Grand's suggestion of Leo's death. Blood may be thicker than water, but do you believe, as Clara does, that it should be thicker than war?

2.   How does Clara's status as an English spy change her relationship with Erich?

3.   Clara talks about all the things that have been rationed, such as coffee and meat, or made more difficult, such as easy travel. What do you think is the hardest thing for her to sacrifice? What would be the hardest for you?

4.   What advice would you give to Hedwig about the conflict between Jochen and her parents?

5.   Though Clara narrates the majority of the novel, we occasionally see events from Hedwig's point of view. In what ways are the two perspectives similar? In what ways are they different?

6.   In part due to Clara's mixed heritage many of her ac-

quaintances ask where she would eventually like to settle down. Where do you think she should go?

7.   Conrad Adler knows that Clara is part Jewish, but she continues on with her life as always, even seeing Adler again. Do you agree with her decision, or would you have handled the situation differently?

8.   Themes of heritage pervade the book, often bringing into conflict ethnic, religious, cultural, and national identities. What do you think it is that makes you who you are?

9.   What do you think Conrad Adler means when he says that Clara has a look of "fire behind ice"?

10.   In a world of spies, secrets, and war, it is difficult to know who to trust, and Clara chooses her confidants carefully. Do you agree with all of her choices? Who in your life would you choose to trust if you were in Clara's circumstances?

11.   Do you think Conrad Adler is a good man, or do you think he is as bad as the political party for which he works? Would you trust him? Why or why not?

12.   There are quite a few revelations as the final pieces of the book fall into place. What surprised you the most?

If you enjoyed

The PURSUIT
of PEARLS

YOU WON'T WANT TO MISS

Jane Thynne's next
CLARA VINE NOVEL

READ ON FOR A SNEAK PEEK . . .

BERLIN, OCTOBER 1937

THE FLASH AND DAZZLE OF FIREWORKS, LIKE MULTI-colored shrapnel, studded the night sky. Vivid bursts of phosphorus erupted in the damp air, bloomed into extravagant showers of stars, then fizzled and died against the dark sheet of the Wannsee below. A faint plume of smoke drifted across the lake as the fireworks fell quiet and night closed in again.

From where she stood, in the deep shadow of the garden, Anna Hansen tried to work out which of the big villas on Schwanenwerder Island had something to celebrate. Fireworks were nothing special here. There were always parties going on in the grand houses. They all had large gardens stretching down to the lake from where, across the water, loomed the inky mass of the Grunewald's eastern shore. Between the shores the dip and ripple of small boats could be heard, rocking in the wind as the water slapped against their sides.

Anna shivered in the night air. It was cold standing here, surrounded by softly dripping shrubs. She shuffled her slippered feet and clutched her dressing gown more closely around her. Though it might have been the bangs and whistles that woke her, in truth she had scarcely been able to sleep, despite an exhausting day. But then, it was always an exhausting day at the Schwanenwerder Reich Bride School. It seemed there was so much to learn for women who were about to marry members of the SS. It wasn't like being an ordinary German bride, though, heaven knows, those girls had their work cut out. But as the Führer said, the women who were to marry the cream of German manhood needed to be something special.

Not that Anna had much choice when she arrived at the Bride School, a stately villa with pillared gates proudly topped by a pair of swastika flags and screened from the world by a ridge of tall pines. Classes there were compulsory—they had been since 1935, on Himmler's orders—and you needed to submit the certificate you received to the SS Race and Settlement Office before your marriage could go ahead. In some ways the School was like a military training academy, with a regime that started at five thirty in the morning and didn't end until the weary brides dropped into their beds at nine o'clock at night. That morning, for example, had begun with the usual outdoor bath, to take advantage of the island's fresh, pine-scented air, followed by energetic gymnastics in shorts and undershirts. After breakfast came Sewing, and then a visit from the local Mother and Child branch for Child Care instruction, before lunch, which was made on a rota by the brides themselves, wearing head scarves and spotless aprons.

Today they had been focusing on Cooking Without Butter because of the shortage, and it had been very dull. Though that was no bad thing, Anna thought, because all these regular meals were making her plump. After lunch came Culture, consisting of a talk on fairy tales. All brides needed to learn fairy tales because the German mother was the "culture bearer" to the next generation. Today's lecturer had explained how in "Cinderella" it was the prince's Germanic instincts that led him to reject the stepsisters' alien blood and search for a maiden who was racially pure.

Culture should have been what Anna enjoyed best. She had been a dancer after all, not so long ago. Chorus line at the Wintergarten. Standing there amid the shadowy shrubs, she ran an absent hand over her rumpled, shoulder-length hair. Her dark roots were showing badly, and the bleached curls were already turning to frizz in the damp air. She sighed. It was hard to imagine a greater contrast than that between her previous life and the one she was living now. Her old friends would die laughing if they could see her. But then Anna's circumstances had changed. Changed drastically. And by some miracle, just as she had needed to escape from a difficult spot, SS Obersturmführer Johann Peters, six foot two with a jaw like granite and eyes as blue as the Baltic Sea, had walked into her life. From the moment Johann had come up to her in that dank little nightclub, she hadn't looked back. If it hadn't been for Johann, she might even have resorted to answering one of those depressing advertisements you saw in the newspapers. *54-year-old lawyer, pure Aryan, desires male offspring through marriage with young virgin, hardworking, low heels, no jewelry.* So when Johann had requested a dance, and shortly afterwards her hand in marriage, she had taken him up on it without a second thought, even if it meant spending six weeks at Bride School in preparation.

The villa that housed the Bride School had been occupied by a single Jewish family until it was transferred to the ownership of the Deutsches Frauenwerk. As Anna walked between lessons, she would look wistfully at the grandeur of the décor, the mahogany paneling of the hall and the line of little bells in the kitchen, which were connected to different rooms in the house. The whole place was full of color: pistachio paint in the hall, almond white on the dado rails, and deep burgundy in the library, which still smelled of leather and cigars. The music room—an entire room devoted to music!—was painted daffodil yellow, and the ballroom, which was lavender blue, had a ceiling like a wedding cake, molded with plaster roses, from where great chandeliers were suspended. Anna liked to imagine the life that had existed there before—all the parties and the fun and the elegance. There were patches on the walls where gold-framed oil paintings had hung, and if you stood quite still you could almost sense the family that had once lived here, evanescent as a waft of perfume down a corridor, or the faint ripple of laughter in the air.

Now, however, the ballroom had been fitted with desks and its damask curtains taken down in the interest of cleanliness. Cleanliness was all-important at the Bride School. Everything had to be hygienic and disinfected, smelling of soap and polish. Dirt, and all soiled traces of the past, must be scrubbed away. Dirt was disgusting, the instructors said. Dust was almost un-German.

Anna's dormitory, where eight girls slept, was a long room on the top floor. It must have been the nursery originally, but it had been redecorated in the same stark, brutal fashion as the rest of the house. Iron bedsteads flanked the walls, and the floors were bare boards. The wallpaper had been whitewashed over, but if you tipped the wardrobe slightly, you could see a remnant of it, pale pink with knotted posies. Anna was observant like that. She had an eye for detail; she always liked to know what lay underneath things.

It had been hard to leave her bed and slip out of the house

unnoticed. Strangely for an organization that believed so fervently in fresh air, the dormitory window was kept locked, and after bedtime the corridors were patrolled by the sewing mistress, Fräulein Wolff. Brides were told not to leave the room except in cases of emergency. Luckily the only person to notice Anna waking that night was Ilse Henning, a good-hearted country girl with a shelf of a bosom and a face as scrubbed as a pine table, who blinked at her in puzzlement, then rolled obediently onto her side. Ilse probably assumed, quite correctly, that her roommate was going into the garden to smoke an illicit cigarette.

That much was true. Yet it was a deeper restlessness that was troubling Anna Hansen. All day she had had the curious sensation that she was being watched. It was nothing obvious. Just a brooding self-consciousness that crawled across her skin, raising the minute hairs on her neck, making her tense, the way a gazelle tenses when it scents the approach of a predator. Several times during the day, both in the garden and in the house, she'd had the distinct feeling of someone's eyes upon her, only to wheel around and find nothing there. She had repeatedly attempted to rationalize the sensation. Perhaps it was the sorry shortage of nicotine that had set her nerves jangling. Or maybe the ugly gardener, Hartmann, the one with the limp and the hedgehog haircut, was spying on her. He was always hanging around eyeing the Reich Brides. What was a creep like him even doing in a place like this? Why couldn't he be sent to the Rhineland or something?

The feeling came on her again as she lay trying to sleep in the dormitory, listening to the distant crump of fireworks, and to shake it off she had risen and crept out into the chill October air.

The moon was obscured by a bank of heavy cloud as she

progressed through the garden, avoiding the gravel path and staying close to the shrubs at the edge of the lawn. Behind her the house was a shuttered and slumbering hulk, with only a single lamp burning on the ground floor. Ahead lay the leaden expanse of the lake, visible only by the lights that glimmered from the few yachts and pleasure boats moored at its shore.

She stopped at the trunk of a large pine tree and pulled out her cigarettes. Around her a dim tangle of laurel receded into a pool of deeper shadow. There was dense vegetation underfoot. Flecks of water from the lake blew against her face, and she hugged her arms to her chest, wishing she had worn something warmer than an old silk dressing gown. Because of the rigid dress code at the School, nightwear was the only area where brides had any self-expression. Most of the girls opted for a floral tent of scrubby toweling, but Anna's was creamy silk with ivory lace inserts, and a matching negligee that smelled of smoke and perfume and acted as a consoling, luxurious reminder of the good old days.

Suddenly she sensed a frisson of movement in the bushes, a spectral shimmer accompanied by a rustle of leaves. She froze, her senses on alert, straining to filter the night sounds. The fireworks had subsided now, and the night's silence was penetrated only by the whine of the high trees swaying and the thrum of a car making its way along the lake road. More faintly, the soft rattle and groan of boats, their timbers creaking, and the water slapping on their sides, carried on the breeze.

There it was again. A distinct crackle of leaves, a few yards to her left. Anna stiffened, her heart lifting into her throat, and whirled to see a white shape and a pair of golden circles trained on her. She almost laughed with relief.

"God, Minka. You gave me a fright! Hiding from the fireworks?"

The cat approached and rubbed against her leg. She was a friendly animal and much loved by the Bride School inmates. Anna squatted down to stroke her head, then took out her lighter, an elegant silver lozenge engraved with her initials. God forbid anyone should find her with it. She had had to smuggle it in here, because smoking was strictly forbidden at the Bride School. The Führer called cigarettes "decadent" and said smokers were unfit to be German wives and mothers. All brides had to sit through a lecture on the poison of nicotine and how the Jews had brought tobacco to Germany to corrupt the native stock. She snapped the lighter open, the flame leapt up and lit the cigarette, and she took a deep drag, impatient for the first delicious hit to coil down her throat. Sighing, she rested her back against the bark of the tree. This was a long way to come for a smoke, but it was worth it.

Beside her the cat froze and lifted her head. She had seen something, but what? A mouse perhaps, or a bird? A fox even? Following her gaze, Anna stared blindly into the murk.

"Is someone there?"

A sudden screech heralded the launch of a single rocket that flared and dissipated in an emerald shower, lighting up the sky. The cat's pupils contracted to slits. As the sound died away, Anna heard something else. The soft crunch of a footstep on the wet earth.

"Who is it?"

The words choked in her throat. As she stared desperately around her into the darkness, frantic thoughts raced through her mind. It had been a mistake to come out here. She should never have left the dormitory. Perhaps it was the creepy gardener, spying again.

"Hartmann? Is that you?"

Two more steps, and then a face loomed up before her. As

Anna peered desperately through the darkness, terror engulfed her. Her knees almost buckled, and it took everything she had to summon a tone of coy flirtatiousness.

"Well, hello, stranger."

The man raised the Walther 6.35-caliber pistol, and Anna's eyes widened, but the sound of the shot was drowned in another exuberant volley of fireworks. A spume of scarlet sparks arced and spangled the sky. The man with the gun watched Anna languidly as she fell, then he turned away and melted into the shadows. For a moment Anna's hand clutched frantically, as if she were trying to haul herself up on empty air, then it dropped back and the lighter slid out of her opened palm, down into the damp grass.

CHAPTER

1

CLARA VINE SWUNG HER CAR THROUGH THE WROUGHT-IRON gates of the villa and braked violently to avoid a peacock crossing the drive. As the bird strutted onto the lawn, dragging its magnificent lapis lazuli tail, Clara was sure she divined an arrogant glint in its beady eye. Still, she was relieved she hadn't hit it. It wouldn't do to damage any property belonging to the Reichsminister of Enlightenment and Propaganda, even if that property did happen to be an unwanted pet. The birds were leftovers from Joseph Goebbels's magnificent Olympics party the previous year, when Peacock Island in the Wannsee had been turned into a fairy-tale playground for two thousand guests, filled with dancing and fireworks. Film stars, singers, and all kinds of celebrities mingled with diplomats and high-ranking visitors. The papers had been full of it for days. After the balloons and the banners had been packed away, some of the birds had ended up here, even though Frau Doktor Goebbels detested them. Their jeweled crowns and magnificent displays concealed a nasty temper, and the stillness of Schwanenwerder was pierced constantly by their shrill cries.

Not that the neighbors would have dreamt of complaining. The Goebbelses' villa, at Inselstrasse 8, was in the most desirable position on this tiny, exclusive enclave. Though it was called an island, it was actually a peninsula, which stretched out from the Grunewald into the lake, connected by a single, narrow road. Surrounded on all sides by water, and wooded with oak, birch, and pine, Schwanenwerder was only a few kilometers from the center of Berlin, yet it might have been another country. It had been colonized a hundred years ago by the very wealthiest of Berlin's society, the bankers, industrialists, and department store owners, who had competed among themselves to build the most tasteful, luxurious country houses and take advantage of Schwanenwerder's restorative air. Since then, in the space of four years, a new elite had emerged to replace them. On the day Hitler came to power, Nazi storm troopers flocked onto the island and raised the swastika flag on its water tower. Most of the homes were now occupied by senior Party figures. Number 8 had been bought by Goebbels at a price far beneath its genuine value from the chairman of the Deutsche Bank, who had been all too eager to sell before his enforced departure abroad. It had a panoramic view of the Greater Wannsee, extensive lawns running down to a boathouse, and a garden ringed with oaks, pines, and fruit trees.

Clara parked the red Opel next to a Mercedes-Benz cabriolet with beige leather seats, checked her lipstick in the rearview mirror, and smoothed her hair beneath her hat. She sat for a second, waiting for her trepidation, like a surge of stage fright, to come under control. Then she stepped out of the car. As she made her way to the front door, a pear, like a tiny, unexploded bomb, dropped beside her into the grass.

The maid showed her into the drawing room, whose French windows at one end led to a flag terrace circled by a balustrade, beyond which was a magnificent view of the lake, edged by the gloomy, impenetrable Grunewald. Now, at five in the afternoon, the sun was a molten orb in a streaked caramel sky, turning the waters of the Wannsee into a sheet of hammered gold. At the end of the garden, Clara could see a private beach and a jetty, where Goebbels kept his motor yacht, *Baldur*. Seagulls squawked and wheeled in the sky, and farther out in the lake, a couple of fishermen drifted in their boats, hunched over their tranquil lines waiting for pike, like figures from a nineteenth-century painting.

Clara crossed her arms and waited, pretending a nonchalance she did not feel, as she tried, yet again, to work out what Magda Goebbels could possibly want with her.

The message had come that morning out of the blue. A messenger had brought the note to Clara directly onto the set at the Ufa film studios in Babelsberg, where she was filming a romantic comedy called *A Girl for Everything*. He had shouldered his way through the makeup girls and the script man, right into the dazzle of the arc lights, to deliver it. The boy's face was a picture of urgency and intense curiosity, as befitted a summons from Magda Goebbels, wife of Hitler's right-hand man and the woman informally known as the First Lady of the Reich. The other actors had looked on avidly as Clara quickly scanned the message, then folded the note and slipped it in a pocket. Her face, she knew, gave nothing away.

Now Clara walked around the drawing room, assessing the pictures and furniture on display. Last year Goebbels had claimed he was embarrassed to have moved into such a large villa because he hated luxury, yet for the sake of the Reich he could not be expected to receive distinguished guests in his old apartment. One look at this room, however, revealed that his aversion to luxury did not run very deep. The place was furnished in solid bourgeois taste: rich Persian rugs and fat sofas upholstered in satin and watered silk, side tables in restrained nineteenth-century style on a parquet floor polished to a high shine. A Gobelin tapestry hung on the wall, and a Bechstein piano stood in the front window. The standard portrait of the Führer, de rigueur in any Party home, hung above a mantelpiece crowded with family photographs, most of which Clara had already seen in the newspapers. There was Goebbels in open-necked shirt and sunglasses, at the wheel of his motorboat. The four Goebbels children, Helga, Hilde, Helmut, and Holde, the girls in matching white dresses and ribbons, and Helmut in a sailor suit, sitting in their miniature pony carriage. Goebbels, it was said, insisted on one baby a year. Four children may be enough for a string quartet, he joked, but not enough for a National Socialist. He had publicly promised another five babies for the Reich.

Catching sight of herself in a gold Rococo mirror, Clara scrutinized the picture she presented with a critical eye. She was wearing a buttoned ivory blouse beneath a fitted serge navy suit with a fur collar, her chestnut hair freshly cut in a neat bob. A new, fashionably tilted navy velvet hat. Red Coral lipstick by Max Factor. Lizard-skin clutch bag. Every inch the screen actress whose career was on the rise, though not so successful that she would be recognized on the street. And all of it a façade. Clara was used to a life of deception now. Sometimes deception seemed like an extension of her own being, moving bodily with her as she walked the streets of Berlin or sat with friends in bars or crossed the sets of the Ufa film studios. The Clara Vine she saw in the mirror was both herself and not herself. What the real Clara Vine might look like, she could no longer say.

Though she couldn't fault the image, still Clara felt uneasy. The near miss with the peacock had done nothing to improve her nerves. Behind her she heard the creak of the door and the heavy tread of her hostess.

"You haven't changed a bit!"

It sounded like more of an accusation than a welcome. As Magda Goebbels entered the room, permitting a transitory smile to twitch across her crimson lips, Clara tried to conceal her surprise at the change in her hostess. Even if she had wanted to return Magda's compliment, it was impossible. Four children in five years had done Magda no favors. Clara had seen her often enough in the newspapers, of course, decked out in satin and pearls, hosting grand Party occasions at Hitler's side, presiding at the Mothers' Union and the Winter Relief charity, partying with foreign dignitaries at last year's Olympic games. But, close up, it was a very different picture. Magda was still elegantly turned out in the height of fashion; she wore a Chanel dress in peach silk, and her platinum hair was scalloped tightly against her cheeks. But beneath the rouge, her skin was putty-colored; her mouth was lined, and the dress bulged at the belt. Her body was waging a war between elegance and middle-aged spread, and it seemed the spread was winning.

They sat on low chairs looking out onto the garden while a maid shuffled in, straining under the weight of a tea tray laden with brown bread spread thickly with butter, sponge cake, and *Lebkuchen*. Magda aligned the handles of the cups precisely and gestured to the girl to pour, wincing as her trembling hand spilled tea into the saucer. Impatiently Magda waved her away.

"I'm sorry about that. She's training. There's a Bride School on the island, and we like to help out by giving their girls a little practice with serving. But I have to say I feel sorry for those poor husbands-to-be."

She waited until the girl had left and closed the door behind her. Then she said: "So, Fräulein Vine. Your career is blossoming, I hear. My husband tells me you are quite the rising star at Ufa now."

"Thank you. And how are you, Frau Doktor?"

"Not too good. I've been at the clinic in Dresden again."

Like most women in Berlin, Magda Goebbels was obsessed with her health. She was always visiting spas and clinics to receive injections purported to calm her nerves.

"I'm afraid I haven't kept up with your films." Magda gestured at the family photographs. "My life is rather busy."

So this was how it was to be. From the first line of the script, Clara could judge the expected dialogue, and she was relieved. Their conversation would be confined to pleasantries. Magda was icy as ever. There would be no reference to what had gone before.

"I've been busy too, fortunately."

"Indeed. You have a new film out now, I see." In her lap, Magda's hands were a tight fist of nerves. "I'm trying to remember what it's called?"

"*Madame Bovary*. It's directed by Gerhard Lamprecht. I'm just finishing another, called *A Girl for Everything*, and in a few weeks I'll begin a new film with Ernst Udet. *The Pilot's Wife*. He plays a Luftwaffe pilot who is shot down, and I'm his wife."

At the mention of Ernst Udet, Magda Goebbels responded the way everyone, from small boys to middle-aged women, tended to respond. Her eyes brightened and her attention was captured. The subject of aviation in general, and Ernst Udet in particular, was an exciting one at the moment. The handsome fighter ace, with his strikingly blue eyes, deeply cleft chin, and jovial smile, was not just a war hero but a national celebrity. He had been the best friend of Manfred von Richthofen, the Red Baron, and after the war he became a film star, moving to Hollywood and taking up stunt flying for the movies. Now back in Germany, in his forties and unmarried, he was something of a playboy. His lean frame had rounded out, but it suited him, and besides, German women liked their men with some flesh on them. His autobiography had sold millions. Lessing and Co, the cigarette company, had even produced a special Ernst Udet brand, which came in a pretty cobalt tin, bisected by a soaring scarlet biplane.

In the past year, however, Udet had been dragooned into the service of the Reich. At Goering's insistence he had been appointed head of the Technical Division of the Luftwaffe. He was supposed to be too busy overseeing aircraft manufacture and development to waste his time stunt flying, but still he couldn't resist it. He was coming into the studio later that week to discuss filming *The Pilot's Wife*.

"Generaloberst Udet! What fun for you! We saw him flying at the Olympics. Such a clever man. Will he be performing any of his stunts?"

"Of course. We've got a day's filming out at Tempelhof."

The fact that Udet's stunts were to be filmed at a real airport, in the real sky, was unusual. Hardly anything was shot on location now. All movies were filmed in the studio. It was as though the Nazis wanted to present their fictional world, perfect in every way, without any interference from the real world and all its complexities.

"Then I shall make certain to see it." Magda speared a slice of lemon and suspended it in her tea. "And I'm grateful you could spare time in your schedule to see me."

"It is a pleasure, Frau Doktor," said Clara neutrally. But her mind was racing. She took a bite of sponge cake and waited for Magda to come to the point.

"I have a little request for you. About a party I'm hosting on Saturday. I wondered if you might like to attend?"

A party at the home of the Propaganda Minister? Clara could think of nothing she would like less. And no offer harder to refuse. "How kind of you."

"I have an ulterior motive, I'm afraid. There are some English guests. Their German is not quite as proficient as one would hope, and I think they find conversation quite exhausting. As you have an English father, I thought you might be able to speak to them and make them feel relaxed."

"I would be delighted."

"Excellent." Her mission accomplished, Magda glanced around restlessly, as if in search of small talk. Her fingers hovered over a biscuit, then withdrew. "And how is your family? You have a sister, don't you?"

"Angela."

"Perhaps I will meet her one day. I imagine she is most interested in the country where your mother grew up. Your mother's family came from, where was it again?"

"Hamburg."

"Ah yes."

Clara wondered how long these cordialities would continue. Their words hung between them like mist drifting over deep waters. Frau Goebbels avoided her eye, tapping her fingers on the arm of her chair like a pianist trying to recapture an elusive melody.

"I wonder . . ." ventured Clara. "Could I ask who these English friends are?"

"Oh, didn't I say? You know them, I think. Unity Mitford and her sister Diana."

The Mitfords. Diana and her younger sister Unity were notorious in London for their fascist sympathies. Diana had caused a scandal by leaving her husband to set up house with Oswald Mosley, the darkly handsome leader of the British Union of Fascists, whose rallies were frequently opportunities for violent clashes between his gang of black-shirted followers and their opponents. Though Clara had indeed met Diana and Unity, they were Angela's friends really, part of a set that adored fancy dress, cliquish societies, and wildly extravagant parties. How curious that their politics should share some of the same characteristics.

"We've met, yes. But it was a while ago."

"Diana's a Mosley now, of course. She married her husband last year in our apartment in Hermann-Goering-Strasse."

Magda's face softened as she recalled the occasion. "They wanted a quiet ceremony, you see, because Mosley's first wife had only recently died. So they decided to marry here in Berlin, and the Führer graciously agreed to attend. Diana wore golden silk. Unity and I were her witnesses. Afterwards we drove out here for lunch, down by the lake, and my little girls presented her with posies of wildflowers. We gave them a twenty-volume set of the works of Goethe. It was so romantic."

At this, it was as if Magda realized she had confided something she shouldn't have. As if she had stepped into some territory that had been declared forever out of bounds. A blush bloomed momentarily in the pallor of her complexion, and her whole body stiffened.

"Anyhow, they're coming over for the day. I had planned a whole day of sightseeing, only . . ." She hesitated momentarily, as if uncertain about imparting any further information. Clara concealed her curiosity with careful sips of scalding tea.

". . . Only I've had to cancel a local outing I had planned for them. I had hoped to show them around the new Bride School just down the road from here, but unfortunately there's been an incident. Well, a bit more shocking than that, actually." Magda flicked an eye towards the door as though the maid might be eavesdropping. She lowered her voice. "One of the brides was found murdered."

"Murdered?" The word rang harshly in the tranquil, tea-time air.

"Yes. In the garden, apparently. A girl named Anna Hansen. Terrible, isn't it? It's so sad for her fiancé." Magda grimaced in annoyance. "And rather inconvenient for us. The visit can't possibly go ahead. It's obviously cast a cloud. It wouldn't be the right atmosphere."

Anna Hansen. For a second, the name snagged in Clara's mind. Then she realized she used to know a girl of that name, though it could hardly be the same one. The Anna Hansen that Clara knew was an easygoing bottle blonde from Munich who would be more at home in a negligee than an SS Hausfrau's apron. Indeed, when Clara first met her, she hadn't been wearing any clothes at all. Anna had been a life model for the artist Bruno Weiss, whom Clara had met through Helga Schmidt, the small-time actress who had been the first person to befriend Clara when she arrived in the city in 1933. After Helga died that year, Bruno and Clara had become good friends, and Clara would often drop in to his Pankow studio to watch him working and bring him meals he might otherwise forget to eat. Since Helga's death, Bruno had been working with feverish intensity, his canvases becoming bloodier and more grotesque, his hatred for the regime erupting in livid clots of paint. It was on such a visit one day last year, bearing rolls and some sausage, that Clara had first met Anna. Her naked form had been arranged obligingly on Bruno's crusty velvet sofa, her legs splayed and a cigarette dangling from a long amber holder in her hand. She had the flexible, muscular limbs that came from a dancer's training. The idea of Bruno's Anna Hansen marrying an SS officer was too incongruous for words.

The inconvenient death of the Reich bride seemed to have caused a palpable chill in the room. Magda rose with unexpected haste and clacked across the parquet floor. "Anyway, Fräulein Vine, don't let me keep you any longer."

She held the door open.

"The party will be next Saturday at seven P.M. Only twenty or so people. Is there"—she hesitated—"a guest you might like to bring? A fiancé perhaps?"

"No, there's no one."

"Then we shall be most pleased to see just you."

With a peremptory nod Magda disappeared across the hall and up the stairs.

Clara walked back to her car, her mind working furiously. She found herself unexpectedly trembling. An invitation, after all this time? Magda had said it was her idea, but could it be, really? Clara tried to analyze the request. There was nothing especially strange about the Goebbelses entertaining English visitors. There were plenty of high-ranking Britons arriving in Berlin, even now, when Germany's march into the Rhineland and Hitler's backing of Franco's faction in Spain had opened the eyes of most British people to the intentions of his regime. Last year, during the Olympics, Berlin had been full of tourists, and last month's Nuremberg rally had attracted another wave of politicians and dignitaries. Yet much as the Nazi elite enjoyed meeting them, conversation could be strained. The truth was, the British were lazy about learning the language. Many of them had nothing more than a few phrases picked up from a Baedeker's guide to help them. They could order a beer in a restaurant and find their way to a nightclub, but that was little use when discussing the extremely delicate matter of friendship between Germany and England in an increasingly difficult international situation.

As she backed the car out of the drive, Clara told herself that her role would be simply to chat with those guests and perform a little polite translation to oil the conversational wheels; she would be no more than an accessory, a party decoration, like those peacocks. Her task would last a couple of hours, at most. How difficult could that be?

Making her way back around the single road that skirted the island, Clara craned her head to glimpse the houses she passed. Most had fences and forbidding gates, or signs announcing that they were patrolled by dogs and security guards. Others had long drives, screened with trees. Between the branches she caught glimpses of handsome, turn-of-the-century villas, with balconies and impressive porches and well-kept lawns. It hadn't taken long for the occupants of this slice of paradise, the Rothschilds and Israels and Goldschmidts, to yield to the offers of high-ranking Nazis and pack up their belongings. One villa had been purchased by the Reich Chancellery and reserved for Hitler's own use. Another was occupied by Hitler's doctor, Theo Morell. Albert Speer, the Führer's young architect, had been seen house hunting on Schwanenwerder, too. It was hard to connect such men with this idyllic place. Now murder, too, had tainted this paradise.

It was fifteen minutes before Clara's Opel Olympia passed through the dense Grunewald, reached the leafy avenues of

Wilmersdorf, and moved along Königsallee into the clanging bustle of Kurfürstendamm, Berlin's smartest shopping street, known to all as the Ku'damm. The noise was always what one noticed first at the heart of Berlin. The high-decibel blaring of car horns, the screech of brakes, the wheedling calls of the newspaper boys. Then the smell, the fumes of traffic and hot oil, the spicy scent of a pretzel cart or a wurst stall. Normally the pavements outside the fashionable cafés were crowded with customers, sipping coffee and watching life go by. Today, however, the tables were mostly empty. The cold of the past few days had reminded everyone that another bone-chilling Berlin winter was fast approaching, and shoppers passed quickly, huddled into their coats and scarfs.

At the junction with Wilmersdorfer Strasse, Clara braked as a traffic policeman stepped forward with his hand extended to allow a detachment of soldiers to pass. There was always some kind of military procession these days. Either it was troops or a formation of the Hitler Youth or the BDM, the League of German Girls, with their flaxen braids and navy skirts. The storm troopers, the SS, or the Hitler Jugend, all with their different uniforms and insignia. War was in the air. Even the collecting tins and the banners talked of the "War on Hunger and Cold" as though the most charitable of enterprises must be undertaken with military aggression. There was a stirring of something just over the horizon that people preferred to ignore, and pedestrians, looking forward to the weekend, kept their heads down, their faces as blank as the asphalt underfoot. They hurried on, hoping that no motorcade of Party top brass would be following the soldiers, requiring everyone to halt and raise a respectful right arm. The Führer supposedly trained with an arm expander so he could perform his own salute for two hours without flagging, but most people found even a few minutes a trial. Clara wondered where the soldiers might be heading. These days, that was all anyone was thinking.

She shivered as she recalled the British newspapers she had flicked through that summer. The dispatch in *The Times*, informing the world how a special German flying unit, formed to support the Nationalists in the Spanish Civil War, had bombed the ancient Basque town of Guernica. For more than three hours Junkers and Heinkel bombers unloaded bombs and incendiaries, while fighter aircraft plunged low to machine-gun those of the civilian population who had sought refuge in the fields. The town was razed to the ground. Hundreds of women and children were killed. Three small bomb cases stamped with the German Imperial Eagle had proved to the world that the official German position of neutrality was a sham. Looking up now at the bone-white sky, Clara tried to imagine the bombers screaming out of the stillness of a spring morning, the terror of the people fleeing as they were strafed from the air. Then she pictured the same happening in England, Hitler's bombers raining their deadly payload on the House of Commons or Westminster Abbey, or Ponsonby Terrace, where her father lived. On Angela's home in Chelsea, or farther out in the quiet suburbs, in Hackney and Greenwich and Barnes. On the Wren churches and Nelson's Column and the National Gallery. She imagined the air-raid sirens, the women and children hurrying out of their houses, the fighter planes diving low to finish off those stumbling figures who had escaped the incendiaries. The horizon lit by the red glow of a thousand fires, gas bombs sending coils of poison into family homes. She shook her head. That could never happen.

As she waited for the traffic policeman to clear the road, she looked across the street, to where a crane was poised like a giant bird, pecking at another excavation. Berlin these days was like a patient under constant operation. Every street was subject to extracting, filling, and fixing. You couldn't move for heaps of bricks, planks laid over holes in the earth, and skeletal steel structures rising into the sky. Everywhere there was the roar of cement mixers and the rattle of drills, erecting the monumental Neoclassical buildings deemed suitable for the new world capital of Germania. There was something grand and futile about these buildings of the Führer, Clara decided. They were like an empty boast, designed to make human beings feel like ants in their long passages and echoing halls. Goering's Air Ministry had seven kilometers of corridors apparently, and it was said that for his centerpiece Hitler wanted Albert Speer to build a dome that rose a thousand feet into the sky, capable of holding 180,000 people. The Führer had also ordered Speer to equip all government buildings with bulletproof doors and shutters, just in case the people should ever lose their enthusiasm for his grand plans.

ABOUT THE AUTHOR

JANE THYNNE was born in Venezuela and educated in London. She graduated from Oxford University with a degree in English and joined the BBC as a television director. She has also worked at *The Sunday Times*, *The Daily Telegraph*, and *The Independent* and appears regularly as a broadcaster on television and radio. She is the author of five previous novels. She is married to the writer Philip Kerr. They have three children and live in London.

janethynne.com
Facebook.com/AuthorJaneThynne
@janethynne

ABOUT THE TYPE

This book was set in Walbaum, a typeface
designed in 1810 by German punch cutter
J. E. (Justus Erich) Walbaum (1768–1839).
Walbaum's type is more French than
German in appearance. Like Bodoni, it is a
classical typeface, yet its openness and
slight irregularities give it a human,
romantic quality.